"Gripping . . . discloses a reality most Americans don't know about. . . . There are some books that are less than they seem to be. This one's a lot more."

—SEYMOUR M. HERSH,
author of *Chain of Command*

"One of the finest espionage novels I've read since the end of the Cold War. Sharp, witty, and chilling; do yourself a big favor and read this."

—NELSON DeMILLE,
author of *The Lion's Game*

"Engrossing and challenging—how do you act when you know what *really* happened on September 11? Baer is so persuasive, one wonders whether he in fact did know. He certainly writes as if he did."

—WILLIAM F. BUCKLEY JR.,
author of *Last Call for Blackford Oakes*

BLOW THE HOUSE DOWN

BLOW THE HOUSE DOWN

A NOVEL

ROBERT BAER

THREE RIVERS PRESS • NEW YORK

Copyright © 2006 by Robert Baer

Published in the United States by Three Rivers Press, an imprint of
the Crown Publishing Group, a division of Random House, Inc., New York.
www.crownpublishing.com

Three Rivers Press and the Tugboat design are registered trademarks
of Random House, Inc.

Originally published in hardcover in the United States by Crown Publishers,
an imprint of the Crown Publishing Group, a division of
Random House, Inc., New York, in 2006

Library of Congress Cataloging-in-Publication Data

Baer, Robert.
Blow the house down : a novel / Robert Baer.—1st ed.
1. Terrorists—Fiction. I. Title.
PS3602.A38B58   2006
813'.6—dc22   2005027754

ISBN 978-1-4000-9836-1

Printed in the United States of America

Design by Leonard Henderson

Map by Mapping Specialists, Ltd.

10   9   8   7   6   5   4   3   2   1

First Paperback Edition

Acknowledgments

Special thanks to Terry Anderson's *Den of Lions;* Lawrence Martin Jenco's *Bound to Forgive;* the 9/11 Commission Report; Murray Weiss's biography of John O'Neill, *The Man Who Warned America;* Many Rivers Films, who arranged for me to get into Israel's high-security prison; and my editor at Crown, Rick Horgan, who patiently kept this book on track.

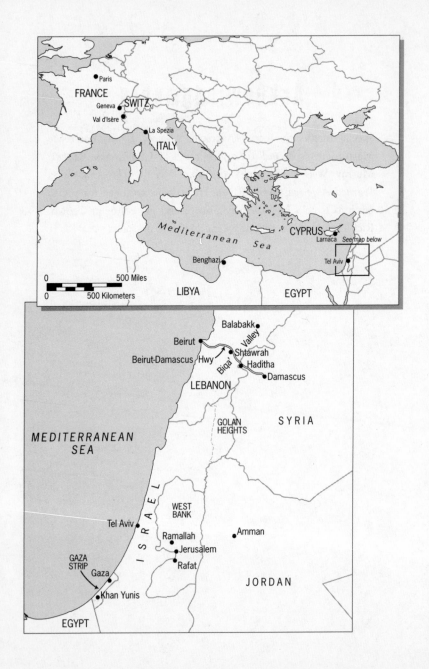

PROLOGUE

Y EARS LATER, after the unthinkable happened, I would remember
where I was when it all started: in a car on the Beirut-Damascus
highway, still a young man who believed the good guys always
won and with no idea that the colleague I was trying to contact on the
radio was already facing his executioner.

"Carson, Carson, this is Lone Wolf. Over."

Damn, still no answer.

"Carson" was Buckley's radio call sign—Bill Buckley, the CIA chief of
station in Beirut. It was March 16, 1984, and I had a meeting with him at
eleven—one I wasn't going to make. There'd been a firefight earlier that
morning in Aley, and a Druze militia checkpoint was backing up traffic.

Bill wouldn't be surprised. Long ago he'd gotten used to my not being
where I was supposed to be, operating solo, disappearing for days at a
time, dragging in who knows what.

When Bill had me come work for him in Beirut in 1983, he assigned me

1

the radio call sign "Lone Wolf." Everybody else had towns in Nevada. The nickname stuck.

"Anyone copy? This is Lone Wolf."

Someone finally keyed a radio. I heard static; then Art, the commo chief, came up on the net: "Lone Wolf, get off net immediately. Return to Reno ASAP."

I switched off my Motorola, wondering what the fuck was going on.

Only when I got into the station did I learn Buckley had been kidnapped two hours earlier.

Bill left the house every day at exactly twenty to eight, and that morning had been no different. He took the elevator to the ground-floor garage, where he checked carefully underneath his car for a bomb before starting the engine, because while Bill was regular, he was also cautious, and the Honda's underside had no armor. Satisfied, he backed out of his parking space—the same space every day—and started for the garage exit.

My guess is that Bill looked in his rearview mirror that morning and saw a car blocking his Honda. He got out to see what the problem was. Someone grabbed him from behind, hit him with something hard on the back of the head, threw him in the rear of the other car, covered him with a blanket, and tore off. Brutally efficient speed, surprise, and force. That's how I would have done it. There were no witnesses. All we had to go by was the open car door.

Getting Bill back was all the station cared about. But trying to survive ate up most of our time. We were operating at something like a 75 percent casualty rate—losing people and assets faster than we ever did in Vietnam or Laos. Washington wasn't calling it a hot war, but that's what it was.

Then, in July 1985, we picked up chatter that the "big crate was broken." In the shadow world of intercepts, our best guess was that the big crate was Bill. There were other hostages, but Bill was the most valuable to his captors. No one was ready to sign Bill's death certificate yet, but it was hard to maintain the fiction he was coming back.

One report with the ring of authenticity had it that Bill had been grabbed by a Sepah-i Pasdaran colonel who went by the name of Murtaza

Ali Mousavi. (Sepah-i Pasdaran is shorthand for Iran's Islamic Revolutionary Guard Corps, the spearhead of the Islamic revolution that Ayatollah Khomeini wanted to spread across the Middle East.) A couple low-level informants told us that an Iranian by that name had recruited the suicide bomber who drove an explosive-packed GMC pickup truck into the lobby of our embassy in Beirut. One bizarre description had him looking almost Western—blue eyes and reddish hair. Mousavi also supposedly recruited the suicide bomber who drove a truck into the Marine barracks near the airport.

There were rumors, too, that Mousavi might be behind a particularly inventive monstrosity. At the peak of the Lebanese civil war, the Christian militia started finding their people dumped near the port with small holes drilled through their foreheads. What they eventually came to believe was that a sadistic dentist had been anesthetizing the victims' foreheads, drilling the holes, then sucking out their brains with an aspirator, one of those things dentists use to keep patients' mouth dry while they're working. I asked around and was assured a dentist's aspirator couldn't suck out a brain. *Maybe,* though, with a stiff suction probe.

The hard part came when we tried to put some meat on the name. We had no stable indices on Mousavi—no birth certificate, address, phone number, even a photo. One of our few leads came from Father Martin Jenco, the Catholic priest who had been kidnapped in Beirut in January 1985 and held for more than a year and a half, at least part of that time in the same apartment with Buckley. During his debriefing, Father Jenco told us that when his blindfold fell off one day he found himself face-to-face with one of his captors: a man with blue eyes and red hair, the Western features we'd heard about before. Father Jenco also thought the same captor might have been the one who spoke fluent English—American English complete with slang. But he couldn't be sure because of the blindfold. Were they one and the same, and was that person Colonel Mousavi?

I recruited a young Lebanese Shia from Beirut's southern suburbs who thought he could get inside Mousavi's network, maybe even tell us whether he really did have red hair and blue eyes. The kid had gotten caught up in the Islamic resistance against the Israelis. By the time I met him, he wanted out. He set about cultivating Mousavi's people, and I met him every two weeks at the Museum Crossing on the "Green Line," the no-man's-land between Christian East Beirut and Muslim West Beirut, the safest place in Lebanon back then.

At one point when the kid was rummaging around in a safe house, he came across a Motorola radio and had the smarts to copy down the serial number. It matched Bill's Motorola—the same one I tried to call him on the day he disappeared.

The kid hadn't gotten far enough inside the network to meet Mousavi and confirm hair and eye color, but as much as there was any certainty in Lebanon, the kid was it. Then, one morning a Lebanese police officer on duty at the Museum Crossing called to say they'd just found the body of a young man. He had a small card in his shirt pocket with my name printed on it. Otherwise there was no identification. Did I know anything about him?

I did, of course, and as soon as I saw the quarter-inch hole drilled in the kid's forehead, I knew how he'd died. I was now convinced the dentist was real, and just maybe Murtaza Ali Mousavi too.

I didn't report any of this to headquarters. You start sending back gruesome details like aspirated brains or betray any hint of an obsession, and they pull you out on a wack-a-vac and send you to some clinic for deprogramming.

But I kept pushing and soon after we picked up a lead that Mousavi's group was operating off a low-power, push-to-talk radio net. Our regular signal intelligence sites couldn't pick it up, so I talked the station into renting an apartment overlooking the Shia southern suburbs to see what I could find on a scanner. After a couple weeks listening, I came across an interesting net. Everyone on it used call signs and coded names, places, and times.

I taped all the important intercepts and wrote down everything I thought might matter. Telephone numbers, addresses, and names—all went in my spiral notebooks. After six months I'd filled three of them. That's when we got the break I thought might crack everything open.

Another informant—a good one—told us that until the start of the revolt against the Shah, the elusive colonel had been a Ph.D. candidate in mathematics at UCLA. Later, we heard much the same from Terry Anderson, another hostage held with Buckley: Not only did his captor claim to have attended UCLA and the American University of Beirut, but he had a strange accent—almost American but with a peculiar rolling *R* as if he'd learned French before English. "Sounds more Iranian than Lebanese," Anderson said.

We immediately checked all the visa and immigration records, but there was no indication that Mousavi had ever applied for or received a visa, either in Beirut or Tehran. I got a friend in the FBI's Los Angeles field office to run out to UCLA. He came up empty on the name, but an FBI informant did remember a French-educated Iranian studying there in the early seventies. He had been writing a dissertation on a subset of non-Riemannian hypersquares, whatever that is, until he dropped out of the program, short of a Ph.D.

When the registrar pulled up the records for my FBI pal, the Iranian student's name was missing—digitally stripped out. The paper application, along with a photo, was gone, too. The registrar had never seen anything like it before. The only useful lead came from a professor in the mathematics department: He recalled a brilliant Iranian graduate student who had "sort of rusty hair." But since the student was a loner and never showed up for lectures, he couldn't tell us much more.

I had been transferred out of Beirut when in late 1991 Bill Buckley's headless, decomposed body was found dumped like a dead dog in Beirut's southern suburbs.

Confirmation that Bill was dead didn't diminish my interest in finding his kidnapper—if anything, it heightened it. But I wasn't in a position to do much about it until my many sins finally caught up with me, and I was yanked out of the field in January 2000 and brought back early to Langley to die a slow bureaucratic death. I was sure the trail had gone cold by then, but I started going through the databases anyhow, and eventually I found a reference to a photo of an "Ali Mousavi," taken in Peshawar, Pakistan, archived to an inactive informant's file. It was a long shot, but I ordered the file from Archives.

It turned out to be harder than it should have been. Archives said they couldn't find the file, so I took the day off to look myself. I never did find it, but I finally turned up the photo: a posed shot of five people standing in a garden. Behind them was a cinder-block house with a couple of half-dead bushes and a barbecue pit. In the middle was Osama bin Laden, clutching what looked like a Koran in his hand. To the left of bin Laden was someone in a salwar chemise. Something about him, his hands maybe, suggested that he was Caucasian, a Westerner, but his head had been carefully scissored out. To bin Laden's right stood a young man in a galabiyah. He couldn't have been more than sixteen or seventeen. On the far right another young Arab wore a kafiyah and held up an AK-47, partly covering his face.

What really got my attention was the person on the far left of the photo: a slight man, maybe five-six, dressed in a rumpled polo shirt and jeans. He looked aloof, as if he were uncomfortable being there or having his photo taken. He was also the only one whose features were too defined to be Arab. Since the photo wasn't in color and the resolution was lousy, I couldn't be sure, but his hair was something other than jet-black. The absence of any caption didn't help either, but I had a hunch I'd never been closer to the Murtaza Ali Mousavi I had been following for fifteen years.

What I couldn't understand, if this was Mousavi, was what he would be doing with Osama bin Laden? If there was any constant in the Middle East, it was that Shia Muslims like Mousavi detested Sunni Muslims, especially uncompromising Sunnis like bin Laden, who considered all Shia heretics best put to the scimitar.

The headless somebody was also an anomaly. For a start, the salwar chemise was caved in, the way clothes are on very old or very sick people. That his head was missing wasn't all that unusual. Faces and other identifiers of CIA officers get cropped out of photos sent in from the field, even when they're marked *Secret*. But the chances of this guy being CIA were close to zero. None of our officers was ever in touch with bin Laden, in spite of the silly myth that he was the CIA's creation. So who was the headless horseman? And who were the other two young Arabs? The picture was intriguing, but it was getting me nowhere.

I needed someone to identify the players. If the dating on the photo was right, John Millis was in Peshawar when it was taken. John had since gone on to become chief of staff at the House Intelligence Committee. I gave him a call.

We met at the Tune Inn, a dive on Pennsylvania Avenue a few blocks from the Capitol—me in a pair of faded khakis and a tattered, wrinkled blue oxford shirt and Millis in his Joseph A. Bank, all-season, light wool suit. We were as mismatched as you get in Washington.

After the waitress brought us our burgers and coffees, Millis pulled the photo out of the manila envelope and took a close look at it.

"I used to walk by that house," he said with a smile. "That's where bin Laden lived. I'd see him out front from time to time—had the impression he was friendly. Where'd you get this picture?"

"I thought you'd tell me. It was sent in from Peshawar when you were chief."

"I don't remember it."

"See anyone else you recognize there?"

"I don't know. Looks like the normal crazies who washed up in Peshawar in those days."

Millis pulled a pair of fold-up reading glasses out of a sleek metal case, fitted them carefully to his ears, and took a closer look. When he was through, he held the photo to one side so I could see and began pointing, starting with the guy to the right of bin Laden.

"This one was a Gulf prince, a true believer who took up digs with bin Laden. He couldn't have been more than twenty. And this . . ." He stopped, held the photo closer, then held it out again so I could see. "This guy on the far right you should know."

"I should?"

I tried to imagine whoever it was without his head wrap, without the AK-47 muzzle blocking half his face, minus the two-week-old stubble.

"A Palestinian," Millis was saying. "He was with bin Laden, and then ended up in Hamas. Nabil something."

I saw it then: Nabil Shahadah. After Afghanistan, he'd gone on to head up the military wing of Hamas. Nabil was the architect of the first suicide bus bombings in Israel, a lord of mayhem.

"And the headless guy? Was he ours?"

"Why would you think that?"

"You know, the head cut out. Why else—"

"Sorry. Like I said, I don't remember the photo."

Millis was losing enthusiasm, all but yawning, itching to leave. The rule is, you never want to lead a source. But I had to get him to focus on the guy in the jeans and polo shirt with the light hair. I picked up the photo again.

"Any of these guys Iranian?" I finally asked, pointing at the man on the far left, the man with the fine features.

He checked his watch, stirred his coffee although it had long ago grown cold.

"How's your kid?" he said. "A girl, right? Sally?"

"Rikki. She's okay when she's in school in England and I can talk with her. She's not okay when she's home on break and her mother takes a hammer to her cell phone every time I call."

Millis seemed not to be listening.

"Think this guy is an Iranian?" I asked again, my finger still under the head of the guy on the far left.

Millis ran his forefinger across the faces and shook his head no. "I don't think so, but that was what, more than ten years ago. Wasn't there a cable or a file that went with the picture saying who's who?"

"There was a reference to a file, but Archives can't find it. They're still looking."

Millis smiled. He knew what the chances were that the file would ever turn up. CIA Archives is the Bermuda Triangle of official records.

Millis slipped the photo back into the envelope, then motioned the waitress to come take her money and started to slide across the banquette.

"Gotta go, Max. Appointments."

"Just look at it one more time."

"Sorry. Maybe another—" His hand hit his coffee spoon as he spoke. The spoon tipped the cup. What was left inside spread itself over the table until I could throw a fistful of napkins down on the mess.

He stood up. "Can I have this?" he asked, his voice suddenly softer. He was holding up the envelope by its corner. "I want to show it to someone. You have a dupe, don't you?"

"Yeah. But the photo belongs to an operations file."

"You said you have a dupe, though, right?"

I should have said no to Millis's keeping the picture. I did have a copy, but letting any part of an operations file go out of the Directorate of Operations is a gross violation, even to a Hill staffer with more clearances than I'd ever have. I let him have it, though. Maybe he would remember something about the guy on the far left, given time to think. Millis was practically family, or so I told myself.

The next evening when I got home, I had a message on my answering machine from Millis: "Let's meet. Call me. I got a name for you."

We never met. Before I could call Millis back, he blew his brains out in a Fairfax motel room.

CHAPTER 1

New York City; June 21, 2001, 11:02 A.M.

"Baton Rouge, Baton Rouge, this is Selma. How do you copy?"
"Five-by-five."
"Baton Rouge, no movement. Che is still at his last."
"Roger that, Selma. Maintain your current. Over."

THE TWELFTH FLOOR of the Deutsche Bank building on Park isn't a bad perch on Midtown: close enough to the pavement to spot the twenty-something MBAs, cell phones glued to their ears, bullshitting about make-believe deals; just high enough to appreciate the grid, the grandeur, how easy it would be to bring it all down with a dirty nuke. But there I go talking shop again.

London's more cosmopolitan. Paris more tarted up. For stolen wealth per square inch, there's no place like Geneva. But Manhattan is where the real money is. Something like half the currency in the world flows electronically through this city every day of the year. Close your eyes and you can almost hear the trillions zinging around the local cyberspace. All that money gives the city a sort of divine energy, and Madison Avenue writes the Bible, selling crap no one can afford to people who don't need it, from Edsels to Viagra and Brazilian butt lifts. No wonder the jihadists go to bed every night dreaming of pulverizing the place. (The fact that one in three Jews in America lives here doesn't hurt, either.)

Personally, I've had my fill of pulverized rubble. Beirut, Khobar, Nairobi—I know the way it smells when it's still smoking and soaked in blood, and how easy it is to make. Load a pickup with half-full acetylene tanks, fertilizer, and fuel oil, and you can take down most anything manmade that you can get under or inside.

I used to think spending the best parts of my life in the worst parts of the world was worth something, but my employer saw things otherwise. I'd reported one too many unpalatable truths, poked Foggy Bottom in the eye one too many times, told my own seventh floor to fuck off in one too many ways. "Intelligence" may be the snake oil we sell, but the one absolutely inexcusable character flaw inside the Beltway is candor.

After a quarter-century in the field, headquarters called me home early and put me out to pasture in an office park near Tysons Corner. The plan was to tie me up watching over a flock of retirees until I shuffled off into my own sunset, but that couldn't happen until I hit fifty, four years from now. In the meantime, I was working off a time card: eight-to-five, no weekend duty, all the "personal days" I needed. That's what I was doing right now: taking a Thursday to see friends in Midtown. Another gaper in the capital of grit. Or so I thought.

"Hey, c'mere and have a look," I said, staring down at Park. I tried to put a little urgency in my voice, enough to pry Chris Corsini away from his high-performance, posture-fit Aeron chair and triple-wide LCD screens. But Chris was a commodities trader. The only things that got him excited were seasonal draws on oil inventories and his annual bonus.

"No, I'm serious. Come here and take a look at these two."

Chris sighed as he pushed himself to his feet. "What's it now, Max, King Kong on the loose again?"

That's what I liked about Chris: Ever since I'd rappelled down the side of Sproul Hall into the dean's office, back in our undergraduate days at Berkeley, he'd decided I was a headcase. But unlike a lot of our classmates, he never held it against me. Maybe I helped balance out the picture-perfect wife in Darien, the three way-above-average pre-teens, and the metallic silver Porsche Carrera.

"There," I said, pointing him toward the corner of Forty-ninth and Park, but Chris wasn't seeing what I was.

"Hmmm, let me think a minute." He was drumming his fingers on the marble sill. "Ah, the three smokers in front of the UBS building across the street! Sky's falling! I'm moving everything into gold."

"Take another look."

"At what, Max? Help me out here a little."

"Those two," I said, directing his eye to a guy and a girl, maybe in their late twenties. "The hip pair in front of Quick and Reilly."

The guy was hip, all right: mini-dreads, black wife-beater, patched black suede pants, Timberland boots, no socks or laces. The girl was basic black, too—faded bodice and denim bottom with built-in creases, carrier bag hanging from her shoulder—except for lavender highlights and a pair of those Puma arsenic-orange and powder-blue sneakers.

"You see something I don't?" Chris asked.

"Can't be sure. Maybe it's that they don't look very comfortable in those uniforms, like they'd put them on for the first time today."

Chris hung by me a moment, made a kind of pitying cluck with his tongue, then walked behind his desk and sat back down. "Max, I'm curious to know how you make it on your own in this world. You're nuts."

Truth told, I had spotted the two of them earlier when I was walking down Park. They were clearly interested in me, so I'd given them both a hard look as I passed by, and they had turned instantly away. That's about as telltale a sign as you're likely to get from static surveillance, and nothing they were doing now was making me change my mind. Every once in a while, the girl would glance over the guy's shoulder, in the direction of the Deutsche Bank, and then say something to him before turning back. The guy never stopped talking into his cell phone. My bet? A walkie-talkie. Without a scanner, though, I couldn't be sure.

"Gotta hop," I told Chris, picking up my jacket. "I need a favor, though."

"What about our lunch? I pushed people all over the place to make room. You're like some goddamn senile cat, scampering off for no reason at all."

It was an old bitch. Bolting for no apparent reason is one of the things I do best—that and manipulation, betrayal, and lying. Only the highest professional standards. The irony is that Chris knew the truest thing about me I'd ever told anyone. We were drunk junior year, burning hemp, sitting on a bluff staring at the Golden Gate Bridge, when he finally got around to asking me how my parents had died.

"I don't know," I told him.

"How can you not know?"

"I don't know if they're dead."

"Give me a break."

And so I told him everything: Mother's two husbands, neither my father; the grandfather who insisted I call him "Sir"; the bonds, the coupons, the trust fund; all the houses we lived in as if Mother were determined to book a season in every climate zone America had to offer. How when I was thirteen, she had signed us up for an archaeological expedition in Baluchistan, straddling the Pak-Iranian border. How I'd woken up one morning two years later to find a note tacked to the center tent pole: "Max—I've left with Ravi [another archaeologist—a real one—fifteen years her junior] to look at a great dig. I shall be back in two weeks. Mother." Not "Love, Mother." Not "Dear Max." Not anything like it. That was the last time I saw her. Those two weeks had stretched to eighteen months before my aunt learned from dear Mother that she'd left me at the end of the world and booked a small tribe to come get me out.

"What the fuck did you do while you waited?" Chris wanted to know. "Live in a cave and eat bat shit?"

"Actually it wasn't too bad. A family took me in. They had a son my age. We rode horses, played soccer. I learned Baluch."

"That's fucking bullshit."

And there's the double irony: Of all the cock-and-bull tales I had told Chris in the twenty-odd years since—the weird excuses for not showing, the weirder ones for leaving early, the improbable investment consulting

firm that provided my Washington letterhead, and on and on—I was sure
the Baluchistan story was the one he least believed.

"C'mon, Chris," I said. He was back to swapping Nigerian crude.
"This'll take ten minutes."

"What in God's name are you talking about now?"

"The favor. All you have to do is stand by the window and watch those
two."

"Why would I want to do that? You really are nuts."

"Maybe. But my hunch is that they're tailing someone in this building—
maybe one of your colleagues; hell, maybe even your boss."

Chris looked at me as if he was deciding whether to call security.

"It happens, sweetheart. Honest. The husband's sitting on his ass at
home, laid off and stewed on midday martinis. Suddenly it dawns on him
that the mother of his children has hooked up with the mailroom boy, so
he calls in a private eye, and bingo! Fireworks hit the fan."

"Yeah, sure."

"It's a fabulous business these days," I pushed it. "Everyone's screwing
everyone." Rule Seven: Create the context before you risk a truth. Rule
Eight: Don't let the context twist in the wind. "Or maybe they're watching me."

"Right, Max. And I'm Princess Di and you're Dodi whatever the hell
his name was. Drop the paranoid act. No one's following you."

Chances are he was right. (The *why*, for one thing, left a hole big
enough to drive the Pyramids through.) But high-octane paranoia is as ad-
dictive as morphine and far more useful. There is no such thing as an accident, no coincidence, no luck—they taught us that on day one at the Farm.

I'll never forget Joe Lynch, the course director, walking up behind the
podium that first morning and, without so much as a nod, asking, "Who
ran a countersurveillance route coming here just now?" All of us wide-eyed
career trainees looked around the auditorium, trying to decide if Lynch
was joking. The Farm is a maximum-security facility with more deer than
people. Only one road of any consequence runs through it. You'd have
to be Vin Diesel with brains to even get inside the place. Still, Lynch had
made his point: Always assume you're being tailed even when you are sure

you're not. It's the only way to keep your edge, not get sloppy, not get caught.

I couldn't tell Chris any of that, of course. Like a lot of friendships, ours depended on a certain degree of ambiguity, augmented in my case—and maybe in his, too—with a healthy dose of harmless virtual reality. A moral no-man's-land.

"Listen," I said, "I was seeing this girl, and . . ."

Chris bit, back on familiar ground once more.

"Bound to happen," he said with a shrug.

"What?"

"Hundreds of women. One Max. One of 'em was bound to get pissed off enough to come after you."

"Chris, listen—"

"I mean it, Max. You really are like a goddamn alley cat. You slink in and out of people's lives. Me, I don't mind that much. I'm not looking to bed you down, but—"

"The point is . . ."

"Remember that chewing-gum heiress who was stuck on you way back when? Get it? *Stuck* on you. What did that last? Seven months? A fucking world record. After Marissa."

In fact, I'd already asked Chris to be my best man when it dawned on me that I liked having sex with the heiress more than I liked her, just about the same time she realized that she preferred the idea of me to me in person.

"Youthful indiscretions," I said. I needed to get Chris back on track. "Lookit, this little piece of work is different. Very vindictive. Worse, she's got the money to indulge her anger."

"What's her name?"

Name? Volunteer nothing, and never give up a detail you absolutely don't have to.

"I cut her off cold," I said. "No five stages of grief with this one. Just checked out. Left her steaming. I wouldn't put it past her to put a tail on me, or worse. Chris, I could use a little help here."

Chris turned serious again. "Come on, Max, we're too old for this. I've got work to do. You can watch the watchers yourself."

"That's precisely what I can't do. If I do something stupid like walk out of here and look over my shoulder, bend over to tie my shoe, or stare into a display window to see what's going on behind me, they'll know I spotted them."

"So? Isn't that the point?"

"Yeah, you do that and whoever is running this little show will bring in a new team I won't spot. It's the way these things work."

Chris wasn't buying into it, but he hadn't said no. It was up to me to close the deal.

"Trust me," I told him, "this chick is totally unzipped, a psycho. She'll do me harm given the chance. I gotta know sooner rather than later whether she's got a tail on me."

I picked Chris's cell phone up off the desk, poked my cell number into it, and put it back down in front of him. "See this little button with the green telephone on it? Push that in ten and tell me what happens. That's all you have to do."

Chris tapped his fingers on the desk, adjusted his neck in his starched white collar, shot his wrist out from an equally starched and beautiful tailored French cuff, and gave his watch a good looking-over.

"Okay, okay. But you know, Max, it's not easy having you as a friend."

He rolled his wrist a few more times just to make sure I didn't miss what was wrapped around it. The watch looked as if it had cost enough to feed an entire Afghan village for years.

"A new toy, eh?"

"A Breitling." He was beaming. "It's got a micro-transmitter in it that works anywhere in the world."

"In case you get kidnapped?"

"No, asshole, I bought it for sailing."

I laughed. "Yeah, just the ticket next time you're blown out of Long Island Sound and end up lost in the Azores."

"One thing, Max. How do you know that that's the way these things work?"

"What things?"

"Not tipping off a tail."

There was something new in Chris's voice—a genuine curiosity. Maybe he was seeing me for the first time as I was, not as he wanted me to be. Maybe he was thinking about dumping his own little side plate. At this point, I didn't care.

"Some guy I met in a bar," I said. "He told me all about it."

CHAPTER 2

"Baton Rouge, this is Selma. Che's on the move. South on Park."
"Roger that. We'll take it from here. Over."

ALWAYS DRESS TO FIT someone else's story line. If that means a sensible black cocktail dress, suck in your stomach, slip it on, and go shopping for a strand of pearls and size-sixteen pumps. I could no longer remember who told me that—some Old Boy, six gins to the breeze, like they all are these days—but it was another piece of advice I'd never forgotten. To Chris, my worn-at-the-elbows linen jacket, baggy olive chinos, and scuffed maroon loafers said gentleman consultant, a guy who didn't need to drape himself in hand-stitched Hugo Boss to set his table. For my fellow pedestrians waiting to cross Park at Forty-eighth, my clothes and dead-on stare—immune to noise, traffic, skyscrapers, muggers, usurious bankers, fee gougers, and prying eyes—typecast me as someone who had wandered out of the Upper West Side on his day off. Trouble was, I didn't know what script the surveillance team in front of Quick & Reilly was reading from . . . if it was a tail, if they could read, if I wasn't just listening to the squirrels racing around that cage I call a brain.

I crossed with the light, then headed for the underground passage to Grand Central Station. I wanted to take a quick look up Park in the direction of the Quick & Reilly pair, but flying on instruments was the only way. If I was going to have any eyes in this game, they would belong to my old pal Chris, twelve stories above me. It was up to him to decide whether or not to use them.

I was out the underground ramp and halfway across the Grand Central concourse, flogging myself with the usual self-doubts, when my cell phone chirped cheerfully in my jacket pocket.

"I told you you're nuts. As soon as you crossed Park, they took off. No one's following you, Max. No—"

"What direction?"

"What what?"

"North, south, east, west? Manhattan's laid out on a grid, you know."

"North. Uptown."

"When did they move? Be exact, Chris. It's important."

I had my eyes on a Middle Eastern–looking student carrying a pizza box just right for a ten-pound load of plastique. Maybe a platter charge to levitate the 11:53 to Poughkeepsie.

"The two of them left just as soon as you crossed Park and headed south."

"They walked north, right? Went on foot?"

"No. Someone picked them up and drove them up Park."

"Someone?"

"A van."

"Hotel van? JFK shuttle?"

"How would I know? It didn't have anything written on the—"

"Did it have a sound stick on top?"

"A what?"

"An antenna. Short. Stubby. Maybe—"

"I didn't—"

"Were other people in it?"

"I couldn't tell. There weren't any passenger windows. You couldn't see in. Max, Jesus, I was looking out a twelfth-story window!"

"You dumb guinea peacock. A 747 could land on Park and you wouldn't notice. But tell me, how often do you see someone picked up in front of Deutsche Bank in a windowless van?"

"All the time. Never. It's not something I ever think about."

"Maybe you should."

"Uh, Max. It's not me who wants to hear you singing soprano in the choir."

"Thanks. You're a dear." I shut off the cell phone before Chris could say anything more.

What bothered me about the Quick & Reilly pair wasn't so much their existence as their tradecraft. They should have been doing sentry duty way down Park or watching from inside that unmarked van they were picked up in. Or they could have used some cover, like climbing in and out of a manhole in monkey suits. Even a vendor's cart. New York City is 40 percent foreign born. If you can't disguise yourself in that thicket of humanity, where can you? The van pickup didn't make sense either. Why not just break off on foot?

The easy explanation was ineptitude, but there was another possibility: They'd exposed themselves on purpose. In Moscow we called it "dolphin surveillance"—now you see us, now you don't. The way it worked was the KGB would start off with a sloppy team on you. You'd have to be blind not to pick up on it. Then, maybe an hour or two later, the team would drop off, disappear completely. You couldn't even find their comms on your pocket scanner. It was as if the whole damn service had taken the afternoon off for a company picnic.

The idea was to lure you into a false sense of security, give you the impression you were sparkling clean so you would go ahead and make your meeting, put down a drop, do whatever. But what really was going on was that the KGB had switched out the sloppy team for the pros. And it wasn't just new people and new vehicles. They enlisted fixed militia posts and the police to call in your movements while the real watchers hung back out of sight. They also switched to military frequencies—so much traffic that a scanner was useless.

That was Moscow, though. Who in New York would even know about dolphin surveillance? More to the point, who would use it on me, a tax-paying American on his own hook in the Free World's Capital of Commerce?

I'd almost convinced myself that the simplest answers are best when I pushed out the door to Forty-second Street and saw a guy exiting two doors down. Early forties, maybe. An elegant summer-weight cashmere sport coat topped by a screaming orange baseball cap. This time, at least, I hadn't completely lost it. There's nothing wrong with keeping your head covered, but a piece of crap like that in a 250-watt color on top of a pricey cashmere jacket?

Chances are, this guy was the "eye"—the point man for the surveil-lance team, the sacrificial lamb who sticks to the target so the rest of the team can hang back out of sight. Follow the orange hat, and they're fol-lowing me. Simple, and way too much work for the little reward I offered. A reasonable person would have simply caught the shuttle to Penn Station, climbed on the next Amtrak back to Washington, and opted out of the game. Chase over. Go home. But for a guy who pretty much lies for a liv-ing, I'm perversely attached to the truth. I had to know if I was being fol-lowed and, if so, who it was. *Who* would lead me to *why*.

First, though, I had to clean myself up—dump my cell phone, not wash my hands. Cells these days are not a lot different from those electronic bracelets used to monitor prisoners serving home sentences. Like Chris's Breitling, they have built-in beacons that constantly transmit your position, your GPS coordinates. Even when a phone's off, it keeps transmitting. A lot of supposedly street-savvy people think that removing the battery fixes the problem, but the pros aren't that dumb.

A couple weeks before, I'd dozed through an afternoon listening to some genius from the National Security Agency explain how he could con-ceal a capacitor in a cell phone to power its beacon. You can't find the capacitor unless you take the whole thing apart, he swore—and know *exactly* (his emphasis, not mine) what you are looking for.

Was my phone tricked? Possibly. Did I want to chance it? Definitely not, but I couldn't just toss the phone in the nearest USPS mailbox. For one thing, I'd be seen and lose the element of surprise. Worse, the FBI carries keys to mailboxes. If that's who was on me, they'd be crawling through my SIM card—the unique chip every cell phone operates off—before I got to Sixty-first Street. I had probably a couple hundred contacts stored on it. I wasn't giving those up to anyone without a fight. I needed a real drop, and I knew the perfect place.

I headed up Madison fast enough to string out surveillance behind me, then darted across the street at Fifty-fifth against the light, grazing a cab. The Sikh hacker celebrated my victory over death by rolling down his window and cursing me in Punjabi. *Bhenchot!* But this wasn't the time to stop and tell him I didn't have a sister, that one child was way too much for dear old Mom. Half a block later, I ducked into the showroom of the Sony building, raced through without breaking stride, and headed straight to the trash can in front of the Starbucks coffee bar on the backside. Surveillance would have had to have been inside the can to see my cell phone filtering down through the crushed cups and napkins.

"Can I help you, sir?"

"A grande double latté con brio with hints of the Costa Rican sunset, and hold the mayo."

"Huh?"

My server, if that's what she was called, had a sterling-silver safety pin stuck through her nose. Other than that, she looked like a Girl Scout from Kansas.

"House brew. Large," I amended. She almost laughed.

Reinforced paper cup in hand, I found a seat and paged through a well-fingered *New York Post*. The idea was to give surveillance a chance to catch up. When I figured that even an AARP flying squad could have gotten itself in place, I carefully folded the paper, returned it to the counter, and headed for the street. Time to move out and draw fire—Plan B.

CHAPTER 3

"All units, this is Selma. Che holding steady at five-five-oh Madison.
    Repeat, Che steady at—"
"Selma, Selma, this is Oxford."
"Five-five-oh Madison, between Fifty-fifth and Fifty-sixth."
"Selma—"
"Oxford?"
"Che just crossed Sixty-first on foot. . . ."

HALF OF EVERYTHING I KNOW about spotting surveillance I
owe to Wild Bill Mulligan, my first boss in India, and it took just
a single lesson.

"Boy-o," he said one day as we sat on the veranda at the Bombay
Yacht Club, "the trick is to always look at the feet, the shoes. And in a
pinch, pants. A good surveillance team carries along reversible jackets,
neck braces, red straw hats, a raft of accessories from shopping bags to
umbrellas, dogs to a watermelon—anything to distract you. Sleights of
hand. But what they almost never do is change shoes. It's awkward. Takes
time. Shoes are hard to carry. Always watch the shoes."

Which is just what I was doing as I made my way up Madison Avenue.
Fortunately, now that I had moved out of Midtown, people were fewer and
farther between. So light was the sidewalk traffic as I cleared Sixty-second
Street that I had time to focus my attention on a pair of extraordinarily fine
and extremely unlikely suspects, neither more than a size six. When they

turned into the Chanel store at Sixty-fourth, I thought, Why not? Browsing Chanel the way I was dressed was one sure way of drawing fire, on me and on anyone else who might find a couple thousand bucks a little steep for a crepe de chine blouse, even if the silk had been spun by free-range worms.

The door had just closed behind me when it popped back open and in walked a doughy guy in his mid-fifties, brick face, bad comb-over, scarlet Ohio State vinyl jacket, polyester pants, and spotless white sneakers. He looked even more out of place in Chanel than I did, but the point is I was almost certain I'd seen him walking toward me ten blocks earlier. If I was right, I was now being tailed from in front, not behind.

In the business, it's called a "waterfall." Whoever is in charge of the operation runs a hundred or more people at you in a constant stream. Two or three blocks after they've passed you by, they peel off onto a side street, get picked up by vehicles and ferried on a parallel street up above you, changing appearance every inch of the way, and then the whole process starts over again. I needed more evidence to be certain, but this little game was starting to take on a distinct smell.

The two size-sixes I'd followed inside were already being treated to a private fashion show, complete with midday flutes of champagne. I might have joined them if a manager hadn't floated in front of my face just then and asked if he could help me in a voice that suggested he'd rather walk naked through a landfill. I was turning for the door when he aimed the same question at Ohio State.

"Just browsing," the man mumbled.

I ducked out in the confusion.

Three blocks later, as I crossed Sixty-seventh Street, I took a peek to my left and sent a silent prayer to Wild Bill. There they were, those Puma arsenic-orange, powder-blue sneakers I'd last seen in front of Quick & Reilly, only now they were attached to the feet of a woman in a long mouse-gray rain-coat and a Phrygian knit cap. Apart from being out of season, the cap, I was sure, was hiding lavender highlights, but the sneakers, you could have spotted from a KH-11 satellite, ninety-two miles up.

.   .   .

By now I was crisscrossing Madison, checking out art and antiques stores. Every run needs a logic that the surveillance team can buy into, and the East Sixties and Seventies are peppered with the kind of places I had decided to make today's theme. Better still, since the shops and galleries are so close together, no one had to work very hard. I'd learned long ago that the best way to manage a surveillance team is to lull it into complacency. Make the chase easy on them, let them take in the sights, and never, ever piss them off. If you do, they're sure to download the flak on you.

At Sixty-eighth Street, I made a right, walked down a few doors, rang the bell at #14—a handsome brownstone and home to the world-famous galleries of Theodore Hew-Chatworth—and waited for the buzzer that would admit me to the stairs that would allow me entry to the second-floor showroom. If anyone was going to follow me in, he would either have to fast-rope off the roof or buzz the same buzzer and walk up the same flight of stairs I was climbing. Theodore was waiting for me himself, ever the gentleman.

"Fuck you, flyface," he said as he opened the door—an improvement, actually, over the last time we met.

We had issues. Teddy was a small-time Texas con man until he copped two-to-five years for accepting tuition payments for a chain of imaginary day-care centers. No fool, he used his cell time to acquire an encyclopedic knowledge of Oriental art and an accent that, except in certain circumstances, would do an Anglican bishop proud. Back on the outside, he headed straight for New York to do his apprenticeship. Today he was one of the nation's foremost dealers in Chinese antiques, but he'd never entirely escaped the con man he used to be.

A decade earlier, a police dog had discovered a handsome cache of heroin, pure China white, packed inside a shipment of vases meant for Teddy's store. The charge didn't stick—Teddy claimed his forwarders in Macau were freelancing—but while they were looking into the case, investigators stumbled upon something that could have put him out of business for good. Antique porcelains are certified by thermoluminescence testing. Don't ask: It's to porcelains what carbon dating is to fossils. What matters is that Teddy and his Beijing partners developed a technique to scam the test so they could sell fake Chinese blue and white as the real thing. It gave me enough leverage to talk Teddy into running ops for us during his frequent trips to China. He never took the assignment gracefully, though.

"Your phone," I said, nodding at the sleek cordless Siemens on his desk.

Phone in hand, I headed down the long side hallway to a bathroom marked *Employees Only,* locked myself inside, and phoned the Special Agent in charge of the FBI's National Security Division. If the Bureau's gumshoes were on me, John O'Neill would know it.

His secretary answered the phone.

I was two sentences into whatever lie I had concocted when O'Neill himself burst onto the line in all his larger-than-life glory.

"Max, you asshole, what are you doing on my turf? If you're up here operating, I'm gonna make sure you spend a cozy night at Rikers."

"Me? You're the one running the op."

"What are you talking about?"

"I got surveillance."

"Oh, bullshit."

"They're like flies at a shit roast."

"Come on."

"Trust me. You can't miss these guys."

"All right. I'll play. Hold on."

He was back in two minutes. "It's not DEA or Customs or One Police Plaza."

It was my turn. With DEA, Customs, and the locals out of the mix, the list of candidates was becoming disturbingly thin. "Are you sure?"

"Well, I could ask again and say 'pretty please' this time."

Point taken.

O'Neill hated silence. "You been drinking?"

"Not yet."

"Well, how about I send a car up and bring you in?"

"Nope, but I might need you later."

"What have you got into now?"

Damned if I knew, but I didn't want to disappoint. O'Neill had once noted that I had a habit of burning my bridges before I got to them, and history was on his side.

"Hey, John, remember that Black Panther, the one who became a Muslim?"

"It still hurts where he took a bite out of my ass."

"I'm going to go see him."

"The fuck you are. If you so much as—"

I hung up, splashed a little tap water on my face, and ran a quick check on the medicine cabinet. Viagra and crystal meth.

"I was never here, Theodore," I said, buzzing myself out his door.

"If only. Where's my phone?"

"I left it on the back of the crapper."

"You fuck."

"Why don't you run it through the thermoluminescencer. That should take care of the germs."

CHAPTER 4

*"All mobile units proceed uptown immediately. Stay close. Oxford
has eye."*

J OHN O'NEILL AND I WENT BACK to 1993, to the World Trade
Center bombing. Our employers were famously antagonistic, and we
had done our best at first to keep the cats-and-dogs skit alive. O'Neill
never stopped reminding me that he caught bank robbers for his living,
while I robbed banks for mine. But sometimes our interests intersected—he
put the bad guys behind bars, I turned them—and Ramzi Yousef and his
fellow truck bombers eventually brought us together.

I think I might have been the one to come up with the idea of pitching
Jamal Mohammad. It doesn't matter now. O'Neill agreed to run it as a
joint op and even got things started by digging up some dirt on Jamal from
his Black Panther days, back when he had been simply Earl Price. The dirt
wouldn't put Jamal behind bars, but it was enough for a gang-plank re-
cruitment à la the Great Hew-Chatworth. And it wasn't like we were asking for the moon. We just wanted Jamal to travel to Tehran every once in a
while. He certainly had the revolutionary Islamic credentials to get in and

out without a problem, no small feat since we were unofficially at war with the ayatollahs there. Just to sweeten the deal, I'd talked our no-vision bean counters into letting him fly business-class. He was going to see the world on our dime, and do so in a seat 20 percent wider than coach.

What we didn't know until too late was that Jamal's sister was an MIT engineer, founder of some fabulously successful niche dot-com company (think "cookies" and pop-up ads), and a devoted and generous sibling in the bargain. No sooner had O'Neill made the approach to Jamal than he phoned Sis, who rang up Mike Lyon, the last lawyer you'd ever want to meet in a courtroom. Lyon's frontal assault on the FBI included a temporary restraining order forbidding it from going within three blocks of the little mosque Jamal ran in Harlem (funded liberally by you-know-who). Washington, of course, caved in an instant: That news cycle would be hell to manage.

By the time the dust settled, Lyon had extracted not only a nice financial settlement for his client and himself but also a promise that the Bureau would never again talk to Jamal without Lyon's permission. Note the word *Bureau* in the previous sentence: I'd been along on that initial meeting, but only as a silent partner. Jamal no doubt had assumed I worked for John O'Neill. While my bosses would rather have committed communal hari-kari than let me anywhere near Jamal, seeing him didn't technically violate the Bureau's agreement with Lyon.

Up until now I'd been operating on Moscow rules: Shake the tree a little but don't saw it down. Fine, I'd confirmed I had surveillance, but if I was going to learn more, I had to "go provocative," as they know it back in Langley. I preferred my modified version: Beirut Rules—hit the bastards with everything short of one of those handy, backpack-size nuclear bombs. Only by really pissing them off could I force mistakes and make them show their hand. Jamal was just the ticket.

I hailed a cab around the corner from Teddy's gallery and had the driver dump me fifty blocks north on West 116th, at the Columbia Law Library. Then I set off on foot down the hill and through Morningside Park, marveling as I went at how the fauna around me was changing from pretty much solid white to solid black. An ethnic two-step was sure to fry the watchers.

The mosque on 116th still looked on the outside like the wall bakery it had been before Jamal moved in and started sprinkling around his sister's money. The sliding window where the previous tenant had sold bread was now covered with a hand-painted sura from the Koran. The Arabic calligraphy was sloppy, but I knew the text by heart—the verse known as the Tawhid, or the Declaration of Oneness: *There is no God but God. . . .*

The two Sudanese in dishdashes sitting on plastic chairs out front didn't seem to notice me as I pushed through the door, but the six-foot-five Mongol in a thigh-length black leather coat standing on the other side definitely did. I'd spent enough time in Central Asia to know he was a Kazak, the preferred hit men of the Russian mob. But what was Jamal doing with one?

Genghis Khan moved fast to block me from going any further. *"Shto?"* he asked, with the open palm of his hand in my face. He said it with just enough menace to let me know that he'd eat my young if I tried going around. When I told him I had an appointment with Jamal, he disappeared behind a curtain. Hanging from the back of the only chair in the vestibule was an empty shoulder holster big enough for a 60-millimeter mortar. From somewhere inside the mosque wafted the sweet voice of Joni Mitchell. "Big Yellow Taxi."

I was just beginning to wonder if everyone had gone out the back door when Jamal strode into the vestibule in a Brooks Brothers pinstriper, slim as a jockey, Palm Pilot in hand. He looked as if he was on his way to a fund-raiser.

"You know, you gentlemen really are dumb as dirt," he said with an evil smile. I had the impression he was looking forward to Round Two with the Bureau. "Trust me, you're about to find out it's not worth the candle harassing me."

"Actually, I'm here from the Department of Education," I said. "You've been found in gross violation of the Federal Minimum Intelligence Act. Come on outside and I'll show you."

Jamal was so taken aback that he actually followed me. So did Genghis.

"See the tanween over the yah?" I said, pointing at one of the accent marks in the sura on the bread window.

Jamal leaned in for a closer look. "So what?"

"It's a grave solecism, it should have been—"

"What the fuck you talkin' about?"

"You've desecrated the word of God, meathead. Get a real Muslim in here next time to do the sign right."

I'm really not as big an ass as I make myself sound. But what I needed right now was for Jamal to get serious about playing the role I'd cast him in. Calling into question his faith seemed to be the shortest route, and it apparently was working. Genghis couldn't have understood a thing I'd said, but seeing Jamal's face was all the guidance he needed. His right hand went under his jacket. He either intended to drop me right there or drag me back into the mosque and do it where he wouldn't have to disturb the neighbors.

One thing I know about gunplay is that when someone intends to shoot you and you don't have a weapon, salvation lies in taking one step sideways and back, then another, and another. You move quickly enough and you don't get hit. Or at least that's what the knuckle-draggers down at the Farm tried to teach us. Just as I was getting ready to start shuffling, out of the corner of my eye I caught a white guy and an Asian woman sitting in a Ford Taurus station wagon parked at the corner of 116th and Frederick Douglass, less than half a block from where we were standing. Exactly where I hoped and prayed they would be, and in extreme discomfort from the locals gathering around them. Allah truly is great.

"See those two there?" I said to Jamal. "I got all the backup I need." By now the white guy was out of the car, talking on a cell phone. He'd been joined by two other white guys, materializing with a speed that suggested an entire Caucasian posse was about to ride over the ridge.

Jamal nodded to Genghis, whose hand reappeared out from under his jacket. Not even Mike Lyon could help with an assault-on-a-federal-officer charge. But I knew beyond a shadow of a doubt that John O'Neill would be getting a call from Lyon even before I caught a cab. And in less than a minute after that, the phones out at Langley would be lighting up like Times Square.

I now knew one other thing beyond a shadow of a doubt, too. The FBI was capable of screwing up with the twosome in front of Quick & Reilly and the rest of the shitty tradecraft I'd caught along the way, but neither it nor the local police nor anyone else I could think of in this nation or abroad would be idiotic enough to field a white surveillance team in Harlem. For that, you needed incompetence on a colossal scale. Langley had to be behind it. I was being followed by my own flesh and blood. All I had to do now was catch the 4 P.M. train back to Washington, get a good night's sleep, and wait until morning to find out why.

CHAPTER 5

Langley, Virginia; June 22, 2001

TALLEYRAND ADVISES EXPEDITING the inevitable. Figuring he knew something about getting out of scrapes, I showed up at headquarters right on the dot at eight, just as the time-card punchers were queuing up for admission. My plan was to stick my head into personnel and see if anything jumped out of its skin. Somebody had to have heard something about New York. Even a wild rumor would be comfort at this point. I'd passed the night imagining the worst, a talent my employer had once praised me for.

No plan survives first contact. When I put my badge in the reader and tapped in my pin code, the red diode flashed instead of the green one. "Invalid identification," the digital reader said. "Please see security officer." Or, in everyday language: "Die like a rat in the road."

The bar ahead of me refused to drop down to let me through. The one behind stopped me from backing out of the stall. I felt like a rodeo steer waiting for someone to jump on my back and start kicking.

Meanwhile, I could feel the stir of wage slaves staring at the back of my head, amazed to find yet another idiot who had forgotten his pin code. How can it be, in a place like Washington? I was about to yell over at the security guard sitting behind the console when this intern in a miniskirt came sidling up to me with a smile that showed her braces.

"Are you Mr. Maxwell Waller?"

"Guilty."

The intern nodded at the security guard, who punched a button on his console, which lowered the bar behind me. When I had retreated sufficiently to make the point, the intern showed me into a room where you get photographed for your badge.

Forget goths and all those scowling indie-label bands with names that seem to have been dragged out of the devil's own handbook. These twenty-somethings waiting for their new badges were a wholesome, cheery lot! It didn't take me long to figure out they were a new career trainee class checking into headquarters for the first time. One guy who looked like an ex–college cheerleader was actually going around introducing himself as if he'd just pledged. An aubergine-skinned girl was telling her neighbor how she was going to put in for Hindi language training so she could reconnect with her roots. Even the most blasé among them couldn't contain his/her excitement at being admitted to the inner sanctum of U.S. intelligence. Mind you, the grins would soon enough be wiped off their faces, but who needs an over-the-hill case officer just stiffed by a magnetic reader to tell them that?

I wished I had a book. Or a newspaper. Or a Walkman. Or maybe even a not-too-old Sharper Image catalog. Instead, I wondered what the bureaucratic warlords who ran the place thought they were doing by making me cool my heels with these frat boys and girls. If they really thought this was going to crack me, how late to Planet CIA had their spaceship arrived? The incident isn't even classified. I'd been locked up two weeks in the basement of Lima's counterterrorism slammer with an unrepentant assassin from the Baader-Meinhof gang. By comparison, the only thing this crew might drive me to do was go floss.

One by one the room emptied. I was keeping company with vacant seats when two suits appeared at the door: Armani knockoffs. Neither of their occupants could have been more than five-six. The knotted muscles underneath the pure Bangladesh Dacron weave suggested the two were security, and so they were. One came over and grimaced as if to apologize for having to walk me up the scaffold. Pleasantries, words of any sort, were out of the question. Silent as a parade of Trappist monks, we crossed the marbled grandeur of the lobby to the director's elevator, which ascends (just like the director himself) nonstop to the seventh floor.

After a brisk lock-step down the hall, my faux-Armani escort deposited me at 7B26, the conference room of the assistant deputy director for counterespionage. A welcoming party was gathered for my arrival, but with the morning sun on the other side of the window, I couldn't make out who was there.

Vince Webber was the first to swim out of the glare. He was sitting at the end of the conference table, examining the back of his hand, acting bored as only a Romanian pimp can. He hadn't changed a bit in all these years—pitted face, diamond Air Force Academy ring, gold neck chain gleaming through a diaphanous white shirt, gold Rolex watch.

Vince, I suppose, had a right to look bored: It was his conference room. After a stint at the NSC kissing ass and a blitzkrieg through half a dozen seventh-floor jobs, strewing bodies all over the place, Vince was now the assistant deputy director for counterespionage—the CIA's premier spy catcher. The director's brand-new Mr. Fixit. And believe me, after Rick Ames, counterespionage needed fixing. Putting a known loser, lush, and political fruitcake in a position to betray *all* the Agency's Soviet assets happens only once (or twice, or thrice) in a lifetime.

Jack Rosetti, the lawyer for the Directorate of Operations, was standing by the window, seemingly absorbed by the woods of northern Virginia as he jiggled the change in his pocket. Suspenders and a bow tie made Jack look at first glance like a Bond Street haberdasher, but he was far too talented to waste his time in the trades. Jack was a bureaucratic survivor. He had fashioned a long and obit-friendly career precisely by avoiding controversy and scandal. Jack Rosetti left no fingerprints. Anywhere. And he certainly didn't want them on this little star chamber. My bet was he wanted to fly right through that case-hardened, laser-microphone-resistant plate-glass window and over the trees.

Mary Beth Drew, ninety degrees to Vince Webber's right, had recently been named chief of security, but she had started her CIA life in the Directorate of Operations. We were in Rangoon together in 1988 when the junta crushed the democratic insurrection. Since then, she'd grown a double chin and cut her hair short in a pageboy. Now in her pressed black pants suit and crisp white oxford button-down shirt, she seemed to have settled quite nicely into the seventh floor. The slight flare of her nostrils told me that Mary Beth knew I was in the room, but she wouldn't break off leafing through her stack of traffic to have a look.

The other half dozen people around the conference table were strangers every one. No surprise. A whole new generation of PowerPoint and one-page-memo wizards had taken over the top floor in recent years. The average age was maybe thirty. They all lived in townhouses somewhere down I-95 in Virginia, an hour-plus commute to Langley, in "planned communities" where the schools are good and crime means running a stop sign. They never went into D.C. for dinner because it was too dangerous. If they'd traveled at all, it was to London or Tel Aviv. The places I'd spent my life in they'd only seen in their nightmares.

Like Mary Beth Drew, Vince Webber pretended not to notice me until I walked right up to him. When he couldn't pretend any longer, he shot up and shook my hand as if I had just dropped out of the sky in front of his eyes. Vince motioned me over to the corner. Looking over at the rest of the assembly, he said in a whisper, "Max, sorry we're not meeting under happier circumstances."

Like Dubai, I thought.

I'd worked briefly for Webber when he was running Iranian ops out of Dubai, just long enough to figure out he didn't know shit about tradecraft. Shortly after I left, the Iranians rolled up all our networks except for one informant, an out-and-out fabricator whose bent and crooked tales were for Webber's ears only. A closed circle that yielded absolutely nothing. I think the reason Vince had never been able to stomach me in the years since was that I knew the truth, but the new Vince Webber was way too polished to let old wounds fester in public.

"This will all work out, don't worry," he whispered as he put a reassuring hand on my shoulder and guided me to a chair.

I'd been assigned the oral-examinee seat, a touch lower and narrower than the others, set just off the far narrow end of the table where the rest of the conferees could contemplate me as if I were some rare and not particularly tasteful zoological specimen. Fair enough, I thought. That much they've got right.

There was a timid knock, a small stir. Whoever had come in late slid a chair up behind someone sitting halfway down the table, opposite the window. The newcomer refused to look my way, but I caught just enough glimpse as he took his seat to see that it was a guy I knew named Jim. Last name irrelevant. He'd been a security officer in Moscow back when I was working in the Fergana Valley. But what was he doing here? Now?

From his seat at the far, power end of the table, Webber nodded at a man sitting midships on the window side. He was wearing a pair of bifocals with thick plastic frames that you don't find at your local For Eyes anymore. The broken blood vessels in his cheeks and nose gave him a pink glow, offset by a green retiree's badge. Just to complete the effect, he had one of those small goatees you see on aging men who drive Miatas and cover their bald spots with Greek fishing caps.

"Mr. Waller," Bifocals started, "we'd like to know what you were doing in New York yesterday?" His voice reminded me of the Bea Arthur character in *The Golden Girls,* a show I'd seen too often on visits to my own golden-yeared aunt.

"On leave. A personal day. Visiting friends."

"We know that much. Please tell us what you did after you visited your friend."

Look confused, I told myself. Bifocals and I and everyone around the table knew the game: Never get chatty. You hand your interrogators a narrative on a silver platter and they'll pick it over at their leisure. Make them work. They'll forget to ask you something or end up saying something they hadn't intended to. It's as basic as not blowing your nose on the tablecloth at the Palm.

"After?" I said, trying to sound genuinely lost.

"You know what I mean." Bifocals was irritated and wanted me to know it. I took a guess that he, too, was from counterespionage. Like the Gestapo, they expected instant submission.

"I am talking about the evasive actions you took in New York, which we are interpreting as an effort to impede an investigation."

Rosetti reluctantly took his queue. "I just got off the telephone with the FBI's general counsel. They're hunkered down waiting for a suit from a Mr. Jamal."

"Hold on, Jack," I said, my turn to be irritated. "Are we wasting each other's time around this table because I dragged a surveillance team through Harlem? I'll confess, then: I did it. They were so inept I had to assume they were petty criminals. I deliberately ambushed them. It's S.O.P. Now, why don't you slap my hand or make me clap the erasers out the window, and we can all get back to work."

The astounding prismatic transformation of Bifocals' face—from pink to red to an almost 911-purple—filled in the first blank for me. The surveillance had belonged to counterespionage. No wonder Rick Ames practically had to pull his dick out and wave it in a circle in Lafayette Square before anyone would pay attention.

Mary Beth peered over her almond-shaped reading glasses at me long and hard before she finally broke the silence. "Dusting off some old Moscow tricks, are we, Maxwell? Pre-perestroika? The bad Russians?"

"Maggie, Maggie, it wasn't just Moscow. That's the way we did things in Beirut, Monrovia, Sarajevo, Kabul—we ran the bad guys into a meat grinder. You remember Rangoon, don't you? Contour flying? Adjust your tactics to the threat?"

Mary Beth glared at me, and with cause: I was not being my kindest. She had lasted less than two months in country—pulled out with a providential case of hepatitis B and dumped onto the admin track instead. She never could spot a tail during her short stay in Rangoon, and so far as I know, she never shipped overseas again. That was one point against me. The other was nomenclature: She detested the nickname Maggie as much as she did case officers. God help us when she transferred back into the Directorate of Operations and took over some mega-station like New York or London.

I wasn't going to let the advantage go, though. I knew her well enough that if I provoked a little more, she would give up something. "New York isn't Moscow, Maggie. I'd assumed we were too civilized to follow each other around in our own country. And, small point maybe, but I don't think aping the KGB is going to make us better spies."

Mary Beth looked up at the ceiling, as if to say, *See what I told you? There's nothing to be done with this cowboy.*

Webber cleared his throat and nodded again at Bifocals, who responded by pushing a black-and-white glossy down the table my way: a grainy photograph of me walking into what had to be a Paris bistro, taken from maybe a hundred feet away.

"Not bad for DEA," I commented.

I'd had only a quick glance, but Bifocals' surprise told me I was right about the origin of the photo, too. He needed help.

"The date time group in the lower-left corner," I said. "It's DEA's. By the way, I didn't catch your name."

"Scott."

I couldn't remember what the bistro was called. There was a bird involved somehow, or maybe a fish. Maybe both: The Flying Carp? Some such. The point is, I used to go there a lot. It was off Rue Mabillon. Judging by what I was wearing, an old double-breasted suit and a frayed wool turtleneck that made me look like a down-and-out French intellectual, the picture must have been at least ten years old. I was in my light Camus disguise back then. Unless I was mistaken, the tattered paperback just barely peeping out of my side suit pocket was *La Peste*.

"Who were you meeting there?" Scott asked.

"Where?" I was momentarily disoriented.

"Paris," he said, with the tried patience of a road-show Job.

"I can't remember." In fact, I couldn't.

"Let me see if I can help. José Marco Cabrillo was having lunch there that day."

That I hadn't expected. I'd never met Cabrillo, of course, never broken bread with him, never clinked Pernods, but I knew him by reputation—a vicious Nicaraguan drug dealer. He'd been assassinated in Batumi, Georgia, a year earlier.

"Ever worked France before?" I said. My irritation was starting to edge toward anger, a bad idea. "Any of you?" I nodded in apology to Webber: He knew that I knew that he had. "On any given day there are thousands of narcos, arms dealers, and pimps lunching in Paris. Lunch is what people do in Paris, and they pay for it by selling drugs, Kalashnikovs, and hookers. The French don't give a damn as long as they're not clipping the locals or cutting too deep into their baksheesh. If you're right about Cabrillo and me in the same restaurant on the same day, it's a coincidence."

I waited for Scott to continue. There had to be more.

"We don't think it's a coincidence," he said. "We have in our possession evidence that you subsequently received payments from the Cabrillo family."

The idea, I assumed, was to throw me off balance. Why else come up with this nonsense? But I wasn't going to give them the satisfaction. Instead, I put on my best you're-all-idiots face.

"We have established a correlation between TDYs you made to Geneva in 1991 and transfers made to a foreign account by a member of the Cabrillo family. Four visits, four transfers. A nice match, wouldn't you say?"

It was unadulterated crap. No one from the Cabrillo family had ever sent me a penny. Nor do I own, manage, or have access to the proceeds of a secret foreign account. Sure, I oversaw a lot of clandestine accounts, but they belonged to the Agency. And the money always went out. It never came back the other way.

"Let me see the statements. The only bank account I have is at Riggs in Georgetown."

Scott looked over at Webber, who nodded again. That's when it occurred to me: They were taping this—audio, not video. Bifocals would have the starring role. Webber might never have been in the room at all.

"The money was wired from Geneva to what we believe is a life-raft account in Nauru, a numbered account," Scott said with his best *Dragnet* menace. "We're verifying it's yours. We will, though."

I think it must have been the "though" that finally pissed me off enough to draw me out from cover. There was something so officious about it, so unctuous, so dead certain that I wanted to shove my fingers up Scott's nostrils, hoist him out of his chair, and snap his neck.

"This has got to be a joke," I said, trying to calm down. "Listen to yourselves: You're telling me that you've pulled my badge, one, because of trips I made to Geneva that just happened to coincide with transfers to an account you're not sure who owns and, two, because I ate lunch in the same restaurant at the same time as a now-dead narcotics dealer."

I knew exactly what was going on. Ames's arrest had set Congress's hair on fire. The burning hair begat the Counter-Espionage Center (CEC, as it's known in the Agency), funded to the grotesque tune of $300 million so the Agency could go through the motions of cleaning up its act. The money and the center and the nearly thousand people who worked there, deconstructing and reassembling old leads, begat the bullshit charges, and the bullshit charges begat today's meeting. It was like some miserably updated version of Genesis: the Langley Bible. The Russians thought they could use Ames to steal the crown jewels, but he'd done a lot more damage by conning us into slitting our own throats in the aftermath.

Their dot connecting, or matrices, or whatever the CEC called it these days had yet to catch a spy. Ames, Nicholson, Pitts, and all the other turncoats were hauled in the old-fashioned way, by recruiting spies in our enemies' intelligence services: messy human beings who knew messy human secrets. Still, they couldn't have been more pleased with themselves. It was all so much more tidy and cost effective than running spies. Webber would never have to explain to the House Intelligence Committee why he happened to have on his payroll a Hizballah shooter who sent a bullet into his pregnant sister's face at point-blank range. The dot connecting had reduced the shock factor almost to zero, but all they'd accomplished thus far was to destroy a lot of careers. Mine, too, apparently, although at this point my career needed only a gentle shove to go careening over the edge.

"And you're stacking these flimsy leads up against twenty-five years of service to this organization?"

Silence. I'd hit a nerve.

I flipped the black-and-white glossy back across the table, unfortunately with a little too much force. It skimmed the table like a Frisbee, rising and hitting Scott in the middle of his paunch, which was draped over the table.

"There's more," Scott said, undeterred.

"More?"

He picked up a yellow legal pad from the table, licked his finger, and flipped a page with it.

"Theodore Hew-Chatworth."

"Harold—"

"Harold what?"

"He was born Harold Pooters. Theodore Hew-Chatworth came later."

Scott looked up and gave me a hard stare.

"Suspected heroin dealer," he read. "Probable contacts to Cabrillo family. Mr. Waller"—the "Mr." was drawn out for effect—"managed to find time in his busy Manhattan schedule to pay Mr. Hew-Chatworth a visit."

"I was borrowing his phone."

"And then there's Mr. Mohammad—"

"Jamal?"

"Offshore accounts. Jamal's real talent. Stopping by for a little tutoring?"

Shut up, I told myself. Say nothing. Definitely not the time to kick the dog.

"And—"

And? It was Jim's turn to take over the show.

"And," he began in a thin, stuttery voice. "And we have reason to believe that Mr. Cabrillo's Afghan heroin trafficking ran through the Fergana Valley, through a place called Osh."

"There's a surprise," I said, completely missing where this was all going.

Scott almost jumped out of his chair to shut me up this time.

"You'll have your chance, Waller!" And then in a much softer voice to Jim: "Could you be more specific?"

"Of course. Specifically, we believe the Cabrillo family, an Afghan heroin cartel, and a smuggling network in Osh"—he turned the page of a pocket notebook and studied an entry—"were assisted by a Russian major based in the Pamirs."

Ah, now I could see where this segment was headed. In the early nineties I'd been detained driving through the Pamirs: the raw edge of the crumbling periphery, as we used to call it, wall to wall with Islamic rebels, drug cartels, and rogue Russian military units. One of the Russian units had stopped my wheezing Neva outside of Osh and found a CZ nine-millimeter semiautomatic tucked behind the radio. Before I could talk the major who led the unit into letting me go, Moscow sent Jim to spring me. That was it: the sum total of the story until this moment.

"And what might be the significance of that?" Mary Beth asked in a stage voice.

"Well . . ." Whoever was sitting just in front of Jim seemed to dig an elbow into his knee. "Mr. Waller's trip through the Pamirs, we believe, was tied to a narcotics deal."

To his credit, Jim looked green at the gills as he spoke. I'd actually come to like him on our flight back from Bishkek. His first child, a girl, had cystic fibrosis. I knew the stakes. He needed a promotion, a fact I was sure hadn't been lost on Webber.

"Is there more?" Mary Beth prompted. "Anything else you feel might be pertinent to our line of inquiry?"

"Well . . ." That same stall, even more painful now. "During the damage assessment, Mr. Waller was, um, unclear about his connections with the Russian major and how he was able to get himself released."

A lie, of course. Jim knew exactly what had happened. He'd spent the night guzzling vodka with me and the major. It was in the morning, too hung over to care, that the major set me free.

I found myself looking from face to face, trying to figure if everyone around the table was in on it. Probably not. I knew Rosetti would eat a bowl of wriggling intestinal worms before he'd stake his squeaky clean on this assembly. For the first time I was confused. Now it really was time to back off.

"So what's next?" I asked.

"A polygraph," Mary Beth said, now back to her normal low simmer. "It'll put us on the road to clearing this up"—in the same way, I suppose, that removing a brain puts us on the road to clearing up brain cancer.

"Fine," I said, "I'll take a polygraph. I'll take as many as you like. And you have my permission to go through my stuff, here, at home."

"Our people are going through your office right now," Scott shot back, feeling at last that he had the upper hand. "I understand you'll have some explaining to do."

Knowing security was ransacking my office on a sunny Friday morning in front of everyone who worked for me wasn't exactly reassuring. I made a quick mental inventory of what they would find in my safe: the three spiral notebooks from Beirut and some other notes I'd collected on Mousavi, Iran, and Buckley's kidnapping. So what? It was a security violation at worst, definitely not a firing offense. Better to worry about where all this was headed, not what was already happening.

For a start, the public ransacking was loaded with meaning. The seventh floor clearly intended to make the break between me and the Agency as visible as possible—a warning to anyone inclined to help me. The ransacking also told me that the entire system was about to come down on my head, and there was no point in my resisting. If I was going to have any chance of surviving, I absolutely needed to find out one last thing before I was escorted to the front gate. I'd have to kick the dog after all.

"Maggie," I said, drawing the nickname out as long as I dared, "do you know how much the Gobi desert grew in the last five years?"

"What?" She knew she was being set up and didn't like it.

"Twenty thousand square miles. You know how we know that? We compared the satellite photography from 1994 and 1999."

"Waller . . ."

"It's only one hundred and fifty miles from Beijing today."

She was gripping the table. "If you think we're here to listen to your—"

"Maggie, I'm talking about an unchallengeable proposition. Facts. That's supposedly what we trade in. So, why are we pussy-footing around here? Do a financial on me, sift through my credit-card bills, decree one more background investigation, or whatever it is you do to ferret out bad apples. But with the evidence you showed me today, you've got shit."

Mary Beth leaned forward over the conference table and pointed her finger at me just the way my maternal grandfather used to when he lectured me on the sanctity of preserving principal. Just like Mother's sainted dad, she also called me by my last name while she delivered her lecture.

"Hear . . . me . . . well . . . Waller. When you walked in this room, you had everyone's sympathy. Now it's gone. And don't count on getting any from the Bureau, either. The mood they're in, they're going to ram a proctoscope up your ass and bolt it in place. I'm through here." She picked up her stack of traffic and walked out.

I still had no idea what shit storm I'd wandered into, but now at least I knew the FBI had been called in, which meant that I was the subject not just of a public humiliation but also of a criminal investigation. I'd worked enough with the Bureau to know they weren't going to buy a flimsy case like this. Cabrillo and the narco charges were for internal consumption, a way to get me out of the building while they investigated me for something else. But what?

We all sat there saying nothing until Webber unfolded himself from the far end of the table, waved his slender pimp hand in a little dismissive circle, and started down my way.

"Let me have a minute with Max," he said in a whisper, taking me by the elbow out into the hall.

Webber's breath smelled of cardamom and some other herb I couldn't identify. Maybe he was using organic toothpaste these days. I wondered what would happen if I ripped his tongue out of his mouth.

"Vince, tell me what just went on in there," I said, forcing a laugh. "Where there's smoke, there's bound to be mirrors."

He didn't even smile.

"You already know," he said. "Your name was bound to come across someone's screen eventually."

The Rick Ames Doctrine again.

"I know you're not on anyone's payroll," he continued, even though he must have seen I'd lost interest. "And if the same lead had come across my desk five years ago, I would have dismissed it right away. I can't today. After Ames, Congress is calling the shots. But listen, Max, the Bureau is going to come to the same conclusions. You know that. They're gonna lose interest, drop the case. I'm going to ride this one, make sure it happens as fast as possible. Just don't go stepping on any more toes, especially Mary Beth's."

Did Webber really think he was going to sweet-talk me out the front door, make me go away and die without a fight?

Webber suddenly pulled his head back with his shark's grin and nudged me in the ribs.

"Hey, Maggie sounds like a spurned woman. Anything you want to tell me?"

"How do I get in touch with you?" I asked, ignoring him. "Give me your cell number."

Webber looked at me for a beat, no doubt wondering what I was up to.

"You know, for an update. Sudden revelations. No crank calls. Promise."

Webber paused for another beat and then pulled out a yellow sticky pad, wrote down a number, and handed it to me.

"*No* one has it," he assured me. "Call me in two weeks and I'm sure I'll have something for you."

"Do you ever wonder what happened to them, Vince?" I asked as I stuffed the paper in my wallet.

"Them?"

"The compromised networks in Iran."

"Dead, I suppose." He sounded as he if were talking about fish bait. "It's a nasty business, Max."

"But we don't have to make it so easy for them."

The shark's grin never left Webber's face as he crooked his manicured finger and summoned the faux-Armanis from down the hall to come collect me.

It was only then, as I walked away, that I realized I had been wrong about the matrices. I was being framed, plain and simple. No one was connecting dots; they were spitting them out like rivets to make a case against me. That's what the circus in New York had been about: goad me, see where I ran, work it all into the story line. Smart as hell, really.

CHAPTER 6

THE POLYGRAPH WAS THE PAS DE DEUX I knew it would be, with me doing the heavy lifting. Assured I was guilty as charged, the operator tweaked his settings accordingly. Just as I had been trained by some of our same in-house necromancers, I declined to react to any of the dozen or so questions posed, and so the stylus did nothing, a flat line. (Strangely, or perhaps not, my Beirut spiral notebooks never came up. What better time to raise the subject than when I was wired to a chair?) By any objective standard, our session finished in a draw, but Langley follows low-rent Vegas rules: In the event of a toss-up, house wins. In my now-fat security file, the results would be entered as "inconclusive." Unofficially, "inconclusive" nicely cemented my new pariah status.

Afterward, the Armani twins sped me out in an unmarked Jeep Cherokee to my little off-campus office park near Tysons Corner. The door to my office was yellow-taped: Do not cross. Crime scene. No one was inside, but I could see from the mess that they'd left nothing untouched. The safe

drawers were pulled open, the files stacked on the floor, next to three reinforced cardboard moving boxes, all ready to be carted off somewhere:
forensics, counterintelligence, the seventh floor. Maybe to the *Washington
Post* for all I knew.

The Armanis were doing wing duty for me: one by either arm. I could
see them taking my measure, probably wishing they could handcuff me.
Behind them, the twenty or so annuitants who worked under me had
formed two lines, a cordon for my perp walk. Their cardigans and pipe-
stained teeth, eerily dated bouffants and comfortable footwear gave the
scene an almost comic element, as if Mr. Rogers had been a spy all along.
I'd spent a year shepherding this herd of broken pensioners, making sure
their contracts got renewed so they could pay for their prescription medi-
cines. Now not one of them would make eye contact with me.

"We will need you to inventory your personal effects," the Armani on
my right said. He seemed to be reading off some mental index card he'd
memorized in Security 101.

I sifted silently through the boxes: a hash pipe from Yemen, the Baluch
prayer rug I'd been dragging around the world ever since my sainted
mother had left me there, all the other cheap souvenirs you pick up overseas and put around your office to create the illusion that your Washington
servitude is only temporary. At the bottom was a framed photo of my
daughter, mugging it up with an Auguste Rodin sculpture in the garden at
the Hirshhorn. I'd taken it during her two-week visit the summer before,
the best time together I think we'd ever had. Rikki was a teenager now,
funny, ironic like her mother. I had no idea what had happened to the
sullen little girl with braces all over her teeth, but she was gone, magically
replaced. At night—Rikki in my bed, I on the sofa—we'd chatter like
schoolgirls before falling asleep. I'd never done that with anyone. It was
like a half-month-long pajama party.

"It's not all here," I said, getting back to my feet. "I had a couple things
in my safe. Mind if I look?"

They whispered to each other, seemed about to call for permission,
then must have figured, Oh, what the hell.

"Okay," one of them said, "but make it quick."

I went right to the bottom drawer, at the back, where I'd kept the spiral notebooks and my files on Buckley and Mousavi. Gone. Everything else was there except them. Webber was probably looking at them at that very minute, searching for the phantom connection to the phantom narcotics network.

"I must have made a mistake," I said as I stood up.

The other Armani had produced a clipboard from somewhere, a form for me to sign, acknowledging that I had done whatever I had just done. The pen was chained to the board, I suppose so I wouldn't be tempted to steal it as my last criminal act inside the place.

The final station of the cross was waiting back at headquarters. I had to be "read out" of the clearances I'd been "read into" over the years—Special Compartmented Intelligence, a nuclear Q Clearance, Talent-Keyhole, one or two others. I'd even forgotten I still had a Q Clearance, but never mind. The industrial-strength matron in charge of last rites dutifully ran through the criminal penalties for talking about this stuff to the unwashed, but I didn't need to hear it. Everyone knew that if you crossed any of the bright red lines laid out in the 1947 National Security Act, you'd win yourself a one-way ticket to the Supermax prison in Florence, Colorado, all expenses paid, and spend the rest of your life on a concrete bed in a 7'1"-by-12'1" cell.

"And by the way, Max, we're sorry to see you go."

I could no longer remember her name, but a few months earlier I'd wandered into an office party celebrating the birth of her second grandchild. The kid's photograph had been stuck on the end of a toothpick and pinned on top of the cake. Grandma cut me a slice herself. Maybe she really was sorry to see me go. But who knew in this insane asylum.

Out in the parking lot, the Armanis kept to the safety and comfort of their air-conditioned Cherokee as I climbed onto the worn seat of my vintage Norton Commando and prayed to all gods known and unknown that it would start. I had a vision that I would have to push the damn bike halfway across the parking lot to jump it—a spark plug needed replacing, or maybe it was the points. What I knew about fixing motorcycles I had picked up in *Zen and the Art of Motorcycle Maintenance* three decades back. Thank God for small favors, the Norton turned over on the first kick: the last bit of dignity I had left to me.

I could hear the Cherokee thrumming behind me as I passed under the sally port and pulled up to the stoplight at Route 123. Waiting there behind a Dodge Grand Caravan with a bumper sticker that read MY SON IS AN HONOR STUDENT AT YORKTOWN HIGH, I felt certain I was doing this for the last time. The crap about putting me on unpaid leave was just that: crap. You don't read people out of compartmented clearances if you ever expect them back. Eventually, security would finish poking through my things and send them back to me, along with the money I'd put into retirement, and that would be it, a quarter-century, framed and out.

The Cherokee flashed its lights once to let me know the light had turned green. I slipped the Norton into first and pulled slowly away. In the mirror, I could see my wingmen already turning around, their job over. They were probably wondering, like me, just what the hell I'd done.

I downshifted hard at the bottom of Route 123, leaned into Chain Bridge Road, and followed it across the Potomac into D.C. Twenty yards ahead of me, a dump truck was bouncing its way along the ripped-up roadbed. With each new rut, the truck threw off more junk. An empty five-gallon tin of Bertoli extra virgin olive oil bounced high in the air, arced maybe within a foot of my visor, fell left, and careened into the windshield of a Camry in the oncoming lane. There was no safe place under the sun. I slowed to a crawl, stuck my feet out to either side of the Norton, and threaded my way through the debris. Inches behind me, some fuckwit in a jet-black Humvee leaned on his horn.

Washington's weather had entered its sultry season. The morning had been sunny, even dry, almost a spring day. But now you could cut the humidity with a knife. A downpour was coming. I'd take a sandstorm any day.

From Canal Road, I headed up Arizona. Across MacArthur Boulevard, I let the bike loose for three long blocks: a roar as beautiful as any jungle cat. I was fishtailing to a halt at the stop sign for Nebraska when a pair of fossils out for an early-evening constitutional gave me a cold stare as scary as anything I had seen that day. Off to my left was a mock Norman château—it had to hold at least eight bedrooms—bathed entirely in green lights: lights woven along the wrought-iron fence that fronted the property, lights strung along a half dozen trees that filled the long lawn up to the house, lights looping from the eaves and curling around the whimsical chimneys. Christmas in June. Too weird.

American University was just taking shape in front of me when I veered off to the right and began working my way back over to Cathedral Avenue. I'd fallen in love for all of five days with a woman who lived in an apartment just off here—a magazine writer, an author of distinguished books. On the morning of the sixth day, she was still working on the same paragraph she'd been slaving over when we met. I was ready to move on to a new story line. Besides, I had to leave for Tashkent before the end of the month. Better to end it early. Chris Corsini was right: I do slink in and out of people's lives.

At the top of the hill, across Wisconsin Avenue, the cathedral shone in all its Gothic-Episcopal rectitude through what was fast becoming an evening mist. I've never been inside, I thought: something to do in retirement. If that's what this is.

The Norton Commando was the spoils of another dream gone sour. When our marriage finally fell apart, Marissa traded in our Istanbul apartment for a little stucco villa with its feet in the Adriatic, next to a lighthouse on a tiny Croatian island called Dugi Otok, a ninety-minute ferry ride out of Zadar. Rikki went off to Canterbury, in England, to middle school, just as her mother had done two decades before. And I got the bike, the only thing I kept. I'd always meant to ride it across Turkey into the Caucasus. Instead, this.

I turned right at Massachusetts, right again on Wisconsin, and left on Garfield. At the bottom of Cleveland Avenue, I threaded my way through two cabs on to Calvert, then shot across Connecticut just as the light was turning red. On Columbia Road, I slipped the bike under a tin outcropping on the building across the street from my first-floor apartment and secured the front wheel to the frame with a Kryptonite lock, implacable enemy of the inexhaustible bike thieves of Adams Morgan. The fat El Salvadoran kid who sat watching the space waited for me to dig a buck out of my jeans.

"Buenas tardes. Comó está?"

"Not so bad," the kid said with a yawn. He had a twelve-inch Quiznos sub in one hand, a Negro Modello in the other. Just another night's work.

The kid's mother and father and eight siblings lived in the basement apartment just below me. Next door to me was two-thirds of a wanna-be Krautrock band. In the floors above, where the apartments got bigger, were a gay ménage à trois, two straight couples with little kids, three full floors of daddy's girls and mama's boys. I didn't exactly fit into Adams Morgan, but I didn't want to live anywhere else. The dim entries, the smell of rancid grease, the ambient din all reminded me of Lima.

I flipped on the television and flipped it off again. Brain poison. Took out a bottle of Johnny Walker and put it back again. Liver poison. Thought about the clubs all along the street and gave up on that as well. Too early. Too late. Too depressing. From the bottom drawer of the dresser I pulled out five years' worth of Riggs bank statements and settled down at the circular table stuck into the little bay at the front of the apartment. Outside, under the sodium streetlight the canary-yellow Norton gleamed through a halo of a steady drizzle.

When I looked up again, the drizzle had turned to rain. An RV blocked the view. 1-800-RV-4-RENT read the sign on the side. Below it, a fiery sunset lit a landscape of mesas and prong-horn antelope. Funny, you never see RVs in Adams Morgan. I went back to the statements: nothing, no surprises, not a thing out of the ordinary I could spot. My check was automatically deposited every two weeks. My savings account never seemed to go up or down. If there was a bubble anywhere, I couldn't see it.

I got the whiskey out again, got a glass—this time I meant it—and was just beginning to pour when I heard a punishing sound from outside: metal ground up and dragged along the macadam. The RV was just pulling away as I hit the street. Out of the corner of my eye, I noticed the El Salvadoran kid was gone. Just down the way, a Metrobus driver was cursing, trying to yank the wreck of a canary-yellow Norton Commando out from his undercarriage.

"Fuckin' just came out of nowhere!" he was yelling. "Right into the fuckin' middle of the fuckin' road. Nobody fuckin' gives a fuck about fuckin' nothin' no fuckin' more!"

I helped him drag the tangle of steel off to the side of the street, then waited while the gawkers drifted away. It didn't take long: These remains were artificial, not human.

I was standing by myself, toeing the crushed gas tank, wishing I had at least thrown on foul-weather gear, and thinking that even Superman didn't mess with Kryptonite, when I felt more than saw someone coming down the sidewalk, walking fast, straight at me. White, black, Hispanic? I couldn't tell. It was too dark to see anything other than that he was wearing a forest-green poncho, hood up, and a pair of basketball shoes the size of canoes. His arms were under the poncho—with or without a weapon, I had no way to know, but I hadn't stayed alive by assuming the best about human nature. I was just about to take a step sideways and kick in his right knee when whoever it was took a sharp right turn and set off across the street.

"Silly, paranoid fool," he said as he passed me, in a voice as void of accent as any human voice could be.

Was he talking to himself? Nuts? Talking to me? I watched him turn left on the other side of the street and head west practically at a run, before he suddenly darted into an alley and disappeared. It was at that last moment, just over his shoulder, that I saw the RV idling three blocks down Columbia, double parked, blocking a lane. The brake lights were on but nothing else. The curtain in the rear window was parted. It was too dark to see if anyone was looking out.

CHAPTER 7

BACK IN THE APARTMENT, it took me a few minutes to find my Majestic lock-picking kit—for some idiotic reason, I'd hidden it inside the toaster—and a few minutes more to get through the lock on the utilities' door. The chirpy gay ménage à trois in 4C had gone out of their way the previous morning to tell me that they would be sunning themselves in user-friendly Laguna Beach while I sweated through D.C.'s summer. The least they could do, I thought, was loan me their phone line. I used a pair of alligator clips to tie into the interface terminal, then rang up Willie.

"Hey, what are you up to?" I asked, pretending to be surprised he was asleep.

"Shootin' hoops. What else a nigga be doin' at two in the morning in the pourin' rain?"

"It's only nine-thirty. Willie, I got a little problem."

"Everyone's got problems, Maxwell. You heard of original sin? 'In Adam's fall sinned we all.'"

"I'm serious."

"So am I. Can't it wait until morning? I'm up at five."

"Remember where you drop me?"

"I'm not senile yet, my friend. You mean—"

I cut him off. Stolen line or not, the phone is your worst enemy. "Yeah. I'll be there. Pick me up in fifteen."

I'd known Willie for twenty years. We'd first met through Stash, an old Air America pilot who'd lost a leg and a foot in Laos. Two appendages shy of a driver's license, Stash hired Willie and his taxi to get back and forth to his make-work job in Seven Corners. I rotated back to the field shortly before budget cuts forced Langley to retire Stash and send him home to die, but I made it a point to call Willie whenever I was in Washington and needed a ride your average cabbie couldn't give you. Willie looked like a mortician's assistant, but he had the heart of a NASCAR driver and the soul of a wolverine.

Stash and I had never told Willie where we worked, but he'd figured it out listening in on our war stories about shit holes like Laos and the Congo. Willie didn't say anything, just shook his head, probably thinking what fools white people are, but when his son had spent half his senior year in high school trying to decide between going to Georgetown to study international relations—a straight shot at the State Department—or heading north to Cornell to become an engineer, Willie talked him into Cornell. He knew a dead-end road when he saw one, and he'd had his own turn with international relations, serving Uncle Sam on the Batangan Peninsula with the 11th Infantry Brigade just about the time William Calley Jr. and his platoon were slaughtering peasants wholesale.

I went back upstairs to my apartment, put on a Levi's jacket, and stuffed a black watch cap in the pocket—the only thing I could find in a hurry to keep the rain off me. Then I grabbed a sterile cell phone I'd stowed under the socks in my top dresser drawer and jotted down its number on a scrap of paper. I used the land line to call Geico and report the accident, hoping I would be put on hold the way I always was when I had something important to discuss. I wasn't disappointed. A digital voice said it would be a twelve-minute wait. As I lay the phone on the floor, I crossed my fingers and hoped she was right. Twelve minutes was just about what it would take for Willie to throw a slicker over his pj's, fire up the Crown Vic, and make it the half dozen blocks to Ontario Liquors.

I took the stairs to the basement and slid past the resident barrio. Univision was cranked up to high volume: a soccer game, Nicaragua against somebody, a tie, injury time. I could have kicked down the back door instead of using the knob and no one would have heard. In the alley, I all but knocked over the El Salvadoran kid. He was peeing against the Dumpster, eyes wide as a raccoon, stoned out of his mind.

I wandered down the alley, lingered by a Dumpster or two myself, and startled enough rats to stock a leper colony. The only way to see me was through a pair of night-vision binoculars, a league I wasn't prepared to play in. Normally, the stoops would have been packed all the way along Euclid and back up Ontario, but the rain had driven the street life inside. Willie was just pulling up as I turned back onto Columbia. He had the car in gear before I closed the door.

"Straight to St. E's or should we give them a run?" he said. St. E's is St. Elizabeths, the local loony bin, home to Ezra Pound and John Hinckley Jr., among other famous nuts.

"Rock Creek," I told him, staring out the back window. "Take Memorial Bridge to the GW Parkway." I was checking to see if anyone had pulled out behind us when Willie tossed a box of Kleenex into the back and flipped down the mirror on the passenger's side. A cobweb covered the entire left side of my face. My ear had disappeared. I never wanted to meet the spider that made it.

I guided Willie along a countersurveillance route in northern Virginia I'd run at least fifty times: a loop-de-loop at the I-395 exchange, a quick on-and-off at the Key Bridge / Rosslyn exit, a U-turn just after Spout Run, enough traps so that a tail either had to show itself or lose you. It was as subtle as a quadruple bypass, but subtlety wasn't the point. The Norton was proof enough that all wasn't well in my little world. No reason to pretend I was out for an evening drive. The only thing I cared about right now was a couple hours of privacy with a person who didn't even know I would be meeting him.

Basically, I was flying blind in the backseat. I needed the rearview and side mirrors to check everything out, but Willie had those. Just to complicate things, there was way too much traffic. Didn't anyone sleep anymore? Worse, the rain was starting to sound like a Bombay monsoon, a steady drumbeat on Willie's vinyl roof.

It crossed my mind to tell Willie what was going on, why I'd gotten him out of bed to give me a ride. If there was anyone I could trust outside the Agency, it was Willie. But how could I ever explain the whole insane run in New York, the alligator clips and the stolen phone line, the call to Geico to convince anyone listening to my phone I was still in my apartment, now this? Spending a life doing anything and everything you can to protect your agents puts you inside a rare subset of existence. It all made sense to me. But Willie wasn't there. Wise as he was, he'd never get it. Espionage is like the world at the bottom of the Marianas Trench. When a creature from it suddenly gets dragged to the surface, no one knows what to make of the thing.

"Phone me in two but not on my land line. On this one." I dropped the number of the ghost cell phone on the front seat.

Willie didn't ask why. I doubt he even wanted to know why, but I knew he would play by my rules.

We had crossed Key Bridge and were headed back through Georgetown on M Street when I warned Willie we'd be making a hard left after the old Eagle Liquor and a quick jog up to Prospect. He inched along, waiting for a gap in the oncoming traffic, until we both saw a space just large enough for the ex-Norton.

"Hit it!" I yelled. *"Now!"* But Willie already had.

The Crown Vic hydroplaned across only inches behind a Navigator packed with high-schoolers and dead in front of a couple in a Lexus. Underwear would be changed early tonight. By the time we hit the alley's cobblestones, the Crown Vic was in a full skid. We just missed slamming into the side of Kinko's.

Low key it wasn't, but there was no way in hell anyone could see Willie slam the brakes just as we turned left on Prospect or me bail out in the fraction of a second he needed to power up again.

CHAPTER 8

I WAITED IN THE SHADOWS under a dripping oak tree until Willie was long gone around the corner. By the time a tail caught up to him, they'd see only the Crown Vic's rear lights going up 35th Street. I waited some more just to see if anything living moved, wishing to hell I'd brought an umbrella. Then, when I knew for sure it was impossible to get any wetter, I jammed the watch cap on my head and set off on foot almost back to where I had come from. Frank Beckman lived on Tuttle Place, in Kalorama, five minutes by foot and a thousand miles in every other way from where my twisted Norton lay rusting in the rain.

I worked my way up through Georgetown, scrambled over the high iron fence on R Street that fronts Oak Hill Cemetery, and followed the slope down through the tombstones and monuments until I hit the bicycle trail that runs through Rock Creek Park. Three minutes later, I was under the Massachusetts Avenue bridge. Another fifty yards along, I forded the creek as best I could—my Nikes were already soaking—waited for a gap in the traffic, then sprinted across the parkway and clawed my way up the steep eastern slope of the valley. I came out pretty much where I expected to: on Belmont Road, a block north of Tuttle Place and two blocks from Frank Beckman's tastefully imposing Georgian mansion.

I first met Frank Beckman in Brazzaville, in the Congo, in 1979, on the evening after the French embassy's chef had been eaten by a crocodile. It was all anyone could talk about. The chef had slipped out of the kitchen between the soup and fish course and walked down to the river. For what? A tryst? A fistful of something to dress the salad with? No one knew. One of the waiters heard him scream. A passerby saw thrashing just below the riverbank, but it was pitch black out on the water and crocodiles were everywhere. There was nothing to be done. The chef's toque was found the next day, snagged on a branch a half mile downstream. That was the other question on everyone's tongue: Had the croc bothered with a red wine sauce or devoured the chef au naturel? Even then, Brazzaville was not the world's most sympathetic place.

I was assigned back then to Dubai, covering the Iranian revolution. (This was 1979, in the pre-Webber days, when the base actually knew its ass from third base.) But mostly I was on the road, going wherever a Farsi speaker might prove useful: Manila, Khartoum, even (of all places) Brazzaville. Headquarters wanted me to pitch the first secretary at the Iranian embassy, a fat, fish-mouthed Khomeini devotee whose father had owned the Cadillac franchise in Tehran back in the days when the Shah was among his best customers.

Frank had been scheduled to take over the station in Brazzaville six months earlier, but a nasty divorce kept him tied up in Washington. When he finally did make it to the Republic of the Congo, just a week before I did, he had wife number two in tow: a tender, Irish-Chinese mix of a thing named Jill, fresh out of Skidmore College with a B.A. in French lit. But if Jill was expecting a honeymoon or even intelligent conversation—in any language—she got little of the sort.

Frank was Kentucky white trash through and through: high school into the army, army into the 82nd Airborne. At eighteen, he was jumping out of airplanes. He enrolled at the University of Kentucky on the GI Bill, graduated in his mid-twenties, joined the Agency a week later, and spent his thirtieth birthday hiding in an attic in Hue during Tet. Somewhere along the way he'd picked up a mid-Atlantic accent, a *sine qua non* for advancement in the Agency. I learned all this in the first half hour I'd ever known him, sitting in what passed for a living room, in what passed for a chief of station residence, in what passed for a capital city in yet another people's paradise of the ever-Darkening Continent. Frank was shit-faced when I arrived: warm gin. He kept drinking it, kept talking—he and Jill had met in Paris the March before when she was tracking Françoise Sagan's youth through the Place Pigalle—but he seemed to have leveled off at whatever level of drunkenness he had aimed for, or arrived at.

As for Jill, the story of their chance encounter and whirlwind romance seemed to hit a sour spot, or maybe it was the climate, or being stuck inside. The French chef had proved a more-than-cautionary tale for her. She had no intention of leaving the house except under armed guard, Frank informed me, and maybe not then.

"*C'est pas vrai?*" I asked. She nodded tartly.

The house was—and here I'm being charitable—a fucking dump. The Agency had given them a furniture allowance, almost a generous one, but by the looks of things, Frank must have used it to offset the ruinous expense of exiting his last marriage. The dining room table was a few planks nailed together and balanced on a pair of sawhorses. Jill's books—Gide, Moliere, de Maupassant, Sagan—formed a precarious tower on top of the only piece that looked as if it might have been up to the standards of her former life. Otherwise, the whole house, or what I could see of it, was done up with local crap, including the painting over the sofa: a Negress on lurid felt, washing laundry in the Congo River. I didn't know Frank nearly well enough then to ask him if it was a joke.

All that, though, was more than two decades ago, in a Cold War no longer being fought, in a part of the world now so ravaged by AIDS and civil unrest that it seemed to be sliding backward off the face of existence. When I ran across Frank a little more than six years later—coming out of the Beau Rivage in Geneva—he told me that the Negress was gone, along with Jill.

"She split," he said. "Homesick, Jill told me. We had a daughter: India. Beautiful, like her name. I almost never get to see her."

If I had been smarter, I would have seen it as a premonition of my own marriage. Like Jill and Frank, Marissa was a half generation younger than me—nineteen to my early thirties, a talented poet, a bright light at the American University in Beirut. We'd met when we were both rock climbing in the Dolomites. She was like a black-haired, olive-skinned spider. I couldn't keep my eyes off her. Nothing daunted Marissa. Not even me, as it turned out. If she hadn't been three months pregnant, I doubt we would have married, but out of it all came Rikki, good from not-so. That, too, Frank and I had in common.

I nodded my condolences over his lost wife and missing child, and asked Frank to talk on. Our colleagues in Southern Air Transport had just been "tasked," as they say in Washington circles, to deliver a thousand TOW missiles from U.S. Army stocks to Tel Aviv for trans-shipment to Iran. Against such madness, Frank's domestic life seemed the picture of normality.

Soon after they were reassigned to New Delhi, Frank said, Jill had talked him into signing a power of attorney so she could buy a small cottage for them back near Saratoga Springs, scene of her undergraduate triumphs. They had been in Brazzaville more than three years by then. With the differential and hardship pay, they'd managed to save a little money, and Jill had never adapted well to a place where the highest form of entertainment was watching geckos crawl across the ceiling. New Delhi wasn't going to be much better. Why not throw her a little bone? There was the daughter, India, too. Better she should be schooled back in the States.

It all made unassailable sense, Frank said, but Jill had other plans. Instead of the cottage, she took the money and bought a condo, and instead of Frank, she filled it with an associate professor of Slavic languages and sent hubby his walking papers. *Et voilà*, Frank was broke again. But America is the land of second acts, and Frank Beckman was its living proof.

First, Frank got his daughter back. India had just turned eleven when he was brought home for good and elevated to the seventh floor, number two in the Directorate of Operations, which made him, with about ten degrees of separation, my boss. Ten months later, long after midnight, India, a runaway, showed up on Frank's doorstep in Herndon, Virginia, after a week of frantic searching. Her stepfather, by now a full professor and department chair, couldn't keep his hands off her, she told Frank. Instead of immediately killing him—his first and deepest instinct—Frank got Jill to sign away her rights to India and set about learning to be a father.

I could still remember almost every detail of Frank's retirement party five years earlier, a barbecue in the fenced-in backyard of his soulless split-level. India was all of seventeen by then. She'd raced through high school as if it were a track event and had just finished her freshman year at Berkeley, animated in the way that only wildly precocious teenagers can be. Over plates of charred chicken earlier in the evening, India told me that she'd already taken courses from two of the people who taught me best.

"Joy of my life," Frank said, with only a slight slur.

We were sitting on his postage-stamp-size deck, watching her bag up the plastic cups and paper plates that littered the yard. India was dragging a recycle bin behind her for the beer and wine bottles. I'd edged out the last of the guests a half hour earlier—a husband-and-wife analyst team that never knew when to leave. Frank and I were cradling snifters, pretending to admire the bouquet and color in the blue bug-light by the sliding glass doors. A bottle of Remy Martin sat on the table between us.

"Joy O' My Life!" he yelled out, louder this time.

"I know, Dad. I know," she called back with a laugh, "and you're the joy o' mine."

I was starting to feel as if I had intruded on some private ritual—a fly on a priest's neck as he blessed the holy elements.

"And Maxie, too," she shouted a split second later to a roar of laughter.

Beside me, I could see Frank flip open the top of an old Sealtest Dairy milk box, the kind my aunt used to keep on the back porch. He rummaged around and pulled out a dirty towel. I could already smell the gun oil.

"I bought it last year," he told me as he folded the corners down. "Didn't buy it, really. Traded a silver Berber dagger for it. Some brother down in Southeast with a taste for antiques."

It was a nice piece, a Beretta six-millimeter with a professionally made silencer, the preferred weapon of Middle East assassins.

"Why?"

"Why—" Not a question. He tilted the Remy Martin bottle in both our directions, wrapped the gun up again, and laid it back in the Sealtest box.

"Why. Because I still wanted to murder the son of a bitch for what he did to India. I figured, What the hell: I retire, I even the score, I die. Case closed."

"And?"

India was waving to us from the far end of the yard, a pair of garbage bags over her shoulder. She was kicking the recycle bin ahead of herself as she worked.

"I decided to get rich instead."

It took a few years, but damn if he didn't.

A miniature guy airing out his miniature schnauzer on the other side of Belmont took one look at me trudging out of the woods, flipped open a cell phone, hit something on speed dial, and took off running, dragging the little rat dog on its side behind him. He'd called security, I bet. The neighborhood pretty much had its own police force and plenty of other help, too.

Motion-detector lights flicked on one by one as I walked by the sprawling coral-stucco Mediterranean at the corner. Across the street, where Tuttle dead-ends at Belmont, two pairs of eyes followed me from behind the tinted glass of a black Cadillac Escalade—private guards for the Embassy of the Sultanate of Oman. Just beyond the embassy, at the intersection with Massachusetts Avenue, sat the Mosque and Islamic Center, wired to the teeth against infidel invaders. For a guy who set out to make his fortune by providing "consulting services" for the oil-rich, Frank couldn't have calibrated his address much more carefully. He had everything but a Bedouin tent parked in the backyard and camel-shit mulch for his boxwoods.

2501 Tuttle Place took up the half of the block that the stucco Mediterranean didn't. Flagstone steps rose on either side to a double front door capped by a limestone half-moon and, above that, a window surrounded by stone scrollwork. More garlands—in stone and wood—were draped over and below the windows that flanked the central ones on either side. On top, three dormers rose tastefully punctuated by a pair of ornamental white orbs. Chimneys bound the house at either end. Improbably enough, an ancient, rusting TV antenna was clasped to the easternmost of the chimneys. My guess is that it was a private satellite communications link disguised to look like some piece of fifties claptrap. In Frank's new world, millions of dollars were measurable in nanoseconds.

English ivy crawled up the redbrick facade at both ends and on either side of the door. At the back, behind seven-foot-high brick walls draped with climbing roses, the garden curved its way past a granite pool to the next street over, to an old carriage house that had once served a great turreted pile of a mansion built in the 1880s by a Nevada silver king and U.S. Senator. The carriage house was all that remained of the estate. Frank had tarted it up into guest quarters for when his clientele weren't traveling in full retinue.

The only thing that spoiled the perfect symmetry of the place was a wing tacked onto the west side: a bedroom, library, and garage stacked one above the other. The garage dated from an era before automobiles took on the general proportion of boats. Frank's beautifully restored Mercedes 600 had no chance of fitting in there. The fact that it wasn't waiting on the street out front meant either that he'd sent his driver home for the night or that he still wasn't in himself.

I checked my watch: 11:07. A little red light was winking at me from inside the old coal chute that once would have served Frank's basement furnace. I was on camera already, and I hadn't even made it to the front door. A block and a half up the street, a car crept slowly down my way, spotlights shining on either side as it searched even the underside of parked cars for the likes of me, perhaps for me in particular. I stepped up to Frank's door, pulled off my black watch cap, straightened my hair as best I could, and pushed the bell.

CHAPTER 9

CHIMES TINKLED SOMEWHERE at the back of the house. Steps approached but then stopped just short of the door. A closed-circuit camera whirred above my head—swiveled left, swiveled right, panned the street behind me, the sidewalks, then zeroed in for a good eye-to-eye.

"It's me, Simon," I said, waving my hand back and forth in front of the lens. "Waller. In the flesh." I must have looked as if I'd climbed out of a peat bog.

Simon, Beckman's butler, opened the door a crack but kept it chained and his shoulder hard against it, just in case.

"Mr. Beckman is out," Simon finally said, after he had ignored me in every meaningful way he could. "I will happily inform him that you passed by, Mr. Waller. Have a good evening."

I stuck my foot in the door before he could close it, but at best, we'd reached a standoff. Simon was too civilized, for the moment, to crush my foot, and I was never going to be able to bust through. Apart from Simon himself, no small challenge, the door chain looked as if it had been forged on Mt. Olympus by Vulcan himself.

"Mr. Beckman is at the Kennedy Center."

"Opera's over unless it's Wagner, and Frank hates Nazis." Simon sighed theatrically on the other side of the door, clapped his hands together in despair, then disappeared somewhere back inside, leaving me alone with my foot in place. That's how I was standing three minutes later when a light from the security-patrol car plastered my shadow against the door. There was no point turning—I would have been blinded—and no time, either. I heard the *flap, flap, flap* of crepe-soled shoes on the steps and felt an eighteen-inch Mag light digging into my lower back, just at the base of the spine. I knew if I moved too fast for his liking, the last thing I would feel was the same light coming down on the top of my head.

Simon's face was back in the door.

"Mr. Waller"—he searched for the right words—"is *known* to Mr. Beckman."

The rent-a-cop behind me gave a slight twist to his Mag before he pulled it out of the small of my back, just to say how disappointed he was not to be doing worse, then turned and started back down the steps. When he was safely in his car, Simon slipped the chain from its mooring and cracked the door barely wide enough for me to enter. He'd already spread two bath towels on the floor and had two more draped over his arm.

"Dry with this," he told me as he handed me one of the towels, "and sit on that," he added, dropping the other on the floor. He reached into his back pocket and drew out a pair of padded-sole athletic socks.

"And put these on. Your shoes"—he was eyeing them as if they were roadkill—"do not leave the towels on the floor. Nor does that jacket. Or the thing on your head. Mr. Beckman will be back presently. You may wait for him in the library. I believe—" But he didn't bother to finish. We both knew that I knew the way.

"And by the way, Max," Simon added as he turned back down the hall. "You look like shit."

Now that I was, in fact, roadkill, everyone seemed to have a "by the way" for me.

One drunken night at the Intercon in Amman back in early 1992, Frank and I had voted Simon the ugliest man on earth. He took it well—he was even more gone than we were, and he'd definitely been standing behind the door when God handed out looks and stature. Simon couldn't have been any more than five feet four, with a lantern jaw that almost grazed his chest. What's more, he was in no position to argue. A would-be soldier of fortune, Simon had fallen on hard times. His nerves had failed him a few months earlier, in the middle of the night, as he headed over the Kuwait border into one of the occupied oil fields.

For three years, Frank and I kept Simon afloat with odd jobs. Then, when Frank decided to remake himself as a multimillionaire consultant and oil trader, he offered Simon the oddest job of all: butler. He had, after all, a perfect British servant-class accent thanks to his father, a men's room attendant at a second-tier London club; and he had stored away his own cache of secrets about the clientele Frank hoped to attract.

There was no question of salary at first. Frank had hocked everything—his house, his retirement, his clothes, china, the silver-plated flatware, his reputation—to even be able to afford the down payment on Tuttle Place. I have no doubt that he called in favors from Jeddah to Doha and points north and south to create the paper facade that would create the illusion that his was a thriving business. But like Jay Gatsby, the new Frank had sprung from his own Platonic conception of himself, and he had made it work. The leased furniture became real furniture; the Benz and driver, a Citation 10 jet, permanent fixtures. The mansion he had bought in a D.C. real-estate trough back in '95 for $6 million had to be worth twice that now, maybe three times as much, and it was only the beginning of Frank's good fortune.

I spread one of Simon's towels carefully on the leather couch in the library, pulled on the socks—an inspired touch on Simon's part—and leaned back to gaze at the Greek marble frieze above the fireplace in front of me: The two phalanxes of hoplites embraced in mortal, hand-to-hand combat were perfectly balanced against each other and perfectly lit, too, by recessed lamps above. When I'd first seen the frieze, I thought it had to be an expensive reproduction. There wasn't a chip on it. The original had to be in a museum, but the brass plaque said otherwise: ATHENS 4TH CENTURY B.C. When I asked Frank, he just shrugged his shoulders.

"Oh, yeah, it's real. Ask my insurance company."

Simon must have approved of my couch hygiene because he placed a double espresso on the table in front of me and padded off again with barely a sound. I downed it in two quick swallows, then got up and grabbed a stack of newspapers off the console table: the *Financial Times*, the *Wall Street Journal*, a new Christie's rare-wine auction catalog. At the far end of the house, across the dining room and central hall, over a living-room fireplace that looked from here identical to my own, I could just make out a Modigliani nude—Frank's newest acquisition. An article about the purchase in a recent *Art + Auction* had set Langley all abuzz.

"Good for you, Frank," I said, raising my empty cup to the distant nude. "You've come a long way from the Congo." I meant it, too. I could still see that Negress on felt, perched over Jill's stringy blond hair as if she might just leap down and have her for a between-meal snack.

I heard a car door close outside, then another. The Benz was pulling away as I got to the window, done for the night. Frank's silver mane was impossible to miss. He must have lost twenty pounds since retiring; he'd even picked back up the spring in his step. Walking next to him was a young woman in a sequined ballgown with a black shawl over her head against what had now eased back to a drizzle. What little castle in the sky did she haunt? She was a stunner by anyone's measure, and no more than half Frank's age from what I could see. His life coach? A girlfriend? Wife number three? Whatever role she was playing, she had her arm in Frank's.

Simon was mumbling something in the hall as a woman's footsteps climbed the stairs. A minute later, Frank stuck his head in the library. "Give me five," he said, but he was already on his cell phone as he turned and started up the stairs himself, two steps at a time.

"Yes, your highness, of course," I could hear him saying. "We'll make sure you have it before noon. No excuses." I picked up the *Financial Times* and pretended I wasn't listening as his voice faded away.

I was still standing there, paper in hand, five minutes later when India suddenly appeared at the door, wearing a Redskins sweatshirt and Levi's. My God, I thought, that's who Frank came in with—his daughter—and I hadn't recognized her, or as they warned us at the Farm, I wasn't looking for what she had so quickly become.

I had seen India maybe half a dozen times since that evening at Frank's tacky split-level—a lunch or dinner when I happened to be near Berkeley, a visit or two to the new mansion when she was home on vacation, only five months ago for a drink at a café near the Gare du Nord when I was in transit from Marseilles to Amsterdam. I seemed to have fallen into the role of a slightly screw-loose uncle—happily, I should add. My mother considered me mistake enough for one womb: I would never have a blood niece of my own. Nor did India have any family other than her father now that her mother had disappeared from the picture.

"Going to relive the glory days with Dad? The time you two camped on the Beirut-Damascus highway?"

It was anything but glory. Frank and I had lived in his car for a solid week on the Syrian border, waiting for the Iranians to deliver David Dodge, the first hostage taken in Lebanon. Instead, they dumped him in Damascus. That was 1983, most of India's lifetime ago. We must have told the story so often that it became embedded in her brain.

"Or are you just stopping by on your way home from a wet T-shirt contest?" India's tone had a definite edge, but her smile was as friendly as ever.

"You think I'm too old to compete?"

"Oh, Max, no. Never."

I took her hands and gave her a quick peck on the cheek.

"I thought you were still in Paris."

She looked at me, held my hands a beat longer, then pulled me in for a hug. India's through with being a girl, I thought. Maybe she never really was one. Some people never get the luxury of a youth. I knew something about that.

"Vacation's over," she finally said. "Time to make a living. Just like the old man."

"Looks like he's struggling."

The frieze was just over her shoulder.

Before she could say anything else, Frank was back, wearing corduroys and a cashmere sweater. The air-conditioning was set at Arctic levels. Simon was two steps behind with a pair of straight-up Scotches, no ice. I could see India wondering where her glass was, but her father gave her his own peck on the check and gently pushed her out the door.

"Good night, dear. I'm sure Max is just stopping by for a minute. You've got work tomorrow."

The library was set off from the rest of the house by a set of paneled pocket doors. I waited until Frank had pulled them shut before I spoke.

"Work?"

"She started last week at the Agency. Can you believe it? Doing traces on the Saudi desk, a whole lifetime ahead of her to ascend to the seventh floor. It wasn't my idea, I assure you. I tried to dissuade her."

He shrugged his shoulders and smiled. It seemed a million years since he had unwrapped the Beretta on his Home Depot deck.

"You might have told me. I could have—"

Frank raised his hand to stop me.

"The stink was on you, Max my boy, the royal whiff. Everyone knew it. My daughter didn't need that."

"You might have told me that, too."

Frank laughed. "You need to hang around the water cooler more. That's where everything happens in an inert bureaucracy."

I was sitting back on my towel; Frank, in a matching end chair beside me. He reached in a drawer of the low table in front of us, pulled out a remote, and punched a button. A sheet of the chestnut paneling slid noiselessly back to reveal a huge flat-screen TV.

"There's supposed to be a program on Al Jazeera tonight about Yemen. The place is circling the drain again, or so thinks Hunt Oil."

Frank surfed up and down the channels looking for it; gave up and flipped through Fox, MSNBC, CNN; then turned the TV off. He sipped his Scotch, frowned, and pushed a button on a side table. Simon must have been waiting on the other side of the library doors.

"It's too late for this. Bring us two Armagnacs."

"I thought you might show up here sooner rather than later," he said when Simon was gone. "Just not so soon."

Actually, I wasn't surprised Frank had heard about the investigation. Washington is a company town; news of government scandals travels fast. It travels even faster in Agency circles where it's such a welcome diversion from the humdrum truth of collective incompetence.

Frank was right: The Armagnac was a much better choice, and Simon left the decanter. I gave Frank the *Reader's Digest* version of Webber's show trial and the FBI investigation. When I got to the part about the spiral notebooks being gone, he stopped me.

"What did you keep those for?"

"Wandering fires."

"Knock off the riddles."

"We never found out who kidnapped and killed Bill Buckley. It's been sort of my grail. You know that. You're not curious?"

"No. If I'd stopped to solve every mystery there was, I'd still be in Kentucky."

"It must have had something to do with the first day I walked in the place and saw those words chiseled in the marble: 'Ye shall know the truth and the truth shall make you free.'"

Frank scowled as I said it: Stirring mottoes weren't his thing, either. I was on to the Norton, the RV, and the guy in the poncho when he stopped me again. "Are you telling me someone's out to get you? A conspiracy?"

"Frank, c'mon, no one blow-torches a Kryptonite lock just to push the bike into traffic."

"Maybe you didn't close the lock tight this time. Maybe that kid you pay to watch the bike watched the combination instead. That's what you get when you live among the savages."

I didn't forget to close the lock, and I didn't live with savages. If Frank would ever walk the ten blocks to Adams Morgan and have a look around, he would know that. But he wouldn't, and I wasn't going to get into any of that with him.

"How about the RV?" I said instead. "Or the poncho guy calling me paranoid? It doesn't—"

"Your famous score-keeping."

"Someone's got to."

"I hate to tell you this, old pal, but Smirch and the Black Hand went the way of the Soviet Union, and I don't really think the Trilateral Commission or the Masons care enough about you to steal your moped."

"Norton—it was a goddamn Norton Commando! Vintage."

"A thousand apologies. Your Norton. Your Commando. Your vintage. Mea culpa."

"I need to know why Webber and this guy Scott or whatever the hell his real name is are after me, Frank. The truth."

"Max, the truth never set a table or put a roof over anyone's head." Something chirped in the room. An ice-blue light flashed on the phone on the desk. Frank was out of his chair in a flash. He didn't turn on the receiver until he was safely on the other side of the library doors.

"Your highness," he said again. I had no way of knowing if it was the same one. He was talking softer this time, running off a string of numbers from a sheet he'd snatched off the desk along with the phone. None of it meant a thing to me.

While I waited for Frank to return, I studied the photos hanging on the wall behind his desk: Frank with George W. Bush, taken at what looked to be the Breakers in Palm Beach. Bush had his arm around Frank's shoulder. Karl Rove and Jeb Bush were standing off to the side, talking. The White House had changed hands only six months earlier, but a photo of Frank with Bill Clinton and Al Gore that used to fill this spot was already gone, banished with the Florida vote and three-day-old fish. Next to the Bush photo was one of Frank with Saudi King Fahd at the Yamama palace. Fahd had his hand out, backside up, beckoning Frank to kiss it. Below that, Frank was cradling a hunting rifle next to Vladimir Putin, probably somewhere on the Russian steppe. Frank had been in Berlin when Putin was a young KGB officer there. They'd met a couple times at cocktail parties, had dinner once together that I knew of. Clearly, Frank had rewarmed their acquaintance. There were plenty of others: Frank and Musharraf, Frank and Tenet, Frank and on and on.

I'd seen variations of the same brag wall in dozens upon dozens of

Washington offices: ex-secretaries of state; ex–directors of this and that, including the CIA that I was so recently ex- of. The Carlyle Group offices on Pennsylvania Avenue Northwest were wall to wall with them. Frank's was no different. He'd been chief of station in a half dozen high-profile haunts in the twelve years between Brazzaville and his summons home to the seventh floor, most of them along the crescent of oil that runs from Central Asia down to Iran and back along the Arab side of the Gulf. He knew the people who counted: presidents, intel chiefs, the royals; their corrupt offspring, too, the grease that keeps the wheels turning. Their home numbers were in his Rolodex. All the walls said the same thing: *I know the people you need to know, I can tie up the deal or fuck it. Don't even think about ignoring me.*

I tried to imagine my own brag wall: terrorists, con artists, pimps, assassins, pedophiles. *Don't ignore me,* to be sure, but not exactly the kind of people to cash out on.

Frank walked back into the library, finished his Armagnac in a quick sip, put his glass down on the desk, and took mine—not quite finished— and set it down beside his.

"Come with me."

We walked across the house, through the living room, until we were standing directly in front of the Modigliani. Like the frieze, it was lit to perfection: a raw, sensual nude recumbent on a daybed, meat-red pillows behind her.

"You heard about this?" Frank asked. He had a look of absolute contentment on his face.

"They couldn't talk about anything else for days out at headquarters."

"So I gathered. See anyone you know in that painting?"

I saw it immediately: the curve of the neck; eyes like little sky-blue diamonds; the button mouth, knowing, ironic, and kind.

"India."

"Amazing, isn't it? I don't particularly like Modigliani, but when this came up on the block I had to have it."

We stood there a moment in silence. Behind us, Simon was busying himself in the hallway.

"Listen, Max, here's what I learned in Brazzaville way back when. You can go for truth, you can go for duty, or you can go for money. I went for the money, and this is what it got me."

He swept his hand around the room: the nude, the frieze, the everything. "You can, too."

He pulled two business cards out of his billfold and handed me one of them: Marc Rousset, Bonnet et Cie, 27 Bahnhoff Strasse, Zurich, Schweiz.

"He's looking for someone to hand-hold some Middle Eastern clients. With Arabic and Farsi, you're a lock."

"He's a slimy fuck, and that's it. You know it, Frank. Everyone does. Didn't Rousset come within an inch of being indicted in France? Bangkok, too."

"And do you think you're going to land a job with Northrop or Boeing now that Webber's lifted your security clearance? Forget it. You're black-balled from coast to coast."

We'd gotten to the heart of the evening. I'd sat through the same thing a dozen times when Frank was on the seventh floor, simultaneously lecturing me and extricating me from some flap. He'd even once hung up on an assistant secretary of state who wanted me fired.

"It's an eat-what-you-kill deal," he continued. "Rousset will carry you initially, but you've got to bring in new clients."

"Why would anybody want to park his money with me? If someone's already got it, he's already got someone to watch it."

"Where do you think I got all this?" Frank said. "I used my Rolodex. The day I retired, I called every contact I'd made during the past thirty-two years. And trust me, more than one panned out."

"That's not the way it's supposed to work."

"Cut out the Boy Scout bullshit, Max. I need someone I trust to handle a couple new clients. One's a Saudi billionaire. He's needy and will suck out your lifeblood. But it's a good place for you to start."

Frank handed me the other card, engraved with the name Michelle A. Zwanzig. In the bottom corner was a Geneva number.

"Michelle's my Swiss fiduciary. Call her in the morning—her morning, not ours. When you get to Zurich, you'll drop down to Geneva and she'll arrange for you to meet the Saudi. Pretend to be obsequious and you'll do just fine."

"It's not going to work. They'll say I'm running. Bailing to Zurich is all the proof Webber will need to make real whatever they've trumped up against me."

"For crissake, Max, no one said you couldn't leave the country. You're not going to ground. Call Webber every day if you want to, make him your pen pal, send fan mail. He used to work for me. I know what makes him tick. He'll be thrilled. You're throwing your hands up in surrender, moving to Zurich. Get off his screen, and this all goes away."

"But the Agency—"

"Don't you get it? The place is over, done with. It's not the Agency you and I joined. You might as well be flipping burgers at McDonald's. Flush every memory of the place you have."

Frank paused a moment and continued. "Grow up, Max. Stop trying to belong. They never liked you, anyhow. You're the lone wolf. The pack hates it when one of their own isn't running along with it."

Frank was picking at scabs, trying to recruit me into his little business empire, whatever that was. He must have seen my face cloud over because he stopped and flicked off the lights on the Modigliani.

"We're still on the truth, are we?" he said, switching tactics. "Haven't you heard the news? People prefer a bad case of the clap to the truth. The polis cut Socrates's throat because he wouldn't lay off it."

"He was poisoned."

"As I was saying."

Frank put his arm over my shoulder, backing me out of the living room, edging me toward the front door. He gave my arm one last squeeze and turned back up the hall.

"It's a lot easier to make enough money to buy a world-class portrait of your daughter than it is to find an honest man," he said from the bottom of the staircase. "Just think about it, okay? You've got the numbers. And, Max, by the way"—the third time's the charm—"trot out the paranoia bullshit, your hunt for Buckley's killer, or your *truth* in front of the Saudi, and he'll drop you like a steaming turd. Copy?"

"Got it."

He had his back to me now, heading up the stairs.

"There are a lot of crazy people out on the streets who look more to-gether than you, Maxie boy."

And with that, he rounded the landing and was gone. Simon had run my Levi's jacket, sneakers, and socks through the drier, my watch cap also. The wool was warm, tight against my scalp. He stood with his hands clasped behind him as I pulled my shoes on.

"Cheerio," I said as I opened the door. He was probably holding a .38 behind his back in case I decided to clarify one more point with his master. He slammed the door behind me and double-locked it before I'd hit the first step. I could hear the camera whirring again above me, recording my exit.

I crossed the street, walked east for a few houses until I was half hidden by the trunk of an ancient gingko tree, then turned back to have a look at Frank's house. A light was on in the bedroom above the library. It threw a shadow against the curtain, too thin for Frank, too tall for Simon. I thought I saw a corner of the curtain move, a hand wave. For a moment I had the impression of one of those fairy-tale princesses trapped in the top of a golden tower. Something scuttled in the ivy behind me. I saw a tail darting for cover. When I looked back up at the window over the library, the shadow was gone, the light out.

The rain was over. Stars had come out. It had turned cool while I was inside. To the north a mile or so, at the zoo, some creature let out a hor-rible, night-rending bellow. An elephant, maybe. Or a rhino or hippo. Some major quadrapod. It was the weirdest thing about living in this part of D.C.: Africa roared all night just around the corner.

I checked my watch. I'd asked Willie to call me in two hours. It was a half hour past that now. I found a pay phone that actually worked at Con-necticut and Florida avenues and dialed him. The phone rang and rang. I hung up and punched in his number again. He finally answered.

"You didn't call." It wasn't like Willie.

"Couldn't," he said. "A funny thing happened. I stopped by a place I know on Fifteenth Street on the way home for a piece of pie and a cup of—"

"Willie."

"Bottom line, when I came back out, the front passenger window was smashed and your phone number gone. Who breaks into a cab to steal a goddamn phone number?"

Now I had to assume two things: I didn't have a sterile phone and, two, I was still of interest to someone.

CHAPTER 10

I RETURNED TO MY APARTMENT the same way I'd left it. The El Salvadoran kid was slumped by the Dumpster, asleep or dead. I held a finger under his nostril until I felt him breathe. God knows what he'd been given to desert his post across the street, but he seemed to have swallowed it or smoked it or snorted it all at once. Next door, inside the Dumpster, the rats were jammin'.

The basement was quiet. So were my three rooms. I looked for signs that someone had tossed the place while I was away but found none.

"Per normal," I said to no one in particular. "I've got no idea what I'm doing."

I sorted through the yellow pages, found a number for Air France, and called to book passage to Paris: Flight 19 out of Newark at 7:45 the next evening. I'd take Amtrak up. I was about to book all the way to Zurich but changed my mind. Why make it easy on them? I'd make the last leg from Paris to Zurich by train.

Did I want to travel light or take part of my previous life with me? It took all of a minute to decide. I grabbed a steak knife, slit the couch across the back, reached in and removed two stolen passports along with twenty thousand dollars American and another three thousand in mixed pounds, francs, and marks. I'd bought the passports—Irish and German—in Macau from pickpockets. A tech friend had substituted my picture for the owners' and put in U.S. entry stamps. I was sure I'd be just fine with my own passport in my own name, but hauling along the stolen passports couldn't hurt. It was sort of like taking two credit cards on a date so you're not embarrassed if one's rejected. *In omnia paratus*—prepared in all things, a motto for Boy Scouts and ex–CIA officers on the lam.

Out in the hallway, the utility room door was still ajar. I slipped inside, retrieved the alligator clips from the top of the interface terminal, and again availed myself of the ménage à trois's line to dial a number on the Lower East Side of Manhattan. I didn't care who knew I was heading for Europe, but I wasn't about to burn an asset. I had this feeling I'd be needing every one of them.

"O'Neill." The voice was full of sandpaper. He'd been pulled from a deep sleep.

"John, it's me. Max. Waller."

"What the—"

"Meet me at Newark Airport tomorrow at five P.M. The Air France counter."

"Why?"

"Just do."

I unclipped the wires, relocked the door this time, and went back to my apartment. I had enough bottles and cans in my recycle bin to build a three-foot tower just inside the door. All the windows were barred against the practical reality of living on the ground floor in the inner city. My pants were dry enough to sleep in. I slid the passports and money in my jacket pocket and curled up under the blankets. For good measure, I kept the steak knife with me under the pillow. I would have slept better with a mini Uzi at my side, but it was field expediency all the way.

As I lay there listening to the night noises—each muffler pop sounding

like a small explosive, each noise on the street like bangers closing in—
the one thing that kept rolling through my mind was this: Do I take the
Peshawar photo with me, or do I destroy it and give up the score-keeping
like Frank told me to do? The answer seemed obvious. Destroying it would
lift a rock off me. It would give me part of my life back. I also knew that if
I did destroy it, the part of my life that kept me going would be missing.

I got up in the dark in case anyone was keeping watch, made it to the
kitchen in a low crouch, and felt behind the refrigerator until I found the
envelope I'd taped there. Inside was the photo. I folded it carefully into
fourths and put it in my pocket next to the passports. Now I could sleep.

CHAPTER 11

Newark, New Jersey; June 23, 2001

N EWARK INTERNATIONAL LOOKED LIKE a cockroach nest in mating season, and Air France was right in the middle of it. The place teemed with families, people going home for summer holiday, and those running away from it, drifters, grifters, the lame and the halt, enough nuns and priests to stuff a sacristy, wailing infants, lost ancients, the whole wonderful-horrible gamut of air-going humanity. At the El Al counter, a black-clad Jew in broad-brimmed hat tugged his forelocks, rocked on his heels, and bemoaned the wholesale price of diamonds. He was carrying a miniature safe under one arm. Just down the way at Ethiopian Airlines, a clutch of dainty-featured nomads clung to empty chicken crates, dejected that they weren't allowed to carry the birds on board with them. A tour director with an open umbrella was leading a parade of golden-years couples to what looked like, by their body language, a sure and certain doom.

"Keep up back there!" she kept shouting. "Keep up!"

Christ, I was thinking, how could you even try to screen all of these people? A punk-rock band queuing up for a flight to Gatwick had more piercing between them, pound for pound, than a 155-millimeter artillery round.

One corner of Terminal B was occupied by college kids on their way to Europe for summer vacation. They and their bulging backpacks and their *Lonely Planet*s and *Rough Guide*s and *Frommer's Budget* books—*Paris on $20 a Day, Monte Carlo on a Shoestring*—were piled everywhere. The shits blocked counters, bathrooms, entrances. They flailed their arms, air-guitaring and lip-synching to private tunes on their headsets; stank, farted, belched; shouted to one another; sighed meaningfully to themselves.

Fin de siècle, the new millennium, the long, rich ride of the nineties— whatever it was, something had unmoored the land, the people; had made travel not a joy or an adventure but some kind of twisted imperative. Gotta go. Gotta go. Gotta go. It made me long for a time I never knew when transcontinental planes had sleeping berths and every man wore a tie.

I carved out a few square feet at the end of the Air France counter, down where they roll out the red carpet for first-class passengers, and kept a lookout for O'Neill. Just to my left, a girl in a Muhlenberg College sweat-shirt spent twenty minutes on her cell phone declaring eternal love to some poor sap forced to spend the summer with his parents in what I took to be Hershey, Pennsylvania. Acne scars dotted one cheek. Her fat thighs had been poured into a pair of jeans that fit like sausage skins. It looked as if her ass was growing out her abdomen. A MEAN PEOPLE SUCK button was jammed into her neon pink fanny pack.

I was pinching the skin under my jaw, the rising turkey waddle, feeling creaky among this golden youth, when someone grabbed my free arm, twisted it up high behind my back, and practically lifted me off the ground before I fell facedown into a pile of luggage ID tags. It was, of course, John O'Neill.

"Max, you're slow. You've lost it."

I bent my head around just far enough to see him beaming to the Air France personnel as if he'd just walked out on the Letterman set. In his free hand, he was holding his wallet, flipped open to his creds. I half expected the crowd to break out into applause.

"This better be good." He was bent closer now, hissing in my ear. "I should have snagged your ass and overnighted it in Rikers when I had the chance. Jamal and his lawyer are all over us."

"Burn him down and bag his ashes." My arm ached.

"His ashes?"

"If you could let go—"

"Party's over, folks," O'Neill called out, pocketing his wallet again. "Training exercise."

"Je lui ai defonce son cul," I called out in turn, in my foulest French, just to piss him off, *"et depuis il ne me lache plus."*

The Air France people turned away in disgust.

I stretched my arm out, turned it this way and that just to make sure the ligaments were still intact, then took out my wallet, sorted through a few weeks' worth of receipts, lifted out a rumpled, soiled scrap of legal pad covered with a long string of digits, and handed it over to O'Neill. His dramatics had the happy effect of cordoning off the space around us. Who knew, we both might be rabid.

"Your dentist's phone number?" he said. "Big deal. I'm sure I couldn't afford his services."

Actually, I was pretty sure he could. I didn't know where John got his money, but he never seemed to leave his apartment without being wrapped up in a couple thousand dollars' worth of threads, and he never had a drink at home when three at Elaine's would do.

"Too many digits," I told him. "Look again."

"Your new extended-extended zip code?"

"How about an unreported foreign account—"

"You lying sack—"

"—in St. Kitts."

"—of shit."

He turned the scrap over and read the name on the back.

"Belongs on paper to a nominee-controlled company in Panama. But it's Jamal's. Get the Panamanians to haul in the nominee, and you got him cold. He's been squirreling money there for years, where Uncle Sam can't tax it. Even a rich sister can't get him out of this one."

Silence.

"We pulled it out of the air."

I knew that would get his attention. O'Neill had zero confidence in the Agency's ability to penetrate American black Muslim groups or for that matter any Muslim group anywhere, but he did know we picked up some enlightening "chatter" from time to time, little bytes like nominee-controlled accounts that we rarely showed to the Bureau.

"How long have you had it?"

"Couple months."

"Why now?"

"I love you. I want to have your child."

"Why—"

The space around us was shrinking by the second, the freshmen mixer creeping in like some unstoppable mold. The fat girl from Muhlenberg College had been replaced by a scrawny, ferret-faced kid in a filthy Hofstra T-shirt who was eating two Slim Jims at the same time.

"Outside," O'Neill said, stuffing the piece of paper I'd given him into his shirt pocket. "Follow me." In his thin black silk socks and soft Italian loafers, he looked more like a Mafia capo than the FBI's top spy and terrorist catcher in New York.

The truth was I'd done a lot of favors, public and private, for John O'Neill over the seven years since Ramzi Yousef had been kind enough (sort of) to introduce us by trying to blow up the World Trade Center. Among other items, I'd helped him investigate the murder of Freddie Woodruff, an American diplomat in Tbilisi. He needed me, too, because the State Department was doing anything and everything to cover up the fact that a murder had occurred at all.

"How the fuck do you shoot someone in a car with an AK-47 and not break a window or pierce the skin?" O'Neill asked one lunch over a pair of single-malts at the Palm.

I had the same question. Woodruff had been stationed with the U.S. embassy in Tbilisi, in Georgia, when an off-duty soldier fired a single round through the back of Woodruff's Neva, miraculously passing between the rear window and the skin of the car. (Okay, there was a hole in the rubber seal, but it sure looked as if it had been made with a pen.) The police called it an accident. O'Neill's and my hypothesis was 180 degrees different: Someone probably stopped the car, pulled Woodruff out, shot him in the back of the head, and stuffed him in the rear seat. But we were a minority. The Georgian version was just fine with the State Department. This was 1994: Washington couldn't get enough of Eduard Shevardnadze, the Georgian president. Better to bury the dead and swallow some half-assed explanation that didn't even bother with ballistics than risk upsetting a Prince of Perestroika. Unless, like O'Neill and me, you cared about the truth.

I happened to be passing through New York back to Washington when we hashed over Woodruff, so I agreed to snoop around the Mothership and see what I could find that might give John a little ammunition to use against State. Two weeks later, when he was down in Washington visiting his own headquarters, I had him out to Langley, forced a government coffee down his throat, and showed him a defector's report that said Russian military intelligence, the GRU, had assassinated Woodruff pretty much as O'Neill and I had figured: opened the back of the Neva, popped him with a subsonic assassination round fired from a derringer, then poked the hole in the rubber seal to make it look like a stray, seeing-eye bullet had somehow done the dirty work. Just another GRU "liquid operation." It wasn't the final word, but it sure made a lot more sense than the lie Warren Christopher wanted us to swallow.

I suppose if you had asked either one of us, O'Neill and I both would have said we were friends. To the extent that he truly liked anyone tainted by Langley, I'm certain it was me. I'm pretty sure the reverse was true, too. I've never known a group with more pokers deeper up their asses than the FBI, but that wasn't O'Neill. Still, friendship among the professionally paranoid—and that included both of us—is a peculiar thing. It always comes with a price, always has a quid pro quo, a truth for a truth. Never stop trading. I'd done my turn. It was his now, and he knew it.

"Why didn't you tell me the Agency was following me?" I began.

O'Neill had left his old blue Buick Regal out front in the drop-off lane, a red gyro light on the dash. We leaned against the doors on the driver's side.

"Because they weren't."

"Come on," I said, "they as much as admitted it."

He was firing up a cigar, a lighter so elegant and razor thin that it was impossible to imagine where the wick and flint and whatever the hell else goes into a lighter might fit.

"Max, you forget. I'm the sheriff up here. I own the town." He took a deep puff on the cigar and let the smoke linger in his mouth. "I know those clowns weren't yours."

"And?"

"Right after you called, I sent a car up to the mosque to see what the hell you were up to. My guy was in place before you got there. He thought the Kazak goon was about to clip you when you came outside."

"He was."

"Why do I think he might have saved me a lot of trouble if he had."

I was eyeing a green Plymouth Gallant about ten yards downstream from us, trying to figure out why the traffic cops weren't moving it along.

"At any rate, he got down the plates of the cars that followed you up there. They were registered to Applied Science Research."

"Big deal. An Agency proprietary."

"Google it. Applied Science Research is a publicly held company. You guys got money to burn, but not like that."

He was right. The Agency owned hundreds of phony shelf companies, usually operated out of the offices of broke lawyers who'd do anything for a buck. But it never owned publicly held companies. Cost aside, it couldn't risk an SEC investigation or a shareholder suit.

"It doesn't make sense," I said. "There was a guy at my show trial— green retiree badge, bifocals. He all but admitted it was his team. He had to be counterespionage."

"Did he tell you that? Or did you assume it?"

"Assume what? Counterespionage?"

"No. That he was one of yours, and not a retiree working for some

Beltway bandit." O'Neill was trying to put his now-extinguished cigar back in its tube.

"He was there, for crissake. The seventh floor. We're not outsourcing counterintelligence!"

But even as I said it, I knew I could be wrong. The Dulles Corridor was thick with Agency retirees working for Beltway bandits with CIA contracts: SAIC, Booz Allen, DynCorp, Titan, McDonnell Douglas. Everyone I knew seemed to be doing it once they hit the magic fifty: Retire on a Friday, back in the building Monday morning with a shiny new green badge. They usually did scut work: hawking new computers and software, compiling statistics, rewriting accounting regulations. But who cared? They doubled their salaries overnight, while the companies that hired them got experts trained on the taxpayers' tab and a straight shot into the vitals of the CIA, where they could work on landing more contracts so they could make more money so they could fund the reelection campaigns of the favorite congressmen who gladly kept the merry-go-round spinning.

That wasn't the seventh floor's view, of course. It billed outsourcing as a slam-dunk win all the way around. The DCI could boast that he was tapping America's "corporate expertise"—buzzwords Congress loved to hear—even as he was tap-dancing his way around personnel ceilings imposed by the Office of Management and Budget. More to the point, hiring retirees in these jobs was a great way to "keep them in the family"—i.e., buy their silence. A six-figure salary on top of an Agency retirement was a fabulous incentive to make anyone think twice about writing a book or tattling to the press about how dismal things are in the Agency. Your classic golden handcuffs.

So maybe we were outsourcing counterintelligence. War would be next. But I didn't have the time to think about that. I needed something solid to grab on to, and my interrogator, Scott, seemed a good start. If I could find out who he was, I might find out why he had it in for me.

"You might have met him out at headquarters—thick plastic glasses, goatee, skinny as a rail except for a paunch that slops over his belt. Red face like, well . . ." I waved in the direction of O'Neill's own broken vessels and capillaries.

"It's genetic."

"It's Elaine's."

"Elaine's is genetic!"

O'Neill was bent over, checking himself in the side mirror, making sure his tie was centered just so.

"Soft as shit and twice as nasty?" he said once he had straightened up. "He might have come to an interagency meeting down at State to talk about embassy security. Gordon, I think his name was."

"He told me Scott."

"As I remember, he was wearing a Department of Army badge, but I could tell he belonged to you."

I didn't bother asking how.

"Did he work for Applied Science?"

"What do you think I did, brace him?"

O'Neill got in the Regal, cranked it over, listened to the engine cough and sputter, then gave up.

The traffic cops were walking by the green Plymouth for a third time without saying anything, not edging it along. Two women were sitting inside, doing none of the things women usually do when they sit together in a car: talk, fix their hair, file their nails, move their hands, move anything.

"Those yours?" I asked, pointing my chin in the Plymouth's direction.

O'Neill didn't even turn around to look. "I don't need backup to meet an asshole like you."

I let it drop. No cause to make O'Neill think I was having a psychotic episode.

"There's one thing I forgot," I said. "Jamal's partner in Panama is a Swedish crook. Goes by the name Lars Larsen. He's holding at least two accounts in his name for Jamal."

"Yeah, and there's one thing I forgot, too. I checked out Gordon. He works for Applied Science."

Son of a bitch. O'Neill had known he was right all along. They'd not only outsourced surveillance but the counterintelligence investigation, too.

"An Agency retiree?"

"Nope. Just a corporate cog. He was hired out of IBM."

It was worse than I'd thought.

"One last thing," I said. "Don't answer this if you can't, but are you investigating the Cabrillo thing?"

"What are you talking about?"

"I got put on unpaid admin leave."

"I heard."

"Some bullshit narco charge."

"Forget the narco charge. That's not what the investigation is about."

The Regal engine caught this time. He held the gas down until whatever was fouling the line cleared up. Then he took the gyro off the dash.

"Where are you heading to, Maxie?"

"Paris."

"A little R&R? Re-upping with tender Marissa?"

"Actually, the end of the line is Zurich. I have a job there. The investigation?"

"Millis," he said.

"John Millis?"

No end to the surprises.

"They want to tie you into the whole thing. Even suggested we hold you as a material witness."

"Whole thing?"

"You don't know? Some bright bulb out at the Fairfax medical examiner's office isn't buying suicide. You'll love this: They found some old classified photograph with your prints on it in his motel room."

O'Neill gunned the Regal once more, just to let me know he was leaving.

"What photo?" I asked. For some reason I was thinking about the DEA surveillance photo of me walking into the Paris bistro. If only.

"You know what one." And of course in that instant I did.

"So what, I gave Millis a photo of bin Laden," I said, feeling my jacket to make sure the Peshawar photo was still there. No point telling O'Neill I had a duplicate.

"Millis didn't know what bin Laden looked like?"

"I thought Buckley's kidnapper might be in the photo."

"Buckley's dead, Max. I'm surprised no one told you."

"Ever wonder who kidnapped him?"

"Ever hear about sticking to your own knitting? No one cares anymore. Case closed."

"Except for Buckley."

"You know, Max, heading for Switzerland isn't the smartest thing." He was looking at me as if I actually thought the dead might rise. "The script you were supposed to follow is stick around Washington and beg for your job back until they throw you some bone and you wag your tail like a good pup. S.O.P."

I didn't say anything but O'Neill was right. Now that I thought about it, I realized Webber had given me his cell phone number only because he expected me to call him and surrender.

O'Neill patted Jamal's corporate account number in his shirt pocket and goosed the gas a last time. The Regal was purring now. "Are we okay?"

"No." It finally hit me full force what O'Neill had said. "Millis committed suicide. His fingerprints were on the trigger." I was holding on to his door handle as if that somehow could stop O'Neill from pulling away.

"Lookit. The problem is the brain splatter wasn't where it was supposed to be. It was like he shot himself twice. Or someone else did. Or someone pulled his brain out his nose and smeared it around the bathroom."

O'Neill rolled up his window and pulled out into traffic.

CHAPTER 12

Something was rattling behind the bird's-eye maple paneling next to David Channing's elbow: some loose screw left behind by a quote-unquote "Old World master craftsman." If they were too inept to screw in the paneling, what did they manage to mess up with the wings or the avionics? You had to be suicidal to fly these days.

Boston was looming below him in the haze, lit by the early-morning sun. Somewhere under the soup was Cambridge . . . *Harvard*. Mother of Christ! And to think that puffed-up jackanapes Summers was going to run the place. He should have been impeached along with Clinton.

He looked over to the galley where Jesse was preparing breakfast.

"Jesse, come here," he shouted. "I need another come-to-God talk with you." He motioned to the seat next to his.

"See what we're flying over, Jesse?"

"Boston, Mr. Channing."

"No. Harvard. You know how much those little snot-nosed kids pay to go to school there?"

"No, sir."

"Thirty-seven thousand dollars, Jesse, more than I pay you in a year, and that's without buying toilet paper to wipe their asses. And do you know what they get for it?" He paused two beats, waited for Jesse to answer although he knew he wouldn't.

"You're right: fuck-all. It's branding, Jesse, branding. They're putting the mark on them so that when they drive away on Commencement Day in their spanking-new BMWs, everyone will know: 'I've never had an original thought of my own. I'm safe. I take tests, I build résumés. I'll never rock the boat. Daddy has enough dough so I'll never be tempted to steal from you.'"

Jesse remained silent looking out the window, his black face impassive. That's why he found Jesse fascinating: He had no idea what he was thinking. Maybe everything. Maybe nothing.

"Who was the last revolutionary to come out of Harvard? Don't bother!" he screamed. "I'll tell you! John Reed! John Fucking Goddamn Reed. Instead of the grand tour of Europe, he took the grand tour of the Russian Revolution, and the poor, dumb sonuvabitch didn't understand fuck-all about anything going on around him. That's Harvard for you."

Jesse kept looking out the window.

"Jesse, Jesse, Jesse. We don't seem to be getting anywhere. Remember how we talked about my great-great-granddaddy? How he stole half the forests of North America? Cut 'em down and made so much money that no one in his family for generations and generations would have to clean his own toilet again?"

"Yes, sir," Jesse said, staring straight ahead. "Yes, sir, I do remember."

"That's my point, Jesse. That's why I get to be a happy cliché and you don't. That's why I own a four-thousand-square-foot pied-à-terre on Central Park West. That's why I have my own island off Maine, why my second cousin is secretary of defense, why everyone's afraid not to take my calls. It's Great-Great-Granddaddy. He understood. He knew that power, real power, has nothing to do with those little Harvard shits. They're the ones I hire, Jesse. They're the ones I pay to clean my toilets because they're so fucking safe."

Jesse lifted an eye at him. He'd been Lysoling and polishing the head to a bright shine while the plane was taxiing for takeoff.

"It's a metaphor, for crissake. Figurative language! Dammit, Jesse, something's wrong. If there's something I can do and you don't tell me, I'm gonna get mad."

"Nothing, sir."

"Go get yourself a drink and me one, too, a champagne. A blanc de noir."

Harvard. The great liberal camp-out. More clueless, whining intellectuals per square inch than any other place on earth. Kennedy's brain trust, the kindergarten that completely missed the Sino-Soviet split and got us into Vietnam. And now it's 2001 and they're still trading in that Fukuyama crap about liberal democracy and the end of history. The global village, globaloney.

It's as if they'd never heard of an intercontinental ballistic missile. As if the Chinese hadn't stolen the plans for our miniaturized nuclear warheads and weren't peddling copies around the world like egg rolls. Rwanda is going to go nuclear before those dumb bastards stir from their slumber. And oil? They think you can go down to the local Starbucks and put all you need on your credit card. When the Chinese own it all, they might just catch on. Just wait: They'll get their wake-up call to the twenty-first century. The sooner the better.

There was a glint off to his left, low on the bulkhead opposite him—some kind of nameplate he had never noticed before. He slid into the seat next to it and bent to read: "The cabin of this Gulfstream G5-400 has been customized exclusively for the comfort of . . ." And then his own name in a flowing script—all of it, for crissake: "David *Oliver* Channing." They'd even managed to work in the logo he had designed himself: a C impaled on a sword.

The loose screw or whatever the hell it was was *ping-ping-pinging* in his head.

He crossed back over to his own seat, called out a number in Falls Church, Virginia, and listened as the recognition software converted his voice into beeps and whirs—another company he owned, which incidentally was a gold mine. The telephone rang seven times before the answering machine kicked in. Count on it: General Dynamics stock might be doing okay for the moment, but it was headed for the crapper. Flush and gone. It was—what?—already 8 A.M. and the goddamn owner of the company was still fiddling with his dick at home. Why didn't he have his secretary answer his private line? That's what civilized people do. Maybe the bastard was caught in traffic. Traffic is a goddamned nightmare in Washington. Everything is a nightmare in Washington, no matter who's in charge.

"George," he yelled when the please-leave-a-message beep finally came on. "I didn't spend forty million for your goddamn G5 so I could listen to screws rattle like some goddamn mariachi band. Fire the sonsuvbitches, or I'll buy the company and fire you!"

Channing roared with laughter as he hit the "off" button. "Welcome to your new day, Georgie." He made it sound like an obscenity. "Hope it's a swell one."

They'd known each other since they were kids: York Harbor, Yale, Skull & Bones. They'd even dated the same girl for a while back when they were classmates at Choate: a Cabot from Miss Porter's who spoke only to the Lodges, who spoke only to God. Stuck-up, lockjawed bitch wouldn't let you have any titty if you begged for it. Where was she now? Six feet under probably. Thin blood. The curse of the Brahmin class. He reached up and found the little pulsing artery in his neck, timed it against his watch: fifty-seven beats a minute. A congenitally slow heart: He'd live forever. Ha!

Breakfast in Bar Harbor, lunch in Sun Valley. Life is good.

They were still climbing. He could see Providence below; New Haven and Long Island, just cresting on the horizon.

"Nils," he said into the intercom, "don't forget to take her low around the bottom end of Manhattan."

He loved Nils, had hired him away from SAS. Nils could put a plane down on washboard rubble, and you wouldn't feel a thing. They were still climbing.

"Nils?"

"Permission, Mr. Channing. I'm trying to get permission to alter our flight plan."

He called out another phone number, knew this one would be answered. No one ever slept at the White House.

"Yes?"

"I want you to call my pilot immediately, and I want you to tell him he has permission to alter our flight plan as requested."

"I'll need—"

"Immediately. I think that still means 'at once.'"

He clicked the phone off, signaled to Jesse for another champagne. Seventy seconds passed by his watch before the plane began to level out. Ninety-three seconds before he felt the first slight shift of a descent.

He called the White House number again. "You're very good," he said, and hung up. He could hear it through the silent phone line: The man he had just spoken to would sell his own daughter into white slavery for the chance to come work for him. And why not? Administrations come and go. Incompetents elected by morons. Morons voted out by nincompoops. There's only one constant in the primeval soup: oil. Buy it from the ragheads. Sell it to the Harvard grads. And let the Hebes keep everyone in line. Better than Great-Great-Granddaddy's trees. Trees are renewable. Sort of. Oil is the endgame.

"There is a tide in the affairs of men, / Which, taken at the flood, leads on to fortune." He could remember the little androgynous prig of a teacher reciting that to them in Fourth Form, in his fake Shakespearean English. Still, something must have stuck because that's precisely what he had done: taken the tide at the crest, seen first from a little perch at State, then a higher one in the Reagan administration, and rode the wave all the way in. Georgie-Porgie had been there with him—dueling assistant secretaries of defense—but Georgie had the imagination of dog shit. Always had. That's why he was a boardroom serf. That's why I'm not.

Channing made a note to himself: *Endow chair.* Surely someone would remember the teacher's name.

The G5 was hugging the coast of Connecticut: Bridgeport, Westport, Darien, Stamford, Greenwich. Sweeping down the East River, he could see the commercial jets backed up on the runway at La Guardia, the helicopters grounded on their rooftop pads, all for him. And then there they were, right out the starboard windows: those twin Bastard Bauhaus atrocities, banality itself posing as architecture. God, they're hideous.

The Weimar Republic. There was that fraud Fukuyama's great goddamn liberal democracy. What a wonderful success *that* was. And let's not forget we have Weimar to thank for the Bauhaus movement that singlehandedly destroyed two thousand years of architecture. Walter Gropius was a Jew, wasn't he? Jew-loving Harvard Rockefellers did the World Trade Center deal. Jew movies, Jewollywood, Jew-loving faggots and niggers conned the rest of the morons into believing it was—What? What?—architecture? Beauty? Truth? Fuck. Skirting the towers in a hard bank, putting them out of his sight, climbing into the thin air over New Jersey—it was the closest thing he'd had to an orgasm in a long time.

"Nils," he said into the intercom, "that was memorable." I'll take him skiing in Chile, he thought: He'd once seen Nils snowboard down a thirty-five-plus-degree chute and never slow down—amazing!

There was a hum up by the front bulkhead, some beeps and rings barely audible. The HP fax, not the clattery Brothers one next to it. Only four people knew the HP number. Jesse jumped up to attend to it.

"Down!" Channing shouted. "I'll get it!"

He gathered the pages as they came out, pulled out a new packet of Hammermill Copy Plus from the drawer below the machine, and fed a stack into the back, just in case.

He waited for the fax machine to beep that it was done receiving, then he took the papers that had arrived, spread himself across both seats, nestled into the kid-soft leather until he was entirely comfortable, and began to read. Pennsylvania was disappearing beneath him.

TOP SECRET

NCIA 2-22-01
25 June 2001

NATIONAL COUNTERINTELLIGENCE ALERT
Number 6-25-01

SUBJECT: NCIA-235
HANDLE VIA COMINT CHANNELS
(DELETION)
SUBMITTED BY

DEPUTY DIRECTOR OF CENTRAL INTELLIGENCE
CONCURRED IN BY THE
UNITED STATES INTELLIGENCE BOARD
AS INDICATED OVERLEAF
25 JUNE 2001

AUTHENTICATED:

EXECUTIVE SECRETARY, USIB

SANITIZED FOR LAW ENFORCEMENT USE
E.O. 12356, SEC. 3.4
NIJ 00-320
BY ____, NARA, DATE 6-25-01
PAGES 12
COPY NO. 4

BACKGROUND

1. (TS) — deleted
2. (S) — Per CEC tasking, subject NCIA-235 was put under discreet physical and technical surveillance commencing 1 June 2001. In view of source sensitivities and specially compartmented programs, surveillance was conducted by ▓▓▓▓▓▓▓▓▓▓ rather than CEC. There was no indication that subject detected surveillance or was surveillance conscious.

SUMMARY OF FINANCIAL INVESTIGATION

3. (S), ▓▓▓▓▓▓▓▓ conducted a full financial on subject, including data as recent as 18 June 2001. FBI, NSA, Treasury, and other cooperating agencies provided independent traces. Positively identified accounts included "premier" checking at Riggs, an equities account at Legg Mason Inc., and two credit card accounts: Visa Platinum and American Express. (See Appendix A for deposit, withdrawal, transfer, and spending records.) All account activity was within parameters of subject's financial profile.
4. (S) Forensic investigation conducted by ▓▓▓▓▓▓▓▓▓ was unable to positively tie subject to José Marco Cabrillo. Neither could cooperating agencies. However, there was a consensus that subject's understanding of covert financial transactions would permit him to conceal financial ties to Cabrillo. Four Para 1 ref transfers to suspect Nauru account were referred to the Internal Revenue Service (IRS), which is currently conducting an audit for consideration of a possible criminal proceeding.

What insufferable shit. He jumped ahead. "Summary of Physical Surveillance . . . On 23 June 2001 at 1230 subject boarded Amtrak Metroliner going to New York. Subject took a taxi from Newark to Terminal B at Newark Airport, where he met at 1717 hours with an unidentified male. They were engaged in conversation for approximately twenty minutes.

Surveillance was able to identify UNSUB's license plate number, which is currently being traced . . ."

Blah. Blah. Blah. Bullshit. Bullshit. Bullshit. He flipped to "Recommendations."

- Task ███████████ to unilaterally monitor subject's activities in Switzerland and other overseas locations.
- Inform the Government of Switzerland that the USG is in the process of considering criminal charges against subject.
- Request cooperative liaison services monitor subject's activities in Switzerland, and in particular contact with hostile entities.

Oh, sweet Mary mother of Jesus, did they understand nothing? The whole point was to get the SOB's copy of the photo. And God knows what else he's carrying around. Didn't they see what he had in his safe? How he'd been showing that photo around Washington? Who could know what the fool might stumble across? Did no one think to call Immigrations or Customs and have him searched before he got on the plane to find out if he had it on him? How hard would that have been? He was already under investigation for narcotics! Now we're going to have to do it in Europe.

But what can you expect from people who aren't familiar with the English language. "Was able"? "Was observed"? "Was interviewed"? Where did people learn constructions like that? Moron school? And the evasions, the words that weren't words, the people who weren't people, the blackouts and whiteouts, things said and unsaid. "Subject NCIA-235," for crissake? What world, what parallel universe did they all live in?

Channing dropped the pages on the coffee table—more bird's-eye maple, pretentiousness itself—opened his eyes again, and found Jesse hovering over him with a tray: blood oranges, peeled and sectioned; sprigs of fresh mint; a Coke chilled in a crystal glass. He counted the ice cubes: one, two, three, four. He nodded to the table, waited until he had put the tray down, then raised his eyes to the partition.

"Vanish." But Jesse already had. He was rolling up points by the minute.

One thing was clear: His little company couldn't do surveillance worth shit. Gordon's florid nose disgusted him. So did his sagging paunch. Who had brought him on? "Find out," he wrote, then added: "FLAY THE IMBECILE." Applied Science was done. "Call Berch," he wrote in the margins.

Waller's networks bothered him. The "UNSUB" at Newark Airport was a mess, an unknown. "Need trace the Regal immediately!" he wrote. "Don't care if you have to break into car and steal registration." A cop? He had a vision of Waller's Rolodex: hundreds of names and numbers, all of them coded in variations of some tongue seventeen people on earth still bothered to speak regularly. *That* he could admire.

Why, then, would Waller go to Frank Beckman, the sluttiest slut in the oil business? *I could rent him for pennies.* Waller had to know about him. Surely, he wouldn't trust anything Beckman had to say. Beckman at least he knew he could find a way to handle: Push a little business his way, make him a little more money so he could add to his nouveau riche I-have-arrived! art collection, and the man would do anything he was asked. Linear motivation—so refreshing. Waller was another matter. Everyone has buttons to punch, strings to play. What were his?

Bloomberg quotes streamed across the top of the flat screen built into the paneling opposite him: sweet, crude, bunker; Nigeria, Caspian, Persian Gulf. Below them, the world passed by in CNN's banner shorthand: suicide bombers in Tel Aviv, retaliatory strikes in Gaza. Jihads brewing in the East, muscles flexing in the West. That was the beauty of this planet: its synergies, its predictabilities. For every action, an equal and opposite reaction. Jews killed Arabs. Arabs killed Jews. With each new death, the world improved, and the price of a barrel of oil climbed, climbed, climbed. Go long all the way. When you made the history, there was no guesswork involved.

For centuries, adventurers had searched for the philosopher's stone: the magic substance that would turn base metal to gold. He'd found it. From now on, G5's for him, graves for the rest. Comedy and tragedy. Survival of the fittest.

Channing scanned his notes one last time, committed them to memory, and fed the fax pages into a shredder tastefully concealed in the base of the coffee table. There was nothing you couldn't have in this world if you dreamed that it was yours. Then he called Jesse and handed him the little box of paper shreds.

"Destroy."

The man looked wide-eyed, nodded his head: Yes! Yes! And disappeared again behind his bulkhead. No wonder he liked him.

"Nils," he barked into the intercom, "are you fucking my wife?"

"Not yet, sir."

Not yet? Ha! Maybe he'd give him the damn G5 when he was sick of it. Nils could fit it with bomb bays and wing cannons—strafe the bastards, pound 'em back into the Stone Age, whoever the bastards were, which was just about everyone.

CHAPTER 13

D ANK WITH THE COUGHS, snuffles, and sweat of the pre-loaded, Flight 19 smelled like a locker room, and it wasn't even off the ground. Half a dozen brats bawled in their mothers' arms and begged for candy, Coca-Colas, a movie, breast milk, anything to relieve the pre-cognate sensation that they were about to be sealed in their own tomb.

Mercifully for the other passengers, Air France had shoehorned the freshman mixer into the final quarter of the plane, where I was headed. Towering backpacks loomed out of the overhead carriers, slammed half into place. Their owners draped themselves over their seats, gabbling on in a language tantalizingly similar to English (a phrase I stole, incidentally, from I don't know where). Twenty rows ahead of me, the rat-faced Hofstra kid cut left across the center block of seats, faded right down the far aisle, and hauled in a perfectly spiraled Nerf football. His all-Slim-Jim diet seemed to be just the thing for an Airbus wide receiver.

It took me ten minutes to push my way through to row 37. All the while, I was steeling myself to spend the night with feet propped on the duffel bag, trying to ignore some pill-popping young shit with his headset blasting Trans Am from Newark to Charles de Gaulle. I'd have no space to think, and I needed to do plenty of that now, starting with John Millis.

Instead, 37G was occupied by a tiny woman with a big battleship-gray coif. I guessed she was in her mid-sixties. She had a fat hardback spread on her lap and a pair of horn-rimmed reading glasses perched on the end of her nose. I found the plane uneasily warm, but my new seatmate looked the picture of comfort in her tastefully tailored two-piece suit. A Louis Vuitton carry-on took up half the rack above us. The other half was filled with a black overcoat folded so the lining was on the outside. The label stared out at me in gold letters: *YSL.* I figured she'd drift off right after takeoff. The perfect seatmate.

"Just be careful putting it back, dear," she said to me with a smile. "I'm sure there's room."

In fact, there was—just enough. The coat had a sable collar. I refolded it as if I were handling the Shroud of Turin. She smiled appreciatively at my ministrations and shifted her legs just enough for me to slip in beside her.

"Patricia Hoag-Carrington," she said briskly, offering me her hand.

I left it at Max and edged back her book just far enough to have a look at the title: *The Histories,* Herodotus. Harvard University Press. Greek and English on facing pages. "That'll keep you busy," I said, hoping she would go back to reading.

"Work," she said with a small sigh. "I teach at NYU. Ancient Greek."

"Of course."

My rule is to never get chatty with the person sitting next to me on an airplane. You let some small piece of information slip, no matter how seemingly innocuous, and your seatmate is one step closer to unraveling larger truths. I've learned to spike any budding conversation by confiding that I compile actuarial tables on cancer victims for Munich Re, the mega–insurance broker. No one yet has encouraged me to go on.

"Did you know," she said, "that Helen never made it to Troy? Hermes spirited her off to Egypt, while Paris showed up at the gates with a body double. Imagine, the most famous war in history, and it was fought under false pretenses."

Aren't they all? I thought. The First Crusade, Urban's famous exhortation at Clermont to rescue the Greeks being slaughtered in Jerusalem by the Muslim hordes. Except they weren't. Our own Civil War: free the slaves or steal a cheap labor pool. The Gulf of Tonkin and the Vietnam War. I kept my mouth shut, afraid I'd open the floodgates.

I don't know why, but I had a sense Patricia's amiability was brittle. I wasn't wrong. We had just leveled out at thirty-seven thousand feet when the dude with blond highlights in 38G kneed her seatback for the third time.

"Swine," she hissed as she eased her seat forward, then slammed it back again with surprising force. The "Fuck!" behind us suggested she had found her target. Satisfied, she turned her attention back my way. Fortunately, the stewardess saved me, looming over us.

"Coffee? An aperitif?"

The stewardess had a thousand-watt smile, but there was something cheerless about her all the same, one of those weird disconnects that always send me rummaging through my own memories of a disconnected childhood.

Patricia and I both ordered wine.

"*Salut,*" I said, intentionally butchering the French.

"*Santé,*" she corrected, and with that, Patricia Hoag-Carrington buried herself in her book and fell silent.

I picked up the novel I'd grabbed as I ran out the door of my apartment. A blurb promised "a riveting read with Tolstoyan sweep and Dickensian vitality." It could have delivered instant nirvana, and it still couldn't take my mind off what O'Neill said about Millis being murdered. Or that Millis had the Peshawar photo with him in the motel room. I stowed the riveting read and opened up the small napkin that came with my wine. With a pen fished from my jeans pocket, I drew a small, neat *M* right in the middle of the paper and began trying to piece together everything I knew.

First, the facts, or what I had assumed them to be until a few hours earlier:

John Millis was found shot to death on June 4, 2000, a Sunday, two days after I let him walk away from the Tune Inn with the photo. To be specific, Millis locked himself in a room at the Breezeway Motel in Fairfax, Virginia, leaned the side of his head into the muzzle of a twelve-gauge shotgun he'd bought only that afternoon at a nearby Wal-Mart, and pulled the trigger. There were powder burns on his hands, all the proof needed that the fatal wound had been self-inflicted, until (if O'Neill wasn't wrong or fucking with my head) someone noticed that Millis's brain had ended up where by the law of physics it shouldn't have.

As for motive, two hours before his death, Millis had walked out of a meeting with Rep. Porter Goss, the chairman of the House Intelligence Committee. The story had it that Goss had convened the small gathering to fire his staff director after George Tenet had showed him incontrovertible evidence that Millis was singing like a canary to the press; but neither Goss nor his chief counsel, who was also present, were talking, at least to anyone who talked to me.

The motive part of the story had never made complete sense to me. In Washington, leaking is a rite of passage—proof that you're in the know and too important to be held accountable for it. Besides, Millis had put his name on plenty of controversial assertions in the months before his death, like the time he told a Smithsonian audience that John Deutsch took first, second, *and* third prizes when it came to being the worst CIA director in history and that Bill Clinton was the worst president ever in terms of supporting the intelligence services. Still, in the absence of any other reason, I was willing to accept this one. Disgrace, if that's what it was, hits us all from different angles.

As for the photo that seemed to tie me to this sad event, or murder, or whatever Millis's death was, it had been part of what's officially known as a "201" file—a Directorate of Operations informant's file. That's what I had been looking for when I took the time off to go through Archives.

The place reminded me of the scene at the end of *Raiders of the Lost Ark* where they're storing the ark in a dark, cavernous warehouse. Just to prove to me that she hadn't been lying, the archivist who declared the file missing dropped the cardboard container on the counter between us from high enough up to launch a dust cloud and with enough *whoof* to let me know it was completely empty. One thing I'd learned in a quarter-century in the Agency is that you never take no for an answer, so I trotted out the lost-little-boy look that my ex-wife used to claim was my only honest expression and asked as meekly as I could muster:

"Would it be possible to see the boxes stored on either *side* of this one?"

And so we went for hours and hours—the boxes next to the boxes next to the boxes—until finally the archivist wrote me out a pass so I could rummage through the shelves myself, and that's when, twenty-four hours later, I came upon the photo in an eight-by-eleven manila envelope marked *Peshawar 387490,* with the lost "201" file number on it but not with the file itself.

Triumphant, I signed a form temporarily transferring the photo to my office. As promised, a courier delivered the Peshawar photo along with a dupe I'd requested (the one I now had in my pocket) to me a week later.

"Salmon?"

I looked up and saw my seatmate almost imperceptibly shake her head: No. "Too dry," she mouthed. Beyond her, our cheerful-cheerless stewardess was holding two disposable plates.

"The other," I answered, which is how I happened to come into possession of a coq au vin, served on a bed of noodles, with a sidecar of carrots and green beans and a prosciutto-and-melon salad. It looked tasty enough, but the first bite told me Air France was outsourcing its meals, maybe to someplace like Guinea Bissau. I just hoped they weren't doing the same with maintenance.

Patricia and I were sipping our wine when 38G wriggled his stockinged foot into the space between our two chairs. We could almost see the odor coming off the threads.

"Should I break his toes?" I asked, hoping to stay on her good side.

"Heavens no," she answered as she eased her seat forward once more and slammed it back again, with even more force than she had before, if that were possible. The sound behind us this time was so pitiable that I suspect she must have driven something—the other foot; a Walkman; perish the thought, even a book spine—straight into 38G's manhood. I turned to steal a peek through the crack between our seats and saw him gobbling pills wholesale out of a makeshift vial and washing them down with some kind of soda pop. Uppers, downers, simple Ibuprofin—who knew. When I turned back, our dinner plates were gone. Patricia had a cup of steaming tea by her hand, thankfully her nose back in Herodotus.

I retrieved the napkin I'd been writing on from my shirt pocket, flipped it over, wrote a "?" this time dead center in the paper square, and started over again. Why was the photo important enough for Millis to have it with him in the motel room? Other than bin Laden, he'd said he recognized only a Palestinian and a Gulf prince. Neither had any contact with the Agency, Millis was sure. I traced Nabil Shahadah after our lunch, and indeed there was nothing in the records indicating we'd ever met him. Millis had no idea about the headless guy in the salwar chemise. And whose name from the photo was he going to give me, anyway?

A lot of other questions nagged at me, too, like the disappeared 201 file. I'd seen Archives lose a lot of documents, but this time I didn't want to let it go as a coincidence. Every time I seemed to be closing in on identifying Colonel Mousavi—whether it was via our own archives or the UCLA registrar's office—the paperwork had gone missing in front of me. What I kept coming back to, and this had been bothering me ever since the Tune Inn, was why Millis had been so damn eager to leave when I asked him who the headless horseman was? And what did all this have to do with Bill Buckley?

I waited until my seatmate had gone off to the restroom, then stuffed my doodle-napkin into my unread novel, re-stowed that in the pouch on the back of the seat in front of me, opened the overhead rack, and slipped my laptop out of the carry-on.

I started typing a chronology of events, from the first embassy bombing to Buckley's kidnapping, events and the details surrounding them I had long ago memorized from my spiral notebooks. I was skimming them for answers when Patricia returned, wiggled once to settle herself comfortably, and went back to her book without so much as a glance my way. Just to be on the safe side, I skewed the screen slightly to the right, but not so much that I couldn't read it or that its reflection could be seen clearly from the window beside me.

I couldn't find a single connection between Buckley's kidnapping, bin Laden, and Peshawar. There wasn't a shred of evidence anywhere in the files that Colonel Mousavi had been in Pakistan in the late 1980s or that he'd met bin Laden. Millis had said he couldn't remember any Iranian close to bin Laden. But maybe he didn't know. Or maybe he didn't want me to know. That left me with the mystery of a twelve-year-old photo. Did Millis know what the connection was? Or was he just carrying the photo with him that last day of his life because he couldn't think of any place to stow it? And how much sense did that make?

Then there was the ransacking of my office by security. Someone clearly had wanted my spiral notebooks. Or were they looking for the duplicate of the same photo, aware that Archives had signed over two copies to me?

In espionage, the hard part isn't connecting the dots; it's figuring out what is a dot and what isn't.

CHAPTER 14

ATRICIA HOAG-CARRINGTON had given up on Herodotus by the time I came back to earth again. Watching me tap on my keyboard was apparently far more interesting even though she couldn't see the screen.

"Doesn't a bottle of ice-cold water sound delicious?" she asked when I looked up at her.

I didn't know what was the matter with pushing the little button overhead that summoned a stewardess, but I was thirsty myself, for something slightly stronger. I closed my laptop down, put it back in its carrying case, and waited for Patricia to slip her legs to the side before turning toward the galley to see what I could rustle up.

At the far end of row 37, the Hofstra rat had a mini DVD camera out. Why couldn't he just snore and drool like everyone else on the plane, I wondered, or watch *Erin Brockovich* for the fiftieth time? As I headed up the aisle, I caught Hofstra doing a quick pan around him. What ever happened to keeping a travel journal?

I've always felt safe in airplanes. Thieves, touts, garden-variety scum—airplanes were the one place where they left you alone. Even domestic crises could disappear when you're encapsulated in a plane. When Marissa and I were fracturing, I actually looked forward to shuttling back and forth across the Atlantic. Thirty-seven thousand feet up was the one place she couldn't call me. But I'd learned another lesson in my twenty-five years in the business, and that was: Trust No One. Even inside the sanctity of headquarters, surrounded only by people who have the highest clearances possible, when you have to take a piss, you carry with you every classified piece of paper you arrived with. That's what hit me now. The Hofstra kid's camera pan meant nothing, but it made me nervous enough to turn back, reach across my seatmate for my laptop, and stow it in my carry-on in the overhead rack.

The stewardesses were half asleep at the back of the plane. I roused one of them to find some of those miniature bottles of Scotch and an Evian for Patricia. She wandered into the rear galley and seemed to open twenty drawers. In the middle of it Muhlenberg popped in and asked for a Coke. I shrugged my shoulders to let the stewardess know I didn't mind waiting. Next, Muhlenberg asked for some peanuts, then a napkin; then she tried to strike up a conversation with the woman. I was beginning to think I might grow old and die exactly where I stood when she finally waddled back down the aisle. The stewardess looked as relieved as I did as she fitted me out with four drink-size hits of Dewar's, a plastic glass, and a bottle for my seatmate. The water was warm, but I wheedled a second glass out of her, filled with ice.

Back at row 37, Patricia was snoring daintily, glasses still perched magically on the tip of her nose, hands folded on the open pages of her book. My novel was lying on the seat, not in the pouch where I had left it. I reached over Patricia, gave the pages a shake, and when nothing came out, I knew my notes were gone.

My carry-on had been rifled, too. It almost fell on Patricia's head when

I flipped open the overhead bin. I could tell by its shape that the laptop was gone, but I stuck my hand in anyway, just to make sure. I must have stared at my carry-on for a full minute, wondering if I'd finally lost my mind, before I broadened the search. The inside pocket where I'd stowed my passport was empty. Who would steal a passport on a plane? Didn't everyone already have one when they boarded? Get robbed on an airplane, and any residual illusions about sanctity vanish completely.

I was returning my carry-on to the overhead compartment when I saw Patricia's Louis Vuitton staring me in the face. It, too, had been shifted slightly. Her black overcoat was skewed to the side. Patricia had been the one, after all, who sent me for water. Even if someone had been looking at her do it, they would have assumed she was searching through her own bag. It was insane, probably, but I eased back the zipper on her carry-on, stuck my hand inside, and began to feel around.

"For great wrongdoing, there are great punishments from the gods." The voice came from below me.

"Herodotus?"

She nodded her head yes.

"I don't suppose it would do any good if I—"

She simply shook her head in the opposite direction as I zipped her bag closed and quietly snapped in place the lid of the overhead bin. Patricia didn't bother to move her legs to let me in. By the time I had climbed over her, reshut my book and stowed it, and let down the table tray, her eyes were closed again, her breathing soft and steady.

I put Patricia's water bottle in the net pouch on the back of the seat in front of her, gave myself a reassuring hug, and was reassured in turn by the slim contours of my two stolen passports, my address book, and the tiny fortune safely tucked in the inside lining of my jacket. And a good thing it was because at that moment the last thing I looked forward to was presenting myself to the French airport police without a passport. They would have sent me on to the vice-consul at the American embassy, who would have forwarded my name to Foggy Bottom, where enough bells and whistles would have gone off that the Mothership would be alerted immediately and Webber could have treated himself to another diamond ring.

Of course, there was still a chance the French would figure out I was trying to enter the country on a stolen passport, in which event I'd be spending the day and night in La Santé, the notorious Paris prison where etiquette calls for welcoming each new invitee with a full cavity search. But that was a chance I was willing to take. I unscrewed the tops from my four bottles, poured them all into the glass, and reached up to flick off my own light. Time to self-medicate.

CHAPTER 15

A SHELL-POCKED ROAD. Rock-strewn fields stretched out in every direction as far as the eye could see. I was standing in the middle of it, wearing a fluorescent orange shirt bright as any school crossing guard, but the strange thing was that I seemed to be invisible. A pair of Russian Mig-27's came toward me full blowers, maybe twenty yards off the ground. As they got closer, I saw I was wrong. They were F-15's, ours. The roar was deafening; their exhaust, like showering in a hot mist of gasoline. They were looking for me. What else would they be doing out there? But even though I couldn't be missed—I stood out like a nun in a slaughterhouse—they hadn't seen me.

A dust storm started up on the horizon straight in front of me, grew larger, came closer until I realized it was a column of Bradleys—fifty of them, a hundred, two hundred, I had no perspective, no angle, no way to judge where the end of the line might be. Even if I couldn't be seen, I needed to move, had to get out of their path, realized now they were bearing down on me at Grand Prix speed. But my feet wouldn't budge. I couldn't tell what it was: My shoes were somehow magnetized to the roadbed. The lead Bradley was a football field from me, then twenty yards. Then someone grabbed me by the arm. I looked over at him. He had flaming red hair. Sapphire blue eyes. He was pulling me, yelling at me in French-accented American English to run, save myself.

"Welcome to Charles de Gaulle Airport," someone squawked from an overhead speaker in three languages, none of them clear. Outside the window, Paris looked to be underwater, but maybe that was just me.

Patricia Hoag-Carrington's temperament remained sour. She rose while the plane was still taxiing, stared hard at me, then snapped open the overhead bin, carefully shook her coat out, took down her Louis Vuitton carry-on, and without ever looking at me again started up the aisle.

"Madame!" the stewardess called out. "Madame! Non!" But to no avail.

Relieved to be free of her scorn, I waited my turn. Herodotus's injunction about great misfortune still sat heavily on me.

The immigration line was moving at a snail's pace. I pulled out the Irish passport, boned up on who I was and where and when I'd been born. Thanks to the miracle of modern document doctoring, Eamon Mooney and I couldn't have looked more alike if we had been hatched from the same sperm cell and ovum. Sleep deprivation must have taken its toll because I remembered my yellow entry form just in time to scribble in the blanks and hand it to the blue-shirted cop along with my passport.

"Ah," he said after a quick glance. "Ireland. Land of Joyce." And waved me through.

After I grabbed my garment bag from the baggage carousel and cleared customs, I took an elevator down to a sub-basement where I'd once met an Algerian baggage handler who claimed to have proof that a Saudi prince was a transvestite turning tricks in that famous Parisian open-air whorehouse, the Bois de Bologne. He wasn't, but I remembered the out-of-the-way café for airport employees where I'd met him. I needed a caffeine fix.

I was sitting by myself, nursing an espresso and reading *Le Figaro*, when I heard the whir of an electric baggage cart coming down the hall in the direction of the café. An African in a blue jumpsuit, airport badges dangling from his pocket, sat behind the wheel. The cart itself was stacked high with magazines, newspapers, and paperbacks all bound up with plastic straps. I was turning back to my own reading when I saw a man lunge at the baggage cart and grab the steering wheel. Drunk, I said to myself, just as the cart swerved and came barreling toward the café, and that's when I knew that what I was seeing wasn't what was happening at all.

Early on in my career with the CIA, I'd taken a monthlong course in a "shoot house." The first day we learned to kick down a door, roll into a room with a mixture of dummy hostages and their captors, and take out the bad guys with a Heckler & Koch MP5 on single shot. It was a walk in the park. I double-tapped all three terrorists, point blank in the forehead, and with the suppressor there was barely a pop. The next day, they turned out the lights and gave me a pair of night-vision goggles. My pickups weren't as fast, but still I didn't hit a hostage. A week later, after they'd ratcheted up the pace, they took my silencer away. Next they set off deafening flash-bang grenades. After that, they made us exercise until our heartbeat hit 145. Each day the pressure went up. The last day, I kicked open the door and was met by a wall of deafening and blinding flash-bang grenades, thundering music, targets moving all over the place. I was dead before I got off a single round.

In shoot-house speak, what they were trying to teach us was "target discrimination." When things go to shit, you have to decide in a split second what the immediate danger is. Then the next. What do the bad guys want you to do. And what's going to save the hostages' lives, and yours. All this raced through my mind in an instant, the way great training always does, as the cart driver bore down on me. I waited until the last second, until there was no space left to correct course, before I rolled to the side and watched him careen into the wall behind me and go flying face first into its mirror panels.

Blood, shouting—I feigned interest until the drunk, suddenly sober, grabbed my carry-on and garment bag, and took off at a half-trot that all but begged me to race after him. Ahab could have run faster, peg leg and all, but that in fact was the point. As he was taking off, I did a lightning inventory of the two bags' contents. My clothes. Toiletries. All replaceable. If I followed, a scene would ensue, one of the parties to which—me—had entered France on a stolen passport. The next thing I knew, the police would be calling the Irish embassy.

I still had what mattered—the photo, two passports, and my money. I'd stick with the plan: Go into Paris, see if I dragged anything with me, catch my breath, and take an afternoon train to Zurich.

I went out the arrivals door and stood in the taxi queue. Two dozen people in front of me, Patricia Hoag-Carrington was just getting into a cab. I half expected something dramatic—a last-minute wave, a flip of that improbable sable collar against what was already a warm Parisian sun—but there was nothing of the sort. Instead, I got to wonder what she had possibly been doing in the airport all that time, especially since she had raced off the plane like a woman on a mission.

Maybe twenty-five yards in front of Patricia, a minibus sat parked at the curb with a sign in the back window: FIRST HERSHEY BIBLE CLUB. I couldn't be certain from my distance—and my track record of late was no comfort—but I thought I recognized a pair of porcine hips and a feral profile clambering onto the minibus. I was about to write if off when Muhlenberg popped up at the back window next to the sign, waved frantically to catch my attention, and blew me a kiss while Hofstra shot me the bird.

Knowing they were together changed everything.

CHAPTER 16

NOT ONLY HAD I HAD BLANKET COVERAGE all the way
from Newark, and from New York a few days earlier; they also
wanted me to know they were on me. That's what that little pop-
up screen featuring Muhlenberg and Hofstra had been all about—a message: We've got you in our sights, we'll always have you in our sights, so
give it up or else. The wrecked Norton and the guy in the poncho in front
of my Adams Morgan apartment calling me paranoid were part of the
same campaign. But give what up? My spiral notebooks, my laptop, my
luggage were gone. Since the only thing I had left was the photo, that had
to be the prize. Whoever was after me knew there were two copies from the
missing 201 file. One was accounted for, with John Millis's blood splat-
tered all over it. That left one at large, and that meant me. Time to tie up
loose ends, then change course.

I went back in the airport, bought a telephone card from the news
kiosk, placed a call to New York University, and got the all-night operator.

"Normal business hours—"

There's been an accident, I explained in my best broken English. A traffic fatality on the road to Lyon. All we've been able to recover was a plastic faculty ID card.

The operator transferred me to the campus security office, which assured me that no one by the name Patricia Hoag-Carrington taught at NYU, adjunct or on staff, classics department or anywhere else.

"But—"

"No one."

My second call was to Chris Corsini, the one person in America who should have gotten used to my calling in the middle of the night.

"Corsini, it's Max."

"Great. It's—what—two-oh-three in the morning." I could practically hear him checking his Breitling.

"Sorry."

"Why do I have the feeling I'm about to board the lunatic express?" In the background, I could hear his wife telling me, him, someone to die.

"I need a real big favor. A name."

"It can't wait, I'll bet."

"I wouldn't be calling . . . I need it in the next twenty-four hours."

"Jesus. Okay. Whose?"

"Wait. Is there a pay phone near you?"

"How would I know? I own my—"

"A 7-Eleven? An all-night pharmacy? Something like that."

"I guess so. Why?"

"Here. Take this down." I read off the number in front of me on my own pay phone. "Find one and call me from it. Five minutes."

"You're sloshed, Max. Fucked up in the head. Or both."

He hung up. I called him back.

"Chris, this is life or death. I'm not fucking with you. I can't take the chance your phone is tapped."

"All right, all right. My God, I've lost my mind, too. Not five minutes, though. Ten. Maybe fifteen."

He called me back in ten. I could hear trucks grinding by on a highway not far away.

"I need to know who was sitting in seat 37G, AF 19 last night."

"Huh?"

"I'll explain later. A woman."

"Shit almighty. You barely get away from one and now you meet some bimbo on an airplane who refused to give you her name. Maybe not such a bimbo after all."

"First thing Monday, call your compliance officer and give him the flight number, the seat number. He can get his private investigator to check airline reservations. Air France is either on Apollo or Saber airline databases. He'll figure it out."

"They'll take me out in a straitjacket."

"Match the seat number to a credit card, and you get a name."

"Why don't you get one of your shady friends to do it?"

Shady friends? Maybe Chris knew me better than I ever realized. But the private security business is a tiny, tight world, and everyone in it is tied to some intel service one way or another. Chances were very good that this little trace request would end up in Langley no matter how carefully I couched it. Outsourcing through Chris was just about my only chance to hide my hand.

"Chris, I really, really need this."

"If I promise to do it, you'll let me go home and back to sleep?"

"Not yet."

"Shit."

"Another number. Take it down." I read off Webber's cell phone, the one I'd cajoled out of him at headquarters. "I need to know every call he made Friday after five."

"Is this legal?"

"Your compliance guy will know the way it works. They get it from the international registry."

"Okay." That's what he said. What he meant was, he'd do it, and I'd pay him back for the rest of my life.

. . .

Next I called Yuri Duplenski in Damascus. The phone sputtered as if it might catch fire any moment. I kept yelling Yuri's name into the static, until finally a voice boomed back at me.

"Who?"

"Max. Max Waller."

"Who?"

I was shouting into the phone so loud, people stopped to stare at me.

"Max?" Yuri finally said. "Max!"

Yuri and I hadn't seen each other since 1984 when he was working for the GRU, Soviet military intelligence, in Beirut. Our last get-together had been a memorable one, though: a vodka binge that ended as so many of them seemed to do when one of us got the brilliant idea of driving up to the Biqa' and firing off a rocket-propelled grenade at Israeli lines. Fortunately, I ran my car into a ditch before we ever got out of Beirut.

At one point I'd considered recruiting Yuri as an informant. I even loaned him two thousand dollars after Moscow started asking about some money that seemed to have gone missing from his till. My loan saved Yuri from a recall to Moscow, maybe worse, and in the normal course of events, I could have used it to reel Yuri in to our side. But I eventually decided he wasn't recruitable. Yuri had big dreams. There was no way the CIA could ever pay out the kind of money he was after. I never got around to asking him for the money back, just swallowed it. I wasn't going to mention it to him now on the telephone. But he and I understood our bonds were deeper than friendship.

"You know how to drink yet, Max?" Yuri had no intention of letting me forget our last ride.

"Yes. No. Anyhow, I need a ride out of Europe."

I'd read in an intelligence report that after the breakup of the Soviet Union, Yuri had left the GRU for the black-arms market and was now operating a fleet of ships and planes around the Med, Africa, and the Middle East. Or maybe he was still in the GRU, selling arms. It didn't matter. In Russia, lines separating state business and criminal business have never been very well defined.

"I got it," Yuri said. "There's a woman after you."

"Actually it's something else."

"Italy. La Spezia," he said. "First stop is Benghazi. Then—"

"I'll take it." I'd figure out later where to get off.

I could hear him leafing through some kind of book, running his finger down a list, cursing the tiny print and his failing eyesight.

"She leaves the day after next at—" He lost his spot, fumbled again with the schedule, and found it once more. "Oh two hundred. An auto transport. Just show up."

"Who do I ask for when I get there?"

"Ask for? Max, you don't need to ask for anybody. The captain will be looking for you. He'll have your cabin ready. I'll greet you myself when the ship docks."

The final call was to Rikki, my daughter. Her fourteenth birthday was in three days. I was going to send her something nice from Zurich. No more. The phone rang eight times before her voice-mail greeting kicked in: a parade of barking dogs. I had no idea what it meant. I waited until they were through, then sang "Happy Birthday" into the phone in Arabic. The woman at the phone station next to mine looked at me as if she thought I might explode myself any moment.

I headed for the elevators but, instead of waiting, raced down the stairs to the basement level again and through the same cafeteria where I'd almost been run over—the place was still a mess. The Algerian baggage handler I'd met there years before had shown me an employee exit at the back of the kitchen, up a small flight of stairs. The door wasn't alarmed, just one sleepy security guard who nodded at me as I went through. Walk with enough authority and you can blow by half the security guards in the world.

Outside, I headed straight for one of the employee bus stops. Eight of them were idling at the curb. I jumped on the one going to Vitry-sur-Seine just as it was starting to pull away. No one got on after me, the most positive note I'd had in a while.

CHAPTER 17

Vitry-sur-Seine, France

I'D BEEN TO VITRY-SUR-SEINE BEFORE. It's tucked into an industrial zone southeast of Paris, one of those innocuously named "cités" where the French hide the North African Muslims who do all the nation's dirty work. We'd caught some "chatter" that Algerian fundamentalist groups were using a place called Carthage Voyages to pick up cash and make travel arrangements. The French busted it a couple times but the owners refused to talk. The French even tapped the phones and still got nothing. I'd gone out myself after hours to have a look, but the owners, whoever they were, seemed to be the model of discretion.

When I got there this time, Carthage Voyages had yet to open, but at least it hadn't moved or—by the looks of the tidy counter inside, packed with brochures—closed down. I crossed the road and ducked into a café full of Algerian and Moroccan workers in blue overalls, smoking their Galois and sipping triple espressos. If there was a word of French being spoken, I couldn't hear it. I ordered my own triple, in Arabic, the closest I could come at the moment to belonging to anything, and settled myself at a table in the front window with a two-day-old copy of *El Khabar,* a mouthpiece of Algeria's military dictatorship.

I was still at it forty-five minutes later, working on a second espresso, when a woman in a burka stepped off a bus at the corner, seemed to glide down the street inside her shapeless tent, stopped to study the window displays at Carthage Voyages, then unlocked the door and began turning lights on. The clock over the coffee bar read exactly nine-thirty as I paid and left.

"May I help you?" the woman asked when I entered. Like her expression, her tone of voice was unreadable.

"I need a ride to Italy. Trieste." (Never tell anyone where you're really going if you don't have to.)

"I don't have a car."

"Later?"

She didn't say anything—just picked up a phone, dialed a number, and spoke Berber-laced Arabic so rapid I could barely catch it.

"Tomorrow morning, six A.M., here," she said finally, a statement, not a question. She seemed used to people who had run out of other choices. Living among French infidels had also taught her not to cultivate curiosity.

I said good-bye and wandered up the street, hunting for a sex shop. I was looking for a woman maybe six feet tall, something in an inflatable latex.

CHAPTER 18

It was hard to tell who looked worse: me after a day of sitting in smoky dives, checking every exit and entrance to see if I was being watched, and a mostly sleepless night on a bench in the RER train station, or my driver. He'd been working since ten the night before, he said. The bags under his eyes spread out like pancakes. I offered to start out behind the wheel, but he shook his head. In fact, I never got a word out of him for the first four hours of the drive. He didn't even offer me his name.

Outside Lyon, he nearly swerved off the A-6, then cut the wheel back so sharply that we almost flipped. Turned out we'd both been asleep at the time.

"*Un café?*" he asked, finally surrendering.

I stood outside for five minutes waiting for the driver to reappear, trying to wake myself up, then went into the Courte Paille to look for him. He was asleep, head down on his crossed arms, at a little table off to the side.

A sip or two remained in his espresso cup. A baguette, two-thirds eaten, teetered on the edge of the table by his elbow. My world being what it had become, I gave his shoulder a small shake, just to confirm that sleep was all we were dealing with. He groaned slightly, raised his head an inch or two, and let it collapse back on to his arms again.

I took the wheel when we got in the car. He was too tired to protest. A hundred kilometers later, just as the road traversed a patch that looked down on a picture-postcard valley, my driver climbed into the backseat and began snoring uproariously.

The day was gray but cloudless, perfect weather for losing myself in the Alps. I'd decided to find an obscure *pensione* somewhere, finally get a good meal, sleep, pay cash, use up the little time I likely had left on the Irish passport, lay low for another twenty-four hours, and find a new car and driver to cross the border and wind my way on down to La Spezia.

By Bourg d'Oisans, the sky had begun to brighten. I stopped at a café tacked on to the side of a Total station for a coffee of my own without bothering to wake the driver. For all he cared or knew, I could have flown to the moon and back.

The café was empty except for a couple sitting at a booth, picking at each other over their pastries. I bellied up to the bar—*au zinc,* as the French say—and ordered a café crème and a croissant. I was on the second jolt of caffeine when the door opened and a head popped in, took a quick look around, then followed its splendid nose inside. Definitely Gallic, but definitely out of place. Even the bickering couple stopped long enough to give him a once-over. He was wearing a bomber jacket zipped up practically to the neck. Nothing unusual there. The temperature was dropping as we climbed—it couldn't have been more than forty-five degrees or so outside. Still, it was obvious that he had a tie and white shirt on underneath. This was the Alps. Summer or winter, you leave your office clothes at home. This guy had to be surveillance, and to butcher the old song, it had to be me.

In one way, I wasn't surprised. The French are good at this sort of thing. Unlike the FBI and the CIA, the French services work together: military intelligence, the national police, and the locals, all in one seamless operation, which means they have eyes and ears everywhere. All they had to do was canvass the airport with my photo, find the bus driver who took me to Vitry-sur-Seine, and hit the streets until they picked up my trail. The burka woman at Carthage Voyages wouldn't rat out her fellow Algerians if the French pulled her nails out one by one, but I wasn't worth a scratchy cuticle to her. Fair enough, but still, I had to wonder who mobilized the French. But that wasn't my immediate concern; now there was no way I could drive into Italy without the French alerting the Italians and the Italians picking me up on the other side of the border.

My driver was sitting behind the wheel, engine running, when I came out.

"Take it slow up to La Grave," I told him as I took his place in the backseat. "Real slow."

He didn't ask why, but he did. The road doesn't give you a lot of choice: It's all switchbacks and steep ascent. But there's slow and slower, and at maybe seventy klicks, we were easily the pokiest car on the mountainside. Drivers behind us were flashing their lights. Some wagged their fingers as they passed us. I was looking for the car that didn't seem to mind dawdling.

My driver noticed them before I did: a pair of Renault 25's, one charcoal gray and the other beige, hanging back behind us, going just as slow as we were. Fat, stubby antennas stuck out of the middle of the roofs of both cars.

"How long?" I asked him.

"Ever since we left the gas station."

The driver started to speed up, but I told him to slow back down. No point in irritating the French any more than I had to or giving them any reason to pull us over. For one thing, the Irish passport now was certainly worthless. Besides, I had work to do. I reached into the plastic bag I'd been hauling along ever since Paris, took out my latex sex kitten—sex Amazon, actually—unfolded her across the backseat, and started blowing. I'd just finished by the time we rounded the final bend. By then, the driver looked as if he was thinking about slamming on the brakes and making a run for it.

. . .

Val d'Isère is a sight in any season. The Pissaillas glacier looms above the town, skiable through most of the summer. Below that stretches the vast Espace Killy, ten thousand hectares of some of the best bowls in the world, named for the French national hero who was nearly unbeatable on these slopes through all of the 1960s. I'd first come here just about the time Jean-Claude Killy's career was on the downside—rock climbing in the Alps with some friends, back when the town of Val d'Isère was a real place. When I returned the next time, in 1992, just as the Winter Olympics were ending, the place had been torn down and rebuilt by a band of marauding Disney imagineers.

I handed the driver five hundred-dollar bills, told him to slow to a baby crawl at the roundabout in the center of town, then ducked out between two tourist minibuses double-parked in front of Killy Sports. As I left the backseat, I sat the sex doll up in my place. I was standing in the recess between the minibuses when the two Renaults circled past me and took off after the cab, back in the direction of La Grave.

Inside Killy Sports, the display counters had all been given over to summer sports—the whole resort had been turned into a sun-and-fun camp for the few who could afford it—but I convinced a surprised clerk to let me into the storeroom where they kept the skiing stuff. While she tapped her heel, I flew through the supplies, not bothering with prices: Gore-Tex pants, Gore-Tex jacket, Gore-Tex gloves, Gore-Tex socks, goggles, ski cap, backpack, high-energy bars, a compass, a vinyl map that seemed to show every knoll for twenty miles around. Amazingly enough, I found a beautiful, top-of-the-line pair of Finnish Karhu backcountry skis, Fritschi bindings, and synthetic skins. Run-of-the mill alpine skis weren't going to work for the route I had in mind. There'd be as many ascents as descents. The free heel and skins would get me up most any slope. By the time I was through, I was out ten thousand francs plus—loose change by Val d'Isère standards.

I must have caught the last lift up the glacier. The restaurant at the top was all but empty now—no wait for the pay phone. Frank Beckman, I was sure, had sent word to both Marc Rousset and Michelle Zwanzig that I was on my way. I had no intention of following up with either of them now. My life had gotten way too complicated for that, but I didn't want them or anyone else sending out an APB because I hadn't arrived. I would tell them I'd been delayed in Paris, family emergency, anything to buy some time. I started with Rousset. His cell phone was turned off. A digital voice answered Zwanzig's phone. The number had been changed; no mention of what the new one might be. Weird. I was staring at her card right in front of me. Three days ago, Frank had assured me she was my route to his Saudi billionaire. I phoned Frank at home to see what was up. No answer. Or on his second line. Or his third one. Or on his cell. Rousset and Zwanzig I didn't care about—that was a sidelight—but Frank's disappearing gnawed at me. He was supposed to be my lifeline. And he was never out of touch.

I looked at Frank's home numbers again. All three were consecutive. I took a chance and dialed the next one in sequence. It was India's private line.

"What are you doing at home?" I asked. "Who's looking after our national interests?"

"I took the day off. Were you trying to get Dad? I think he's already left."

There was something clipped about her voice, uneasy. I didn't think it was me.

"I tried his other numbers—thought I'd take a chance on—"

"Where are you?"

"The French Alps. A skiing holiday."

"June, Max. *Été*."

"The Pissaillas glacier. There's supposedly some new snow."

"Right. Listen . . ."

I didn't like the edge in her voice.

"Are you busy?"

There was a long pause. It sounded as if she was pacing back and forth. I thought of that glimpse I'd had of her a few days earlier, behind the curtain in the room above the library—the princess trapped in a tower of gold.

"Max, they're after you."

"I know. But who?"

"Not now. Not on the phone."

"Is it work?"

There was another long pause—no pacing this time. I thought maybe we'd been cut off.

"Some people were here last night to see Dad. He shushed me out of the room, but I could hear them through the air-conditioning vent in my bedroom."

Another vision: India, lying on her side, ear pressed to the metal grill.

"What did they say?"

She laughed just for a moment. "I heard Dad call you a well-hit three-wood in a tile bathroom."

"Huh?"

"He's mad at you about something. I don't know what it is."

"It must be the truth thing."

"What?"

"Nothing," I said.

"You've got to go someplace safe." The laughter was gone, the strain back. Whatever she'd heard had been enough to scare her, for me, maybe for her father and even herself. I wanted to tell her that the only safe place I knew of was the one where I would be in the greatest danger, but why scare her more.

"I will."

"Promise?"

"Promise. Listen, thanks."

She didn't want to hang up. Sometimes you can feel it over a telephone line.

"India—"

"It's okay. I'm fine."

"If you're worried about something . . ."

"What?"

"I don't know. We'll talk when I get back."

"Good old Uncle Max, looking out for little India." At least she sounded better. The tension was out of her voice.

"That's me, but you're not so little. Got to go. I've got your number. I'll call in a week."

"You don't know how much this means to me," Chris said when he answered, "not calling at two in the morning."

"That's me. Thoughtful. Webber?"

"Got it. But they gave me three months of calls. You want them all?"

"Yeah, sure. Here, copy down this number."

I gave Chris an e-fax line secured with a PIN code. It ran off a spoof, or triple-eight server, meaning if someone was tapping Chris's fax line, they wouldn't be able to trace his fax to me.

I was almost afraid to ask the next question, about Patricia, afraid to break my streak of luck.

"Did you get her name?"

"Joan Hanahan."

She'd lied to me. No surprise there.

"I'll bet she paid cash." That's what I would have done if it were me putting a surveillance team on an airplane.

"No. She paid with a corporate credit card. Visa, I think. I've got the number here somewhere. . . ."

"Don't need it. Just the name of the company."

I could hear Chris open a drawer and shuffle through it.

"Applied Science Research."

That was sloppy. But after the circus in New York I wasn't surprised.

"Don't you wanna know who owns Applied Science?" Chris asked. "Eight big pension funds. But here's the strange thing. There's also an outfit out of the Caymans. Its shares look like they're protected by a half dozen dummy companies. It stinks."

"Who owns the Caymans company?"

"I'll dig around."

"Chris—"

"I know. You love me."

"Who wouldn't."

CHAPTER 19

ACK OUTSIDE IT FELT like winter. Anyone in his right mind would have taken the lift back down to Val d'Isère. Not me. I stepped into my bindings, tightened up my pack, lowered my goggles, and pushed off down the glacier east toward Italy, *Il Bel Paese*.

My goal was the Colle del Nivolet, the end of the paved road that winds up into the Italian Alps out of Turin. It didn't look that tough when I planned the route: The Colle sits more than twelve hundred meters below Val d'Isère, less than ten miles away, across terrain I had traversed before. But I was almost thirty years younger then. Or maybe it was the round earth, flat-map syndrome. Or the fact that I was now running on fumes. Anyhow, by night, on skis, in my mid-forties, it was a miracle I made it.

Melting and freezing, freezing and melting had left the top a slick of ice. I needed crampons and an axe more than skis. Clouds kept obscuring the moon. At one point I was sure I was about to slide down a five-hundred-foot chute on my back. It turned out to be only five feet, but it scared the hell out of me all the same. I went up and down at least three thousand feet, taking my skis on and off as the glaciers appeared and reappeared, until my quads were on fire. Then a small release sluiced me over a cornice. Fortunately, it wasn't much of a drop. If there hadn't been a moon and if I hadn't been lucky, my frozen carcass would still be up there, lodged in a crevasse, waiting to be discovered a thousand years hence by some alien race with silicon chips for hearts.

But I was lucky, and I finally did make it to the tiny Italian outpost of Chiapili, a little after dawn. Thirty minutes later, I hitched a ride with a milk truck down to Ceresole Reale, at the bottom of the lake by the same name. From there, two hundred American dollars found me a ride to Turin and another two hundred—same driver, different car—to Genoa. In the Piazza Principe, I caught the last bus of the day to La Spezia, and by one-thirty that morning, I was doling out twenty American dollars to a half-drunk cabbie, who got lost four times before he found the port. At one point we ran out of gas and I had to give him money to put twenty liters in the tank.

Even then, I must have wandered around the docks for half an hour or more before I found a lineup of a couple dozen virtually brand-new Mercedes, Porsches, and Audis, and followed them right on board. *An auto transport,* Yuri had told me. Maybe he'd gone legit.

CHAPTER 20

I'D SPENT MY LIFE in shitholes where the water is undrinkable, where the rats carry bubonic plague, where you're lucky if you just catch malaria, and I'd never been sick a day. Two hours after we left port on Yuri's rust bucket, I was hit with a fever that I was sure was pneumonia. I slept for forty-eight hours, shivering and sweating. Probably longer. My cabin didn't have a porthole. I couldn't tell day from night. I slept right through Benghazi and a couple other ports.

By day three, the fever felt like it was breaking, but I still couldn't eat or even leave my bunk except when I had to. On the fourth day, I stepped unsteadily out on deck, took a brief stroll around, and did a double take. We'd left La Spezia sailing under the *Xerxes II*. Now we were the *Demopolis*. I had this suspicion we were carrying more than just cars.

I was an albatross, bad luck. The crew ignored me. It was fine with me. I had time to try to sort out the story to date. Here's what bothered me: I'd had blanket coverage all the way from Newark, and at least a day in New

York a week earlier. Both times it was Applied Science Research, a company I now knew (thanks to O'Neill) Webber had on contract to do his dirty work. I then get to Paris, and someone calls in the French. It couldn't have been Applied Science Research on its own. The French still have too much common sense to outsource espionage. There had to have been some kind of nod from the CIA. Webber again? He had been assigned to Paris and would have known who to call. I didn't have a shred of evidence it was him, but it was the only thing I could think of. Who else would mobilize a resource like that? Still, it didn't add up. Webber wanted me out of the Agency, sure, but now that I was gone, why keep up the chase?

Then there was the mystery of robbing me. The first time, on the plane, they got my laptop. The second time, in the café, my clothes. The only thing of value I had left was the photo. I'd already established that. The only reason for calling in the French that I could think of was to set up another chance at grabbing it. But who other than me cared about a twelve-year-old snapshot? Webber? Not likely. O'Neill was right: No one in the government, CIA or otherwise, gave a damn about Bill Buckley.

Still, it had to be the photo. And if the interest in it had nothing to do with Buckley, then it was someone else. Or something else. I was sweating in a dark cabin, churning through all the possibilities I could come up with, when the blindingly obvious occurred to me: Ask someone in the photo. I could immediately cross off bin Laden. The Taliban would cut my head off as soon as I tried to cross the border into Afghanistan. That left me with Nabil Shahadah, the only other person in the photo I knew by name.

Shahadah wasn't going to be easy to find. At least three Israeli commando teams had been shot up trying to get to him before me. Now drones armed with Hellfire missiles flew over Gaza 24/7 ready to incinerate Nabil the first lock they got. Still, I couldn't see another choice. If I didn't get an answer to the picture, I'd live the rest of my life as the Flying Dutchman of ex-spooks, pursued for a reason I couldn't begin to understand. First, though, I needed to put down a red herring.

CHAPTER 21

ASK THE AVERAGE PERSON what he thinks "going off the grid" means, and he'll tell you something about catching a Greyhound bus in Wilmington, Delaware, getting off in Bozeman, Montana, hiking up into the mountains, building a shack out of bark, and going without electricity, a phone, or anything else that links you to the digital cosmos. He has it only half right.

Going off the grid in my world means two things. Step one: Systematically erase all "stable indices" in your life. No credit cards, no checks, no cell phones, no calls to family or anyone else who could be tied to you in any database. I'd already executed most of step one, or more accurately, the thief on the plane had: getting rid of my true-name passport. The cash had freed me of credit cards. Carthage Voyages and Yuri was another step in the right direction. There was no database in the world that could connect me to them. (I'd never reported either to headquarters, although I have to admit I couldn't eliminate the possibility that Yuri had reported his contact with me to Moscow.) Skiing into Italy meant I left no border prints, either.

Step two is just as important: Create a virtual identity in another place, preferably another country. You need to give your pursuers something to do, waste their time and money, and irritate the hell out of local authorities with leads that don't go anywhere.

I dozed off for yet another long sleep and woke to find the boat stopped dead in the water, engines idling. It was dark, eleven at night by my watch. I was half amazed in my stupor at the humanlike cries of the seabirds, and then I realized they weren't birds at all. We were docked. Larnaca. Cyprus. I grabbed my jacket—everything I now owned—and went up on deck. The *Demopolis* or whatever we were now called was deserted. A parade of roaches the size of field mice led the way down the gangplank.

I'd spent enough time in and out of the harbor to know that this close to midnight, immigrations and customs would be closed, or at least dozing. I could have walked out of the port unchallenged, but I needed to start establishing a virtual persona here. I pounded on the door of immigrations for at least ten minutes until some bleary-eyed guy with his shirttail out sleepily recorded the arrival of Eamon Mooney, stamped the Irish passport, and let me through without a word.

From there, I checked into a suite at the Flamingo Beach Hotel, then went back out to cruise Larnaca's run-down waterfront until I came to Scottie's, a scabby imitation-pub watering hole for sunburnt and homesick Brits. At the end of the bar were three twenty-something girls partying, one brunette and two blondes. I sat next to the bemused blonde in a pink spaghetti-strap tank top.

"Eamon," I said, sticking out my hand, nodding to her two friends.

"What kind of Yank has a name like Eamon?" she asked. Australian to the bone.

I pulled out a wad of bills, bought a round of drinks for the four of us. The brunette and the other blonde took their drinks and wandered off, leaving Alice to me.

Alice was from Alice Springs, although maybe that was just to help her remember both sides of her story. She'd just quit her waitressing job and was blowing her savings on a one-way trip to London—via Cyprus—where she hoped to figure out life.

By the time the bartender started to pull down the metal shutters an hour or so later, Alice was too sloshed to walk on her own. I helped her out the door, and by the time we got to my hotel, I was practically carrying her. The desk clerk at the Flamingo didn't give Alice a second look.

Up in my room, I tucked Alice in and sat down on the corner of my bed. She was asleep before her head hit the pillow.

I called my old office near Tysons Corner, hoping someone would be working at least to closing time. Jake was—just the guy I'd hoped to talk with.

"Max, what happened to you?" He pretended to be pleased to hear from me.

"I'm in Larnaca. On my way to Jeddah. I need a favor."

Silence.

"I need to see Rafik Hariri. Know anyone who knows how to get in touch with him in Jeddah?"

Hariri was Lebanon's prime minister, although he'd made his fortune in Saudi Arabia. Even after he became prime minister, Hariri spent a good part of his life in Saudi Arabia. A lot of Lebanese considered him a paid agent of the Saudi royal family.

"I wouldn't go near him, especially you, especially now."

"I'm on to something. Something I've been after for years. Hariri holds the keys. Isn't there some ex–case officer who works in Hariri's Jeddah office?"

In fact, I knew exactly who I was talking about: Bill McGuiness. I could see him clear as day charging down the halls, always looking straight ahead, never acknowledging anyone. Ex-Marine. Silver-blond hair. Every other word was *fuck*.

"You mean that crazy bastard who snarled like a mad dog?" Jake said. "Bill something."

"That's it. Bill McGuiness. Got a telephone number for him?"

"Sorry."

"It's okay. I'll find him. But if you can think of anything, I'm at the Flamingo in Larnaca."

What was going to happen within the next five minutes was that Jake would walk into his new boss's office and relay my conversation word for word. The new boss would then call the Counter-Espionage Center, setting off a blizzard of one-page memos about Max Waller's going off the reservation. The seventh floor would go on full alert, especially after Counter-Espionage produced my spiral notebook and the Peshawar photo as Exhibit A. What better evidence that I was still after the Buckley grail.

Headquarters would easily buy off on the story line that I was on my way to Saudi Arabia to see Hariri. Hariri ran his own private intelligence service. As prime minister of Lebanon he could tap into all sorts of official Lebanese intelligence bases. He was in a position to dig up something on Buckley. But just as useful for my misdirection, as far as the seventh floor was concerned, I couldn't be in worse company.

After Bill McGuiness was fired for gross incompetence, he spilled every secret he knew to Hariri. He came close to being indicted. On top of it, Hariri was despised on the seventh floor. In Jeddah in the early seventies—back when he was a procurer of girls and liquor for the Saudi royal family—he'd openly cultivated connections to the CIA, using them as a platform to claim to the royals that he was a conduit to Washington. (Hookers aside, Hariri's reporting turned out to be all lies, and headquarters eventually dumped him.) Now that he was a prime minister and a triple A-list player in Washington, pouring millions into K Street lobbying firms, Hariri had set himself up as the avowed enemy of the CIA, dumping on it at every party he attended. The way headquarters would look at it, having Bill McGuiness, Hariri, and me together in Saudi Arabia was the perfect storm.

There'd be meetings all day tomorrow at Langley, followed by calls to the Cypriots and the Saudis. My bet was Alice's wake-up would be a cop pounding on the door. They wouldn't find me, but I wanted them to think they knew where I was going and why. It would take them a month to figure out I wasn't on my way to the Kingdom.

Just to make sure no one missed the lead, I wrote Alice a note and propped it on the dresser: "Had to pop over to Jeddah a couple days. Please stay. Restaurant etc. is at your disposal. Eamon."

Downstairs, I left a thousand-dollar deposit with the desk clerk and asked him to make me a reservation to Jeddah on the first flight. While I waited for a cab to the airport, I borrowed the desk clerk's computer and logged into the e-fax site I'd left with Chris Corsini: one last unfinished piece of business before I disappeared.

Chris had come through: an eighty-six-page list of all Webber's cell calls for the previous three months. The evening Webber sacked me he'd called three numbers. One, in San Diego, he'd dialed six times. A quick reverse-directory check told me it was Applied Science. That's exactly what I'd expected. The second number was one in Maine. The reverse directory listed a post office box as an address, but no name to go along with it.

The third number Webber had called that evening I didn't need to look up: It was Frank Beckman's house.

CHAPTER 22

Tel Aviv, Israel

A S THE YOUNG IMMIGRATIONS GIRL at Ben Gurion Airport read my German passport and tapped in the name and birthday, I kept my fingers crossed that, one, she didn't speak German (mine was seriously flawed); two, she didn't notice I didn't look like a Horst Friedrich Arends; and, three, the Germans were as lazy as the Irish and hadn't sent a notification around that the passport was stolen. In the middle of her tapping she made a call, turned away from me, and whispered into the telephone handset. I figured I'd been spotted and wondered how many years I would get for trying to enter Israel on phony paper. But the call apparently had nothing to do with me, and she waved me through without looking at me a second time.

I didn't tell the Palestinian taxi driver I wanted to go to the West Bank until we were out of the airport and it was too late for him to tell me to fuck off. June had been an especially bad month for taxis getting stoned and shot up in the West Bank, even ones with Palestinian plates. I didn't mention the word *Rafat,* where Nabil was from and where I was going, until we were well past Jerusalem.

The driver knew Rafat was a fire-breathing Hamas stronghold. Several commanders of Hamas's military wing and a half dozen suicide bombers came from there. The Israeli army entered it only in force and backed up with heavy armor. The driver agreed to keep going only after I handed him $250 and promised to pay him another $250 when we got back to Tel Aviv.

Two hours east of Tel Aviv, we cut off the main highway and bumped down a dirt road. A thirty-minute drive over barren, hardscrabble hills, and we came to Rafat, which sits on top of a windswept ridge. It looks pretty much like every other poor village in that part of the West Bank: unpaved, dusty streets, stone houses, groves of terraced olive trees in ground more rock than dirt.

The driver had to ask three times before we found where Nabil Sha-hadah's father lived, and then we found it only by spotting the heap of rubble and grove of ploughed-up olive trees in front of the house just below his. I didn't need to be told the story. As soon as the Israelis found out Nabil was a new impresario of suicide bombings, army bulldozers showed up and flattened everything that belonged to him. The house, I'd read somewhere, had been built by Nabil's father in the hope that Nabil would marry one day and come back to Rafat to live. I suppose Nabil's father was lucky; if Nabil had been living at home, the father's house would have been bulldozed, too.

Razing houses, displacing families, and generally spreading misery among the brothers and sisters, the fathers and mothers of suicide bombers was Old Testament justice, the way the Israelis looked at it. An eye for an eye, tooth for tooth, a message to any would-be suicide bombers: You spend eternity in a celestial garden, but your family pays the price in the here and now. Long ago the Israelis had figured out that the Palestinians' Achilles' heel is the family. Palestinians—all Arabs, really—are bonded to their families in ways we can't begin to understand in the West. Find some way to tap into those bonds, and you knock the wind out of the resistance. Or so the Israelis were counting on.

.   .   .

Nabil's father, Muhammad, was standing out in front of his house when we pulled up. With his sad eyes and in his dirty dishdash and frayed silk cap, he looked tired, defeated maybe, another victim of a war that seemed to have no winners.

I told Nabil's father I was a German journalist doing a profile on his son.

The father shook my hand and motioned me to a cement bench running along the side of the house. He pulled up an old rickety table as his wife brought us two cups of tea that were more sugar than tea and a plate of cookies. She went back inside to leave us alone to talk.

"Nabil was a good boy," the father said. "A good student, a good son."

It sounded practiced and probably was. Nabil was a hero in the Arab world. Hundreds of journalists came to Rafat to interview his father.

"A brilliant electrical engineer, I heard," I said, encouraging him to talk.

One of the first things they taught us about interrogation at the Farm is to enter the logic of whoever you're talking with. If you're interrogating Icarus, don't confront him on how smart it was to jump off a cliff with wings made of feathers, wax, and linen, and fly into the sun. Instead, ask him about the various qualities of wax, the best feathers, the weight of the linen. You always want to make someone feel you're on his side.

The father motioned me to get up and follow him inside. There was a small bookcase filled with college textbooks. I pulled one out. Neatly written on the flyleaf was *Nabil Muhammad Shahadah* and a year, *1994*. I pulled out a loose piece of paper; it was a drawing for the firing mechanism of a rocket-propelled grenade.

I looked around the room; there was no memento from Nabil's time with bin Laden. I remembered that after Afghanistan—he'd been there less than six months—Nabil returned to Rafat, finished high school, and went to Birzeit University. Three years later, he had his degree in electrical engineering. He had joined Hamas at some point when he was at the university, but the Israelis first found out about him, or rather his handiwork, when they were hit by a series of roadside bombs set off by remote-control detonators— detonators designed and built by Nabil.

"Nabil always held a suit so well," the father said, pointing to a picture of his son hanging over the sofa. "He was a handsome boy. He has so many of them." He motioned me to follow him again, this time upstairs.

In a back bedroom the father opened a closet door to reveal a rack of suits. He shook the hangers gently, dusted the shoulders of the suits with a cloth from his pocket.

Back outside, I told the father I intended to find Nabil and interview him.

"I haven't talked to him in two years," he said.

"But you know how to get in touch with him, don't you?"

"No."

The father was probably lying, but I couldn't blame him. He was just being cautious. Nabil had a friend in Hamas who talked with his own father by phone nearly every day. Israeli intelligence didn't know where the son was hiding, but they did know which part of Gaza he'd gone to ground in. So they arranged to have phone service cut off for that area, then convinced an informant to carry an explosive-trapped cell phone to the son. The phone rang, the informant answered, and he handed it to the son, telling him it was his father. The son couldn't resist: "Daddy, is that you?" Instantly, the Israelis detonated the phone over the signal, peeling half the son's head away.

"Maybe I could find him through a friend," I offered. "One of them must know where he is."

The father looked at me as if I were some sort of improbable daydreamer.

"They're all dead or in jail," he said.

"Surely there must be one."

"No."

"Wasn't there a boy from Salfit that Nabil almost got arrested with?" I said. I'd read about him in an intelligence report. "They were friends."

"Hassan Saleh? He's in Bir Shiva. He'll never get out. And you'll never be allowed to see him."

He was right about not getting out. Saleh was serving a life sentence for organizing a pair of suicide bombings in Jerusalem and one in Haifa. Bir Shiva prison was where Israel housed its "national security" prisoners, the Hamas and Islamic suicide bombing networks.

"Let me try," I said. "If I see Nabil, can I give him a note from you?"

The father looked at me for a moment and then called his wife. They went off in the corner of the garden and had an animated conversation, then came back and sat down. The father asked me for a piece of paper and wrote a one-page letter to Nabil. He handed it to his wife so she could read it. She folded it up and gave it to me. They must have decided writing a note to their son wasn't going to make it any easier for the Israelis to find him.

Before I left I pulled out a disposable camera I'd bought at Larnaca Airport and took a picture of them for their son. It was the first time they smiled since I'd arrived.

CHAPTER 23

Bir Shiva, Israel

A BLAST OF WIND roared off the Negev desert just as I exited the taxi in front of Bir Shiva prison. Plastic trash bags were plastered against the outer chain-link fence and the rolls of razor wire that topped it. The sun was almost blocked out by the swirling sand. A hundred feet south of the prison I could just make out a Bedouin encampment, camels and all.

The guard in the booth at the outer perimeter was on the phone talking. I pounded on the door to get his attention, waving a letter from the Israeli Prison System. He slid open the window, took it, and called someone on his walkie-talkie.

"Wait," he told me, pointing to an open shed covered by a tin roof.

Peri, my retired Shin Bet friend who had arranged the letter for me, advised me not to bother going to see Hassan Saleh. An unrepentant mass murderer, he wasn't going to tell me anything useful.

"I can make him sit down with you, but that's all," Peri said.

I didn't really have any other choice. It was the only name Nabil's father gave me. The rest of Nabil's group was either dead or, like Nabil, on the run.

"He'll never say a word," Peri insisted. "Don't waste your time."

Peri didn't need to say it, but I knew he was also nervous about being the one who was getting me into Wing Six. Leftist journalists, especially the Scandinavians, were known for passing messages from inmates to the outside. If the prison officials suspected that's what I was doing, I'd wind up in a cell myself.

I shared the waiting shed with a Palestinian family who looked as if they'd been there for days. At noon, when the sandstorm finally seemed to pass, the old lady opened a satchel of partially burnt wood and charcoal and prepared tea. She saw me watching and prepared a cup for me. By the time the tea was ready, the wind had picked up again.

We huddled together in the shed, barely able to hear one another over the wind. The woman told me she was there to visit her son, who was doing three years for theft. When I told her I was waiting to see someone in Wing Six, I'm sure she thought I was lying or crazy. No visitor ever got to see the prisoners in Wing Six, including parents. Prisoners weren't allowed to make or receive phone calls, either.

More than an hour later the Israeli guard walked over to the shed and crooked a finger my way: "Mr. Arends, you can go in."

At the main guardhouse they took everything: cell phone, keys, belts, even my Bic pen, giving me one of theirs for the interview. The guard let me take in my yellow eighty-by-eleven pad after he fanned it to make sure nothing was in it. Fortunately, I had the photo of Muhammad Shahadah and his wife and their letter to Nabil in my pocket.

The guard waved me into an air lock. After the door closed behind me, the one in front clicked open and a voice came over the loudspeaker in German telling me to come through. On the other side, I walked through a metal detector and then an organic strip searcher, which detects explosives secreted on the body.

I felt as if I was about to enter the *Death Star* and come face-to-face with Darth Vader. Instead, a striking, petite woman in a sky-blue prison-guard uniform met me on the other side. She looked Moroccan. We walked side by side, not saying a word, until we came to a two-story blue pastel building surrounded by rolls of razor wire and an electrified fence. Wing Six.

The woman and I waited silently in Wing Six's air lock for another five minutes while they locked down the prisoners. A guard then led me out into the prison exercise yard while my escort stayed behind. A thick metal screen and razor wire covered the yard. No Hollywood helicopter rescues from this place.

A minute later Hassan Saleh appeared, shackles on his legs, cuffed from behind. The guards pushed him through into the exercise area, then waited while Hassan turned his back so his shackles could be removed through two holes in the bottom of the door. Freed for the moment, he walked over and sat down in the chair next to mine. He didn't offer his hand or say a word.

Saleh was a small man with small hands. His prison uniform hung on him loosely. His green eyes, the color of antifreeze, were fixed on mine. Both of his hands were badly burned, no doubt from chemicals.

I started by telling him I was doing a profile on him for *Der Spiegel,* the German weekly. I could have told him I was writing an article on floor waxes for *Good Housekeeping* for all the reaction I got. I hadn't expected this guy to be a complete mute. My experience had been that prisoners locked down for three years welcomed conversation with a stranger, even with a journalist. Not this one.

I threw out a couple banal questions, like were the prisoners treated well, was the food okay, did the guards speak Arabic. The more I willed him to respond, the harder Saleh studied the mesh wire above us. Finally, I pulled out the picture of Nabil's father and mother and nudged Saleh with my foot. "Look at this."

Nabil's father had told me he'd known Saleh from when he was a child. Saleh had played with Nabil in Nabil's parents' living room. When Saleh was arrested, Nabil's father had gone to Saleh's parents' house to offer his sympathy.

Saleh took the picture from me and stared at it. He then looked back up at me.

"Your brother graduated from high school two weeks ago," I said, another piece of information I'd gotten from Nabil's father. He told me Saleh and his brother were very close. "He's doing fine. He'll be at the university this year."

Saleh now blinked. "What do you want?" he said, speaking for the first time.

"Let me ask you what you want. Would you like me to call your brother and tell him you're okay?"

"You know what they do here? They steal your time. But we do just the same. We read. We recite the Koran. We strengthen our faith. We steal our time back. I'm not just okay, I'm at peace."

I noticed the guard was pacing impatiently back and forth on the other side of the mesh wire watching us, no doubt surprised I'd gotten Saleh to talk.

"Do you want me to call your brother or not?"

Saleh didn't answer.

"I already have his phone number."

Saleh looked over at the guard, leaned closer to me, and whispered in my ear. "Okay. In two days it's his birthday. Wish him happy birthday."

"I will. Now a question you won't like. How do I find Nabil Shahadah?"

Saleh stood up abruptly and motioned to the guard that he wanted to go back to his cell.

As the guard started to unbolt the metal door to the exercise yard, I held the picture of Nabil's parents up to his face.

"I saw them yesterday," I said. "They haven't talked to Nabil in three years. Are you telling me you don't care whether Nabil gets the picture or not?"

"I don't know who Nabil Shahadah is."

I pulled out the letter Nabil's parents had written from my pocket and handed it to Saleh.

As Saleh read it, he shifted from foot to foot, no longer calm. The guard was now in the exercise yard walking toward us.

"Let me write my parents' telephone number," he said, grabbing my eighty-by-eleven pad. He quickly wrote something and then handed the pad back.

The guard led him away as I read what he'd written: *Gaza. Beach Camp. Port Video.*

CHAPTER 24

Gaza City, Gaza

ONE PALESTINIAN REFUGEE CAMP looks pretty much like another: unfinished cinder-block houses intersected by dirt roads, mounds of rotting trash, posters of suicide bombers pasted on the walls. But the Gaza Strip's Beach Camp is different—narrower streets, more rubble, more menacing. Although the Israelis regularly hit the place with drones and F-16's, Israeli assassination teams stayed clear of it. It was too dangerous.

I walked up and down the Beach Camp's main street, looking for the Port Video, but it wasn't where it was supposed to be. Either it never existed or it was long gone. Back on the coast road, I found a man in his sixties, manning a vegetable cart. He thought about it, rubbing his chin, and then pointed at an abandoned building three houses back along the road I'd just come down. "Maybe it was there, I think," he said. "It closed a long time ago."

I went back up and had a look, but there was nothing to show it had ever been a video store or anything else. Rebars stuck out of the unfinished third floor, waiting for an addition that there would never be enough money for. I kept having the feeling I'd wandered onto a Becket stage set.

Across the street, I noticed a gaunt kid in a ripped Che Guevara T-shirt and military fatigue pants, maybe all of fourteen, toothpick arms folded across his chest. He was leaning against a wall, watching me.

I walked over to him. "Do you know where I can find Nabil Shahadah?"

Instead of answering, the kid pushed himself off the wall, sauntered a few steps down the pitted mud road, and disappeared into the interior of the camp. I waited ten minutes but he never came back.

Saleh had lied to me so I'd go away, I figured. It was that simple: a video store that wasn't a video store for the journalist who wasn't a journalist. But maybe it was more than that. Maybe I was being set up. The obvious next move was to head back to my hotel and get back into Israel as fast as I could. Instead, I decided to make another attempt to find Nabil in the morning.

It was too humid to sleep. The electricity was off. There was no breeze. Only the mosquitos were stirring. For company, I had a late wedding party outside my window. Around one in the morning I gave up on sleep altogether and went out for a walk, south along the road toward Gaza's fishing port. I was nearly out the door before I remembered to grab my pad and photos. Never, ever leave anything in a hotel room.

It was better walking along the beach. There was a puff of a breeze off the water. Thousands of lights twinkled offshore—fishing boats—none of them more than two miles out because of the Israeli blockade. I was a hundred yards down from the hotel when I noticed someone following me. I crossed the street diagonally and caught a glimpse of him: the kid with the toothpick arms from that afternoon. He followed me across the street, gaining on me.

"Come," he said in English.

He turned away from the beach road into a poor neighborhood. I followed him through a maze of cardboard shacks, sheet-metal lean-tos, and more rough cinder-block houses with open sewers running beside them.

We came to a trash dump watched by two Fedayeen in fatigues, sitting in the back of a Toyota pickup with a .30-caliber, belt-fed machine gun cradled between their knees.

The kid left me there, just turned and seemed to disappear through one of the cinder-block walls that ran alongside the dump. The humidity and stench had my stomach roiling. Happily, I'd eaten almost nothing that day.

One of the Fedayeen motioned me to an old Toyota Land Cruiser, indicating I was to get into the backseat. The other Fedayeen got in with me, forced me on the floor, and threw a blanket over me.

We drove around for a full hour, cutting through back streets, onto an open highway, and then across a washboard dirt road. At one point, the Toyota bottomed out over what felt like a trench, slamming me hard against the floor.

When we eventually stopped, someone pulled me roughly out of the back, pushed me against the side of the car, and yanked the eight-by-eleven pad and photos out of my hand. Two new Fedayeen, faces covered with kafiyahs, walked up to us. The taller was carrying a stubby AK with a grenade launcher under the barrel. The short one grabbed me by the arm and led me down a couple of narrowing alleys and through the ground floors of two plywood houses until we came to a house that had been used as an abattoir, and not long ago. Dried blood covered the walls and ran across the floor into the alley. There were no windows. The minute the Fedayeen closed the door behind me, I was cast into pitch black.

I stood there I don't know how long—I was afraid to even sit down— until a grinding noise started up outside, as if something large were chewing on the corner of our bunker-building. With that, the taller of the two most recent Palestinian escorts came through the door with a hand metal detector. He waved it over me, looking for a beacon or transponder. Satisfied, he signaled for me to follow him.

The room I was led into was darkened, except for a television. In the glow of the screen, I could see a man sitting in a plastic lawn chair. He was alone.

A video was playing—jerky, grainy footage taken by a handheld camera. I could hear the cameraman talk to someone behind him, telling him to be patient. "He will be here soon," he said. It looked like Gaza, with the fence and the guard tower of a settlement in one corner of the frame.

A bus appeared out of the lower left of the picture, bumping along a gravel road, throwing up plumes of dust. A couple seconds behind it came a Pajero, gaining on the bus. The camera panned left, following the bus to what was now clearly a Jewish settlement surrounded by razor wire. The Pajero inexplicably slowed, and the bus passed through the gates of the settlement.

"This is where he loses his faith," the man sitting in the chair said. "But not for long. Watch."

The Pajero swung around to the main road, turned right, and picked up speed fast. Just for a moment, you could see the face of the driver—a boy, his head barely above the window. You couldn't see where he was headed until the cameraman panned right and picked up an Israeli military jeep, mesh over the windows, a long whip antenna. The jeep suddenly stopped, the doors flew open, and two Israeli soldiers started to sprint away from the jeep. The Pajero was maybe ten yards away from the jeep when it exploded, sending plumes of dust and rocks in all directions. Seconds later the two Israeli soldiers ran out of the cloud of debris, sandblasted but alive.

The man switched off the TV and turned on the table light next to him. It was Nabil Shahadah. A dozen years older, but I recognized him from the Peshawar photo.

Nabil was a small man, still rail thin with unruly hair and a great hedge of a mustache that looked to be dyed jet-black. His body, though, couldn't hide the hard years on the run. A wound or maybe arthritis had taken over his knees. He grunted, pushed himself to his feet, and walked stiff-legged over to the hot plate in the corner to turn on the gas burner to make coffee. He worked silently until the coffee was ready, then carried a cup over to me and settled down again with his own.

"The target was the bus, wasn't it?" I asked.

Nabil nodded.

"It looked like there were children on it."

"There were," he said, bristling. "Do Israeli F-16's differentiate between children and our martyrs?"

I knew I had to let it go. That's not what I'd come for. Still, I was curious. During the Iran-Iraq war, the Iranian suicide bombers hit only military targets. In Lebanon in the eighties, it was the same thing—military targets only. Then Nabil and Hamas changed the rules when they started targeting buses. It was now slaughter for slaughter's sake, a pornography of violence.

"Why did you want to see me?" he asked. "The Israelis couldn't have sent you. They're not that dumb."

"Give me back my stuff. I want to show you something."

Nabil yelled at the darkened doorway. When one of the Fedayeen came in, Nabil whispered in his ear and sent him off. The Fedayeen was back in two minutes. I handed Nabil the photo of his parents and the letter.

"I saw your parents two days ago. I took their picture. But I'm not going to lie to you that I came here for that. I need you to help me find someone."

I probably imagined it, but Nabil looked as if he was softening, holding the picture of his mother and father.

"What is it you want?" he asked, turning back to me.

I pulled out the Peshawar photo and handed it to him. He looked surprised. I could tell he'd never seen it before, probably even forgotten he'd been photographed that day. For Nabil, Peshawar must have been a lifetime ago.

"You're standing on the far right," I said. "The man I am looking for is on the far left. The slight guy with the fine features. I'm pretty sure he's Iranian. Maybe a Pasdaran officer."

"He was. But I don't remember his name. On the other hand, it doesn't matter."

"Why?"

"He's dead."

CHAPTER 25

WE SAT ON A BLANKET on the bare cement floor and picked at a plate of flatbread, olives, and yogurt, and drank tea. Blackout curtains covered the window, but I could tell it was turning light.

"The Iranian." I said. "Frankly, I find it hard to believe he's dead."

It wasn't going to help to tell Nabil about my history with the photo. But if Mousavi really was dead, I was more confused than ever as to why Millis had dragged it along with him to the Breezeway Motel. Or why anyone wanted to grab it from me now.

"Whatever this man means to you, he's dead. I'm sure."

"Someone misinformed you maybe."

"My people were there. A bombardment in Lebanon, two years ago. A 155-round landed on the house he was sleeping in."

It was all a waste of time coming here, I thought. I was out of questions, frustrated, not sure where to go next. And yet a minute later, I don't know what it was—training, twenty-five years of running informants, curiosity—but I realized I'd come too far to stop asking questions now.

"Tell me about the day the photo was taken."

Nabil said he was coming back from Karachi and stopped by to see bin Laden. Bin Laden had guests. They were closeted in a back bedroom when he arrived.

"First to come out was bin Laden. Then an old man, a foreigner. He was wearing a salwar chemise."

Nabil picked up the picture and pointed at the man with the missing head.

"I think it was him. He had a cane, but you can't see it in the photo."

"A foreigner?"

"An American. He spoke to me in English. He had an American accent."

That surprised me. Even during the Afghan war when bin Laden was nominally allied with the United States, he was a strict Wahhabi and avoided Americans. Europeans, too. Nabil must have been mistaken. Maybe it was a foreigner who spoke American English.

"Who was he?"

"I don't know."

"Why was he there?"

"He couldn't stand for very long. Bin Laden was worried about his health. But the man seemed perfectly at ease, like he'd known bin Laden for a long time. I wondered if he was one of those Americans who seem happy only when they're away from home. I have no idea why he was there."

"He spoke English with bin Laden?"

"No. He spoke to bin Laden in Arabic. And later he spoke to me in Arabic. Fluent, classical Arabic."

That was even stranger.

"Then I heard him and the Iranian speaking in Farsi. They spoke very fast. It sounded to me like the American's Farsi was fluent, too."

"Wait. The American knew the Iranian?"

Now it was getting really interesting. For a start, only a handful of Westerners speak both fluent Arabic and Farsi. But throw in the fact that he knew the man who may have kidnapped and killed Bill Buckley, and I was starting to understand why someone had cut this man's head out of the photo. Who in the hell was he? I still wasn't convinced he was American.

"Did the Iranian have red hair?" I asked.

"Maybe. I can't remember. There are a lot of Iranians with red hair."

"His eyes?"

"I don't remember. It was a long time ago."

This wasn't going anywhere, and my interest shifted back to the American. The easy answer was he was a journalist. The war was hot. Bin Laden was a scoop. But then again I'd never heard of an American journalist speaking fluent Arabic and Farsi. And they certainly don't make friends with Iranian Pasdaran officers. Something about that day was critically important. I just couldn't nail it down.

"Wait a minute," I said. "Who took the picture?"

"Khalid."

"Khalid who?"

"I never knew his surname even though he was always at bin Laden's house. He was a Kuwaiti. And like the Iranian, the American knew Khalid. He kept putting his hand on Khalid's shoulder. The American had a camera with him. He asked Khalid to take the picture. 'To memorialize the passing of the torch,' he said. I remember because I didn't know what he meant. Khalid drove away that day in the same car with the American and the Iranian."

"Don't you find this all very strange?"

"I don't have an answer. You need to talk to the other person who was there that day. A Kuwaiti. A prince of the Al Sabah." He pointed to the young man, almost a boy, immediately to bin Laden's right.

I'd forgotten the Gulf prince. Neither Millis nor I could place him, and I'd just assumed he was some inconsequential hanger-on.

"The prince knows Khalid. And he has this very strange story, which I know only part of."

"Where is he now?" I said.

"In Lebanon. The Biqa' Valley."

Lebanon wasn't my first choice of places to go—hell, it wasn't my second or third choice, either. The Pasdaran still had free range of the country, and if they thought I was back looking for Buckley's kidnapper, they might try to put an end to my hunt for good. But now with this new piece of information that there was an American—or whoever he was—in touch with both bin Laden and a Pasdaran officer, there was no way I wasn't going to go see Prince Al Sabah and ask him what he knew about it.

One of the Fedayeen was waiting outside to lead me back to my hotel. When I turned to say good-bye to Nabil, he was still sitting in his plastic lawn chair, looking at the picture of his mother and father. In a way, we weren't that different, both of us shoved in a corner, our room for maneuvering narrowing by the day, both hanging on to a photo.

CHAPTER 26

"Max, you bastard, where'd you get to?" Yuri sounded genuinely pissed.

"I met a girl in Larnaca. We got to drinking, and, well, you know, when I woke up, your boat was gone."

"You went at it for twenty-four hours? Wow."

I knew I was running this girl thing into the ground. But the fact is that in this business you pretty much have to orient your life around a lie—or "cover for action," as headquarters calls it. If you're in Moscow and you own a dog, you spend your two-year tour walking Moscow's streets and parks. It gives you a reason for being out late at night, getting up at the crack of dawn, wandering around strange neighborhoods picking up shit. Antique collecting, jogging, amateur archaeology—they all work the same way. I can't remember when, but by default my cover for action became women. It seemed to still be working, at least with Yuri.

"I need to get to Lebanon," I told him, "but not through the front door."

It wasn't just that I didn't want to fly from Tel Aviv to Amman, Jordan, and from there on to Beirut on an overstretched German passport or an even more overworked Irish one, although that was certainly part of it. I also had to consider that I'd used Rafik Hariri to bait the Saudi trap, and I didn't want anyone thinking I was now heading to the prime minister's office in Lebanon. That's the problem with misdirection: You unknowingly burn bridges you might need later.

"Okay. Okay. I'll fix it," Yuri said. "I got a car leaving tonight. Call this number in Ramallah, and they'll tell you where to go."

You make a Russian your friend, and he sticks with you the whole way, potholes and all.

The number Yuri gave me led me to a garage just outside Ramallah—more accurately, a shed with a pit decorated with portraits of suicide bombers and presided over by a lone mechanic changing the transmission on a twenty-year-old Peugeot. After the mechanic made me a glass of tea, he took me around back to a sparkling Mercedes that looked as if it had just come out of the showroom.

"A 2001," he said, polishing the door handle with a rag.

Twenty minutes later a Palestinian in his twenties showed up, wearing Top-Siders, Quicksilver jeans, and a polo shirt. He put me in the passenger seat and we headed off east, to Jordan. Two miles from the border, we stopped by the side of the road so the driver could switch the yellow Israeli plates for green Palestinian ones.

As soon as we crossed the Israeli line, he stopped again and exchanged the Palestinian plates for Jordanian ones. Jordanian customs was a breeze—five minutes flat. The driver seemed to know everyone by first name.

We were halfway to Amman when it finally dawned on me what Yuri did for a living these days: He fenced cars. The new Audis and Porsches and Beemers waiting to board the boat in La Spezia, the new Mercedes I was riding in were all stolen.

By the time we passed through Amman and were heading to the Syrian border, I was dead asleep. I woke up just enough at the next checkpoint to give the driver my German passport (at least I thought it was the German one), but I might just as well have handed him a four-day pass to Disney World. Yuri's networks clearly included Syrian immigrations and customs.

By the time I emerged into the land of the living again, the car was bouncing along a rutted dirt road. Dusk was turning to dark, but it was light enough to see we were ascending up into the anti-Lebanon range. Below was Zabadani, the old Iranian camp that was used to supply the Pasdaran in the 1980s, a stark reminder that I was about to jump from the frying pan into the fire.

When we got to the top of the pass, the road was hardly a cow path. We slowed down to a crawl, driving off the path to avoid boulders. My driver obviously knew the road. At the very top, someone had plowed a path through the remaining patches of snow. There wasn't a Syrian or Lebanese border guard in sight.

The road improved as we dropped down the other side into the Biqa' Valley. In Hamm, the first village, the road was even paved. Thirty minutes later, in Balabakk, the driver dropped me off in front of the legendary Palmyra Hotel. He might have said ten words the entire way. Nearby, the Roman ruins glowed in the light of a nearly full moon.

Before I went up to my room, I ordered a taxi for the next morning to take me to Beirut. I wasn't going to Beirut, but there was no sense in telegraphing that I was really going to Shtawrah.

CHAPTER 27

Shtawrah, Lebanon

SITTING ASTRIDE THE BEIRUT-DAMASCUS HIGHWAY, Shtawrah is the dividing line between East Biqa' and West Biqa', ground zero of one of the most continuously dangerous places in the world. I'd come by service taxi, an hour door-to-door from the Palmyra. Not a long trip, but one I didn't want to make often.

Shtawrah's Ritz Hotel is the epicenter of the Biqa' Valley's drug trafficking. Walk into its lobby and you'd swear the electricity was off. The only light was one behind the front desk. But the clientele like it that way. The biggest hashish and coke deals in the world are struck in the Ritz's black alcoves, where the principals can't be seen.

There was no doorman, no concierge, no desk clerk for that matter. I wandered around the hotel, starting to feel as if this meeting wasn't going to happen. Just as I was getting ready to head back to Balabakk, a young man materialized out of the dark in front of my eyes: bespoke silk suit, no tie, a shirt that had Harvie & Hudson written all over it. His slight bone structure and dark skin told me he was from one of the Arab Gulf states. He quietly introduced himself as the nephew of "the sheikh."

"Would you follow me, please?" he asked softly.

"The sheikh?" I asked. We were feeling our way down a darkened corridor. I'd seen the prince only once in a twelve-year-old photo, and I still had no idea which Kuwaiti prince he was. There are tens of thousands of them, and Kuwait was never my strong suit.

"Prince Sabah Al Sabah," my guide told me in an even quieter voice, "the grandson of the Amir of Kuwait." My guide rattled off about thirty names, taking me all the way back to the Prophet. He was halfway there when I conjured up his post-Peshawar bio: Miserable student at Sandhurst. Drinking, gambling, wenching in London. Made it through thanks only to the low bar set for Gulf royalty. I remembered that he'd found his way to Lebanon to fight with the Palestinians but ended up an opium addict. He'd almost died after a liposuction operation at a fat farm in Marbella. Great, I thought, a day with a dope-head tub of lard.

My guide glided to a stop in front of a door at the far end of a second-floor hallway, knocked once, then motioned me through and closed the door and himself behind me. Even by the low light, I could see that I'd imagined the wrong Kuwaiti prince entirely. The one sitting on the floor, with his elbow on the sofa, reading, was trim, an athlete—little changed from the photo. Then I finally remembered the right Sabah Al Sabah: another grandson of the Amir, except this one graduated Sandhurst in the top five and was a star on the polo team. A runner, too. I'd read somewhere he'd finished in the top ten in the Marine Marathon in Washington, D.C., only a couple years before under some other name.

As soon as the prince saw me, he jumped up and walked over to shake my hand. He was wearing a cotton crew-neck sweater, neatly starched khaki pants, and American loafers.

"Thank you for coming to Shtawrah." He pointed me toward the sofa he'd been leaning on. "I feel safe only in the places where I know what the politics are."

He didn't have to say anything more: Syria controlled Shtawrah and the Biqa' with an iron fist. For the moment, the prince's politics coincided with the Syrians', and that was all the protection he needed.

As the prince took a chair, the rest of the story came back to me. He'd come to Lebanon immediately after graduation from Sandhurst to fight with the Palestinians. Except, unlike most princes, he really did. I'd seen news footage of him running across a Beirut street, firing a Kalashnikov at a Christian position. I wondered now if Nabil hadn't been just out of camera's range. There'd been a nasty fight with the Amir, his grandfather—something about trying to raise money from the Kuwaiti royals for Hamas and the Palestinian Islamic Jihad, followed by a self-imposed exile in the Biqa'. A voice in my head whispered, *British wife, scholar, a book on the Israeli lobby in the U.S.* I didn't trust the last part, necessarily. My synapses were starting to short-circuit. In any event, he was too poised and thoughtful to square with his reputation.

He seemed to be waiting for me to clear my memory banks before he began.

"I'm delighted the Americans have finally come to talk with me," he said, satisfied at last that he had my attention. "I thought I was going to have to surrender like the Germans and the Japanese before you would listen to my story."

It sounded to me as if Nabil had figured out I was CIA and not a journalist. It didn't surprise me, and I didn't see any point in setting the prince straight.

"No surrender needed here," I said.

"Tell me, why did the U.S. stand by bin Laden for so long?"

I figured he was referring to the phantom bin Laden–U.S. connection. I'd heard about it plenty of times from plenty of Arabs.

"We didn't exactly," I said. "He shows up in Peshawar, offering money and recruits to the Afghans. We were in no position to turn down help, so we left him alone. A sin of omission, not commission."

The prince shook his head. "Remember, I was there. I saw with my own eyes the planes coming in from all over the Middle East, believers and guns. Americans were on the tarmac receiving them."

"What does that have to do with bin Laden? I don't recall we gave him any weapons."

"I'm not talking about weapons. This war was fought and won thanks to a green light from the United States. Bin Laden was allowed to stay in Peshawar because of you."

Good point.

"Bin Laden can't keep a secret, you know," he said, rising and taking the seat directly opposite mine. "That's what you came to talk to me about, isn't it? Nabil said you were interested in his American connection."

"That and a couple other things," I said.

"It's always been a subject of curiosity for me, your relations with Saudi Arabia. I'm not casting blame, mind you. There was a time you had no choice but to support bin Laden and the extremists in Saudi Arabia. Anyone could see that. The Iranian revolution threatened to consume the Arab side of the Gulf, chaos would follow, and they'd get their great Shia crescent. The United States had to give the Saudis a backbone, a jihad to avert the people's eyes from their weakness, so you gave them the Afghan war, and it worked brilliantly. The Shia uprising fizzled. Balance was restored. But now the Middle East is out of kilter again. The Sunni believers think they have the upper hand. They are convinced that they can restore the Khalifate, *truly* convinced. But that's not what you came to hear."

"I'm hoping you remember this day," I said as I pulled the Peshawar photo out of my pocket and handed it to him.

"The way we were. My good friend Sheikh Osama," the prince said, pointing to bin Laden in the middle. "And there's Nabil and that Iranian. I never knew his name. I don't think I ever talked to him, more than a word or two. And here's . . . the American," the prince said, pointing at the headless man in the salwar chemise.

Two sources over time and space; I was starting to believe he really was American.

"Why were you there?" I asked.

"I was seeing bin Laden that morning. There were several of us. It was strange to see an American there."

"Go on," I said.

"He spoke beautiful Arabic, with no accent. Later I asked bin Laden about him. 'An American,' he said, 'he's the price of admission.'"

"'The price of admission'? That doesn't make any sense," I said.

"I asked bin Laden what he meant by that. He only smiled. I immediately thought the American must be CIA. Why else would bin Laden be so coy? You must know about bin Laden's connections with the CIA. Surely it's common knowledge at Langley."

"Some things are off the books," I said. I was starting to suspect I was more right than I knew. Officially, at least, the CIA had never met bin Laden. I personally knew every case officer serving in Pakistan in those days. I was in and out of Peshawar when bin Laden was there. If anyone had ever met him, I would have heard.

"I'm sure he was CIA." There was a defensive edge to the prince's voice.

"What was his name?" I asked, humoring him more than anything.

"Oscar. Ormond. No, maybe Oliver."

As much as I wasn't convinced a case officer had ever met bin Laden, the name rang a bell. Oliver isn't a common name, at least not in the CIA. But I remembered an Oliver from a long time ago: an Old Boy, there from the start, the OSS. We'd met at some party early on, when I was just a career trainee, spent ten minutes exchanging pleasantries first in Arabic, then Farsi. Mine were still rough on the edges; his, flawless. He'd told me that after Harvard, he spent WWII in Iran with the OSS. He was handling the Qashqa'i tribe. After the war he'd planned to go back to the university and spend his life studying Avestan and Pehlavi texts in a musty library. But the taste of the real Orient put an end to that. He joined the OSS's successor, the CIA, and for the next forty-five years moved from one station to another across the Middle East.

I remembered him putting a bony hand on my shoulder just as our conversation was ending. "You know what I figured out?" he said. "The Arabs don't hold a candle to the Persians when it comes to civilization."

Oliver had buttonholed me a second time at Langley on his way out the door for good, disgraced by some closed Congressional investigation. It must have been ten years after that first meeting. He had aged decades. His bones seemed to rattle every time he coughed. I could recall his going on about the Babylonian captivity—the seventy years that the Jews dwelled in the Iraqi desert before being freed by Cyrus. He kept insisting that no one could understand modern Judaism without understanding how much influence the Persians and Zoroastrianism had on it. We had to learn to use that. The Persians and Jews united could contain the Arab Bedouin, with their brutal, desert ways, if only we would encourage them. I wondered if he was mad, flipped, his brain fried from too much sun. He would have sat me down for an hour lecture if I hadn't been running off to a meeting. Oliver Wendell Something, like the Justice. Brow like a triumphal arch. Someone would know. It had to be the same guy. How many Americans speak fluent Farsi and Arabic? It would have helped to have a head to go with the body in the photo.

"Did he have a cough?" I asked.

"He did. Hacking."

That moved me one step closer to the Oliver I knew. But what would the Oliver I knew be doing in Peshawar that day, and, more to the point, with bin Laden? Had he met bin Laden by accident, accompanied him home, and somehow got himself in the picture? It wasn't impossible.

I remembered something else about Oliver: He was fabulously wealthy, rich enough to pay informants out of his own pocket, which meant it was possible not all of his networks were documented. Rich enough, too, to roam all over the Muslim world on a whim. If I had the right Oliver, it's possible he met bin Laden and there was no record of it.

"Forget the old American for right now." The prince interrupted my thoughts. "You're missing the point. There's someone else you need to concentrate on. The man who took the photo—Khalid Muhammad."

"You don't mean Khalid Sheikh Muhammad—KSM?"

KSM's popping up in a picture like this is sort of like having an old girlfriend show up at the altar at your wedding.

"KSM?" the prince asked.

"That's how we refer to Khalid Sheikh Muhammad, the uncle of Ramzi Yousef, the mastermind of the 1993 attack on the World Trade Center. We use his initials."

The prince waved my shorthand away. "Americans and their acronyms. You think you're going to reduce the world and then make sense out of it. Yes, that's who I'm talking about."

"What was he doing there?"

"In those days he was always by bin Laden's side. He's Baluch. His family is from Iran, though, originally."

"I thought Pakistan, from near Quetta."

"No, definitely the other side of the border, the Iranian side. The Kuwaiti government has been watching him ever since he showed up in Peshawar in the mid-eighties. At first we didn't pay any attention to Khalid. He was just another believer who took up arms to fight the communists. Then we started to pick up some hints he was cooperating with the Iranians, with the hard-liners, the Quds Force. It fit with half his family living in Iran."

The Quds Force was the intelligence arm of the Pasdaran, Mousavi's organization, whose sole mission was to drive the United States out of the Middle East.

"Are you absolutely sure KSM works with the Pasdaran?"

"We watch these people closely," the prince said. "The Baluch from Iran have always been a problem for us. We never know which way their loyalties blow. The important thing is you understand who Khalid Sheikh Muhammad is. He would have been like any other Baluch in my country, a nuisance, no more, except his father had bigger plans. He encouraged Khalid to go to college in the United States, some agricultural school in the South. Things didn't turn out as the father had hoped, however. Khalid finished the university, came back to Kuwait, and went straight to Afghanistan to wage jihad against the Russians."

"Everyone was doing it," I replied.

"There is a twist, though," the prince went on. "Khalid told his brother he'd been trained by the CIA and was going there under its protection."

"He was lying. We didn't train anyone in the U.S. to go fight in Afghanistan, just as we didn't run bin Laden." I was impatient now and needed to know more. "Anyhow, I don't get the connection between the Pasdaran, bin Laden, KSM, and this man who you think is CIA."

"It confused us, too, at least at first," the prince said. "It made no sense."

"Maybe because KSM's a liar," I said, more to myself than to the prince. "A fantasist."

"Remember, I know Khalid," he replied.

The prince recounted how he'd first run into KSM at the Intercon Hotel in Peshawar. They'd struck up enough of a relationship for him to see that KSM always seemed to have money—odd because his family was poor. KSM and the prince became close. KSM eventually told him that he'd been approached when he was at school in North Carolina by an elderly gentleman who spoke fluent Arabic and had come there to recruit "consultants on the Middle East." The offer seemed innocuous enough and KSM accepted. When he graduated, the man bought him a ticket to Peshawar. Every two months, he would appear himself, pass KSM an envelope stuffed with cash, and debrief him on the war in Afghanistan.

"Don't tell me this is the old man in the picture, the one with his head cut out? The one you think is CIA and is called Oliver?" I asked, still not ready to believe any of our officers had ever met bin Laden, let alone KSM.

"This is what I've been trying to tell you. The old man in the picture was a CIA agent, Khalid's case officer."

The story was getting more improbable by the moment. KSM one of ours, an informant? This was going to take a while to sink in.

"Are you sure you don't know who the Iranian was?" I asked, still trying to piece this all together.

The prince shook his head.

"It's important. There's this Pasdaran colonel I've been tracking for years. If they're one and the same . . ."

"Do you know the name of the martyr who drove a truck into the Marine barracks in Beirut? Of course not. Some things will never be known. Don't you think it's enough that a Pasdaran officer is keeping company with a man who once tried to bring down twelve airliners?"

I didn't need to answer. KSM's dreams were clear enough to everyone. In 1994, when he was in Manila, he planned to blow up twelve American airliners over the Pacific. He'd also plotted to assassinate Clinton and the pope. When I first heard about KSM, I thought he was a fraud. He didn't appear to be capable of executing any of his plans, either back then or now. But it was an entirely different matter if he was really in league with the Pasdaran.

"Khalid found a way to make money." The prince's voice momentarily surprised me. I'd wandered into some other zone.

"What do you mean?" I asked.

The prince told me how the Kuwaitis had pieced together from telephone taps that there was an underside to KSM's plan to blow up twelve airplanes: He was betting on the stock market—options. Several months before the attack was to occur, he'd bought deep-in-the-money puts on airline companies that would have been affected had the attack succeeded. The trades were made through numbered accounts in the Caymans and banks in Puerto Rico.

"I'm sorry, your highness, this all has the markings of someone's fabrication. I've dealt with crap like this for the last twenty-five years. And right now my bullshit detector's in the red zone."

The prince opened up a portmanteau and pulled out a six-inch sheaf of documents.

"These are transcripts of intercepts: Khalid's calls back to his family in Kuwait. They're genuine, believe me. My brother has the actual taped conversations."

"Your brother?"

"He's the adviser to our intelligence service."

You had to love small, tight families like the Al Sabah.

The prince picked out a transcript of one of KSM's calls to a telephone booth in Kuwait City on June 16, 2000. After KSM asks about family and news from Kuwait, he says he's sent "six chips" to Kuwait by courier.

"Six chips?" I asked.

"Prepaid Swiss cell SIM cards to be used by his network for the next operation. We intercepted all six. The amazing thing was that they were all in sequence. Now we're able to intercept most of Khalid's calls."

"Did you tell the CIA station about this?"

"Of course. My brother gave the chips to the station to copy. He also told them about the call options. But there's been no response."

The prince handed me more transcripts. The details were amazing:

KSM's phone calls across the Middle East, and to Germany, Spain, Italy, even the United States. In my twenty-five years with the CIA, I'd never seen better stuff.

"Tell me again what the station said."

"I just told you. Nothing. Not a word."

Unless I was completely misinterpreting the stuff the prince was showing me, this was insane. It was rock-solid intelligence that could be acted on.

The prince picked out another transcript and turned it so I could read it. In this one KSM says:

Do not move until liquids are in place.

"What liquids?" I asked. "Nitrocellulose?"

KSM had been planning to use nitrocellulose to bring down the twelve planes in 1994.

"No. We think it's some other highly volatile substance. Something that could be added to jet fuel. Maybe methyl nitrate."

We both stared at the words, hoping they might somehow translate themselves into something comprehensible.

"Are you sure your brother gave all this to the station?" I asked again.

"He did. And I'm also sure he never heard back. Not even a 'We're looking at it' or 'Please keep investigating.' Gross incompetence? We don't know."

"Can I have these?" I asked.

"That's why I showed them to you," he said. "You have to bring them to someone's attention in Washington who will understand their value. But we haven't talked about the most important thing. Khalid isn't working alone. He has an American partner."

"You don't mean Oliver? He's barely alive in the photo. I'm sure he was dead by 1994."

"No. Another American. We don't have his name."

"How do you know this?"

"Again, Khalid's calls back to his family," the prince said. "He talked about his American partner. But here's the really scary part: Khalid is about to try again."

"Blow up airplanes?"

The prince nodded. "There's no smoking gun yet, but it's the best conclusion we can come up with."

"He wouldn't have discussed this on the telephone," I said.

"We would never have believed it ourselves if we hadn't arrested two Saudis transiting from Iran in October 2000. They confessed they were working for Khalid Sheikh Muhammad."

The prince pulled out another set of documents from his portmanteau—the confessions of the two Saudis.

I skimmed through them. Indeed, both independently confessed they worked for KSM. But what really got my attention was where they both said that a Pasdaran officer had arranged their transit through Iran, including a week's stay in Tehran. They were taken to a camp where Pasdaran explosives experts briefed them on techniques to blow up planes in midair.

I studied the prince's face. If the confessions were genuine, they were a damning piece of evidence, a *causus belli* against Iran. It was plausible, too. Someone as bloody-minded as bin Laden would never let religious differences get in the way of a tactical alliance with the Pasdaran. We'd even seen evidence of it in 1996 when we found out he had met an Iranian intelligence officer in Jalalabad, a powwow that led to an agreement to conduct joint terrorist attacks. Nothing came of it, but only because Iran's ayatollahs stopped sanctioning terrorism shortly afterward. If now the Pasdaran wanted to mount an operation independently from the Iranian government, why couldn't they outsource it to someone like bin Laden, especially to help recruit suicide bombers? No one had a better pipeline to that bottomless pool.

"Is this real?" I asked. "There's nothing about stock options." I was still stunned I was seeing intelligence this good.

"Khalid wouldn't have told them about something like that. The options are a side deal between him and the American. The Iranians and two Saudis care only about slaughtering Americans."

"Are you absolutely sure about the options?"

The prince picked out another half dozen transcripts of KSM's calls. The conversations were elliptical and involved code words, but you could make the case that KSM was giving instructions to arrange the trades through *hawalas*—money changers. Airplanes weren't mentioned, but I took the prince's word that they were somewhere in the intercepts.

"Fascinating stuff," I said, "but if our station in Kuwait is not buying it, I'm not sure my carrying the bad news to Washington will make a difference."

"The reason we're sitting here together is not to pass the time. I'm giving you the intercepts to give to your government so it will listen and stop the attack—and the bloodshed that will ensue if Khalid and the Pasdaran succeed. You Americans always get history wrong when Muslims are involved." He was studying me hard as he talked. "Khalid is not Hamas. He's not even a good Muslim. He's a murderer, pure and simple. If he succeeds in doing what we think he will try to do, he will hurt our cause. You'll blame Muslims in general. The Jews will play you the way they always do, make you blame *their* enemies—the Arabs—and not yours."

I felt as if his eyes were burning a hole somewhere in the back of my brain.

"You don't think I know all that?" I asked. "I'll try."

The prince grabbed the transcripts from me and looked through them until he came to the one he wanted. It was a New York City area code and telephone number.

"New York?" I asked.

He nodded. "This is fresh information not passed to the station in Kuwait. This number should help you. It belongs to one of Ramzi Yousef's contacts who was in on the World Trade Center. He was living in Queens then."

"Here's a second number," he said, showing me another page of the transcripts.

I recognized the country and city code: Tehran.

"Khalid's contact number. Maybe this will convince the U.S. this is serious."

"Where's KSM calling from?"

"Usually Karachi. But in this instance . . . well, look for yourself."

The transcript the prince handed me was dated February 16, 2001—a call from KSM to a phone booth in Kuwait City. At one point in the handwritten transcript KSM says, "I'm in the country of the 'Aja'im"—a common term for Iranians.

"The number Khalid is calling from is a main Pasdaran number. You should have a record of it. But before you do anything, you need to see my brother. He's coming to Lebanon next week and will bring more intercepts."

"The more stuff he brings, the better."

"I understand. There's something else he will tell you about: Khalid's American partner owns a company in Maine called BT Trading."

CHAPTER 28

Balabakk, Lebanon

A S SOON AS I GOT BACK TO BALABAKK, I borrowed the Palmyra's only phone, which might have been new in 1921. My first instinct was to look for the crank.

India answered on the third ring.

"Max? You were supposed to call me a week ago. I absolutely have to see you. I can't tell you what's going on, not on the phone. Can you come back here?"

"Not now. What is it?"

The silence stretched out so long, I gave the phone a shake to see if it had gone dead.

"Dad has a problem."

"He can't find a Scottish castle with central heating?"

"Max, this is dead serious. He owes money. I have to talk to you about it."

"Sure. I should be back in a couple weeks."

"I think it's all going to crash before then. They want someone to run some stuff out to Riyadh in the next twenty-four hours. Any chance you could meet me there?"

"Not right now."

"I'd heard you were in Saudi Arabia."

"A rumor I started."

I could hear the panic in India's voice, but my traveling to Riyadh was out. The fact that she'd heard the rumor that I was in Saudi Arabia was enough to tell me they'd taken the bait. I thought about asking India to come to Balabakk, but I knew our embassy in Beirut would never let her. Damascus might, though. People going TDY to the Middle East often stopped there on their way back to buy rugs. I didn't want to risk saying any of this on the phone, especially from the Palmyra, where the phones were sure to be tapped by Hizballah.

"Remember your dad's and my stories about the time we camped out in this part of the world?"

She had teased me about it only maybe a month earlier. I counted on her remembering.

"Sure. The border—" India caught herself, but I was sure she had the place down.

"I'll be there Saturday at noon. Alternate twenty-four hours later, same place. Third alternate forty-eight hours after the primary."

"They'll have my head."

"You won't be crossing any borders you're not allowed to."

"Let me think about it."

"Think about it all you want, but I'll be there," I said as I hung up.

Frank out of money? As if I needed another reminder that life is fragile.

CHAPTER 29

Haditha, Syria

A FREEZING WIND BLEW IN off the barren hills. India was exhausted but radiant. She looked like a schoolgirl who'd just pulled off the prank of a lifetime as she ran up and gave me a hug. We were standing in front of a Dunkin' Donuts next to the duty-free store. The nearest Syrian checkpoint was fifty feet away, but no one was paying any attention to us.

We had an hour, maybe two at the outside, no more. She was taking a plane out that afternoon, to Geneva and on to Washington the next morning. A whirlwind round-trip. I stepped back to have a look at her, and as I did, her mood swung from giddy to serious.

"What is it, India?"

"They're going to burn you. There's a journalist—a guy with the *Times*. He's writing an article that you've hired yourself out to a foreign intel service—"

"It's bullshit."

"What if they accuse you of working for somebody like Mossad? It could get you killed here."

"They just want to shut me up. Is it Vernon Lawson?"

I didn't even wait for India to nod yes. Lawson was one of the tame journalists the seventh floor at Langley used to spread disinformation and punish its enemies. He'd even written a couple books on the CIA—big hits, packed with lies but with the ring of truth. No question, Vernon Lawson would be delighted to out me on page one, above the fold.

"Did you talk to your dad about Lawson?"

"I tried to."

"Webber's behind it, right?"

"I never said—"

"You didn't have to. He was there, wasn't he?"

"Dad kept quiet."

I could tell she was protecting her father.

"What's happening with your dad? He doesn't know you're here."

"I wouldn't dare tell. I told you, he's mad at—"

"So why are you here?"

"I think Dad's going under."

He was about to make me his right-hand man, I selfishly thought.

"I don't want to talk about it now," she said, turning her face away from me. She wiped her sleeve across her eyes.

When she turned back to me, her eyes were red. I put my hand on her shoulder, and she pushed it away.

"You said something to someone that pissed Dad off."

"Did he tell you what?" I asked, deciding to let her father's money problems drop. She would tell me in her own time.

"He wouldn't say," she said.

"They're both pieces of shit," I said, more to myself than to India.

"Who?" Anger. Hackles way up.

"Not your dad," I said, correcting course, although I was starting to wonder. "Webber. Lawson."

Calmer again. "Webber's gunning for Chief/NE." NE is the Near East Division in the Directorate of Operations. "It's out in the open. Dad—"

India stopped talking as a Syrian armor convoy of T-64 tanks rolled past into Lebanon. The roar of the diesel engines and metal treads on the road was deafening. The decks were stacked with the crews' belongings, everything from old pots to sacks of flour. The tanks looked as if they hadn't been painted in years. The Syrian army definitely hadn't fared well since the end of the Cold War.

The last tank was rumbling by when I noticed two Syrians in uniforms walking toward us. A third joined them. We weren't going to be left alone after all.

"Time you go back to Damascus."

"I'm not done lecturing you, Max. You can't stay—"

I gestured with my chin toward our welcoming party.

"Three choices," I said. "We part here now. I ask the Syrians for political asylum and go to Damascus with you. Or we go into Lebanon."

"I've always wanted to visit Lebanon."

"You can't. You're on a plane tonight to Geneva."

"A full-fare ticket. I'll rebook for tomorrow—tell them I got caught in traffic on the way to the airport."

"There is no traffic in Syria."

"Well, then the taxi had a flat tire."

"You do understand going into Lebanon is hideously transgressive."

Transgressive in more ways than one. India could get fired for entering a country she didn't have headquarters permission to enter. It was stupid of me, too. If you're traveling on a stolen foreign passport in a name not your own, the last thing you want to do is hang around with someone traveling on an American diplomatic passport. But I wanted more time with India and decided to flush caution down the toilet.

The Syrians were maybe half a dozen feet from us.

"Know a good place to have lunch?" India asked. "Some scenic spot in the Biqa'?"

We sat in the front seat of the service taxi. In the back were two Syrian grunts—one with a caged bird—and an old woman dressed all in black. Sharing a ride with foreigners didn't lighten their dispositions.

"My God, if Dad found out," India said under her breath. She was practically giggling again.

In Bar Ilyas, we found a new taxi to take us to Balabakk. This time we sat in the backseat. For the next forty minutes, I listened to India off-load on what a miserable bureaucratic hell my ex-employer had become. Her day was spent running traces for the station in Saudi Arabia, names the case officers sent in just to make it appear they were doing something.

"How did you last so long, Max? It's mind-numbing."

"Saudi Arabia's different. We don't do any spying there."

"What about the good old days you and Dad liked to hash over? The romance, the adventure."

"It'll be different when you get overseas," I told her. "Hold on." I'd been mouthing the same platitude for years to new recruits. It never felt so false as it did just then.

We'd reached the outskirts of Balabakk. I pointed to the military barracks on the hill just east of town.

"That's where Bill Buckley was held," I whispered into India's ear. For all I knew, our cabdriver was the one who separated Bill's head from the rest of him.

"Who's there now?" she whispered back.

"No one. The Lebanese army took it back from Hizballah, and the Iranians left town. Well, more or less." I didn't add that we never would have come to Balabakk for lunch otherwise.

The Palmyra Hotel's restaurant was completely empty. The waiter showed us to a table next to the immense fireplace, still filled with old embers. I ordered a bottle of wine: a Kasara red, Reserve du Couvent, a vineyard not far from Balabakk. What greater irony in life than that one of the world's best wines grows in the birthplace of Islamic terrorism.

India handed me my glass, took hers, grabbed my arm, and pulled me back into the lobby so she could take another look at the photos and letters of the Palmyra's famous guests: Agatha Christie, T. E. Lawrence, Cocteau. She kept going until we were out in front of the hotel, on the terrace overlooking the Roman ruins. India sat down in a dusty old wicker chair and motioned me to the one next to her.

The waiter followed with a low table that he placed between us, then left and came back with the rest of our bottle of wine and a platter of fresh vegetables and mezzah.

Her father's daughter, India sat mute until the waiter had gone away again.

"What are you doing here, Max?"

"Here? I'm staying here. The rooms are nice. We'll visit the ruins after lunch. Over there is the largest cut stone in the world," I said, pointing at the temple of Jupiter. "Did you know—"

"Here. Lebanon. Tell me."

"A truth for a truth?"

"Just tell me."

I did. But not the truth Nabil or the prince had told me. She'd have to see the prince's documents to even start believing. Or maybe I just didn't think this was the time to get into it. I gave the old story instead, the reason I kept coming back to Balabakk, the search that had led me to the photo that had somehow led me here.

We couldn't see the barracks from where we were sitting, but I motioned behind me in its direction. I told her how after Buckley was kidnapped, I'd spent the next two months working the Biqa', sure he was being held there, but still coming up empty-handed, not picking up a single lead, not even a rumor. There was no way to get inside because it was guarded day and night by the Pasdaran. We only found out Bill had been there when one of the hostages escaped and told us. It didn't matter, though, because the Iranians moved all the hostages the same day.

"That's the last solid piece of intel we had on Buckley until his body was found in the southern suburbs," I said. "It's never let me go. The mystery. The truth. I don't know which. Are they different? At any rate, since you asked, that's why I'm here."

The bottle was empty. I went inside to get the waiter to bring us another one.

"Now your turn," I said as I sat back down.

India tried to stand up. I didn't know where she thought she was going.

She held on to the chair to steady herself, and fell back, spilling wine on her Levi's. She laughed, covered the stain with a napkin, and settled in.

"You know what I hate most about my job?" she said.

"The parking lot?" I joked.

"The sleazebags."

"They're everywhere," I told her.

"You know who I'm talking about."

"Webber?"

"The very same."

"A man for all seasons."

"He hit on me."

"Oh, come on. The guy's asexual at best."

"Keep telling yourself that, Maxie, but that's not it."

"It?"

"Why I can't stand his sleazeball guts."

"Why, then?"

I reached over, poured for both of us. The mezzah sat untouched between us.

"He's dangerous."

"Tell me," I said.

"Can't. You're out. Rule 2201, Subset C-3."

"What happened to truth for a truth?"

"I get boxed in two months."

"The polygraph. That *is* a problem."

She looked over the ruins and back at me.

"You'll protect me?"

I nodded my head and put my hand on hers. She laughed, shifted her chair slightly in my direction, and propped her feet on my knee.

"There's some case out in California," India began. "Two Saudi Takfiris showed up in San Diego, up to no good, and Webber stole the case—turned it over to some contractor to monitor them."

I immediately thought about the two Saudis arrested in Kuwait. Were they connected?

"They were tied up in the East African embassy bombings," she continued. "Turki came to Washington especially to tell us. He said they were part of a bigger team. They're preparing some big attack."

The chief of Saudi intelligence, Turki Al Faysal was hard to ignore. He came to Washington rarely, only then when he had something important to say.

"Maybe Turki's blowing sunshine up headquarters' ass, hoping to squeeze some more toys out of us." True to training, I was fishing for detail.

"Max, this is serious. There's a Saudi case officer in touch with them in San Diego. Under cover of Saudi Civil Aviation."

"Did Turki say what the targets were?"

"Maybe a Texas refinery."

Destroying a refinery. Why not? If this had anything to do with KSM, you could make a fortune on gasoline options. More than on airline options.

"Turki was missing a lot of detail," India continued. "That's why he wanted us to watch them. But Webber won't bring the Bureau in until we've got more to go on."

"What happened to NE?" The Near East Division was where the case should have ended up. That's the way it was supposed to work.

"Webber was at the meeting with Turki. He grabbed the case and turned it over to a contractor. Chief/NE fought it and lost. They supposedly have a surveillance team on these two guys."

"A contractor doing that kind of surveillance? Jesus."

"I see the invoices they're sending to the desk. A hundred sixty thousand a week. It's grotesque what—"

"The contractor's sending the invoices through the Saudi desk?"

"Yup. We pay for it. Counter-Espionage runs it. Cute, huh?"

"Is it Applied Science Research?"

"The contractor? Could be. Does it make a difference?"

My guess was that Frank hadn't told India about what happened to me in New York, or if he had, he'd kept the facts to a minimum. Applied Science Research seemed to mean nothing to her.

"How about the Saudis?" I asked. The wind had gone flat. The sun beat down on us as if it meant to melt us in place. India's face was flush with the heat.

"One's gone—maybe to Europe. Webber insists the contractor can handle the other on its own."

"You didn't happen to hear about two Saudis arrested in Kuwait?"

Sitting on the Saudi desk, she should have seen the traffic from Kuwait. Or maybe it was compartmented and she wasn't on the distribution list.

"Two Saudis arrested in Kuwait? How would you know—"

"My turn. How do you know all this about the Saudis in San Diego?"

"C'mon, Max, I'm not deaf and blind."

I found myself thinking about something Frank had told me: that it was India's idea to sign on, that he'd objected.

"Why did you join the CIA?" I asked her.

"You know. Dad told you, I'm sure. His big idea."

"And who got you on the Saudi desk?"

"Dad. The Old Boys' network, its nine lives." She was flicking her fingers up—one, two, three, four—counting each life with a little meow.

Jesus, I'd been slow. Frank had placed India right where he needed her, the Saudi desk. His own in-house, in-family agent. Obvious, especially considering his business partner was a Saudi. And that was only the beginning. That's why Frank offered to set me up with Rousset: another cog in his networks. Frank Beckman, collector of relationships. I'm not sure when I had felt quite so totally stupid, so scammed.

"India, they don't talk about stuff like this at morning staff meetings. Especially about Webber taking down Chief/NE. Where'd you hear that?"

"Same source. Dad."

"How would he know?"

"Webber, Webber, pudding and pie, kissed the girls and made them—"

"What the hell are you talking about?" I asked. She was kicking her feet against my knee.

"I'm talking about Webber, Max. 'He just needs some direction, India, dear—a little mentoring.'" Her imitation of Frank's voice was pitch-perfect, not the Kentucky accent I'd first known but the new one that had been born along with the Tuttle Street mansion. " 'My darling—' " India stopped it there, exhausted or embarrassed, for herself or her father, I couldn't tell.

Of course. When Beckman was head of the Afghan Task Force, Webber had been deputy in Islamabad, Pakistan. They must have worked closely together. I'd always thought Webber was too openly ambitious for Frank's tastes—Frank always seemed to like a little mouse with his cat—but clearly not. The place was more incestuous than I'd ever imagined.

"Hey, I was thinking the other day. Ever hear of an old-fart case officer named Oliver? He's dead now."

I gave India the quick synopsis of what I could remember about him.

"Oliver Channing," she said when I was through. "Dad worked with him in Beirut years ago. I can remember a photo Dad used to keep in his bedroom in the old house. Incredible brows. Dad used to joke that someday they were going to swallow his whole face. He's dead but it's the son who gives me the creeps."

"Your dad knows Oliver's son?"

"I can't figure out why he gives him the time of day. Every time David Channing comes to Washington, Dad has dinner with him at the Four Seasons. It's the only place in Washington the guy will eat."

"What's wrong with him?"

"He acts like he's got all the money in the world, but he's on the make. You can smell it. He dresses nice, but he still reminds me of a used-car salesman."

"Ever hear of your dad doing business with him?"

"Maybe. I know Dad traveled to Geneva or Zurich once or twice to see him. In fact, I'm stopping off there."

"To see David Channing?"

"No, silly. To drop something off for Dad, something I picked up in Riyadh."

"Michelle Zwanzig's office, right?"

"How do you know?"

I told her about how Frank had given me her card.

"The stop in Geneva is about your dad's problems, isn't it?"

She either didn't hear or still didn't want to talk about it. Instead, she waved at the waiter and pointed at our empty bottle of wine.

"Maxwell. Maxwell. Maxwell. What kind of name is that?" India's foot was digging into my thigh now. "It sounds like a cup of coffee. A very common cup of coffee! But you're the least common thing I can think of."

She was laughing so uproariously at her own joke that she failed to notice when she knocked over the wine bottle on the low table between us. No matter—it was already empty.

"Better get you a cup of espresso," I said. "And a good walk."

"There's my uncle again. Always looking out for little ole me." She reached over, took my hand in hers. "Max, there's only one cure for a woman in this condition." Her eyes were wide as saucers. I followed them as they traveled across the room, past the front desk, and up the stairs to my room above.

"Uh-uh," I told her. "No." I didn't know if it was a joke or not—she seemed to be quaking as she said it—but I felt as if I would be violating some primal law of the universe.

She laughed again, more like a choke really, then rose heavily to her feet and wobbled away from the terrace. By the time I caught up with her, she was halfway across the road, walking toward the ruins.

"Well," she said, taking hold of my arm again, "you're probably right."

"It's not like—"

"I know, I know," she said, patting my hand. "It's not like you don't want to, but . . ." She checked her watch. "Anyhow, it would be better if I spent the night in Damascus. Morning flight. Beauty sleep."

"There's one thing," I said, putting my hand on the small of her back and directing her toward a taxi.

"There always is."

"A favor?"

"Tell me."

"You're right about David Channing. I've got a suspicion something's not right with him. Can you find out anything about him?"

I didn't have all the pieces, but something was gnawing at me about the Channings.

"Max—"

"A truth for a truth."

"That would be two, and you know I can't spy on Dad's business partners." The effects of the wine seemed to have evaporated as fast as they'd come on. There was nothing unsteady about her now.

"Just see if you can find out the name of David Channing's company. The Rolodex, a letter. There's got to be something lying around. I've got a name in mind, but I want you to find it on your own."

India looked at me silently, then gave me a tight hug. I had no idea if this last request had registered, but the thought of her leaving made me desperately lonely. I could still feel her in my arms as she got into her taxi. In all this mess, it seemed that she was the only innocent one.

I watched the taxi round the corner, then headed for my room to pack. Our little lunch had burned Balabakk for me. It was time to move on.

CHAPTER 30

Beirut, Lebanon

THE ALBERGO HOTEL sits in the heart of Ashrafiyah, the old Christian Beirut. It's one of the hippest boutique hotels in the world. A tiny, discreet lobby. Leather books—real ones. Real antiques in the bar, too. The last time I'd had a drink there, I'd been half afraid to put my glass down for fear I would leave a ring on a buffet that once belonged to a Medici. Like all hip hotels worldwide, the Albergo's rooms are cramped—the less-is-more aesthetic—but the furnishings and little extras make up for the lack of elbow room.

The desk clerk standing behind the Louis XVI écritoire was elegantly lean: a black wool suit despite the summer heat, with a straight collar and a bright starched white shirt. When I told her my name was Jacques Dumet, she wrote it down neatly in the vellum ledger. She didn't ask for my passport, and I didn't offer her one. My German passport had done all the work it could handle.

As soon as the clerk gave me my key, I went out and caught a taxi to Hamra to an Internet café. I ordered a beer and logged in.

Ever since we'd worked on the World Trade Center bombing together, John O'Neill and I had used a kitchen-redecorating chat room to park messages for each other. O'Neill was Captain Crunch. I went by Subzero.

"Time to replace the counters, Captain Crunch," I wrote. "Call me ASAP on 011 961 1 33 97 97 or 212 ███████. Subzero."

The first was the number of the Albergo; the second, the one the prince said was tied to Ramzi Yousef, the mastermind behind the World Trade Center bombing. I knew O'Neill would immediately trace both. If the prince was right about the New York number, O'Neill's interest would be piqued enough that he would have to know more.

O'Neill called three hours later.

"All right, what is it now? If you're chained to a radiator in some Hizballah basement, I'll be sure to send a card at Christmas."

"Did you trace that New York number?"

"Yeah, you already know that."

"Whose number was it?"

"Fuck off. You already know that, too."

"It's not public, is it? Wanna know how I got it?"

"Okay, you win," O'Neill said. "How did you get it?"

"Can't tell you now, but there's a lot more, trust me."

"Awright, sweetheart, what do you want?"

Unfortunately, I had to cut another corner. There was no way to say it in code and have him understand me.

"Tell me about a David Channing. His father, Oliver Channing, used to work for us. His son may own a company in Maine."

"Why am I going to do this for you?"

Again, I didn't want to say KSM's name over the phone, but I wasn't hearing any give in O'Neill's voice. "You know the guy from Manila you'd love to get your hands on?"

I was counting on O'Neill connecting the "guy from Manila" with KSM.

O'Neill was part of the FBI investigation into KSM when he was plotting to bring down the twelve airplanes in 1994.

"I got his arrest warrant sitting right on my desk."

"Wanna know where he is and what he's doing?"

This time I could hear O'Neill sigh.

"How long you going to be at this number?"

CHAPTER 31

EIGHT DAYS LATER, I sat in the darkened bar of the Albergo and watched John O'Neill enter like a vicar walking into a child brothel. He kept reaching into his linen sport coat as if he were going for a gun. He wasn't, of course, but this was Beirut. The gesture rattled the hotel staff.

"Someone's going to call for backup if you do that again," I said, walking up to him.

"It's my cigar case."

"Pull it out, then. Kill the suspense. You're in a smoker's paradise."

"I can't."

"Can't?"

"I stopped. Doctor's orders."

"You never took a doctor's order in your life."

"I'm a new person. I want to live to be a hundred."

He didn't look it: bags under his eyes, drawn face. It couldn't have been jet lag or lack of sleep: O'Neill was an alien out of *Men in Black*. "You get to sleep when you're dead," he liked to say.

I suggested we pace through the tiny courtyard in front of the hotel as we talked. The Albergo itself was above intrigue, but you never knew if the lobby was wired.

O'Neill got things started by bitching and moaning about the hoops he'd had to crawl through just to show up: the embassy, the ambassador. In the end, they'd let him into the country only after he swore he would come to the meeting in an armored car, with bodyguards. I could see both cars parked across the street. The bodyguards milled around, hands in their vests.

"Listen, John—"

He wheeled on me before I could finish. "Max, what are you up to? Self-immolating? I can't believe you hooked up with Russians."

Russians? The only thing I could think of was that Webber had caught wind of Yuri, turned it into a full-blown counterintelligence investigation, and shoved the whole thing straight up O'Neill's nose. I didn't want to distract him with an explanation.

"I don't have time for that bullshit. Remember Applied Science Research, the clowns who followed me in New York?"

"Max, that's over. They followed you. They got crap. Ancient history."

"Did you hear they're working a case in San Diego?"

"Who's 'they'?"

"Applied Science."

"So what?"

I told O'Neill what India had told me about the two Saudis, about how Webber was intentionally withholding the information from the Bureau. The only thing I left out was my source, and her father.

"I'm gonna have his balls," O'Neill said when I finished. The words were right, but nothing else was. There was no punch behind them, none of O'Neill's usually blustering outrage. Time to worry about that later, too.

"Tell me about David Channing."

"No, first you tell me why I'm here."

"You're here because I know things you want to know. The same old game."

"Like what?"

"Like Khalid Sheikh Muhammad is planning to fly an airplane into a refinery—to make money."

"Woo-woo," O'Neill said, twirling his forefinger at his temple.

"Bin Laden's going along for the ride."

"Double woo-woo."

"You're not listening."

"Of course I'm fucking listening. You opened the door to the Woo Woo House, Max, and you heard the inmates screaming, and this is what they had to say. Big. Fucking. Deal. KSM? C'mon. Get real. He's afraid to set off an M-80."

"But what if—"

"What if *nothing!* It's crazy. You're crazy. The whole fucking Middle East is battier than goddamn Carlsbad Cavern!"

None of it sounded like O'Neill. Some bad impersonator had climbed inside his skin.

"Let me finish," I said. "What if KSM was just a front? Bin Laden, too. What if the people really doing the operation were the same ones who fought in the trenches in Beirut for fifteen years, the same people who truck-bombed the Marines, people who could put together a network and really carry off an operation like this? That scare you?"

"Yeah, if I were paying eight ninety-five to watch some rinky-dink, Hollywood version of the Great Global Conspiracy. Maybe you checked into the Woo Woo House, too." He took a long look around the over-planted courtyard and out to the street beyond. "Maybe you're already there."

"What's the matter, John?" I finally said. "They're on your ass?"

He sighed, huffed, reached for his cigar case again, and pulled his hand away in disgust when he realized nothing was in it.

"None of your damn business."

"Want more?"

"I got more than enough already."

I handed him the other phone number the prince had given me, the one in Tehran.

"Trace it," I said. "It's a Pasdaran ops number that Khalid Sheikh Muhammad calls from. I'm pretty sure his real masters are a couple crazies in the Pasdaran, not bin Laden."

"Oh, fuck. You're not still after Buckley's kidnapper, are you?"

"That's how it got started. No more."

That wasn't exactly true, but right now I needed O'Neill. He was my only connection to Washington. If he didn't believe my story, no one would. And my gut feeling was that the prince and his brother were on to something.

"Go home and check it out," I said. "If it's a good lead, call me and tell me it's worth pursuing."

"Oh, hell," O'Neill said, staring down at his palm as if I'd just spit in it. "Goddamn hell."

"David Channing?"

"What do you want to know about him?"

"How he makes money."

"Commodities. Oil. Pork rinds. Calls, puts. Hedge funds. He's deep in debt, though. A guy over at the SEC said they're about to investigate him. What does he have to do with KSM?"

"John, I still need one more favor."

He looked at me as if I were about to ask to borrow his pecker to screw his girlfriend.

"A last one. I mean it. Go through Millis's phone records for the afternoon of June 2, 2000. He was at lunch with me until at least two-thirty. See who he called after he got back."

I honestly thought he would say no, just leave. I'd emptied the cookie jar, run out of things to trade. It was down to trust now, the thinnest reed of all. In fact, he did turn to go, but I grabbed him by the arm before he got two steps. My jar wasn't empty after all.

"John, I wouldn't ask you if I didn't have to. But I can't get into Millis's House numbers. My bet is that if I find out who he called after I saw him, it'll mesh with something in the intercepts of KSM's calls."

"You have transcripts of KSM's calls?"

I nodded.

"Where are they?"

"You know the game. I play only if I get to be a player. I give you the transcripts now, and that's the last I'd hear from you."

"With or without them, it might be."

I knew what was going through O'Neill's mind. Even when you think your informant has gone over the edge, you make yourself listen on the outside chance that he comes up with one last piece of the puzzle that unlocks everything. Ninety-nine percent of the time, it's a fool's game, but the best intelligence officers keep playing.

"Okay, fuck," he said. Brushing my hand off his jacket. "If I can get my hands on them, how do I get them to you?"

I gave O'Neill the same e-fax number that Chris Corsini had used.

"Don't expect anything soon." O'Neill said, straightening his cuffs. "Unlike you, I got a daytime job."

"Listen," I told him, "I'm about to connect the dots. I'm not that far away. But—"

"No, *you* listen, Max: Stop adding two and two and getting twenty-two, okay? It'll only get you into more trouble. And stay the hell away from that Russian. Got it?"

O'Neill grabbed me around the neck, gave me a side hug, and started to walk away.

"Are we okay?" I called after him. He was more like himself now, but the whole performance was off a beat.

"Nothing I can't handle," he said without breaking stride.

"Sure?"

"Sure I'm sure. I'm John Fucking O'Neill."

O'Neill was halfway to his armored car when I thought of something else. "Wait," I called, racing after him. "What about Channing's company?"

"BT Trading, whatever that is. Some shell company registered in Maine."

Bingo. Here we go.

I was walking back to the hotel when I noticed an old BMW 316 parked down the street. The plates were gone. Even from a half block away, I could tell it was spray-painted. None of its three occupants were looking in my direction. One had a black vest on. Nothing entirely wrong about the picture, but nothing right about it, either.

CHAPTER 32

RECEPTION WOKE ME THE NEXT MORNING. Someone had dropped off a note. The bellboy brought it up.

Dear Max,
My brother is in Beirut tomorrow tonight. Let's meet. I'll
send my car around at eight.
Prince Al Sabah

I should have already left Lebanon, satisfied with what the prince had given me. Each minute I stayed was a roll of the dice. But I was intrigued by what the prince's brother would be bringing from Kuwait, especially if he knew something new about BT Trading. It looked now like it was a good decision.

The rest of the day I spent on the Albergo's eighth-floor terrace, trying to come up with a working theory from the bits and pieces I already knew, or thought I knew. Essentially, Frank Beckman retires and starts digging up old contacts to make his fortune. Most are informants he ran during his thirty-two-year career, but one is David Channing, whose father seemed to have a knack for meeting people all over the Middle East, especially on the far ends of the continuum. My guess, and here I was stretching, was that David Channing had taken over Oliver's networks when the old man died and that he was now Frank's conduit to those same people. After what India had told me, Webber was likely part of the package, too. That would explain why Webber framed me. Frank realizes I have a photo of Oliver Channing with bin Laden (that KSM took) and decides I have to be discredited and fired, and the photo destroyed. Webber takes care of Frank's dirty work.

A lot of question marks remained in the margins. Was the prince correct that an American was working with KSM? If so, was it Channing the younger or (and) Beckman? And if so, had he/they been working with KSM on the investment side back in '94 when he was plotting to bring down those twelve airplanes? (Frank was just getting his feet wet then in the private sector. This would have been a chance for him to make a big enough bundle to launch his business in grand style.)

I admit believing Frank was involved in bombing twelve passenger airliners was a deeply cynical link in this chain of thought. Christ, I'd known Frank forever. I'd had my ass saved by him. But I couldn't avoid it. Frank's frieze, his India-Modigliani, the Tuttle Street mansion—they all sat there at the edge of my memory, gnawing on my score-keeping. So did the fact that Frank had tried to tie me up with a crook like Rousset and everything India had told me about Frank and Lawson and Webber. Moral flaws run through me like the Amazon, but Frank had betrayed me in ways I didn't expect or deserve.

When the sun started to set, I borrowed a laptop from the front desk and went back to my room to check e-mail.

There was the usual spam, an e-mail from the landlord telling me a pipe had broken in my bathroom and that he'd let the plumbers in to fix it. Nothing from Marissa. Worse, nothing from Rikki. I'd been gone so long, under the radar and off the grid so many months, that they both must have figured I'd finally disappeared from their lives for good. Channels of communication were closing down fast. Marissa, I wasn't worried about. We kept up the usual incivilities of exes. I could disappear for years and not afflict her with my absence. Rikki was something else: I was afraid I might never repair things with her. We'd ended last summer's visit so well. This summer there wouldn't be a visit. More necessary losses. Or maybe not so necessary. Maybe that was just my excuse to myself.

I scrolled down and found a message from the e-fax site. It had to be from O'Neill. I got in the site, typed in my cell phone number, and watched it unlock an Adobe document: eight pages of calls for Millis's phone from June 1 through June 4, the day Millis was found dead.

I scanned the sheet until I came to a call made at 13:56 on June 2. It was to Frank Beckman's home number. Millis must have called Frank minutes after he got back to his office after having lunch with me. The next call to Frank was at 07:32 on June 4, the same day Millis was found with his head blown off in the Breezeway Motel.

Granted, Millis and Frank knew each other from Millis's Peshawar days, when Frank was head of the Afghan Task Force. It wouldn't be odd if they called each other from time to time. But what was the call on June 4 about? I would have thought Millis had other things on his mind.

CHAPTER 33

THE PRINCE'S RANGE ROVER and driver were waiting out front, engine running, when I walked out. I was just about ready to get into the passenger seat when I spotted what looked like the same three guys I'd seen the day before sitting in the BMW. One guy was wearing the same black vest. Only now they were standing by a late-model Mercedes in front of the Al Dente restaurant. All three were wearing sandals. Christians, and especially Christians living in Ashrafiyah, don't wear sandals. Invading Muslim hordes wear sandals. The rest of their clothing was way too shabby for Ashrafiyah. None of them had beards, but that didn't mean anything.

I motioned for the driver to sit tight, then went back inside the Albergo and asked the receptionist if I could see the manager. I was told he was in the dining room on the eighth floor.

The manager was French, maybe fifty, as slim and elegant as the rest of the place: Lanvin tie, the whole Gallic works, shining like a lighthouse all the way across the room. I asked him if I could have a word in private, and he led me out to the terrace, which overlooks Martyrs' Square, the old city, and beyond that the Med. It crossed my mind that Buckley's penultimate act of freedom was doing just this: taking a last look at the sea.

"I need to use a private office."

"My office is completely at your disposal." It's hard to beat a deluxe hotel, as Mother used to lecture me.

I followed the manager downstairs and waited while he unlocked his office. Then I surprised him by closing the door behind me, with him on the outside. First, I scanned all the documents the prince had given me in Shtawrah and downloaded them onto the manager's computer. I logged onto the Internet and went to www████████com, a site run by a CIA proprietary with software that allows you to hide scanned documents in images. Then I picked out three photos from the hotel's website and distributed the documents between them. When I was through, I wrote an e-mail to John O'Neill:

Dear Mr. and Mrs. O'Neill:
We are pleased to confirm your reservations for 24 September.
The Albergo.

As soon as the e-mail was launched, I erased it along with the scanned documents, then used the hotel's photocopier to make a copy of the documents for the manager to overnight to O'Neill. The originals I was going to walk out of the hotel with. If it wasn't my paranoia running wild—if in fact those three guys outside were waiting for me—I wanted them to have something to grab. Never disappoint a mugger. The last thing I did was to make out an Aramex international air bill addressed to O'Neill at his office.

The manager was waiting outside the door when I came out, seemingly unperturbed that I'd taken over his office for almost thirty minutes.

"There is a possibility someone will come and ask for this package you're about to send for me," I said. "Don't give it to them under any circumstances."

He nodded gravely as I handed it to him along with the air bill, like a partisan about to be sent over enemy lines.

The Albergo ran like a Swiss clock. It was famous for it in small circles. As soon as I turned around to leave, the manager would give the packet to an incorruptible bellboy who would run off to the nearest Aramex office, which would dispatch the documents to either the London or Paris flight. Within hours, my packet would be in the air, out of reach of whoever was waiting outside to talk to me.

As I headed for the door, I considered the possibility that the gang outside could simply push their way through the lobby when I was gone, image the Albergo's computer, and come up with the e-mail and scanned papers, but I didn't see it happening. The overnight package and the prince's originals, I thought, should be all the misdirection I needed.

As things turned out, I probably overreacted. The Mercedes was gone from in front of Al Dente. There wasn't a person in sight in sandals or underdressed in any way for overdressed Ashrafiyah. The entire streetscape was the very picture of upscale, old, Christian Beirut. I took a deep breath of relief, crossed the street, and let myself into the back of the prince's Range Rover.

As I got in, I saw three photos on the seat, all facedown. Two were eight-by-ten black-and-white glossies. The first one was of an overturned car, the prince lying beside it, eyes closed almost in repose, some kind of mottled scarf around his neck. The photo looked as if it had been taken on the Shtawra-Balabakk road. The second photo showed the same car, same road, from the other side. A second man lay faceup. Half his head seemed to have been blown off or scraped away. The other half looked enough like the prince that I guessed it was his brother, the adviser to Kuwaiti intelligence.

"Let's go!" I yelled to the driver as I picked up the third photo: an old Polaroid, color, four-by-four. The man kneeling in the foreground was some emaciated version of Bill Buckley. Standing behind him was the Iranian from Peshawar. A little younger but definitely him. In the sunlight, his red hair seemed to be on fire. Then I looked closer. Someone had colored the hair red with a Magic Marker.

"Go!" I screamed again at the driver.

He turned around, but it wasn't anyone I'd ever seen before. He was still staring at me as he slipped the key out of the ignition, opened the door, and began to walk away.

I was lunging to do the same when a gray Internal Security Forces Toyota Land Cruiser screeched to within an inch of the Rover's front fender and the two occupants jumped out. Neither was in uniform, but one carried an M-16.

"Passport!" one of them yelled at me, sticking his head through the back window. He was clean shaven. He could have been a cop. How was I to know?

I was pulling the German passport out of my back pocket when he jammed his pistol into my temple. "On the floor!" he yelled, this time in French.

He opened the door, climbed in, dug his foot into the back of my head, and assured me that if I moved so much as a fingernail, I'd be pudding; then he threw a jacket over my head.

I was trying to figure out what the immediate future might hold—arrest, interrogation, torture, more; I'd been trained for them, even had more than a taste of each—when the other door opened and someone slid calmly in.

"Mr. Waller, you know what you are? The inoculation. The inoculation against the truth. You run around the world, wildly exposing some insane plot about bombing airplanes, a plot hatched by a redheaded Iranian. They write you off as mad. 'Poor, poor soul,' they say when another such story passes by them. 'Some fool actually listened to Waller.' If you didn't exist, I would have had to invent you."

The accent was American, but with a peculiar rolling *r*. Terry Anderson had been right on the money: like someone who learns French before English.

"So you see, Mr. Waller, the Bible is a liar. You have a small piece of the truth right now, but you don't look very free to me."

He was sliding out the far door when someone reached in and swiped me across the side of the head with the butt of a rifle—a love tap, really, just enough to stun me and send blood streaming down my shirt collar and jacket while he rifled my pockets. By the time I realized I was alone and could finally get up, the ISF jeep was gone, as was anyone who had bothered to watch what was happening. A chic lady dressed to the nines walked by, looked at me in the backseat of the Range Rover, turned away in fright, and clattered down the street in her high heels. Beirut was back to being a prosperous Phoenician entrepot.

The envelope with the prince's documents was gone. So were the three gruesome photos, the German passport, every other piece of identity real or false, and my money.

Either Nabil was wrong about Mousavi being dead or someone was still trying to drive me over the edge.

CHAPTER 34

Geneva, Switzerland

ANOTHER ADVANTAGE TO DELUXE ACCOMMODATIONS: Everyone is too polite to mention the obvious. Anywhere else in the world the glowing-red bruise up the right side of my face would have gotten me sent around to the service entrance with the help, but the desk clerk at the Beau Rivage actually smiled when I walked up to his white-marble-and-gilt counter.

"I have a reservation," I said, pulling out the fifteen thousand dollars Yuri's Russian partner had sent me off with. "If you don't mind, I'll be paying in cash." That loan I'd forgiven Yuri almost twenty years earlier had turned out to be the best investment of my life.

The desk clerk took a five-thousand-dollar deposit without a murmur and gave me a room facing the lake.

The room was everything a five-star rating promises. The basket of fruit spilled over with kiwis, apples, blood oranges, even pomegranates. Orchids ascended elegantly out of an exquisite Japanese pot. A vase of tulips. Linen sheets—at least an 800 thread count. The bathroom had a walk-in shower with two heads on each side and a bench.

I fell asleep as soon as my head hit the pillow, telling myself I'd need only a fifteen-minute nap. It was dark when I woke up. The traffic along the quai in front of the hotel was light now. I checked my watch: a little after midnight. Another fifteen minutes, I told myself. I woke with a start to daylight: six-thirty. For a moment, I thought Murtaza Ali Mousavi had been a dream, but the dull ache in my head was anything but spectral.

Mousavi, or whoever it was in the prince's Range Rover, had been right. The truth hadn't set me free. I was more ensnared in it than ever, but in an odd way, my one-sided meeting with the man I had been chasing for nearly two decades had freed me from the past. Bill's murder wasn't avenged, but somehow I could begin to focus everything I had on what waited ahead, not on what lay behind. It was time to act. I reached over and dialed O'Neill's number without leaving the bed. He answered on the first ring.

"Did it arrive?"

"Did what arrive?"

"The package from Beirut."

"What are you talking about? I didn't get a package from you."

They'd gotten to the Albergo manager, convinced him to turn over the documents, mugged the bellhop, burned down the Aramex office, blown up its plane. Possibilities were endless.

"What about the e-mail?"

"I got an e-mail from the Albergo. What was that about?"

"When I get to New York, I'll show you how to read it. You gotta get me in the U.S. I'm on U.N. docs. Phonies."

Fortunately, I'd caught Yuri on his cell phone. He was in Urumqi, China. It took all of ten minutes after I called him for one of his Russian partners to get to the Albergo and another two hours for the partner to se-cure the U.N. refugee laissez-passer. I would have preferred a good-quality forged passport, but that took time, and time I didn't have.

"What in the fuck have you got yourself into now?" O'Neill asked.

"Here. Write this down. Joseph Konrad—Konrad with a *K*—K O Z E N I O W S K I. Can you get me in?"

"How the hell did you come up with that name?"

I'd asked the Russian partner the same question when he handed me the laissez-passer. "Patron saint of dark hearts" was all he answered, but I was in no position to argue. I did say no when he tried to send me to Bratislava. Geneva it had to be. No other options. He needed another four hours to get the United Nations High Commission for Refugees to agree to get the Swiss to agree. By the time Yuri's partner reserved me a room at the Beau Rivage, my head hurt too much to argue.

"Can you get me in?" I asked O'Neill again.

"I don't know."

"John, I used to parole people through immigrations all the time. Do it. I've got evidence of an ex-colleague making a killing using foreknowledge of terrorist attacks."

I didn't. Or maybe I really did. The point was to do what I had to do as quickly as possible and get out of Geneva, show up in New York, and drop everything in O'Neill's lap.

"Your kind of evidence, not mine," I added. O'Neill didn't laugh, and I didn't have to drive the point home. The way the FBI worked, there had to be the hard promise of a collar before they would even consider paroling someone into the country on an alias passport.

"You already have a lot of the stuff in the e-mail I sent," I continued. "And I'm about to put my hands on a lot more." Another promise I wondered if I could keep.

"I'll get our guy in Paris to come down and see you."

"No, the deal is I give it to you in New York."

O'Neill had been grinding his teeth at the other end of the line loud enough to let me know how put out he was. "Let me see," he finally said.

I called India an hour earlier than I promised myself I would.

"Max? You woke me up."

"I need to ask you something."

"Are you out of Lebanon?"

"Is your father really having financial problems?" I asked, ignoring her question.

"Call me back on my cell," India said, and hung up.

She answered on the first ring.

"Sorry," she said. Her voice had gone from sleepy to downcast. "I didn't want Simon listening in. Or Dad."

"It's bad, isn't it?"

"You can't believe what's happening here. He was on the phone all night talking to Saudi Arabia, trying to raise money. There's a bunch of margin calls he can't make. I can't stand being here. By the way, where are you?"

"Switzerland. Why don't you call Michelle Zwanzig and ask her what's going on. You wouldn't believe what people tell their fiduciaries."

"I already know. Channing screwed him. The bas—"

"Did Michelle tell you that?"

"No. I read Dad's e-mails. Max, it's awful. He could go to jail." I heard a muffled sob.

"You don't have an inkling of what he's up to?"

"He locks himself in the library. Whenever he comes out, he says that it's going to be okay, that he's about to close on a big deal."

If she only knew. Listening to India, I now was close to convinced that Frank Beckman had gotten rich from tip-offs on terrorist attacks. KSM lets Frank know about a plane about to go down, and Frank shorts the company that owns it. A tanker is about to go up in the Straits of Hormuz, and Frank goes long on crude futures. The newspaper stories would cast it as part of the ideological struggle between Islam and the West, but for Frank it was the oldest story of all: money. But I wasn't going to air this over the phone with India.

"You need to confront Michelle. My bet is she knows what's going on." Saying that made me think of something. "By the way, do you have any accounts with her?"

"One or two. I have no idea what's in them. Dad set them up, and he stored some of my stuff with her. Trust papers, wills. That sort of thing. She has it in her office, I think, in some sort of safe-deposit box."

"Come here, then. To Geneva. Tell her you need to look at it. Maybe some of your dad's stuff is in the same box, and you'll figure out what's going on. Maybe something that will shed light on Channing, too. You're a client, India. You have a right."

"I don't know. She'll call Dad. Anyhow, I don't have any idea where the key to the box is."

"There's a key?"

"Somewhere."

"You need to know the truth, India. I can't tell you on the phone, but you need—"

"What are you saying?"

"Just come here tonight." I was almost begging now.

"Tonight? Max, I can't! I have duty Saturday. There's dinner at home that night. It's with—"

"India, I wouldn't ask if it weren't important. Try. Think about it. Call me at the Beau Rivage if you can't make it." I gave her the name I was registered under. "Otherwise I'll be at the airport."

"You don't like to give a girl much time to think about her wardrobe, do you?"

"And India . . ."

"More?"

"Find the key."

My next call was to the concierge.

"Michelle Zwanzig. Can you find me her address and telephone number?" I'd lost her card along with everything else.

He called back in five minutes. "Unfortunately, sir, it's unlisted."

"Are you downstairs?"

I found the concierge, pulled him aside, and slipped him five hundred dollars to find out her address from the police. An old girlfriend, I explained, hoping to make the task more palatable. I added that I was in town on short notice and wanted to surprise her. I was pretty sure he'd come back with the number. Switzerland is a country of snitches, and concierges are all tight with the cops.

Back in my room, I was flipping through the TV channels when I heard a tap on the door. The concierge was as efficient as the rest of the hotel.

Michelle Zwanzig's office was on the other side of the lake just off Rue du Puits-Saint-Pierre. That would put it just behind the Hotel Les Armures, where Marissa and I had once stayed in better days, before we were married. We always thought Rikki had been conceived there, proof that sperm and egg can't be too drunk to find each other.

"A hotel car, sir?"

"What? No." I was too distracted at the moment to even think of giving him a tip, but I immediately regretted it. His inclination would be to file a report with the police about me—the passive aggression of the servant class. I caught up with him in the service stairs and pressed another hundred into his palm.

To pass the time, I went downstairs to the business office, sat down at one of the guest computers, and logged on. I wasn't expecting anything more from O'Neill except perhaps an instant response that he couldn't parole me into the U.S. or anywhere else on Planet Earth. Instead, there was a message sent from Marissa's address, marked "Urgent" in the subject line. What now? I wondered. What in the middle of all this? It had to be money. I felt like shit when I read it.

> *Max, please call immediately. Marissa suffered a stroke.*
> *Rikki needs you as soon as you can get here. You need to*
> *come to Istanbul.*

Marissa's father had sent it, followed by six others, all ending with a plea to come be with Rikki.

I e-mailed him back a pile of nonsense with just enough verisimilitude to it that I thought he might believe me: I was in Central Asia, places unnamed, hush-hush. Terribly sorry. I'd come with the first plane out. He had gotten used to similar evasions when I was married to his daughter.

Then I picked up a hotel phone and called Rikki, not at the Istanbul phone number her father had left but on her cell.

"Hello?"

It was her voice, tentative, the way it used to be around strangers.

"Rikki."

"Da—"

"No, honey. Don't say anything yet. Are you in the hospital room?" She whispered a yes. "With your grandparents?" Another yes. "Maybe you could step out into the hallway. A boyfriend calling."

I heard her footsteps, what I guessed was a hospital cart being pushed by, monitors beeping.

"I'm at the end of the hall," she finally said, "by the window."

"Sweetheart, I just e-mailed your grandfather. I didn't want him to get upset on the phone, but I can't come now. It's—"

"It's all right, Daddy. You can't be around all the time. I know what you do."

I hope you don't, I thought. Oh, Jesus, I hope you don't. I let the implication sit there, though, another small lie to add to my skyscraper of deceit.

"How's your mother?"

"Better," she said. There were tears in her voice. "She's only thirty-three, Daddy. A stroke! How does that happen? Her face is paralyzed on the left side. She looks so old. She can't really speak yet."

The words were gushing out now, a torrent. I heard about how Rikki had been swimming in the Adriatic and came back to the villa just before supper to find Marissa sprawled on the kitchen floor, about the lighthouse keeper and his first aid, about the helicopter that flew them to Zadar, on the Croatian coast, and the airplane her parents had chartered at ruinous expense to bring Marissa to Istanbul for treatment. I knew Marissa's age, of course, but hearing Rikki say it shocked me, too. She'd seemed so old for nineteen when we married. She seemed so young for this, now. Marissa's grandmother had died at the same age, dropped dead at the stove. I was hoping Rikki couldn't see her own fate sitting out there, less than two decades ahead.

"I don't know what to do, Daddy," she finally said. "School starts in two weeks. I can't go back; I can't leave her."

"Yes, you can, sweetheart. You can. You have to. Your mother would want it. I know she would. Grandma and Grandpa can look after her. She'll get better. You have to go on with your life. You're too young to be a nursemaid."

I was gushing now, running my own words together. We didn't have much time. I wanted to say everything I could.

"Daddy, Grandpa is waving at me from the door. I think we're going. He looks upset."

"He's just impatient, honey. He's not angry at anyone. Not at you. Go. I love you."

"I love you, too."

I could hear her footsteps starting back up the hall.

"Rikki!"

"Yes?"

"I'll get to England. In September. I'll see you there."

"Will you?"

We were cut off there. Whether it was Rikki hanging up or the network failing, I didn't know. But I thought that if I didn't get to England the way I said I would, she would remember me the same way I remembered my own mother. The thought of it made me shiver. She'd have someone to hate forever.

I had never met Michelle Zwanzig. Indeed, I never would have heard of her if Frank hadn't given me her card and told me she would be my conduit to the Saudi billionaire. But I was sure she was chatty as a clam. All Swiss fiduciaries are. They hold private fortunes in their own names, based only on blind trust and total discretion. When their clients ask for their money back, Swiss fiduciaries are expected to have it. Still, I wanted to see her office. I couldn't use my real name; Frank had probably warned her about me. But maybe we would meet, and I could elicit something from her, tight-mouthed or not. At the least, I would get a look at the layout. Always better to do something than nothing.

Private Investment Services was located on the third floor of a sixteenth-century four-story Palladian on Rue Soleil Levant. There was no plaque out front, nor was Zwanzig's name on the building list.

I rang the buzzer for the *rez-de-chaussée*.

"Yes?"

"I'd like to talk to Private Investment Services."

"About what?"

"A new account."

"Do you have an appointment?"

"No."

I wished the damned lady would come out and show herself. It's virtually impossible to recruit someone through a squawk box.

"Please wait."

I took a quick survey of the lobby and the hallway leading upstairs. A closed-circuit camera perched up in the corner covered the front door. The camera looked to be fed with a standard hookup. Disrupt the power supply, and you could fry the camera by crossing the wires. By the time the security company arrived, the electricity would be back on. If it was the weekend, they wouldn't get around to replacing the camera until Monday morning.

The problem was the front-door lock—a sophisticated Swiss laser-cut. I'd never be able to pick it. I had no way to tell what lock Zwanzig had on her own door, but it was probably the same one. If I decided to go in, I'd have to drill them both. No problem so long as the invisible *rez-de-chaussée* lady was away, but I'd still need to get in and out fast. Strictly a bash-and-dash entry.

I'd been standing there at least ten minutes before the squawk box came alive again.

"Private Investment Services thanks you very much for your visit, but at the moment they are not taking any new clients."

I considered asking her to relay the message that Frank Beckman had told me to get in touch with Madame Zwanzig, but I'd been throwing caution to the wind ever since I left Washington, and for the most part, I'd done nothing but pay for it. Besides, now I knew my way to Private Investment Services. In my own way, I'd even cased the place. The day hadn't been a total waste.

The next morning, I had nothing to do, so I prowled Geneva instead—ate, walked, had more coffee, watched the storm clouds gather over the lake, piling on top of one another like some fraternity phone-booth prank. I was on the Quai du Mont-Blanc when they finally broke and an ocean of rain fell from the sky seemingly all at once. Maybe ten seconds later, a Beau Rivage doorman walked halfway down the block to meet me with a huge umbrella.

I was just inside the lobby, mopping my hair, when I heard a familiar voice—"Mr. Kozeniowski!"—and looked up to see India standing at the reception desk. She was far more drenched than I.

"Don't you own a raincoat?" she whispered.

"Sarcasm is unattractive in the young. And by the way, where's yours? How did you get so, so . . ."

"Wet?"

I nodded.

"The storm. The run from the train station. It was the last block that put me over the top. Wet-wise."

"Ever hear of taxis?"

"The train is so much easier. At least when it's not raining."

The Beau Rivage had been Frank's favorite hotel. It's where he told me that he and Jill had separated, where I first learned that he had a daughter, where I first heard her name. Frank must have brought India here later when he could really afford the place, but if the staff knew her, they weren't letting on.

"Luggage?" I asked.

"They put it in your room until mine is ready. Hope you don't mind. I need a shower."

"By the way, how did you get here so soon? I checked the schedules. The first plane—"

"The one before it. It was sitting on the tarmac at Dulles when I got there. You underestimate me."

So I had. We headed to the elevator.

I offered to have coffee or tea sent up, but India immediately popped into the bathroom, extended one delicate arm out the slightly cracked door with a plastic dry-cleaning bag containing all her dripping wear, and stepped into the shower while I called laundry.

A half hour later steam was still pouring out under the door.

"Hey!" she called out. "Let's celebrate. How about a bottle of Bollinger? And why don't you get into something dry. " As she spoke, the bathroom door cracked open again and a terry-cloth robe came flying out.

The Bollinger and India's newly dry wear arrived together twenty minutes later, just as she was stepping out of the bathroom—or steam-bath, it was hard to tell—wrapped in a towel. Her flushed, angular face and the raven hair plastered close to her scalp would have driven Modigliani straight back to his easel.

We stood quietly by the window, sipping our champagne and watching sheets of rain buffeting the lake. Finally, I pointed to the tidy pile on the desk.

"Your clothes," I said, but she just shook her head no, took my hand, and starting leading me toward the bed.

Looking back on it now, I think that's the moment in this horrible skein I felt the sickest over. I fed India the bait, and she took it, hook, line, and sinker. I'd recruited her.

CHAPTER 35

THE TRUTH JABBED ME in the brain like a cranial probe. The faxes, the transcripts of KSM's calls, the methyl nitrate, Frank's options trades had all been boring deeply into my thoughts while India slept softly on my shoulder. Then I remembered a seminar on methyl nitrate I'd attended at the FBI Training Academy in Quantico maybe two years earlier. I knew little about it before, and still don't understand the chemistry today, but the practical effects were staggering. It was completely plausible for KSM to introduce the stuff into the fuel system of a plane. The plane would blow up into millions of pieces and devour the evidence in the conflagration. He could do the same with a refinery—somehow introduce it into the flow, and the whole thing blows apart. The only calling card methyl nitrate leaves behind is a bright ocher hue as it burns, not the orange-red flash of burning gasoline or jet fuel.

"Time the explosion to happen over the ocean, and only the albatrosses and fishies will know," the instructor had told us. "Forensics cannot detect methyl nitrate residue, unlike with conventional explosives."

I sat bolt upright in bed. KSM was going to use "liquids" that would never be traced. And it was so much easier than trying to get plastic explosives on a plane. It was a foolproof way to protect his options trade. It couldn't be anything else. The question now was when.

India was awake. "What time is it?"

The room was dark. There was no traffic on the Quai du Mont-Blanc. I looked over at the clock on the nightstand. A little after three, I told her.

"Max, are you okay?"

"I will be. First tell me again about Vernon Lawson." Intuition leads. Facts follow. Somewhere in my descent-into-hell dream I'd been having, I'd seen the face of the journalist-whore who was ready to deliver my balls on a platter to readers of the *Times* and anywhere else willing to pick up the story.

India sat up beside me, plumped pillows for both of us, and as we sat there skin to skin in the dark, she told me what had happened.

It must have been almost six in the evening, she said. She left work early, stopped by a place in Georgetown to pick up some catfish. It wasn't just Simon's night off. The cook was gone, too, and the driver. She was going to bread the filets, then fry them up with red beans and rice, a favorite of Frank's from the old days when money didn't grow on trees.

The library doors were open when she got home. She could see two men sitting with her father. Frank rose immediately to greet her and close the doors before she tried to join them, but she got a good look at the guy I was certain was Vernon Lawson. Her physical description matched him to a tee.

"And Webber," I asked, "did you get a good look at him? Where was he sitting?"

"I'm not sure . . ."

"Sure of what?"

"Sure that it was Webber."

"But—"

"I never said that, Max. I never . . ." She let it trail off.

I was ransacking my memory. Hadn't she told me before that Webber was there? Or was it my need that made me hear it that way?

"Whoever it was was sitting off to the side, maybe behind the desk. I didn't get a look before Dad closed the doors."

"India—"

"All I can tell you is what I remember, you understand? You weren't there."

I put my arm around her, pulled her closer to me. She had gone cold all of a sudden. I rubbed her shoulder and neck until whatever it was had passed.

"I didn't care that he didn't invite me in," she began again. "That's Dad. The Old Boys taking care of business."

As she was starting up the stairs, though, she heard my name, or thought she did. Frank shushed whoever said it. That's when India went up to her room and pressed her ear against the floor vent. The third one—not her father, not the journalist—was saying that I was on the dole of some ex–GRU officer. The FBI was dragging its heels, refusing to issue an international fugitives warrant, but it wouldn't do any good even if they did. No one was going to execute it.

As she talked, I tried to imagine what a voice sounds like filtering from the floor below through an air vent. India had told me in Balabakk that Webber had hit on her. Did he send a mash note, a mash e-mail? If not, wouldn't she recognize his voice? And if not from that, then from some staff meeting, an orientation lecture?

"The journalist, Lawson, he said that the *Times* was ready to run his story that you'd gone to work for a hostile intel service. Then the other person said—"

"Said what?"

"Said that the story had to run as soon as possible. He told Lawson to find whatever confirmation he needed to write it."

"Are you sure?" I interrupted.

"He was adamant about it. You had to be stopped."

"Stopped from what?"

"No one said. Anyhow, Lawson didn't seem to know or care. He just wanted to burn you."

"But it didn't run. Or at least not so far."

"Believe me, Max. I don't know why."

Another dead end.

India reached over, patted my hand. "What did you say to Dad to make him so angry?"

"When he called me a well-hit three-wood in a tile bathroom?" It still hurt. Maybe because he wasn't that far off.

"A truth for a truth: It's your own rule, Max. Dad used to say you were damaged goods. I was always intrigued. I never knew what he meant. Are you?"

Am I?

"He said something had happened to you when you were a kid. I don't think even he knew what it was, but he said you would never get over it."

"He was right."

"Did you?"

"No. Not really, I guess. Just compensated around it the way people do in life."

"So," India said.

"So?"

"Are you going to tell me?"

"My mother," I began, "was born with the biological capacity to reproduce but with no maternal instincts. She despised me from conception. It was unfortunate. For me at least."

And so for the second time in my life, I told the story.

"Your aunt?" India asked when I was through. "The one who came and got you?"

"My mother's sister. The only one who even knew where we were. The only family I ever cared about. She died last year."

"And your mother?"

I shrugged, turned my palms up. "She used to contact my aunt occasionally. No more. Alive. Dead. I hope the latter."

With that, we sat in silence holding hands. I had been drunk, stoned, a twenty-year-old college student unpracticed in deceit when I'd told Chris the story. Now I was sober, a liar par excellence, in bed with a woman not much older than I was then, a graduate of the same university. Life has weird circular harmonics, I've found, if we just listen to them. But we move on, too. We become different people. And that night in Geneva, thinking about what I had just recounted and all that had happened over the last months, I felt as if I could almost see my entire life's story coming together: the Baluchs and KSM; Beirut and Buckley; Webber and Frank Beckman and John O'Neill; Murtaza Ali Mousavi and his dentist and Millis's displaced brain; abandonment, loss, and recovery; the search for truth that would never, ever let me alone.

Isn't that what every introductory perspectives course teaches in art school, that at the horizon, all points converge?

I'll tell the story one more time, I thought, to Rikki, when she's old enough to understand. Only a few years more. It can die with her.

India was shaking quietly beside me, on the verge of tears, I realized. To forestall, I asked her if she knew either Rousset or the Saudi billionaire, her father's partner. She'd heard him mention them but never met either.

"It doesn't make sense," she said. "Dad knows Rousset is about to be indicted in New York for selling Kazak oil to Iran. He stopped doing business with him at least a year ago."

That was another dot clear and bold. If Rousset was about to be indicted, there was only one reason for Frank to give me his number: burn me, dirty me up in some illegal oil deal, dispose of me for good.

India got up, put on a robe, and went to the minibar. She poured herself a straight-up Scotch. "Want one?" I didn't. She got back into bed, farther away than she'd been earlier, no more skin to skin.

"Dad's in even worse trouble than I told you."

"You never told me anything."

"I shouldn't be saying any of this."

She did anyhow. India didn't know exactly what had happened, but she was beginning to piece the picture together. Frank was deep into commodities speculation and the options market. Airlines. Insurance companies. Especially oil. A lot of the money he played with was borrowed from his

Saudi partners, as was a lot of the advice he acted on, such as how much crude they were pumping on a day-to-day basis. If his Saudi friends told Frank they were about to cut back on production or there was a problem with a field, he bought calls on oil—bets that the price of oil would go up. If they were ratcheting production up, he bet the other way. It was easy money, and for several years Frank made an absolute killing. Even when he was betting someone else's money.

My intuition was looking better and better: Like some incorrigible capitalist Delphic oracle, Frank had built his fortune by seeing into the future.

Trouble was, after a while, he started tapping other sources of information. Half a dozen times, when his Saudi partners went long on oil, he went short and got creamed.

"I know," India said, catching my glance. "I'm curious how Dad and his partners bet against the market and got it right so often."

Actually, I didn't think there was any question about it now: insider trading. Channing's networks fit right into their uncanny success.

"How do you know all this?" I asked. She was just out of college. It wasn't the sort of research a daughter usually undertakes on her father.

"I already told you. I read his e-mails and faxes. He's all I've got; I have no choice but to be interested."

It served my interests, too, I thought.

"So what's he going to do?" I asked.

"He's playing the spot oil market hard."

"With his Saudi friend?"

"Not this time. With David Channing. The trades are in Dad's name to hide Channing's hand."

"Did you ever hear the name BT Trading?"

"No. Never."

India and I talked until six in the morning, running through all the possibilities. We both knew we weren't getting anywhere.

"Did you find the key to the safe-deposit box?" I finally asked her.

"Keys," she corrected. "They were in Dad's desk drawer—two of them."

"Bring them with you?"

She nodded.

"Get dressed," I said, throwing the sheets back.

I had coffee sent up while she washed and dressed.

From Cornivan, Geneva's main railroad station, to Annemasse is a twenty-minute trolley ride. The trolley passes through a border crossing, but neither the Swiss nor the French bother checking passengers.

In Annemasse, we took a taxi to Bons-en-Chablis, a French village that had yet to be gentrified. It probably wouldn't be for a long time because you couldn't see Lac Léman from any part of it. The taxi dropped us in front of Electromanager du Lac, a well-known fence for illegal arms.

I'd never been in the store before, but as with Carthage Voyages, I'd read about the place in cable traffic. Geneva station and the French police independently used it to keep tabs on anything from arms to stolen plutonium. It was a nice deal for Jean-Marc, the owner; he got protection for his fencing in return for passing on an occasional tip.

Jean-Marc emerged from the back room when he heard the bell above the door ring. A slight man, maybe forty, with horn-rim glasses and a tweed coat, he didn't look much like a black-arms dealer.

"I work with Pat," I said, sticking my hand across the counter to shake his.

Pat Graner was the chief in Basle, Jean-Marc's case officer.

"He should have called."

"I know," I said, shrugging my shoulders in apology. "No problem. Call him now if you like."

I knew it was Pat's habit not to get into the office on Saturday until after eleven.

"Where are we?" India asked when Jean-Marc slipped behind the curtain, no doubt to make sure I really worked with Pat.

"This guy's an informant," I said.

"Oh, fuck, I might as well go home and resign."

"They'll never know you were here."

"What are we doing?"

"Finding out why your dad's in trouble."

"Here?"

"No. At Michelle Zwanzig's."

"Max?"

Jean-Marc was back before I could respond. He must have decided not to call Pat after all. "How can I help you?"

Jean-Marc didn't flinch when I asked him for a spin dialer, an ultrasound generator, and a five-inch pneumatic gun.

"Max?" India asked again when he disappeared. More of an edge this time. As if she could hear glass breaking in the distance.

"Props."

"No, seriously."

"Break-in stuff."

"Christ almighty, I'm outta here." She actually turned around to leave, but she didn't resist when I took hold of her wrist.

"It's not like we're going to use it against someone we don't know. It's your dad's own office."

"Forget it. Sneaking over the border into Lebanon was one thing; breaking and entering is entirely different."

"You're not going in; I am."

CHAPTER 36

A T A LITTLE AFTER FOUR that Saturday afternoon, I rang the *rez-de-chaussée* bell. No answer. I rang it again.

India watched from across the street, leaning against an arch. A knapsack at her feet, she looked like a well-heeled college backpacker in Switzerland on summer vacation; I looked like a *Gastarbeiter* in a blue monkey suit. I turned and gave her a smile as I rang the doorbell once more, then pointed to the arch and watched as she ducked out of sight. There was no answer. This time I rang the third-floor doorbell, Zwanzig's office. It was Saturday; Zwanzig wouldn't be there—fiduciary agents never work on Saturdays. After five minutes of this, I pulled the cordless drill out of my pouch and jammed the bit in the keyway. The pins sheared off one after the other. The racket reverberated up and down the cobblestone street, but no one paid attention. I was just another locksmith replacing a broken lock on a weekend call.

Once the lock gave and I was inside, I pulled out the cylinder and replaced it with another one. The clerk at the hardware store, the same one who sold me the drill and the monkey suit, assured me that all the cylinders for this particular lock were the same. He was right. I loved the Swiss.

When I was through, I went back outside, let the door lock behind me, and tried the new key. Aces. Now I was the only one who could get inside the building. I couldn't see India now, but I was sure she was there, just where we'd talked about. She wasn't happy about it, but at least she'd agreed: If an alarm went off outside the building or if she heard the police coming, she was to shoot the gun at the third-floor window, Michelle's office, then walk away.

India had laughed when I'd walked across the Quai du Mont-Blanc a half hour earlier carrying a dead pigeon in a plastic bag. She'd thought I'd gone completely nuts, and when I began stuffing the bird down the barrel of the pneumatic gun to show her how it worked, she was sure of it. But she understood when I explained. If an alarm goes off and the police come, the smashed glass and dead pigeon explain the alarm: a simple avian flight malfunction. It wouldn't take care of the closed-circuit camera, but I figured we'd be out of Switzerland before anyone checked the feed.

"I'm going to shoot a dead bird at a window?"

"That's how it works, dear. The good news is that no policeman in Switzerland would have the nerve to haul you in for it. He'd be laughed off the force. Just be sure to clear the area before the police actually arrive."

As the pigeon gun suggests, this wasn't exactly a professional break-in. To do that you need a hundred people on the street: a ten- to twelve-person surveillance team watching each and every person with twenty-four-hour access to the building just in case someone makes a surprise visit to the target site, and a dozen other watchers with radios on the approaching streets in case the police answered a silent alarm you didn't know about. And then there's the actual team: a specialist for electric alarms, another for motion detectors, a safe cracker. I had to work with what I had.

I let myself in again and walked up to the third floor. Zwanzig's lock gave up as easily as the one downstairs, and I didn't have to worry about replacing it. The big question now was what was waiting inside. Normally, a break-in crew sticks a fiber-optic probe under the door to take a look around for the alarm system. Jean-Marc didn't have one, and I didn't have a week to wait for him to get one. Instead, the hope was that the ultra-sound generator would disable a motion detector. Open the door slowly. Push the generator through. Turn it on. Pray. I did. There was no alarm, or at least no audible one. And I was inside.

As I suspected, Zwanzig's office was as neat as a pin: a wall of three-ring binders, two tasteful etchings, a kid leather couch and matching chair, and in the corner a four-foot-high safe with a dial. I looked everywhere, even behind the pictures and in the closets, but there were no safe-deposit boxes. Either India got it wrong or Zwanzig transferred her clients' paper into the safe. Now I would have to try my luck with the safe. I attached the dialer and started it spinning.

In the meantime, I went to look for Zwanzig's computer. Her drawers were as tidy as the rest of her office, pencils neatly aligned in one compartment, pens in another. But no computer, no laptop, no Palm Pilot, no nothing. I went through all the closets. Nothing there, either. The spin dialer was still spinning—running through all the possible combinations could take a couple hours. While I was waiting, I started in on the three-ring binders.

The labels on the outside all seemed to be about watering holes for posh souls: San Remo, Gstaad, and on and on. Inside the folders, though, the contents had nothing to do with vacations. The first thing I came to in the Gstaad folder was a telefax from Zwanzig to UBS AG, the Swiss mega-bank, ordering the transfer of six million dollars from a numbered account in Venezuela to a Qatari prince's account. The entire binder was full of similar transfers, some for even more money, some for much more. I pulled down the binders one after another looking for transfers connected to either Frank or Channing. I even looked for something with Webber's name on it.

I heard the spin dialer click. It had picked up the first number of the safe combination. I stood watching it as number two caught. Number three fell in place another minute later. I pulled down the handle and the safe swung open.

I didn't know what to expect, but if Michelle Zwanzig had left the kind of stuff I'd found in the binders in open view, she had to have something pretty incredible sitting on those shelves in front of me, maybe even the keystone I was looking for, the one that would nail down my suspicions with facts.

On the top shelf of the safe was an eighteen-page computer-generated sheet of "calls," option swaps and credits to banks. I quickly skimmed through them. They were all related to oil futures, oil service companies, oil companies. Whoever owned the calls was paying only two cents on the dollar. If Halliburton stock rose more than ten dollars, the owner was going to make a fortune. If the price of oil went up five dollars, Exxon was a gold mine.

I kept looking, still sure there had to be something related to airline stocks. But there wasn't. I rifled through the paper on the shelf underneath. Nothing about airline options there, either. So much for my theory about a reprise of KSM's plane-bombing scheme. Instead, I found a dozen letters from David Channing, instructing that profits from calls be paid to a score of accounts around the world. I looked for anything with BT Trading on it, but there had to be six inches of paper on that shelf. It would take me at least an hour to go through it.

I'd started looking through the papers when the window behind me shattered. The pigeon didn't make it through—I'd thought the bird was too light—but the broken glass was all I needed. I couldn't hear a klaxon. But India had to be warning me that the police were on the way.

I jammed as much paper as I could from the safe into a plastic shopping bag I'd brought along, then pulled off the spin dialer and stuffed it in the safe along with the ultrasound generator, the monkey suit, the drill, and the rest of the stuff I'd come in with. Then I squirted Gorilla Glue into the safe's key locks and behind the dial. The repair company would scratch its head for a day before it drilled the thing open. More than enough time to get out of Switzerland.

I ran downstairs and out the front door and almost tripped on something. I looked down and saw a woman in her seventies with a beet-red face and a bleached Heidi haircut. She was maybe five feet tall and not even a hundred pounds. She had a key in her right hand.

"*La clef ne marche plus*"—the key doesn't work anymore—she said, looking at me for an explanation.

Just as I recognized the voice behind the squawk box, she took a hard look at me.

"*C'est vous!*" she screamed. She pulled a cell phone out of her purse and screamed into it even before dialing. "I've caught a thief! I've caught a thief!" People on the street stopped to look at her, and then me. I considered running but I knew that within a block I'd have a hundred people after me.

I looked behind me to make sure India had taken off. I couldn't see her.

"Thief!" the woman screamed. There was a crowd gathering around us.

I was about ready to surrender when I heard India's voice. "What are you saying?" she yelled as she pushed her way through.

The woman turned around, surprised that anyone would dare interfere with the course of Swiss justice.

"Leave him alone. You're crazy," India said.

"He—"

"He didn't do anything," India said, her voice now calmer. India's French was flawless.

"*Mais—*"

"*Mais merde!* We're here waiting for Ms. Michelle Zwanzig. Floor three. Private Investment Services. She represents my family." There was something almost regal in her manner. She expected an apology—no question about it. Now.

"Give me your cell phone and talk to her yourself," she said, her voice now back to normal.

The woman dialed a number, no doubt Zwanzig's home. India took the phone from her.

"Michelle, it's India. India Beckman. Dad wanted me to come see you. . . . Yes . . . No, I don't know why. Documents for your safekeeping, I suppose. I have them with me. Dad told me this time; he must have thought you would be here. We'd been ringing your bell. The downstairs door was open. My friend went inside to see if he could ring up to your office. And now this lady is accusing him of breaking in. She's insufferable." She was actually stamping her foot as she said it. "Would you mind talking to her?"

India handed the phone to the woman.

"Yes, madam . . . yes, madam . . . You're sure you know the young lady? Of course, thank you, madam."

She put her phone back in her purse, looked at the two of us, certain something was not right, and apologized.

As she watched us in puzzlement, we walked down the hill arm in arm, me with my shopping bag crammed with who knows what, India with her backpack minus the pigeon gun. Somewhere in the ether overhead, I was certain, Frank Beckman and Michelle Zwanzig were in earnest conversation. We had to get out of Switzerland fast.

CHAPTER 37

I WAS ON THE COUCH, watching India packing, when there was a knock on the door.

"*Service,*" a muffled voice said.

I looked at India. She shrugged her shoulders to tell me she hadn't ordered anything. It couldn't be the Swiss police. It was too soon for them to have figured out what happened.

"*Service, s'il vous plait.*"

"*Un instant,*" I said.

I motioned for India to go into the bathroom and close the door. Then I turned off the lights and drew the curtains. I knew the interior. I was betting whoever was in the hall didn't. I crouched low beside the door and threw the latch. As soon as I turned the knob, the door flew open with a hard kick and someone threw himself into the room. I swung my leg around in an arc and caught him in the shins. His momentum carried him across the room. I could hear the crack of a chair leg breaking over by the windows. I was on him, my foot in his crotch, by the time he recovered and tried to scramble to his feet. One downward thrust, and he lay still on the floor, panting. The door to the hall must have banged against the wall so hard it closed again. The room was still too dark for me to see who I'd pinned to the floor.

"Was she a good fuck?" Raspy, through clenched teeth, but I'd know Frank Beckman's voice anywhere. He must have already been in Geneva when he got the call from Michelle. How he found India and me so quickly I had no idea.

I stepped hard on his crotch. This time he screamed until I eased up.

"I said. Was she a good fuck?" He was breathing hard, gasping.

"Frank, I just want to know one thing: Did you know why you were buying airline puts in 1994?"

The puts were a hunch. Until I had the time to go through the documents from Michelle's safe, I wouldn't know for sure Frank was into them. Still, it was a bluff that couldn't hurt.

"Fuck you."

"You don't care that you have blood on your hands," I said.

"Let me up."

"Let's try another question. . . ."

"Fuck you."

"What is it now, tankers, refineries?"

"Let me the fuck up."

I stepped harder on his crotch. He screamed again.

"Who's running Khalid Sheikh Muhammad, you or Channing?" I yelled.

Frank didn't respond this time.

"You got Webber to frame me. You knew I was getting close with the photo, that one day I'd find out KSM took it, that he was your inside guy."

I was talking mostly to myself by then. Maybe I'd been doing that all along. Frank had passed out somewhere along the way. He wasn't making a noise. I took my foot off him. A few minutes later he started to stir, groaning. It was clear he wasn't going to talk. I bent over him, patted him down. I was thinking of that Beretta he'd bought to kill India's stepfather with. I wouldn't have been surprised if he'd brought it with him on this trip, too. What else are private jets for?

"I thought about it," he said, reading my mind. His body was limp, jelly.

"You'd be better off thinking what your next move is. One is: Don't think about going to the Swiss police. I'll lay it out right here. I've already e-mailed Danny Pearl at the *Wall Street Journal* with half the story. I get rolled up and he gets the rest. Move two, you stop whatever is going down: airplanes, refineries. If you don't, it'll be a cinch tying you to it with the paper I got."

When I was through, I pulled him up, half carried him to the door, and pushed him out into the hall.

Then I opened the door to the bathroom. India lay curled on the floor, sobbing.

CHAPTER 38

I WENT DOWNSTAIRS to the business center and called Chris Corsini.
"It's me, Max."

"Why are you bothering me? I thought we had an agreement that you got your last favor."

"Here, take down this number." I read off Webber's cell phone number, the one he had given me my last day at headquarters, the same one I'd already given Chris to get Webber's calls. "Do a quick credit check on him. Call me back with his bank and bank account number."

"This isn't legal, is it?"

"It's okay. I owe the guy money and I lost his financial coordinates. If I don't make the transfer today, I'm cooked."

"Right. I think I've heard that before, too."

But Chris called back right on cue, ten minutes later.

"Whoever Webber is, he has only one bank account, domestically and in his name at least: the Bank of America in Falls Church." He gave me the number.

"One more favor, Chris. I'm running out of time. Look up the IRS's fax number in Philadelphia."

"Jesus, Max, what are you up to?"

"You don't—"

"You're right. I really don't." Happily, he seemed to have the IRS number on his Rolodex.

As soon as I hung up with Chris, I pulled out a three-by-five card I'd grabbed at the last minute from Michelle Zwanzig's office: the pin code to her UBS account. It had been taped to the inside of the safe door. Using it, I logged onto her account and transferred twelve million dollars from David Channing's Morgan Stanley account to Webber's checking account at the Bank of America in Falls Church, Virginia. I printed a copy of the transfer and faxed it to the IRS.

Next, I called John O'Neill, hoping he, too, was still speaking to me.

"Can I get back in?" I asked him. "I gotta see you now."

"JFK okay?"

"I'll see you there."

"I won't be at the airport. A friend, though."

"Okay. But this can't wait."

"One other thing: I got you immunity."

"What for?"

"You know. Millis. But that doesn't mean they can't tag you. If there's any chance of cleaning up your act, do it now."

Too late for that.

"John—"

"Oh, no . . ."

"One last request ever."

"I mean it. You're like the clap, like some herpes virus. You just keep mutating and erupting all over the place."

"I need a meeting. Justice. CIA. FBI. Set it up, will ya?"

"Fucking nuts," O'Neill said as he hung up.

. . .

I'd lied to Frank; I hadn't e-mailed Danny Pearl anything. But I did now. David Channing's options buys. Not enough to write a story, but if anything happened to me, Pearl would never let the story go.

When I got back to the room, India's bag was waiting by the door, but she was gone. I was lying on the sofa two hours later when she let herself back in. She looked as if she'd been crying for days.

"I have to leave."

"I know," I told her. I tried to put my arms around her, but she backed away. "Our flight's in—"

"Now, Max. Now. I can't stay here anymore."

"What did he say?"

"A lot. He's giving me forty-eight hours to get my things out of the house."

"It's time for you to move out, anyhow."

"Yeah, but not this way."

CHAPTER 39

**NATIONAL SECURITY COUNCIL
WASHINGTON, DC 20504**

September 6, 2001

INFORMATION

MEMORANDUM FOR CONDOLEEZZA RICE
FROM: RICHARD CLARKE
SUBJECT: PRESIDENTIAL POLICY INITIATIVE/REVIEW—THE
MIDDLE EAST: NEW CHALLENGES, NEW OPPORTUNITIES

CONDI, WE CONTINUE TO NEED IN THE MOST PRESSING WAY A
PRINCIPALS LEVEL REVIEW OF THE ADMINISTRATION'S
APPROACH TO MIDDLE EAST POLICY, BOTH IN ITS BROAD FOR-
MULATION AND IN ITS SPECIFICS. GOD'S IN THE DETAILS. . . .

H E BARKED OUT A NUMBER, listened to it convert, waited for the ring. Beyond the window, acres and acres of sagebrush rolled down to Sun Valley in the distance.

"Institute for a Fair Peace. Donald Sherley's office."

The man had a secretary answer his cell phone?

"Institute for Fuck-All. David Channing's office." He spoke in a high, mincing voice.

Sherley was on in an instant.

"David!"

"The memo is idiotic, for crissake. I-di-ot-ic!"

"Now, David—"

" 'New Challenges, New Opportunities'? How about 'Do We Really Need to Let the Crazies Take Over the Middle East?' "

"I hardly—"

"And the figures for the Shia are all wrong. Kuwait thirty percent? Change it to fifty-two percent. Who the hell's going to know. Certainly not State or the limp-dick CIA. Same for Iraq. Round the sixty-two-point-five percent up to seventy. The Saudis? Three-point-three percent Shia? Can't anyone do math? Make it fourteen percent and add a footnote in twenty-four-point Helvetica bold that the Saudi Shia sit on ninety percent of Saudi oil. And drop Qatar. A cat's litter box I don't give a shit about."

"Our litter box, David."

"You fucking dope. I don't know why I give your pathetic goddamn institute a single penny."

He threw the memo across the room, pages flying in every direction; sent his red pen scudding after them.

"Jesse!"

One, two, three, four . . . Jesse showed up in five seconds flat, the gold standard. He loved the man, loved the effect of the full-butler outfit and his chalky black skin against the seamless, concrete-gray walls, loved the way Jesse was framed just now in one of the large angular windows. He loved Idaho in this late-summer light; loved the cold evenings, the wolves he could hear howling late into the night; loved the fact that Jesse was *not* fucking his wife the way Nils had been fucking her. (Not cause enough, of course, to dismiss Nils—the man was a *brilliant* pilot—but he would have to pay the piper eventually.)

"Jesse, have you been studying your catechism?"

"Yes, sir. Indeed, I have."

"Wonderful. Wonderful! Take a seat!"

He did, in a severe side chair centered beneath a Chuck Close self-portrait: huge, hugely ugly. A Donald Judd sculpture—a vast peaked monolith—stood against the blank wall opposite him. Channing paced back and forth in front of him like a deranged schoolmaster.

"The key to long-term stability in the Middle East, Jesse, is . . ."

"Destabilization of the existing status quo, sir."

"To be replaced by . . . ?"

"Shia republics from Iraq to Oman, sir."

"Contained by . . . ?"

David Channing heard some kind of jangling coming from one of the nearby spaces, the *click click click* of heels on the heart pine floors. His wife.

"Go away," he shouted out.

The heels kept clicking, kept coming in his direction, like a goddamn tsunami. He waited until she was almost in sight to speak again.

"That decrepit motel next to the ski lift—I want you to go over there right now and buy the closest unit to the lift. I want the parking space. I'm sick of having to haul my skis all that goddamn way every winter."

"Did you have a figure in mind?" Vanessa Channing's voice was pure honey—she hated hauling her skis, too. She'd been lobbying for one of the ex-motel-unit condos all summer long.

"A hundred ninety-five thousand. Not a penny more."

"Good luck," she said.

"Two hundred and fifty, then. You and Nils can use the condo for a love nest."

"Go fuck yourself."

"If only I could."

Vanessa signaled Jesse to disappear, but he was already halfway to the kitchen wing. Something had to be done—canapés made, pillows plumped, the cook weaned off his cocaine, at least for the evening. Guests were coming: an ex-ambassador, an ex–movie star, an ex-senator. That's how she thought of Sun Valley: the land of exes, of honorables, of once-had-beens. She wanted to throw up half the time she was here.

"You're pathetic, David."

She was wearing jeans, a denim work shirt, enough diamonds to buckle the fingers of a weaker woman.

"Me?" he screamed. "Me? Donald Judd is pathos? Glenn Close, Chuck Close, whatever the fuck his name is—that's pathos? Nine pages in *Architectural Digest* is pathos? Look out that window. Look all the way to Sun Valley. I could buy it all!"

"Aren't we forgetting that Daddy's money is about dried up? That you've run through it like goose fat through a dog? Thank God he died when he did."

"Shut up. Shut up! What about the voice-recognition company?"

"Shitty hardware," Vanessa said. "You've heard how the damn thing grinds away. Shitty software. The company's in the tank."

"It's not."

"Of course it is. I read the financials. Someone around here has to actually understand a balance sheet."

"You don't know—"

"Michelle talks to me, David. I'm the one she does talk to. I don't treat her like a rug."

He was picking up the memo pages scattered across the floor, collating them, stacking the pages together as he went.

"I've got work to do," he said as he stood up.

"Your little institute?"

He'd turned, was walking away. She put a hand on his shoulder and spun him around.

"Your pretensions, David, are sickening."

"What?"

"Your butler-in-livery. Your Jew-baiting. Your Harvard-is-shit. It's all sickening. Don't you understand, David? You're a garden-variety bigot all wrapped up in big theories. And now you're going under because you don't understand diddly-squat about making money."

"You don't know anything."

"You lost Oliver's money. Every penny."

Somehow Vanessa had grabbed the *Times* off the table and rolled it up without his seeing her do it. She hit him with it once on the side of his face and once on his ear. When he looked up again, she'd turned to leave, her heels click-clicking.

The bitch.

He walked down a long, cork-lined hallway until he came to his desk and, beyond it, nothing but blue sky through the floor-to-ceiling window. A plasma screen rose like Lazarus out of the ash-black desktop. He studied the oil quotes, short and long trades, spot prices, wet buys: a day out, a week out, a year out.

Channing had just finished when the fax he kept locked in his wall safe (the safe encased in tons of concrete, the concrete reinforced by hundreds of yards of stainless-steel tie-rods) began to chime. He could hear the fax humming, gurgling softly. When it was through, he spun the dials and picked out a single page, handwritten, as beautiful as any Michelangelo:

Primzahlen unter a (=) a/la

. . . followed by a string of numbers. The numbers looked randomly generated, but he would bet his wife's plastic surgeon's bill that they had been prompted by an algorithm written in ten minutes. That's why his father had nicknamed the man the Genius. No one could do numbers theory like him.

"He was a supernova, David!" He could hear the old man saying it even now. "His dissertation, non-Riemannian hypersquares, was all of two pages, yet they had to send it around to five universities"—here, his father would always hold up five fingers and fan them just to drive the point home—"*five*, just to figure out what he was talking about."

That was back when he and Dear Papa still talked to each other. The Halcyon Days. Hah.

David Channing pulled out his Palm Pilot, typed in the sequence of numbers the Genius had faxed, and decoded them: CH_3-O-NO_2. What the fuck is that? Is he playing a joke?

He picked up the phone, called Nils, and read off the chemical compound's notation. Nils had majored in something like that, somewhere in some other country.

"Methyl nitrate," Nils said.

"Hah."

Of course. Odorless. Colorless. More powerful than nitroglycerin.

He wrote a note to himself: "Find out temperature methyl nitrate burns."

He thought of his father. The venerable fraud had fancied himself the superior of Acheson, the Dulleses, Kennan, Kissinger. Naturally. Not one of them could see beyond the Soviets; beyond Marx and Engels, Lenin and Stalin; beyond their ridiculous "dominoes" and containment. Only Oliver Wendell Channing saw the world as it was. Just ask him.

"Communism lasted seventy years. As a threat, it was around for less than four decades. A smoke-cured ham has a longer shelf life than that. Islam is more than thirteen hundred years old. It's about something. It has a God. It has true believers, not a corrupt nomenklatura, not apparatchiks."

David couldn't remember anymore if his father had written that or only said it, but my God, he'd heard it all ten thousand times if he'd heard it once. The same song and dance. The portentous tones, like Moses shouting from the Mount. The portentous pose, like Horatio at the bridge, like the little Dutch boy at the dike. (Rhymes with kike.) If ever there was a stuck record, Oliver Wendell Channing was it. But he had to give one thing to the old son of a bitch. All on his own, he'd plugged himself into that primeval muck, the Middle East. He had a Rolodex that wouldn't stop. But he didn't have a clue what to do with it. His daddy's trust fund was just fine.

"You're dying, Father." David could remember the moment, the time, the place exactly. The wine steward was just walking away from the table; their waiter just circling back to them. A hush seemed to have fallen over the dining room of the Harvard Club as if some wraith were floating through. The wraith, in fact, was across the table from him.

"Of course I'm dying," his father had answered, collapsed into his suit. "That's why I've asked you here."

"What?"

"Death, David. A last meal, father and son. Everything in—"

"Set things right?"

"I couldn't wait for my own father to die, but we're . . ."

At long last, the old man had handed him the opening he had been looking for forever, and he had no intention of letting it slip from his grasp.

"Dad, your Don Quixote act never worked for me. All your books—well, they go in the bonfire."

Oliver Channing started coughing, spitting something into his napkin.

"You never understood a fucking thing about the world," David Channing said, not paying attention. "All those people you fell in love with are savages and will always be savages. All the obscure languages you learned—golden keys to empty rooms. You never had an idea what to do with all those people you collected."

Oliver Channing wanted to fight back, but all he could do was muffle the coughs with his napkin. He stopped for a moment, pulled the napkin away, and saw blood. He thought he had days left. Maybe it was just hours.

"That's all going to change," David said. "I'm going to make something out of your life."

David Channing could remember folding his napkin, could remember that he was half out of the chair. He could see the wait staff bearing down on them with platters of food when his father finally said it: "You win." And thus the Genius was his—the still center of the turning dance.

Channing took the fax and studied the chemical formula one more time, then folded it and fed it into the shredder tucked beneath the desk. His ear still hurt where his wife had hit him.

CHAPTER 40

New York City

O'NEILL WAS AS GOOD as his word. An FBI agent was waiting
for us at immigrations. You couldn't miss him. The loose linen
jacket didn't even pretend to hide the Glock and shoulder holster.
With only a hello, he walked India and me through immigrations, customs,
and out of the terminal to catch a taxi.

Both of us were exhausted. India had cried halfway across the Atlantic,
until there was nothing left inside her. A death in the family, I told the stewardess when she asked. Wasn't that right?

India fell asleep in the taxi heading into the city. I woke her when we
got to the Mercer, walked her inside to the lobby, and told her I'd be back
for her in a couple hours. She didn't protest, didn't say anything. She must
have done something like this a hundred times with her father, wait for him
to make a meeting, never asking who or why.

. . .

I looked at the address twice, 9 Pell Street, and again at the number above Joe Shanghai's, a downscale Chinese restaurant in the downscale part of Chinatown. O'Neill had sent word with his FBI baby-sitter that I was to ask for him at the "receptionist." Easier said than done. I pushed my way through the noon crowd waiting to get in and waved my hand back and forth to get the attention of the young Chinese girl behind the register.

"I'm here to join Keith." It was the name I'd been told to ask for. She looked at me dumbly. I figured she didn't speak a word of English.

"Keith!" I yelled. "Here?"

"Keith? Upstairs. Sixth floor." A flawless Brooklyn accent.

I hit the steps. A lawyer's office took up the entire second floor. Above that, the building was all apartments. The place was eerily quiet after the hubbub down below. I got to the fifth floor and that was it. No sixth, but there were stairs to the roof and the door wasn't locked, so I opened it and walked out. O'Neill grabbed my shoulder from behind.

"Three buildings that way," he said, pointing across the roofs.

I heard him slap a padlock on the door I'd just come through. No one could get out on the roof now unless he'd brought along an axe or a sledge hammer.

Three buildings down, just as advertised, we clambered back inside. Again, O'Neill locked the door behind us, then led me to a third-floor apartment. The place was bare except for a table in the living room with four chairs around it. I looked in the kitchen. The refrigerator door was open. Cabinet doors were open and empty, too. The whole place reeked.

"What are we doing here?" I asked.

"NYPD," O'Neill said, sitting down at the table. "I still have friends there."

"That wasn't an answer."

"Somebody's all over me," he said.

"Like?"

"It doesn't matter."

"You sound like me. You'll tell me if you want. Did you get the meeting set up?"

He nodded. A surprise. I thought I'd run that well dry, too.

"Tomorrow," he said.

"We'll go down together."

"I'm not going."

"Don't tell me you got something more important to do."

"July eighth was my KMA."

"KMA?"

"Kiss-my-ass day. Twenty-five years in the Bureau. And I took it. I re-tired August twenty-second."

"What the hell do you mean? You were in Beirut just—"

"On my own hook."

"All the bitching about the embassy?"

"It's called creative reality, Max. I paid for the fucking bodyguards, too."

"I don't get it. Why?"

"Because someone had to tell you face-to-face, you stupid CIA fuck, that your ass was in the wringer."

"You flew to Beirut on your own dime just to do that?" I still didn't get it. I was sure O'Neill had a heart, but it wasn't of gold.

"Maybe I started to believe you, too. I told you, you're making me as crazy as you are. And goddammit, if you have to know the truth, bin Laden's going to hit us. Out or in, I'll never let it drop."

"Wait a minute. My immunity, how did you—"

"*I* left, Max. My friends didn't. I've got a few favors I can call in."

This was a showstopper. O'Neill was the one guy I'd really walked through this stuff—months of explanation, of cajoling and convincing, down the drain.

"Don't sweat it. You have the paper. You'll do just fine."

He pushed a stuffed manila envelope across the bare tabletop. I could make out the outline of one of those plastic CD cases on top.

"Your e-mail. Too bad I never got past the lobby at the Albergo. Those photos make the place look almost civilized. I take it the docs are there."

"No one's going to understand this stuff on its own. I need a live body to back me up."

"You want the truth? I was forced out. They don't want me there, no matter what I have to say. I'm not invited to this game."

The wheels had started to come off the previous summer, O'Neill said, when his briefcase was stolen at a retirement seminar in Orlando—"from the goddamned conference room with a dozen agents sitting around. That was one hell of a miraculously lucky thief. Amazingly, the fucking thing popped up a few hours later with nothing gone."

"Why didn't you tell me when I saw you in Beirut?"

"I was still getting used to the idea. Things got really strange after I started asking around about your two Saudis in San Diego."

"Strange?"

"Yeah, strange. Webber went apeshit, denied everything, went straight to the acting director, complaining that I was spying on the Agency."

"What did he say?"

"I don't know. I never talked to him about it, but just about then someone at the Bureau gave my file to the *New York Times*. There were . . . irregularities."

"You could have fought it. Told the truth."

"Fuck you and the truth, Waller. But if you got to have it again, there was a money problem. Nothing big. Just big enough."

O'Neill always insisted on paying when I came up to New York. I'd always assumed those doubles at Elaine's were going on the Bureau's tab. Maybe not.

"The perfect tempest in a teapot," O'Neill sighed. "The fuckheads won't stop chewing on it. I thought I heard some kind of echo on my phone this morning."

"John, the only time you can hear a tap on your phone is when the Bangladeshis are doing it."

I'm sure it was my imagination, but O'Neill looked smaller.

"You'll love this," he said. "Less than twelve hours after I packed my stuff out, the Agency finally cabled us about the two Saudis."

"How'd you find out?"

"One of the guys looking for them told me."

"Looking? You mean they're missing?"

"Yep, as of 0900 this morning neither the FBI nor the CIA has any idea where they are. Hard to believe. The day after I walk out the door, that pack of bastards you used to work for tells us. You can't make this shit up."

"What about the Applied Science surveillance?"

"No clue. Oh, by the way, I was thinking about you. The week before I left, they arrested some dirtbag out in Minneapolis—a Mr. Moussaoui. He was taking flight training. I actually called up and asked if he had blue eyes and red hair. You know, Max, you really are like catching the clap."

"Well?"

"No. He's French-Algerian. Not a French-speaking Iranian."

"Back to basics: Who's going to be at the D.C. meeting tomorrow?"

"The guy for the Bureau is Chuck Appleton. Not the sharpest tool in the shed. The Bureau's line is that with you and me pushing this penny, they don't want to put any credence in it. DOJ is sending someone from Violent Crimes and Terrorism. He won't say a word, just listen. I don't know who the Agency's sending. But count on it, he won't be a friendly. Oh, and there'll be this politico from the National Security Council—Don Sherley. He'll be chairing the meeting. It's his first week on the job, maybe his first day."

"Don Sherley? What the fuck."

O'Neill rolled his eyes, seemingly as amazed as I was.

I couldn't believe the guy was back in play. Truth told, I'd thought he'd lost his security clearance for good. He'd been around in the Reagan years, a deputy assistant secretary of defense. Every time he flew to Tel Aviv, Sherley downloaded top secret cables onto his laptop, and each time, Mossad got into the laptop and copied everything. The Bureau thought he'd done it on purpose, but since he never handed any secrets over directly, they couldn't make a case.

Sherley had disappeared for a few years at the start of the first Clinton term only to surface again at the helm of a right-wing think tank called the Washington Institute for a Fair Peace in the Middle East. The institute was known for pushing wacky ideas like Arab nationalism equals fascism and democracy was going to bring down the Silk Curtain just like it brought down the Iron Curtain. No one paid it any attention until the blowhard op-ed columnists at the *New York Times* and *Washington Post* picked up the refrain. And until the new administration moved into the White House. The institute's latest hobbyhorse was invading Iraq, turning it over to the Shia, then spreading a Shia revolution down the Arab side of the Gulf.

O'Neill was reading my mind.

"You know who funds the institute, don't you?"

I didn't.

"David Channing. His father gave the seed money. Sonny boy picked it up."

"Oh, fuck."

They'd more than stacked the decks; they'd dealt themselves all aces. If Sherley was chairing the meeting, he'd be sure to shit on everything I brought to the table.

"I ain't going," I said. "It's an ambush."

"You got one chance. You have to."

He was right. I knew that. But I sure as hell wasn't going to deliver the prince's intercepts and the Geneva stuff to Sherley. I might as well burn them right now. I handed O'Neill back the package he'd brought with him, along with the plastic shopping bag of documents from Geneva that I'd been thumbing through on the plane while India sobbed beside me.

"These are better off with you than me," I explained. "In New York, they just mug you for money."

O'Neill shrugged.

"Wait a minute." There was one Geneva document I wanted to keep with me. I fished it out, then gave him the bag again.

"You know what you're doing?" he asked.

I thought I did, maybe for the first time in a long while. But I'd been wrong before.

"They'll be in my safe, thirty-fourth floor. Even my new secretary doesn't have the combination."

"Wait a minute. What thirty-fourth floor? What new secretary? I thought you were out on the street."

"Me? C'mon. Security chief, World Trade Center. I started this week. Expense account as long as my arm."

O'Neill smiled as he said it, but he seemed to be trying to decide something, waging some private battle with himself. I couldn't tell if he lost or won.

"Listen. I got an idea," I said. O'Neill was starting to shift in his chair, ready to leave. "A channel check. When you get back to the office, call the Chatworth Galleries on Sixty-eighth—"

"That thief's not out of business?"

"Tell him you've got a package to drop by."

"What? I'm selling my Ming vases?"

"Just do it."

"Not until you tell me what for."

"You think your phone's tapped. Let's see."

He grunted, shifted again, then decided to say whatever was on his mind.

"Max, the guy who met you at the airport told me you're traveling with someone. Your daughter, he said."

"Ex-colleague."

"I know who she is. Be careful."

"Come on, John. She's an old friend. I've known her since she was a kid."

"Did she tell you that she started two weeks ago in the Counter-Espionage Center, working for Webber? I think he's the guy who framed you."

O'Neill went down the stairs with me. I watched him as he walked up Pell. His Buick Regal was parked in front of a fire hydrant.

CHAPTER 41

Washington, D.C.

A T WASHINGTON NATIONAL, I started to take India's hand as we were walking down the long corridor to the terminal, then decided it wasn't even worth pretending. I don't know if she sensed what I'd learned while she was sipping tea at the Mercer, but she smiled so hard, I thought she might start crying again.

"I'll call," I said when we got to the moving ramp over by the Metro stop. I took her hand after all. Maybe O'Neill had the story wrong. Maybe I wanted to touch her one last time.

"Can't you tell me where you're staying?" she asked.

I paused, then told her. She'd never heard of the place, but the address didn't impress her.

"You'll be okay with those?" She was staring at my carry-on, thinking the documents must still be inside. "I'll hold them for you if you want."

"No," I said. "Thanks, but you never know when—" There was no need to finish, nor any way to.

India nodded, turned, and started down the ramp. She wasn't my mother, though. She turned, waved a big good-bye, even blew me a kiss. I waited until she was out of sight, then found a pay phone and called Willie.

"Ever hear of this whorehouse on Rhode Island Avenue?"

CHAPTER 42

A COP FRIEND HAD INTRODUCED ME a few years earlier to
the Amble Inn at 18th Street Northeast and Rhode Island Avenue,
maybe forty blocks and five thousand real-estate zones from
Frank Beckman's Tuttle Place mansion. The inn was a sanctioned whorehouse, the only one in D.C. The girls rotated in and out, mostly from up
and down the eastern seaboard. The police provided protection and laid
down a little covering fire when things got nasty, and everyone did a little
business and felt better or worse depending when they were through.

I wasn't in the market for what the ladies at the inn and their pimps
were selling, and I hadn't exactly crept back into Washington unan-
nounced, but I still needed to fly under the radar as much as I could, and I
figured even the refrigerator was wired in my apartment. The Amble Inn
was about as close to getting off the grid as D.C. offers.

Willie rolled his eyes when I gave him the address and offered to lend
me some money.

"You do know what you're getting into?" he asked as we were nearing 18th Street. "Trust me, I can find you nicer at the same cost. A better chance of sleeping through the night."

Willie waited outside while I checked to see if they would give me a room.

The Indian desk clerk behind a Plexiglas window had equal doubts about my sophistication, especially when I told him I wanted a room for four nights and offered to pay in advance.

"Here?"

A sign just to the left of the clerk's window laid out the house rules: NO SWEARING, LOUD NOISES, FIGHTING, OR SPITTING. Below that, another handwritten sign spelled out the rates: twenty-three dollars for two hours, forty dollars a night. Overhead, two cameras recorded my arrival at the Amble Inn for posterity.

"You're alone?"

I nodded.

"You're not planning on causing any trouble, are you?"

"No."

"Good," he said, pushing a key through the tray under the Plexiglas window. "Enjoy."

I stepped out onto the front stoop and put my forefinger to my ear and my thumb to my mouth to let Willie know I'd be calling.

Two cans of St. Ide's malt liquor sat open on top of the window air-conditioning unit. Across the street, a Baskins-Robbins outlet glowed in the night. Next to it, a dozen people trickled out of the International House of Prayer for All People. Their stooped shoulders and frantic smoking suggested an Alcoholics Anonymous meeting. Just below my own window, a single dim bulb barely illuminated a sign that read AMBLE INN: REAR PARKING. RCA RADIO & TV.

The TV was a Zenith; the radio wasn't at all. The carpet, a sinister floral swirl, was pocked with cigarette burns, as was the top and, oddly, the sides of the flimsy dresser. Otherwise, the room wasn't half bad. The sheets had actually been changed. The bathroom had a fresh towel. The toilet flushed and refilled. For twenty dollars an hour I could watch all the porn flicks my heart desired. The comforts of home.

I could hear the door opening in the room next to mine, the squeak of bedsprings, a metronomic thumping of the headboard against the same wall my headboard rested against. "Too big," a woman's voice kept saying in a relentless monotone. "Too big." All night long.

CHAPTER 43

A T TEN THE NEXT MORNING I went out to call the galleries of
Theodore Hew-Chatworth. Teddy picked up on the first ring.

"We're closed. All day," he said, hanging up the phone.

I called back. "Teddy, don't hang up."

"Who is this?"

"Max. Why are you closed?"

"It's none of your business. But since I've been dying to make your day,
we were robbed."

O'Neill was probably right about his phone being tapped.

A half block to the east of the inn, the convenience store tacked on to a
Shell station offered up an almost drinkable pot of coffee and microwav-
able sausage biscuits. I bought one of each, plus a four-pack of lightbulbs,
five cans of jumbo lighter fluid, a combination lock guaranteed to "beat the

bad guys every time," and a large spray can of air freshener. I was almost out the door when I remembered copy paper. A package of it sat all alone on a shelf, under a banner that read COMPUTER SUPPLIES.

Back in my room, I propped the bathroom window open and left the gas can sitting on the sill so it wouldn't stink the place up too badly. Then I started calling around to medical-supply stores until I found one in Northeast D.C. that sold those little pen-size drills emergency-room docs use to make holes in fingernails after they've been slammed with a hammer or in a door. While that was being delivered, I popped down to the Burning Dog next door, nestled among the half dozen people already slouched at the bar, and offered fifty bucks to the first person who could produce for me two live rounds of ammunition.

No one said anything. No one even looked my way. I wasn't surprised. Washington, D.C., might be the world's foremost provider of deadly weapons, but it's illegal to sell a single round of ammo inside the city limits, especially to a middle-aged cracker who wanders off the street. I left a fifty on the bar and went to the bathroom.

When I came back, a pair of nine-millimeter rounds were sitting on the bar and the fifty was gone. I did it five more times.

The medical-supply driver didn't seem to find it odd at all that a guy living in a whorehouse was ordering a pocket-size drill and paying cash for it, which was just fine with me. I sat by the window in my room, cradling the lightbulbs carefully in a pillowcase, and made a bb-size hole in the top of the glass. Next, I pried open the rounds, tipped the charge out onto a piece of creased paper, and used the crease to pour the gunpowder through the hole I'd just drilled. Then, ever so carefully, I removed the lightbulb over the sink basin in the bathroom, replaced it with my new one, and plugged the sink with its stopper.

An ice bucket or something similar would have helped with the next step, but since I didn't have one, I had to settle for the Gideon Bible, spread just enough to stand on end in the bottom of the sink basin. When that was stable, I filled the bottom of the basin with two inches of lighter fluid. Then I took a stack of the blank copy paper, stuffed it in a manila envelope, rested that on top of the dry end of the Bible, and shut the bathroom door behind me.

When I was ready to leave, I used my new combination lock and the hasp already screwed into the jamb to secure the door behind me. You gotta love a hotel that encourages you to bring your own lock with you.

CHAPTER 44

T**HE RUSH-HOUR TRAFFIC** had just about cleared downtown
D.C. as I walked down 9th Street and turned east on D, just across
from the FBI headquarters. I stood for a few minutes by the door
of the Caucus Room, sizing up the situation. The Caucus was one of those
clubby Washington steakhouses that try to give the impression that politics
is left at the door when the truth is just the opposite. I was about ready to
start across the street when a jovial party burst out the door beside me and
fell into a waiting limo: lobbyists dining expensively on some industry
group's money. The guy with the chiseled face in the middle of the pack
had to be a senator: They all look the same these days—at least all the first-
term males do—but I couldn't place him.

By contrast, the agent waiting across the street seemed not to belong in
Washington at all. With his sunken chin and off-the-rack green blazer, he
reminded me of an H&R Block accountant from Norman, Oklahoma.

"Chuck Appleton," he said when I walked over to meet him. O'Neill was right: The FBI intended to slow-speed the meeting. We shook hands, and I followed him down D Street and around the corner to the RMS entrance.

RMS was the Residences at Market Square, a high-priced block of the new Pennsylvania Avenue, diagonally across from the Justice Department and a half block east of the FBI headquarters on D Street. I knew about the apartment we were headed to, number 730. Everyone who was halfway inside the loop knew about it. Number 730 was occupied by a cheery homosexual who did dirty jobs for the Agency and the Bureau and got to live rent-free in return. ("Rent-free" but not inconvenience-free: When the condo got claimed for off-campus get-togethers such as this—which it frequently did—the occupant of record had to kill time someplace else.)

I told Appleton that since we were early, I'd wait outside until everyone showed up. He shrugged his shoulders and went up. Probably figured I was going to have one last smoke.

Five minutes later Don Sherley came rolling down the street, briefcase in hand. From the time he came into view until the time he got to where I was, he checked his watch twice: a man in a hurry.

He didn't see me as he turned into the building.

"Don," I said, grabbing his arm.

He didn't recognize me. It had been at least ten years since we'd last seen each other.

"Max Waller," I helped.

"Of course." He flashed me a pained smile. "Good to see you."

"I need a minute." I still hadn't released his arm.

"I don't know if we should be talking before the meeting."

"Just a minute," I said, letting go of his arm.

He relaxed.

"I'm delighted you found the time to attend," I said. "But maybe in the meeting you should let me talk—you know, give me my fifteen minutes and not say anything. In fact, why don't you keep quiet the whole time."

"Excuse me?" He tried to back away a step, but I grabbed his arm again and held it tight.

"I know about your accounts with the fiduciary agent."

"What are you talking about?"

"The accounts you have with Michelle Zwanzig."

"You're crazy."

I pulled out a transfer from UBS to the Institute for a Fair Peace and shoved it in his face.

"Don, I have more. Think the IRS might like to take a look into your accounts?"

In fact, I didn't have anything on Sherley. It was another bluff. Still, I couldn't help but think Channing had somehow, somewhere bought Sherley off. Channing would never trust anyone he didn't own.

I was right. The color faded from Sherley's face. "How did—" He grabbed for the paper, but I pulled it away at the last moment and held it an inch from his grasp.

"Don, a truce is all I'm asking for. Let me take the meeting where it needs to go, you keep your mouth shut, and the paper disappears. It really shouldn't be a problem."

There were five people in the living room when I walked in. A man with a bad comb-over and a bulging stomach stuffed inside a summer-weight three-piece suit sat in a straight-backed dining-room chair, reading a magazine. Appleton was in an armchair in the corner of the room, his eyes half closed. Sitting on the sofa was Mary Beth Drew and a woman I recognized from the general counsel's office. We'd crossed swords years ago, but I couldn't remember why or her name. Sherley was standing at the window, looking out.

Bad Comb-Over stood up, walked over to me, and extended his hand while simultaneously tucking his card into my shirt pocket. "Jeff Forrest, Department of Justice." He seemed to be the only one happy to be there.

I was looking around for someplace to sit when Mary Beth materialized at my elbow.

"Max," she whispered, pulling me halfway back out into the hall, "this better be good. I heard you have it papered."

"It is."

"I don't see anything."

"Didn't bring it."

"Oh, fuck," she said, loud enough to make a couple heads snap up. "He's going to crucify you."

"Sherley?"

"I don't know who told him. It was out of the blue. He insisted. But he's toast. Trust me."

"Who?"

"We've got one chance," she said, turning back into the room without answering my question. She sounded like O'Neill. "You'd better make it good."

I didn't know how "I" had turned into "we," but there was no time to figure that out, either.

Officially, this was Chuck Appleton's show. The FBI borrowed the condo we were meeting in, which meant they owned the chair, but it was clearly Forrest who'd come to listen.

Forrest looked over at Sherley to get things going, but Sherley was absorbed examining the carpet. He motioned for Forrest to start. I sat down on an ottoman.

Forrest cleared his throat. "All of us appreciate your coming here, Mr. Waller. We're sure you've had a tiring several months. So let's get under way."

"In 1984 I was assigned to Beirut when Bill Buckley . . ." I began, looking toward Sherley to make sure he hadn't changed his mind about staying out of it.

Across the room from me, Mary Beth made a tight, circular motion with her index finger: *Speed it up.*

I ignored her. With or without the paper, I had to have history and context on my side. They had to know about my hunt for Murtaza Ali Mousavi, how he'd grown up in south Tehran, his hatred for the U.S., his capacity for slaughter, how the Quds Force was still in the terrorism business. I had to leave it all in, even the fact that Mousavi might or might not be dead. The meeting would mean nothing if they didn't understand that Mousavi wasn't a one-man act, that he represented a faction in Tehran that would stop at nothing. They had to understand how the whole business tied into Nabil, how the Middle East had turned into a grotesque carnival of violence, revenge, and slaughter. Only then could I get to Beckman and Channing. The paper was worthless until they bought off on the story line. Context was everything. It always is.

I was as far as Bir Shiva prison when the DOJ attorney stopped me.

"This is fascinating, but could we move on to financial aspects of the case?"

It was then that I heard a noise and looked to my left to see Vince Webber walk in from a bedroom. Mary Beth's "he." Webber had been listening the whole time.

"With your permission," he said, nodding toward Forrest.

"Of course."

"I believe that before we continue, we need to establish Mr. Waller's bona fides. We need to know *whom* he represents before we are able to evaluate *what* Mr. Waller has to tell us."

Webber had been looking directly at Forrest. Now he turned his gaze to me. "I'm sure Mr. Waller will appreciate this. It is standard operating procedure at the Agency."

"Naturally." The DOJ attorney was settling into the role of the Greek chorus.

Webber opened an envelope and pulled out what looked like a cable.

"Mr. Waller, maybe you could help us out here. From September second to September seventh of this year, you were a guest at the Beau Rivage Hotel in Geneva."

I nodded.

"The Swiss cantonal police tell us you paid in cash, nearly five thousand dollars. Where did you get this money?"

"You apparently already know where I got it."

"We do. Yuri Duplenski. What is his profession, if I may ask?"

"A businessman."

"No, he's not. He works for the marketing arm of the Russian Ministry of Defense. He's a Russian official."

"So?"

"So, it seems to me that you have some sort of financial tie to the Russian government. We believe this needs to be clarified before we proceed."

"We?"

Webber waved his arm around the room. "Yes, we. The same people who are meant to believe you've uncovered some mysterious plot."

I caught Mary Beth out of the corner of my eye. She seemed to have rolled up into herself like a porcupine under attack.

"Yuri Duplenski is a friend," I said.

"Ah, then when you were an employee of the Central Intelligence Agency, did you report contact with him?"

"No."

"Why not?"

"He wasn't recruitable."

"Wasn't the regulation then, as it is now, that you report all contact with suspect intelligence officers?"

I thought about Oliver Wendell Channing and his thousands of unreported contacts, the ones his son was now making money off of. But it didn't matter. Webber wasn't waiting for an answer.

"Let's move to the Biqa'. Who did you see there?"

"A member of the Kuwaiti royal family."

"We know. Were you aware that he has been soliciting funds for Hamas and Islamic Jihad?"

"Half the Gulf is."

Webber nodded at the DOJ attorney, who chimed in on cue, "We're considering an indictment against the party in question."

Good luck, I thought, but maybe I was the only one in the room who knew the prince was dead.

"How were you introduced to the prince?"

"Does it matter?"

"It all matters." Again, he didn't wait for an answer. "Back to Geneva. Is it not a fact that you misrepresented yourself to an Agency asset in order to procure materials to execute an unauthorized break-in at the office of a Swiss national?"

Where did that come from? It was either India or the fence in Bon-en-Chablis. Sherley had come out of his pout. He was all but smirking.

"It's a complicated story."

"Dishonor always is." Webber was opening a PowerBook G4 as he talked. "Unfortunately, as we've found time and again, it's also contagious. I'd like everyone to take a look at this DVD."

He turned the PowerBook so everyone could see. A shaky image lighted up the screen: the interior of an airplane. I knew what was next. I appeared in the picture, carrying four small bottles of Dewar's, two glasses, and a bottle of water. I watched myself shake my novel and yank open the overhead compartment. The resolution wasn't good, but it was clear that in the next minute I'd be tumbling Patricia Hoag-Carrington's carry-on.

I stood up, feeling myself lose control, exactly what I had planned not to do.

"Webber, it's not going to work. You know what was inside that safe—"

"Ah, yes, your safecracking. Well, Mr. Waller, this is a colorful part of the story I've been waiting for. Please go on." Webber swept the room with his shark's grin.

"I need a moment with Agent Appleton," I said.

In the back bedroom, I grabbed him by the lapel: "Get me a one-on-one with Forrest."

"Well, gee, I'd have to—"

"Just make it happen. You go back in there and tell them I'm not putting up with this shit anymore. I didn't come here to be fucking prosecuted. If they don't want to listen to what I have, fine, I'm out of here."

Before he could say anything, Mary Beth walked in. "What are you doing, Max? I knew this would be a hard sell, but Jesus . . ."

"So go light a candle. What's Webber doing here?"

"We're this close to nailing him—income taxes, everything." She held her thumb and her forefinger a millimeter apart. "We know about his deal with Applied Science. He was featherbedding. There was an odd transfer into his checking account that made us suspicious. You wouldn't believe the money—" She stopped herself. I'd built that particular tent, but I wasn't going to say anything now. "We're not ready to move on him right now. When he insisted on coming, I couldn't say no. It would have alerted him."

"He's in this with a guy named David Channing, and Beckman, too," I said, a little too breathlessly.

"Forget Beckman. It's what these guys have their finger in that I care about right now. Goddammit, Max, you should have brought the paper. I would have made sure it got in the right hands."

"I got it. Don't worry."

"Based on what I've seen, I'm worrying. Big time. Five," she said, turning away.

"Five what?" Her back was to me now.

"Five P.M. tomorrow. Same place. Not the same people. I'll keep Webber out if I have to bring a gun to do it. But you better deliver next time."

When I walked back in the room, Sherley and Webber were gone. Apparently they didn't care that I wasn't finished.

"What now?" I asked.

"You're coming with me," Appleton said, looking apologetic.

"Thanks. I can find my own way home."

"No, we've been instructed to hold you on a material witness warrant."

The only thing I could think of was that Sherley had gotten on the phone and had my immunity withdrawn. Or maybe he'd been planning it all along. Channing had to get something for his money.

"You're not going to cuff me, are you?"

"Nope. It's not like we don't know this is all bullshit," he said, a cockeyed smile on his face.

We walked out of the Residences at Market Square. A black Crown Vic was waiting for us, parked at the far end of D Street, in front of the 9th Street entrance to the Bureau parking garage.

Appleton insisted I buckle my seat belt before he drove off.

CHAPTER 45

WE WERE FORTY BLOCKS EAST on Pennsylvania Avenue, tuned in to an Orioles game, heading through the far eastern reaches of D.C., when Chuck Appleton slapped his hand to his forehead, said, "I need to get some things," and pulled up in front of a Superfresh market with half the bulbs burned out in its overhead sign.

"Wanna come in with me?"

"I'll wait."

Two black kids were leaning against the plate-glass window, eyeing us, undoubtedly trying to figure out what a couple of dead-on white guys were doing in their native terrain.

"Yeah, you better stay with the car," Appleton said. "It's a—"

"Questionable neighborhood?"

He nodded, closed the driver's-side door carefully behind him, and disappeared into the store. The O's had men on first and third, none out. Appleton had left the engine running so I could listen to the radio without draining the battery and fill him in on what happened. For the a/c, too. He was nothing but thoughtful. The shopping list was short, but I knew he would be a while. Appleton was the kind of guy who did comparison shopping even when he was on an expense account.

I gave him maybe three minutes, then got out of the car. Our two watchers hadn't moved a muscle.

"Yo, lost?" It was the shorter one, maybe all of thirteen, his warm-up pants two-thirds of the way down his butt.

"Either of you know how to drive?"

"Shit, yeah. What's it to you?"

"Want to take this baby for a spin?"

"It's a fucking Ford, man. Like ten years old. My granddaddy's granddaddy's car!"

I went around to the driver's side, flipped down the visor, and pulled the government credit card out of the pocket on the back. Behind the kids, I could see my FBI keeper in the express lane. He was picking a deck of cards off a rack. Gin rummy till the cows came home.

"Your granddaddy's car come with its own credit card?"

The kids seemed to fly across the sidewalk into the front seat. Fortunately, the taller one took the driver's side. His spindly legs actually could reach the pedals.

"Wait a minute," I said to them.

"Wha?"

"The light." I leaned in and put the gyro on the dash and flicked it on. "You got to go in style."

I took a half dozen quick steps back into the shadows and worked my way along the wall into the alley beside the store. The kids were a block down Pennsylvania Avenue, the light flashing, laying down rubber every inch of the way, when Appleton walked out of the Superfresh.

"Shit," I could hear him saying. "Shit. Shit. Shit."

If the kids could just keep from ramming the Ford into the side of a Metrobus, the FBI would be chasing me through the worst parts of D.C. all night long.

CHAPTER 46

I DUCKED DOWN AN ALLEY, in between two houses, past a caged, derelict liquor store until I came to a pay phone in front of a 7-Eleven. I tried O'Neill at work, then his apartment. No answer on either number. I found him at Elaine's. Some things never change.

"How's your morning tomorrow, John?"

"What? They didn't give you the Congressional Medal of Honor?"

"I need the stuff, now."

"I'm not in the office until three."

"It can't wait. I gotta see you first thing tomorrow, pick it up, and be back here by five."

I could hear chatter in the background, what sounded like ice cubes tinkling in glasses. O'Neill was well into happy hour. Happy hours.

"Sorry. There's no way I can change my rendezvous."

"Listen. You have no idea the ambush I walked into. It got real nasty. They lifted the immunity."

"Look, Max, I want this shit out of my life. The sooner, the better. In fact, don't come up here. I don't want to be seen with you. Give me an address and I'll FedEx the shit—no, better yet, find some Kinko's down there that'll let a crazy fuck like you hang by the fax machine for thirty minutes, call me first thing in the morning with the number, and—"

"No fax. No FedEx. I come get it, you understand. If I have to, I'll duct-tape it to my body and swim back to Washington."

There was a long sigh at the other end, a swallow.

"Who's bothering you, John? The Bureau?"

"My old comrades in arms. They came to see me this afternoon. More shit. This time it's about some money I borrowed while I was still in. All aboveboard but that's not stopping them."

"John—"

"It's you, Max. Don't you get it? You're toxic. I tried, right? But everything that touches you turns into fucking melanomas. I'm not going down with you on this one. I've got a new life."

I could hear a woman saying they were late, something about reservations, purring in his other ear.

"Okay. Okay," he finally said. "When?"

"Seven-thirty."

"Eight-fifteen in my office. And I mean it. If you're not there by nine, I burn it. The chimes start ringing and I light the fire."

"John!" I could tell he was about to hang up.

"What, for crissake?"

"Don't blow me off."

"I don't understand why you don't just come up tonight. Maybe one last drink."

"I got one thing to take care of first."

CHAPTER 47

B UT, SIR, THE TABLE IS FOR ONLY TWO," the maître d'
sniffed.

"Someone must have made a mistake," I said. "If you wouldn't
mind adding a place."

The maître d' swept his hand around the dining room of the Four Seasons, inviting me to take a look for myself. He was right; the place was
packed. It was lucky Sherley had made a reservation. It was even luckier
that I knew Sherley would go sniveling to Channing about my blackmail
threat. And it was just as lucky that I remembered India telling me that David
Channing would eat only at the Four Seasons when he was in Washington.

I spotted a single empty chair in the far corner, off by a service station,
and pointed it out to the maître d', who summoned a waiter to move it.

I settled myself in one of a pair of matching wing chairs near the entrance, grabbed a magazine someone had left on the table between them,
and held it half over my face as I waited. Not for long. Sherley came racing

down the steps just over my shoulder, neck craned like some demented ostrich, until he spotted a man who looked as if he might actually own the Four Seasons. The two of them blew right past the front station, heading for what had to be a regular table. I arrived just as they were summoning the maître d' over to ask about the third place setting.

Sherley bounced to his feet, napkin clutched in his right hand, as I pulled out the extra chair and sat down. I thought he was going to pick up his water glass and throw it at me. His dinner companion, though, was unruffled. He took one look at me, one look at Sherley, then rose himself, put a hand on Sherley's shoulder, turned him so he pointed toward the lobby, and gave him a little pat on the shoulder.

"I think the two of us will be fine, Donald. Just fine. Surely you have more important matters to attend to in your new exalted position."

Sherley looked almost stricken as the man patted him again, harder this time, then gave him a shove in the small of the back. *Go.*

"David Channing," he said, extending his hand as Sherley began to trudge back up the stairs. Oliver Wendell's son in the flesh. Not quite the massive brow. Not quite the massive presence. Not half the money, either, if O'Neill was right.

"Would you care to join me?"

I nodded. "Only so you don't have to dine alone."

He ignored me.

"A glass of wine?" he asked. "White?"

Before I could answer, he summoned the waiter over and ordered a Bienvenue Bâtard Montrachet. "René, be sure it's either a 1995 or '97."

This guy was very good. Why not sit back and enjoy the performance.

"I understand you just returned from Beirut, Mr. Waller," Channing said. "It's always good to hear the perspective from the ground."

"Trust me, it hasn't changed. The same clans run the place."

He looked at the bruise on the side of my head but didn't say anything.

"We hear that Syria's grip on Lebanon is faltering. It would take only a nudge to loosen it completely. They're itching to make a deal with us, don't you think?"

"The Syrians don't really talk."

Channing signaled the waiter again, this time to order pâté and caviar.

"Well, of course, you've stopped seeing the reporting. We think that some fillip in the Middle East will bring them around. Offered the right deal, they'd close down Hizballah, don't you think, Mr. Waller?"

"What do you mean, a fillip? Something like Israel complying with U.N. Resolution 242?"

Channing threw up his hands, palms up. "I'm not so knowledgeable as you, of course, but maybe U.S. boots on the ground in the Middle East. The big stick. Make the rats scurry back into their holes."

"Invade Iraq?"

"Maybe. Maybe not that dire. But who knows."

"I met a guy not long ago who met your father."

"Dear Dad knew everyone." He said it the way someone might describe a fish he'd just bought for dinner.

"He liked your father. Said that he was smart, that he read and thought about things. Perfect Arabic and Farsi . . ."

"All that and five bucks gets you a cup of coffee at this place." He was sweeping his hand grandly around the dining room. "My father was a romantic. What did he retire out of the Agency as? A GS-13? Not that he needed the money, of course, but I never could figure—"

"Mr. Channing?"

"Mr. Waller?" A smile was on his face.

"Perhaps we could cut the shit."

"At the Four Seasons? But let's do. Tell me why you invited yourself to dinner."

He held a hand up as he said it. René had brought the wine. Channing took the bottle to look at the label. "It's a Chevalier Montrachet."

"Mr. Channing, unfortunately, we've run short on the Bienvenue Bâtard."

A blaze of anger ran through Channing's eyes. I thought for a moment he was going to smash the bottle on the floor. Instead, he waited until René had filled our glasses, then dismissed him with a quick twist of his hand and turned his attention back to me.

"You were saying?"

"Not saying. About to say. There's a difference." I waited a beat before going on. I wanted to see if I could throw him off his stride. "You know the myth that Brzezinski turned Karol Wojtyla into Pope John Paul II and brought the Soviet Union down?" Channing nodded as he spread his caviar. "People actually believe it because they believe that people can make history. I thought you were one of them."

"Thought?" For a trim man, he was eating the hors d'oeuvres greedily.

"That's the point. You didn't. I was wrong. It's only about money."

"Here's what I'll tell *you*, Mr. Waller." He took a sip of his wine, let it linger on his tongue before swallowing, then dabbed at his lips with a napkin. "I was wrong, too. I thought the Lone Wolf was cunning. But he's not. You believed you could take me, but you don't have the sense, the pieces, anything else. You're not connected to the machine. Too bad I won't be able to see you again and ask what the ride down was like."

Channing pushed his chair back, stood up, and turned to leave. As he did, I instinctively palmed the caviar knife, slid it up my sleeve, and followed him out. What was I going to do with a knife? Cut Channing's throat and declare I'd done a public service? He was on the third stair back up to the lobby when I threw an arm over his shoulder like any old friend. He looked over at my hand and saw the knife.

"I think we missed a couple points," I told him.

I turned him around, and we walked down the steps and into the bathroom tucked underneath them. Some guy in his eighties—cashmere blazer, pink turtleneck—was dowsing himself with perfume in front of the mirror.

"My friend enjoyed his Montrachet too much," I explained. "If you would give us a minute."

As soon as the man was out the door, I let Channing go and crammed the caviar knife into the crack between the door and the jamb, hard enough so that someone would need to give the door a good kick to open it. Channing looked at me, trying to measure just how crazy I was.

"You know, maybe I should kill you right now," I said, shoving him into a stall.

I could see Channing looking at the door and then at me. Would I retrieve the caviar knife and plunge it into his throat?

"You don't have shit," he said, calling my bluff.

"Wrong. I know about BT Trading. I know about the calls on oil. As soon as the refinery gets hit, the Saudi gas-oil separation towers, the tankers, or whatever it is, you're nailed. Cold. Done."

"You can't—" Channing barked.

"You don't care if we invade Syria or Iraq or remake the Middle East. You don't give a shit about history. You just want to blow the house down so you can pick up the pieces."

"You don't—"

"I do. I have the evidence, understand? The bright, shining dots any idiot will be able to connect. The only way you get out of this is if you call it off."

There was a pounding at the door. Channing looked in its direction, for the first time sure I wasn't going to kill him.

"One question. Are all the dead just unfortunate collateral in paying off your G-5?"

Channing straightened up, smoothed down his hair, adjusted the knot of his tie. "You have the paper, you say? Fine. Use it."

I pulled the knife from the doorjamb and walked out.

CHAPTER 48

A QUEUE OF CABS WAITED OUT IN FRONT of the Four Seasons. I climbed in the first one, gave the driver the address of the Amble Inn, and sat back while he hit the lock switch.

We rode in silence until we passed through the blinking stoplight at 18th and Rhode Island Avenue and I saw the swirl of red, white, and blue lights from the two D.C. fire trucks pulled up in front of the inn. Smoke poured from my bathroom window. A ladder stood propped against the wall, a fire hose snaking up beside it.

I could see it all unfolding in my mind's eye: the lock popped out in the hall or the hasp just ripped off the jamb, the room tumbled, finally a gloved hand (no prints) flicks on the bathroom light and opens the door just as the bulb explodes and burning embers tumble into the little pool of gas in the sink below. Was the gloved hand surprised? I wondered. Did it try to grab the envelope off the Gideon Bible in that fraction of a second before it realized its flesh would melt if it tried? Did it have any idea the paper inside was blank? No, it would have happened too fast. I still had surprise on my side.

But the point was, only two people knew where I was staying, India and Willie, and between them, it was no choice at all.

"Change of plans," I told the driver. "Tuttle Place."

CHAPTER 49

THE LIGHTS AT 2501 TUTTLE PLACE were all on, blazing. Frank was entertaining. I walked past the house and turned down the side street, along the brick wall that surrounded the garden. You couldn't see it from the street, but I knew on the other side was the swimming pool, beyond the flagstone patio with the frolicking Henry Moore bronze. It was where Frank liked to eat when the weather was good. I could hear music coming from the patio. Patsy Cline.

I pushed through the rosebushes that ran against the wall, found a chipped brick for a foothold, and hoisted myself up until I could throw a leg over the wall. The closed-circuit camera was staring right at me, the red light blinking. I was counting on no one monitoring it. Everyone would be helping with dinner. They could watch the tape the next morning, after it was too late.

I paused on top of the wall to listen. Someone was telling a joke—a male voice I didn't recognize. A woman laughed. India.

The music was too loud for anyone to hear me drop down onto the other side of the wall into the azalea bushes. I paused again to listen. The granite pool gave off a muted, shimmering light. I could smell citronella torches.

I stepped out of the azaleas and heard a sound you can never mistake: the chambering of a shotgun shell.

"I wouldn't go any further."

I half turned to see Frank sitting in a wrought-iron pool chair with a short-barreled twelve-gauge riot gun across his knees. Going by what he was wearing—a black cashmere blazer, chinos, and a bow tie—I'd interrupted dinner. Someone had been monitoring the cameras after all.

"Don't you think you've gotten yourself in enough trouble without breaking and entering? If I cut you in half, the FBI would throw a party."

"I'm sure." I made one small step back, edging toward the wall.

"Far enough." I heard the safety click on and off. "Why don't you take a load off your feet, Max. Sorry there's no chair. Sit on the edge of the pool. The light's better."

Frank raised the riot gun at my head.

I went over and sat down on the edge of the pool. The underwater lights were enough to light me but not Frank. I couldn't see him now.

"You know, I thought you were a lot smarter," Frank said.

"Me, too. I misread you by a mile."

"Did you?" he snorted.

"Was this place worth it, the pool, the Modigliani?" I said.

"What did you find in Michelle's safe?"

I heard laughter from the patio, this time loud: India's voice again, then a man laughing at what she'd said. I wondered if she knew I was sitting there. Odds were she did.

"I asked what you found in Geneva."

"Enough to nail you."

"Have you been through the papers you stole?"

"Not yet. I will, though. They're perfectly safe."

"Any fool would keep it in a safe place. But frankly, you've been sloppy, Max. For a start, I can't believe you never wondered about the coincidence of that Nicaraguan wiring money to the Nauru account every time you happened to show up in Geneva. Did you ask Webber to see the transfers? Just to put your mind at rest: There *were* transfers. Each time you came to Geneva, I managed to paper it with a fake transfer from Cabrillo's account to Nauru."

I was starting to lose my footing. Right now Frank should have been on the phone to the FBI to come get me, not confessing how he'd framed me.

"Cute," I said. "But I was never on Cabrillo's payroll. It was a dumb ploy."

"They served my purposes; they were enough for Webber to pry you out of the place."

Shit. He's going to shoot me, I thought. Why else the confession?

I tried swallowing, but my mouth felt like it had been swabbed with cotton. Frank would say it was self-defense. Not even a manslaughter charge. I looked at the water glimmering at my side and wondered if I could roll into it without getting shot, swim to the bottom of the pool, and then I don't know what. Lie there until I drowned? Never mind, I'd be dead before I hit the water.

"It was easy."

"What?"

"Framing you. Michelle knew Cabrillo's banker, who for a consideration ginned up the fake transfers. No money got sent anywhere, but it was good enough for DEA to call Webber."

I looked at Frank, still wondering why he was telling me all this. Wasting words, gloating over having beat me—this wasn't his style.

He started to laugh as if he was really enjoying himself. He stood up, keeping the riot gun on me, and moved his chair closer to where I was sitting. He was in the light of the pool now.

"Maxie, we haven't been at a cotillion dance all these years."

Frank flipped the safety back on and put the riot gun down at his side against the chair.

"Max, don't you see? The photo, Millis's brains on the wall of the

Breezeway Motel, my imminent fall, India's trip out to Lebanon—you fell for it, hook, line, and sinker."

"What are you talking about?" I stammered.

"The photo you carried around the world, obsessively believing it was the key to Buckley's murder. Ever wonder how you got it?"

"I dug it out of Archives."

"Did you ever see the 201 file that went with it?"

"Lost."

"Wrong. The 201 never existed. That was mistake two. You never checked around to confirm if it was a real 201. You wanted it to be Murtaza Ali Mousavi's picture so bad, you never confirmed anything. All you cared about was moving an inch closer to your grail. You wore it on your sleeve."

"What are you saying?"

"It was me who found the photo and cut out the head. I had someone fiddle with the records and insert the photo into the system for you to find. Bait."

"I don't believe it."

"Wait a second," he said. He left the shotgun resting on the chair. He had more trust in me than I had in him.

Frank was back in five minutes. He handed me the Peshawar photo, but here the headless man in the salwar chemise had a face—Oliver Wendell Channing's.

Frank had sat back down. He was smiling, no doubt amused by my confusion.

"Why?"

"Because the only way to stop Channing was from the outside."

The shock of what Frank was saying must have drained the blood from my face, but suddenly it fell into place. I'd been manipulated, lied to, seduced, betrayed, and set up—the same thing I'd done day to day for the last twenty-five years.

CHAPTER 50

I WAS TRYING TO PUT IT ALL TOGETHER in my head when Frank put his hand on my shoulder. "Let's have a drink."

We moved to the table next to the Henry Moore, and Simon brought us a pair of Bas Armagnacs.

"Let me tell you how it happened from the beginning."

In late 2000, Frank was in Islamabad bidding on a natural gas pipeline when he ran into an old informant who'd fought in the Afghan war. After dinner, the informant pulled out a box of old photos. They were pretty much all the same, mostly mouj posing with AK-47's, except the one: Oliver Wendell Channing posing with Osama bin Laden and three others.

"Christ, we all knew Oliver was a loose canon," Frank said. "Worse than you. He never reported nine-tenths of the people he met. He spent his vacations in the back of beyond, in places we weren't supposed to go to. By the end he was completely out of control. I wasn't all that surprised to see him in a picture with bin Laden."

A week after Frank got back from Islamabad, he ran into Millis at a dinner on the Hill. The two hadn't seen much of each other in years, but they had Peshawar in common, so Frank told Millis about the photo. When he was through, Millis spun Frank around and pushed him out of earshot of everyone. The National Security Agency, Millis said, had just intercepted a call from David Channing, Oliver's son, to Khalid Sheikh Muhammad, who by then had an arrest warrant on him. There wasn't anything substantive in the intercept, but it was clear David Channing hadn't called a wrong number.

Curious, Millis went out to Langley to ask about David Channing. No one wanted to touch it. David Channing was too big a political player in Washington to go after lightly. Also, it was an election year, and Channing was showering money on the neocons. If they got the White House, whoever had crossed Channing was sure to pay. The seventh floor had no intention of sticking its nose in *that* manure heap.

Millis was savvy enough to know he couldn't go after Channing based on one call to KSM. He was about to let it drop, write it off as a coincidence, but then one afternoon a CIA analyst knocked on his door with a story to tell. In 1996, after the Manila police rolled up KSM's networks, the analyst did a profile on options purchased around the time the planes were supposed to go down. It was just a hunch, but he came across a cluster of trades going short on the airline stocks, betting their stock would fall. The analyst couldn't decide whether it was one person buying the puts or it was all just a coincidence. They'd been made through dozens of traders, enciphered accounts, layered transactions, and complicated swaps. He enlisted the National Security Agency to see if they could reconstruct the calls to and from the traders, intersecting them with the purchases of puts. It wasn't easy. The buy orders came in on different phones, from all around the world, but there was one thing that got his attention: a phone number in Bar Harbor, Maine.

Right after KSM's accomplices were arrested in Manila, someone calling from the Maine number contacted a trader, who immediately canceled some airline put options. The analyst reverse-traced the number to BT Trading, and followed BT Trading to David Channing. That's as far as he'd gotten. He knew he'd walked into a mine field. Without backup, he wasn't going to go any further. When he heard about Millis's nosing around head-quarters asking questions about Channing, he decided on his own to go see Millis.

"Why didn't Millis and the analyst take it to the FBI?" I asked.

"You'd have to see the stuff," Frank said. "It was too dense and com-plicated to open a criminal case. Instead, Millis decided to enlist me. I was on the outside. I didn't have to file reports. I traveled in that world, options trading."

Frank dug around and found out that Michelle Zwanzig was Chan-ning's Swiss fiduciary. To get a foot in her door, Frank opened an account with her. Not that it did any good. She never talked about Channing's busi-ness. The only thing Frank was able to do was get the layout of her office and a look at the outside of her safe.

"So that's where the key thing came in," I said. "The McGuffin to en-courage me to break into Michelle's office and make sure I invited India to Geneva."

Frank smiled.

I wondered for a moment if Frank had been listening on another line when India and I had talked. If so, he must have worked hard to keep from laughing, but Frank was already back on Channing.

He said he'd thought about presenting the evidence to the seventh floor himself, but he would have gotten the same reception Millis got: blind fear of 1600 Pennsylvania Avenue once the election was settled. Neocons are nothing if not vindictive.

"Besides, the evidence was still too flimsy, and there's no way an inside investigation could have been hidden from Webber," Frank said.

"You knew about Webber that long ago?"

"Everybody knew he was angling for a job with Channing. That's the only reason Applied Science got a contract with the Agency."

"I knew it," I interrupted again. "It was Webber who shit-canned the stuff from Kuwait, the SIM chips and the interrogation of the two Saudis they arrested. 'Not credible.' I can see him brushing it off his desk with a flip of his hand."

"You're wrong about one thing, though," Frank said, stopping me. "Webber doesn't know about Channing and KSM's plans. He's really just the cleanup crew. Once Millis and I decided that the seventh floor wasn't going to act, we read three people into this. Maggie was one of them; the other two you won't ever need to know. We knew the investigation had to be done from the outside—you."

It only now occurred to me that I'd been outsourced, put on the same level as Applied Science and the thousands of Agency retirees working on the Dulles Corridor. Only I was never given the choice.

Frank must have seen my look. "Max, what would you have done?"

"You had no idea I'd pick up the thread, find my way to Nabil and the prince. Without them I would never have ID'ed Oliver Channing in the picture."

He answered me with a question: "After O'Neill told you the photo was found in Millis's motel room, would you have acted otherwise?"

"But it wasn't found there, was it?"

"No, we got someone in the FBI to pass on the lie to O'Neill."

"How did Millis die? I can't believe he was murdered."

"Maybe he wasn't. But the stuff about his brains not being where they were supposed to be—more bullshit we fed O'Neill."

"You set up O'Neill, too?"

"I knew you'd run to O'Neill after you were shoved out the door. We needed him to tell you about the surveillance and make you believe Millis had his brains sucked out. You trust O'Neill."

"I need to know: Was it you who arranged to have O'Neill's briefcase stolen, forcing him out?"

"I don't know anything about the briefcase. What I do know is that Channing is behind the current investigation into O'Neill. He found out about your meeting O'Neill the day you left for France. Channing needs him discredited."

"Back to how Millis died."

"We don't know, and we probably never will know," Frank said.

"Of all the case officers you could have picked, why me?"

"Your obsession with Buckley and Mousavi. Your obsessions are what drive you."

"Oh, come on, Frank. You couldn't be sure of that. I could have just picked up and disappeared. It was a crazy gamble, thinking I'd pick up all the clues you left and follow them."

"I know about Baluchistan. Betrayal and abandonment. It's something you can never let go of. After you got to Europe, I made you believe I'd betrayed you. Not answering your phone calls was the start. As the clues of my betrayal mounted, I knew you would come after me but in the end find Channing. I was the bait."

"Webber's visit to you with Lawson—it never happened, did it?"

Frank shook his head no.

"India was in on it from the beginning. She never went to work for Webber, did she?"

"Another piece of disinformation we slipped to O'Neill. Like I said, you work best when things get personal."

"But using India as bait? That was cynical."

"It wasn't supposed to happen," Frank shot back. "I blame myself for that. If it's any consolation, I was madder at myself than you when I burst into your room at the Beau Rivage."

I thought about how Frank must have run her into me on the Syrian-Lebanese border and in Geneva, feeding her a script.

"You offered her up on a platter," I said, more to myself than to Frank. I hoped my life never came to the point that I ever sacrificed Rikki like that.

"Where's Rikki these days? Mind the glass houses, Max."

"And India carried it off beautifully, right to the end," I said, ignoring him. "She even tipped off Applied Science where I was staying."

"That wasn't her. Maybe not even Applied Science."

"Who, then?"

"We don't know. Someone. It doesn't matter. They want the documents."

"Who else besides Channing is in on this?"

"We don't know that, either. David Channing definitely has a following in the White House. I have no idea who knows what."

"They want to invade the Middle East, don't they?"

"They're only missing a pretext. Channing's well enough plugged in to know that if bin Laden and KSM run some planes, let's say, into Saudi Arabia's oil facilities, this president seizes them. But the point for Channing is that oil goes through the ceiling, and he makes a killing."

"What about Iran's role?"

"Another unknown."

"Is Mousavi dead?"

"There are two choices: Mousavi is alive and working with KSM. Or Mousavi is dead and someone picked up the torch for him. Let it go."

"One more question: Mousavi—did Oliver Channing recruit him?"

"Yes and no. We think he cultivated Mousavi when he was a student in Beirut. He helped Mousavi get a visa to UCLA."

"Why's there no record of a visa?"

"There was. David Channing just saw that it got scrubbed clean, or almost all of it."

"Oliver didn't have anything to do with Buckley's—"

"Unlikely. The guy was a harmless romantic."

I was about to ask if Frank thought David Channing had ever met Mousavi, but Frank was right. This wasn't about history.

"Where's India now?"

"She's gone off with a friend. The young. Late-night rambles."

"A friend?"

He left it at that.

"So what's the next move?" I asked.

"The ball's in your court, my friend. Let's hope you don't hit it back into the net."

"If you'd told me . . ."

"I'll take the blame for that. Just go get the paper and come back with it."

He stood up with me, threw an arm over my shoulder, and led me up the terrace steps and through the house. Half an hour earlier, I had been certain I was going to die at his poolside.

"I'll make sure you get Maggie's hearing tomorrow—a real one. No setup. No Sherley. No Webber."

CHAPTER 51

THE WAITING ROOM FOR THE CHINATOWN EXPRESS (or Dragon Coach or Today Bus—it goes by many names) sits in the basement of a modest two-story townhouse, two doors down from the 6th and I Streets Synagogue and across the street from the redbrick Fujian Residents' Association and the barely standing Teddy's House of Comedy Restaurant and Tavern. This is Washington at its most eclectic.

A television was playing low by the door: some grainy black-and-white movie that looked as if it ought to be starring Ray Milland. One of those church-social-size coffee urns steamed and sputtered on a Formica-topped table. The half dozen chairs were taken up by a motley collection of students, wizened Chinese-American ancients, and a pair of hard-looking women. I thought I recognized one of them from Rhode Island Avenue. Maybe the smoke had driven her to high ground.

The rest of us stood against the walls, trying not to think about what we were doing waiting for a bus at three-fifteen in the morning. The price was right, though: twenty dollars one way to Manhattan, thirty dollars round-trip. If the traffic cooperated, the trip took only an hour longer than by rail. It was the safest way I could get up to see O'Neill to get a copy of the documents without leaving a trace. Unlike the shuttle or the Metroliner, there was no chance I'd have to show an ID. And the buses ran all night long.

I was surprised when I stepped out on the street to see more people waiting: what looked like a rock band complete with drum set, a pair of mothers each with sprawls of children, two guys who might have been pimps for the two women inside. Our Chinatown-to-Chinatown express was going to be standing room only if we picked up many more passengers in Baltimore and Philadelphia.

Just at the edge of the crowd, leaning against the side of the stoop of the building next door, was a dark pile of some sort—clothing or people. I walked over and bent down for a look. An old woman was leaning against the steps, asleep, her face half covered by a worn black shawl. The rest of her seemed to disappear into its folds. In the woman's lap, cradled in her arms, also wrapped in black, was a little girl: four, five, six years old; I've never been able to tell.

I'd seen this tableau a thousand times, from Khartoum to Kabul—grandmother and granddaughter, destiny's orphans—and my response was always the same. I looked for bulges, barrels under the shawl, wires, anything out of the usual, anything to suggest that what I was seeing was what I was supposed to see, not what really was. That's how you stay alive in my world. Then the rock band shifted its drum set so that the streetlight fell on my human pile, and I felt as if I were seeing some kind of tableau of my own life.

I had no way of knowing. She could have been Afghan or Iranian. There were too many ruts in her face to say anything for sure, but in that instant when the street lamp first hit her, I was willing to bet the grandmother I was staring at was Baluch. She had the nose, the eyes, the forehead of my friend's mother who had taken me in when my own mother set across the desert for a life without me. She might even have been my stepmother if I hadn't known for certain that she had been dead twenty years, but yes, I did make that leap, just for a second, beyond time, beyond this overwhelming doubt, beyond the suspicion beaten into me by every experience I could think of, to some innocent land where miracles do happen.

Then the grandmother shifted slightly in her sleep and the little girl opened her eyes with that stunned amazement kids have when they're pulled from dreams, and I truly was floored. It was Rikki, a look I loved from that brief moment when she had been that age and Marissa and I really were a family. Christ, I wanted to see Rikki so badly, the one true thing I knew anymore. Maybe next week. Or the week after.

I was thinking that maybe I had found that miracle land after all; thinking that I would sit with these two on the way to New York, that we could talk, swap life stories; that for once I might really tell the truth, the whole truth, nothing but the truth, and that maybe the old woman would tell me a truth in return—tell me how we had all come to live in a world as fucked up as this one, tell me how I had fallen into a life that piled betrayal on betrayal on betrayal—when I heard a rumbling and a rush of air behind me and turned around to find the bus, door open, ready for us to board. The Chinatown express was a luxury liner.

"Grandma," I said in Baluch, hand on her shoulder, shaking her gently. "It's here. Time to get on board. I'll help you."

"No," she answered, unsurprised to find someone speaking her tongue in Washington, D.C. "No. We're waiting."

The little girl's eyes were open wide now, too. Waiting for what?

CHAPTER 52

I F ANYTHING CAN GO WRONG, it will. Murphy's Law. It's the first
thing they teach you at the Farm, maybe the one eternal truth down
there. Fifteen miles south of Wilmington, Delaware, a fuel tanker a few
hundred yards in front of us swerved to avoid a pair of deer that must have
been standing stock-still in its lane, jackknifed, caught a van broadside
traveling two lanes over, and exploded into flames. We got a front-row seat
to the aftermath from behind a barricade of Delaware state-police cars.

The two deer on the right seemed to have been dismembered. On the
far left, someone—man or woman, it was impossible to tell—had somehow survived. He or she or God knows what was collapsed in the arms of
an EMT. In between were the twisted hulk of the van and the still-burning
fuel tanker.

I sat there thinking of the fragility of it all—of the tanker driver, of
whoever might be ashes in the embers of the van, of the one thing I knew I

couldn't stand to lose myself: my daughter, Rikki. Maybe it had taken me this whole winding route to understand that. Now I did.

By the time a Medivac helicopter had lifted off with the sole survivor and tow trucks had cleared the highway, our four-hour trip had turned into a five-hour one. At 8:15 when I was supposed to be meeting O'Neill, we were still working our way crosstown from the Holland Tunnel. When the doors finally opened at 88 East Broadway, it was 8:32. I took off running. O'Neill said he'd light the fire at 9 A.M. I knew he meant it.

I was in full stride thirteen minutes later, dead in the center of Foley Square, when a shadow descended like some Biblical judgment, followed by the roar of engines.

What in the name of hell, I remember thinking, is an American Airlines passenger jet doing a few hundred feet over Lower Manhattan? I heard the explosion and looked up. The first thing I noticed were the flames shooting out of the North Tower: a bright ocher. *That's not the color of burning jet fuel.* And that's when I knew: I was too late.

I turned and raced north for blocks looking for a taxi. Traffic was at a standstill. I stopped at a phone booth. The line was busy. I moved to the next one. Broken. Another block north some woman was just hanging up a pay phone as I ran by. I grabbed it, punched in a call-card number, and dialed England. I was waiting for a rock anthem to finish so I could leave a message when the second plane hit.

"Rikki!" I shouted into the receiver. "Rikki! I promise. I'll be there. I'll be there."

In August 1996, in Jalalabad, Afghanistan, Osama bin Laden came to his door to greet a man with a close-cropped beard and dressed in a starched white shirt with a straight collar and a lightweight synthetic suit. Bin Laden led the man into his sparse living room, where they sat on either end of a couch. The two were alone. What they had to say they wanted to remain between them, but bin Laden was delighted by the visit.

Recently expelled by the Sudanese, who had seized all his property, Osama bin Laden had arrived in Jalalabad basically broke. Rumors about his having a huge inheritance and trafficking in narcotics and "blood diamonds" were simply not true. He had been reduced to living off the Taliban's meager hospitality, but bin Laden had another problem: The Sudanese also had betrayed most of his networks to Western intelligence. By August 1996, bin Laden needed all the friends he could get. Now, an unlikely one had come to his door.

The visitor's Arabic wasn't fluent, but it was good enough for bin

Laden to understand the proposition the man had crossed Afghanistan in the midst of a civil war to deliver: Al-Qaeda and Iran, he said, should conduct joint terrorist attacks against the United States.

A month earlier, bin Laden had sent a feeler to Tehran, suggesting Iran turn its attention from fighting the Taliban and destabilizing Central Asia to attacking the United States. Still, the idea of a cooperative effort must have startled him. Bin Laden was a Wahhabi Muslim, a sect despised by all Shia, but especially by the Iranians.

Rather than respond right away, bin Laden changed the subject. Afghanistan, he told his visitor, was pitting Shia Muslims against Sunni Muslims, and Israel and the United States were using the divide to destroy Islam.

The hour was late by now, and the visitor said he would have to go. As they rose, bin Laden put his hand on the man's shoulder and told him he would accept Iran's offer but only on the condition that their cooperation remain a secret, kept even from his own Qaeda inner circle. The visitor shook bin Laden's hand to close the deal, telling him they would be in touch.

When news of the meeting hit the CIA, alarm bells went off, at least with the Iran watchers. Bin Laden's visitor was an Iranian intelligence operative with American blood on his hands. Less than two months before, he'd been involved in the truck bombing of the Khobar Towers barracks in Saudi Arabia, which killed nineteen U.S. servicemen. Surely, this new partnership promised a new, even more lethal strike against the United States. The only questions were where and when. Those were answered on August 5, 1998, when truck bombs took down our embassies in Nairobi, Kenya, and Dar es Salaam in Tanzania, killing more than 250 people.

After the embassy attacks, the Justice Department indicted senior Qaeda members on charges of conspiring with Iran to commit terrorism against the United States. But there was one thing hauntingly odd about the indictments. While bin Laden and other members of Al-Qaeda were named, including some known only by alias, no Iranian was. Not even the one bin Laden had made his original bargain with in Jalalabad. The same thing would occur three years later when indictments came down for the Khobar attack. Iran was named, but no Iranian.

By then, I admit, I was beyond dismay. When I served in Lebanon in the eighties, there seemed to be, in effect, a blanket immunity for Iran. We knew which Iranians bombed our embassy and the Marine barracks. We knew the names of Iranians kidnapping Americans. And it wasn't as if the Iranians were trying very hard to cover their tracks. The first American hostage kidnapped by the Pasdaran was moved out of Lebanon and held in Evin prison in Tehran. When Bill Buckley was held in Balabakk at the Sheikh Abdallah barracks, he and the other hostages could see their Pasdaran guards from their cells. We knew the names of the local Pasdaran commanders. But they were never named, let alone indicted.

I remember thinking that the odd relationship had reached some kind of crescendo when the Reagan administration clandestinely sent missiles to Iran—through Israel no less—that ended up in the hands of the Pasdaran, the same crew killing and kidnapping Americans in Lebanon. But things got even stranger when Oliver North, Reagan's point man on the Iran-contra arms-for-hostages deal, gave a Pasdaran officer a tour of the White House late one night and later met in Europe with another Pasdaran officer who had been involved in Buckley's kidnapping. This was truly crazy, insane. Then along came the meeting in Jalalabad, and Khobar Towers, and the embassy bombings, and 9/11, and the bizarre grew commonplace.

The blue-ribbon commission that investigated 9/11 did finger Iran, at least to a degree. Iranian intelligence assisted some of the hijackers transiting Iran to Afghanistan, making sure their passports were not stamped. Khalid Sheikh Muhammad, the mastermind behind the slaughter, had a cozy relationship with Iran, too. KSM, as he's known in intelligence circles, stashed his family there back when he was wanted by the United States for trying to assassinate President Clinton and blow up twelve U.S. airliners over the Pacific. When three of the future hijackers flew from Beirut to Iran in 2000, a particularly nasty Hizballah operative with close ties to Iran was on the same plane.

All that's in the 9/11 report, as is the fact that KSM apparently wasn't a member of Al-Qaeda. In the commission's word: "KSM states he refused to swear a formal oath of allegiance to bin Laden, thereby retaining a last vestige of his cherished autonomy." Did he then have an "allegiance" to Iran? The commission doesn't offer an opinion, only recommending that

Iran's role in 9/11 be studied further. It should. But what's striking in the 9/11 commission's report is the same thing that was striking in the indictments for the embassy bombings and Khobar Towers: No Iranian—or even the Hizballah operative traveling on the plane with the 9/11 hijackers—is named.

Stack up the intelligence we had against Saddam Hussein next to what we had on Iran, especially if we go all the way back to the Tehran embassy takeover in 1979, and it's obvious that the United States went to war against the wrong country in March 2003. Why? I don't pretend to know for sure, but maybe the answer has something to do with a grand balance-of-power scheme: Depose Saddam and give Iraq to the Shia, sow conflict between the Shia and Sunni across the Middle East, and drive a fatal wedge between the Indo-European Persians and the Semite Arabs. Divide and conquer—an ancient strategy.

Amid the blind stumblings of the Iraq war, the evidence for a master plan is thin, but there is some. In 1996, a group of neocons who would go on to become architects of the Iraq invasion wrote a paper entitled "A Clean Break: A New Strategy for Securing the Realm." It's mostly drivel, but in one telling part the paper calls for bringing down Saddam and containing Syria, all of which has come to pass. Once again, though, there was no plan for Iran. It's as if the neocons like the country just the way it is.

Or maybe the far left has it right: The White House warmongers are all about power and money, especially oil money. After all, Exxon's revenues soared to over $100 billion a quarter in 2005, and even Dick Cheney's Halliburton climbed out of the red in the wake of the Iraq war.

Whatever the actual truth, the absence of convincing evidence leaves the field open to a fictional one. That's what I try to get at in *Blow the House Down*. Like any fictional truth, this one stands, I hope, on a firm foundation of reality. Aside from the above indictment of Iran, here are the facts I've drawn from:

- The FBI forced John O'Neill into retirement by giving his personnel file to the *New York Times*. O'Neill died on September 11. He was last seen running towards the South Tower, where his office was on the thirty-fourth floor.

- Freddie Woodruff's murder remains open on FBI books. The Bureau is unsure whether he was murdered or died from a stray round.
- Two Saudi officials—one suspected of being a Saudi intelligence agent— were in contact with two of the hijackers in California almost two years before 9/11.
- John Millis was assigned to Peshawar in the late eighties, at the same time bin Laden was living there. On June 2, 2000, Millis was suspended as House intelligence committee staff director. He committed suicide the same day.
- One of Beirut AP correspondent Terry Anderson's captors spoke with a French accent and claimed to have attended the American University of Beirut.
- Another American abducted in Lebanon, Father Lawrence Martin Jenco, told investigators after his release that one of his captors had blue eyes and red hair.
- In October 2000, the Kuwaitis detained two of the 9/11 hijackers transiting from Iran. The record of their interrogation has never been made public.
- The character of Prince Al Sabah is based on a real Gulf prince who tried to warn the United States that KSM planned to use commercial airliners in suicide operations inside the United States.
- The Securities and Exchange Commission and the FBI found no evidence that anyone benefited financially from 9/11, but experts acknowledge that the use of encrypted trades, fiduciary agents, and multiple accounts makes it nearly impossible to determine whether anyone has benefited from foreknowledge of a disaster like 9/11.
- By January 2000, the CIA knew two bin Laden terrorists and future hijackers had entered the United States and taken up residence in California. The CIA failed to tell the FBI until August 2001. The 9/11 Commission concluded that had the FBI arrested the two on material witness warrants—both men were involved in the attack on the U.S.S. *Cole*—9/11 might never have happened.